VIA FOLIOS 73

The Bitter Taste of Strangers' Bread
An Italian Immigrant in America

Elena Gianini Belotti

Translated from the Italian by Martha King

BORDIGHERA PRESS

Library of Congress Control Number: 2012936292

First published in Italy as *Pane amaro*
Rizzoli, 2006

*Bordighera Press dedicates this English publication to
the memory of Martha King.*

Printed in the United States.

Published by
BORDIGHERA PRESS
John D. Calandra Italian American Institute
25 West 43rd Street, 17th Floor
New York, NY 10036

VIA FOLIOS 73
ISBN 978-1-59954-032-0

In memory of my father Basilio,
emigrant, musician, and stone mason

1

Hunched over, a tattered cloth covering his cramped shoulders, Gildo shut his eyes tightly, as though darkness might protect him from his brother's sadistic attack. Giacomo twirled the scissors around Gildo's head, grabbed a handful of hair, pulled it mercilessly, almost ripping it out of his skull, and snipped it off close to the skin. Now and then, snorting with impatience, Giacomo would whack him on the back to make him sit up straight, and Gildo would jump, straighten up, and then slump again.

Giacomo went about his task quickly and carelessly, skipping from the back of his head to the front, from his temples to the nape of his neck, so that his brother's head, bristling with random strands of hair among patches of bare skin, seemed devastated by illness. Hair fell on the cloth covering his shoulders, on the uneven floor, and on his forehead, nose, and mouth, but the boy didn't bother to shake his head or blow it away, almost as though he didn't notice. He didn't even react when Giacomo, a novice at this craft, pricked his ear with the scissors. He barely flinched, blinked, shut his eyes, and immediately opened them again.

The two brothers did not exchange a word. After the shearing was over, the parts of Gildo's face, neck, and ears, tanned from outdoor work, were in sharp contrast to the newly exposed white skin. Finally, armed with comb and razor, Giacomo finished the clumsy homemade job that left his brother looking like a homeless beggar. He shook the cloth covered with curls, studied the disfigured head, gave him a slap on the back, and as though to justify the slipshod work, commented that anyway hair grows back again. Gildo stood up and gently caressed his head. He couldn't see what he looked like because there was no mirror in the kitchen, but that tentative feel of his ruined head was enough to make him fall into silent despair. He struggled to hold back his tears, considering them a shameful adolescent weakness, and headed for the door.

His mother, slicing bacon to add to the cabbage, was also feeling the pain she had been helpless to prevent. She knew very well how much Gildo loved his beautiful brown curls, like every boy his age. When he attended school—as far the obligatory third grade—the teacher had made the boys shave their heads two or three times a year as prevention against lice and scabs. But it was different with little guys. Being handsome or ugly wasn't a matter of concern, and as their shaved heads all looked alike, it wasn't important. They teased each other—Baldy! Baldy! They laughed and cuffed and whacked each other's craniums, and that was the end of it. Now that she thought about it, she wasn't sure that Gildo hadn't suffered from that repeated practice, although he never complained. This fourth child was so different from the other nine, the only one with her blue eyes, and the one who most resembled her in character: quiet, mild, shy, always with his head in the clouds. And to her unending sorrow, his dreamy slowness and hesitation in everything aroused his father's violent fury and the cruel spite of his older brothers. She trembled when fights broke out between the brothers, or her husband's anger flared, because Gildo would be forced to surrender. He couldn't deal with their violence, any violence at all, without it destroying him. Retreat was his only defense.

In the fireplace she laid some chestnut logs over a few twigs and set them afire. Then she poured water from a pail into the copper pot for the polenta, tossed in a handful of salt, and hung the pot on a chain over the fire. She swept up the hair scattered on the floor and tossed it into the flames. It crackled brightly, filling the kitchen with its acrid odor. She had expected Gildo to rebel against the scalping; or rather, she had hoped to see him react at least this once. Instead he had put himself in Giacomo's hands like a lamb. But in his mildness she sensed a resentment he was too proud to show.

Gildo would have preferred to keep his hair for the crossing overseas, and to shave it before they arrived only if he had picked up lice or some skin disease on the ship. His father had firmly declared that was what he intended to do, and as Lorenzo did before going to the army. Someone suggested Gildo take a bottle of gasoline and a fine-tooth comb to get rid of the parasites at the end of the voyage, if he should get them. He was so young and already unhappy and discouraged enough without having to face another humiliation. And anyway, he was neat and knew how to keep clean. But her son had stubbornly refused, almost as though wanting to see his misery to the very end, to be a miserable wretch in the hands of others.

That story about hair, passing from mouth to mouth, reached the little village of Abbazzia da Gazzaniga. Someone who had just come back from America advised those who were getting ready to go to cut their hair because they would be packed like sardines into a small space and could easily get infested. And they could be turned back for a silly thing like that. The American officials who checked the emigrants at the port were very strict, and if the inspector was feeling out of sorts that day he was as likely as not to turn away some poor devil just because he had red eyes, a boil on his neck, or four lice on his head. According to that fellow in Abbazzia, they aren't polite or shy over there, but are as hard as granite, without an ounce of pity. Most of all it was important to leave in good health. A doctor checked you when you got on the ship also, and a cough was enough to get you sent back home. You might get over it in a week, but you had to wait a year before you could emigrate again. To be turned back was a catastrophe, not to mention the money tossed to the four winds.

The water in the copper pot was boiling. She slowly added corn meal, stirring it with a stick. She poked the fire, scrapped a few cinders from the ashes, and placed the pan of bacon and chopped onions over them. Soon they began to sizzle. Giacomo must have gone to change the cow's straw because she could hear him cursing the stubborn animal that wouldn't budge. Early in the morning, after doing the dishes, Maddalena had washed her father's and Gildo's underwear, and stretched it to dry next to the fire. Then she had sewn pockets in the jacket linings where they could hide their money while traveling.

Indirectly they had heard stories that gave them the shivers. A man from Ranica, who went to Switzerland every year for seasonal work, told an acquaintance, who repeated it in town, about an unfortunate thing that happened to a poor young fellow from Leffe. He went to sleep on a train and someone stole his wallet from his pants' pocket with every cent he owned. He didn't realize it until he got to the station at Varenna, and was so desperate that he had tried to throw himself in front of a train. Luckily friends snatched him back in time; he had screamed that he wanted to die, and cried for his mother like a baby. After seeming to have calmed down, he suddenly took off running like crazy along the tracks in the other direction. His friends went after him and grabbed him again. He struggled to get free and, sobbing, begged them to let him go because his life was over. Right there on the platform they took up a collection and made him go on with his trip. You had to keep your eyes open. Certain criminal gangs can easily worm their way into groups of emigrants, so confused and lost that stealing from them is child's play. Some of the emigrants hid their money in their shoes, socks, or underwear. But the best thing, according to those with experience, was to sew a pocket inside your jacket, always keep it buttoned, and never take your hand off it.

Gildo and his father, Cipriano, had come back from their work-stint in Switzerland with their clothes in tatters. She had almost ruined her eyes patching and mending for days, but with pathetic results. Gildo had grown so much that his clothes no longer fit. She had wasted time letting out the stitching and lengthening hems. Why couldn't his father have bought him a sweater, a shirt, a pair of trousers, and a jacket his size? He had bought the other children a couple of shirts, a sweater, and second-hand heavy jackets for the cold weather by pawning the gold chain and cross and a pair of earrings that her dear mamma had given her as a wedding present. She would get them back as soon as they sent money from America.

Heaving a sigh, she put another log on the fire. Her husband's drinking vice had brought the family to ruin, but she couldn't say a word without him flying off the handle. It was almost dinnertime and Cipriano still hadn't come home. He was probably at the tavern as usual, and no doubt would come back drunk.

That man at Gazzaniga had also said it was better to carry their things in a suitcase rather than a sack—and certainly not bundle up their things in an old sheet—in order to make a good impression. But there was no money for that. He had also advised taking a piece of laundry soap for washing their clothes on the ship, and keeping a decent change of clothes to put on before arriving so they didn't look like tramps, which sorry to say was the impression Americans had of Italians.

She stirred the polenta, tossed the cabbage in the pan—one of the last from the garden—put on the cover and worried about what she would cook until the vegetables came up in the spring, which weren't even planted yet. She went to the door to see what her children were doing; they were always busy with something. Egidio was in the woods cutting firewood, Attilio was getting water from the brook, Mario was sawing chestnut logs on the trestle in front of the cowshed and stacking them under the lean-to. She could hear the voices the younger two, Adele and Lodovico, off gathering bits of frozen grass for the rabbits among patches of snow. Not a sign of Gildo. He must be hiding in the thick chestnut woods, and she didn't have the heart to bother him on his last few days at home. It was Sunday and she would have preferred to respect the holy days of obligation, but certain tasks couldn't be postponed, and after mass in town everyone set to work.

She turned back to the fireplace, gave the pot of polenta a shake, stirred the slowly simmering cabbage, and cut eight thin slices from a block of stracchino cheese. The crust of polenta in the pot, dipped in milk, would serve as her dinner. For her husband a rabbit thigh was browning next to the fire. She couldn't let him go without meat on Sundays. As head of the family he expected it, and if he didn't find it he was likely to turn the house upside down. He complained about having polenta for dinner and supper every single blessed day, and raved about the Swiss white bread and Gruyère.

She sighed again, thinking about Gildo who hadn't said a word when his father, like a general who expects total obedience, announced that Gildo would go with him to America. But her son's face had turned dark and his hands trembled. Like someone who feels he is dying. It wasn't fair. He had already done his part; why not take Mario who had just turned fifteen? Or Egidio, who was almost thirteen? He couldn't say they were too young, because he had dragged poor Gildo off to work in Switzerland at that age.

For two years Mario had been working as an errand boy in a factory in Albino, and Egidio had been taken on by a carpenter at Tribülina. With the excuse that they were learning a trade they were paid practically nothing, and if it depended on their earnings, the family would never get out of debt. It was a terrible sacrifice to work in a foreign country, because of the hard work so far from home, and the bad way those people treated Italians. But it paid so much better. The two younger ones would have been more willing to go to American than Gildo, just because they had not yet experienced the bitter taste of strangers' bread, so thick and hard it breaks your teeth, and it would all seem like a big adventure to them.

Even the girls did their part to support the family. After Cipriano lost his job, Carolina worked in a spinning mill in Gandino, too far away to come home even on holidays. And from the time Maddalena was nine she had worked in the spinning mill in Cene. She came home Saturday evenings and left on Sunday afternoons, and she never complained about the bleeding sores on her hands from dipping silk worms in boiling water.

Her oldest son Lorenzo couldn't go with those two when they left for Locarno in Switzerland because he had been about to go in the army. He was still in the service now, and in December, after his three years were up, he planned to join his father and brother in America. Giacomo had already received his notice, and when he was finished with the army he too would board a ship. But why hadn't his father taken him to Switzerland instead of Gildo who had been just a boy?

If she understood it right (because her husband never explained anything to her and flew into a rage if she dared ask a question), it was dangerous for a boy to leave the country if he was about to go to the army. If they ran into guards on the paths that led to the border, Giacomo would have risked a prison sentence, or even worse.

No one in the valleys ever bothered to get a passport to work in Switzerland, because it was right over there, behind the mountains, close by, and it didn't even seem like leaving Italy. They left in the spring after the snow thawed, hired to build a road, along with other men and boys from around here. Her husband was the oldest: at forty-eight no one would have hired him if he hadn't brought his son with him. They told how they had taken a train as far as Lake Lecco, had gone by ferry to Menaggio, walked along the road to Porlezza and crossed the border at Valsolda, right at the top of Lake Lugano, and from there walked to Locarno.

After they left for Switzerland Giacomo found work on a crew to build a new church in Albino. Although the pay was poor, he had the advantage of coming home every evening. Very different from Switzerland where sixty men slept in a bunkhouse, packed in like animals, suffocating in the summer and freezing in the winter. The work was backbreaking, the food skimpy and bad, and the Italians, more than the other emigrants, were looked down upon, exploited, mocked, and treated like beggars. Cincalì, they were called, because they shouted Cinc! Cinc! when they played morra. The only good thing was that they spoke Italian in Ticino Canton.

She asked herself why her husband bullied Gildo like that, almost as though wanting to make his life as difficult as possible. He acted like he hated him, a hate she couldn't fathom: perhaps because he was so different? Or because he was docile, meek, and quiet, and Cipriano wanted his sons to be tough, aggressive, and strong?

When she had dared ask why he was taking Gildo with him to America instead of one of their other sons, her husband became infuriated and accused her of protecting him like a mother hen. That's why he's so strange, he shouted, always so quiet and moody you never know what he's thinking and sometimes you just have to believe he's an idiot. Maybe she had made him an idiot with all that babying. He was weaned, after all. Sneering contemptuously he had told her that right after they arrived in Lucarno they had gone to have a beer in a tavern near the station, and right there, right at the table, Gildo—who knows why?—broke out sobbing like a two year old in front of their fellow countrymen and other customers they didn't know. It's embarrassing to have a kid like that. And the more he told Gildo to shut up the more he had cried, and wouldn't stop until he slapped him.

Well, that's no surprise, she thought bitterly. The poor boy must have been dead tired and scared to death, and his father couldn't think of anything better to do than hit him? His father's outbursts terrorized Gildo, his tendency to fly off the handle at the slightest thing and his habit of kicking and hitting him whether drunk or not; and also his cruel way of teasing and ridiculing him in front of his brothers and strangers. That contempt hurt more than the physical pain.

During those three years in Switzerland they hadn't returned home even once, and they rarely sent money toward paying off the debts. Her husband had admitted that the pay was good compared to Italy, but their daily expenses were so high they had to spend almost everything they made and weren't able to save a thing. She suspected that her husband drank up his pay in the tavern at night. And probably drank up Gildo's too.

She could imagine what Switzerland looked like, over there beyond the snow-capped mountains. Every year at the beginning of summer, men from Val Seriana and Val Brembana drove their herds of cattle to graze on nearby Engadina Mountain, and took them back in September. She could imagine Lake Locarno like a basin of blue water a hundred times bigger than the lake at Endine, which she had once seen when a girl. During those three years they were away she had prayed every day for her son who, with his thin boy's arms, worked with a pickaxe from dawn to dusk, loaded dirt on a cart, collapsed with exhaustion on his cot every night. Gildo had come back taller and more robust, almost a man, with muscles, and hair on his chin and cheeks, and hands as worn and calloused as an old peasant's. He had changed so much that she didn't recognize him at first.

But what she could not imagine was that other country in another part of the world. It made her dizzy thinking about the distance and vastness of that unknown land where her son would wander around like a lost soul, with even his father against him. And more than that, without understanding a word of that language. And then the sea that none of them had ever seen, an immense expanse of water to cross for weeks, prisoners on a ship battered by storms. But you could earn good money over there and make your fortune, they said, so to emigrate was the last thing left to keep alive, to pay your debts and make your creditors happy who grew angrier every day. When she had gone to Signor Ghilardi in town to pay a small amount of what they owed him, his sneer, his sarcastic comments, and his arrogantly waving those few bills under her nose had intimidated her. Even so she had plucked up enough courage to ask for a receipt.

So many from the valley towns had gone to America. The first to go had lured others, and in letters to their relatives they all wrote that the work was hard, of course, but they lived comfortably, the people were civil, everyone knew how to read and write; they were appreciated, there was a future for anyone willing to work, while in Italy you could only die of starvation. And everyone— some more often, some less—sent money home.

Bepo, who had emigrated almost ten years ago, enclosed a photograph in his last letter to his wife, which amazed everyone. He was sitting in a magnificent automobile on a seat of shining leather thick as a mattress, with his hands resting on the steering wheel. On either side of the powerful hood shone copper headlights. The wheel spokes sparkled like sunrays. Bepo, who had gone around in rags when he lived in Abbazzia, and had barely managed to scrounge a living, was wearing an elegant black derby and a starched shirt with a silk bow tie. Between the lapels of his jacket you could glimpse a vest and the silver chain of a pocket watch. His face, adorned with a grand mustache that no one had ever seen before, oozed pride and satisfaction. One of the peasants had once seen an automobile, but never one like that, which certainly cost a pretty penny. Bepo must have made a fortune in America. Why in the world, then, his wife said, did he keep suggesting she and the children join him, but after ten years they were still there?

From the knot of curious admirers scorched by envy, pushing and grabbing to get a good look at the amazing photo, rose the voice of Evaristo, crippled from birth, who went hungry working his corn patch, but because of his physical defect wasn't able to emigrate. He said that behind the automobile you could see something like a blanket. What, a blanket? the others exclaimed, flabbergasted, and someone grabbed the photo and looked at it intently: Yes, he agreed, the backdrop was a white blanket, and if you looked at it closely you could make out a piece of fringe in the lower corner. They exchanged bewildered looks and one of them expressed the others' doubts when he speculated that the automobile was a fake, without a motor, probably made out of tin or wood or even papier-mâché, placed in front of the blanket in the photographer's courtyard and used by who knows how many other emigrants who wanted to fool their relatives and other gullible folks back home. Some went away disillusioned, and another, who pretended to have it all figured out, said he was sure that the auto was really a piece of painted junk, because there was no crank in front for starting it up. Now it was clear why Bepo's wife and children had never left home.

Luckily not everyone told lies about America. Early in December, before her husband and Gildo came back from Switzerland, her German cousin Delfina who lived in town got a letter from her brother-in-law Tranquillo. Four years earlier, in 1906, along with a group of men from Val Seriana, Tranquillo had emigrated to the end of the world, to the furthermost corner of immense America, to the state of Washington, right below Canada. He had sent a photo that didn't seem faked. He was standing with some of his companions in work clothes, their shirts rumpled and mended, trousers patched at the knees, muddy boots on their feet and shapeless hats on their heads. In the first row two of them held up a bicycle by its handles and seat, their faces happy and satisfied like they were showing off a trophy. One pointed at the bell. Maybe it wasn't Tranquillo's bicycle, but never mind, it meant that one of them had been able to afford it, and so they weren't so bad off.

He said there was work there and would be for years. They were building new roads all over the state and needed more hands. It was hard work but paid well. So if someone in town felt inclined to roll up his sleeves and grab a pickaxe, he should pack his things and leave. Except that in winter (which was colder than the Alps) the ground was frozen with snow and ice and the digging stopped, while in spring the company would take on a large number of skilled and unskilled workers. Giacomo wrote a letter to his father in Switzerland about it, and Cipriano decided to go back home and get ready to leave for America.

Going bankrupt four years ago they had lost everything they owned, swallowed up by their creditors: land, livestock, the house at Molinello with all the furniture, including the beds and mattresses. And the villagers' respect. For more than twenty years her husband had had a contract with the neighboring communes to maintain the roads from Albino to Pradalunga, Nembro, and Cene, as far as Gazzaniga: to dig ditches for water run-off and keep them clean, to repair potholes, to rebuild the roadbed when necessary, to shovel snow in the winter and spread gravel when it scattered and turned into a quagmire, to repair the low walls and bridges damaged by frost. When they were big enough, in the final years before the catastrophe, Lorenzo and Giacomo had helped their father; they worked hard but grudgingly because of his hot temper.

In addition to keeping up the roads, they did occasional jobs, such as hauling sand, cement, crushed stone, and gravel removed from the Serio. The roadwork took care of daily expenses, but when the communes cancelled the contract because his drinking had made him unreliable and he didn't do his job, everyone else backed off and no one gave him extra work. So he went bust. He was able to earn a little with what few possessions he still had — shovels, hoes, pickaxes, sledgehammers, spades, wheelbarrows, a mule and a cart — until he left for Switzerland with Gildo.

Only what she had inherited survived the disaster: a two-storey stone building with a cowshed in the chestnut woods halfway up the mountain, where they lived stacked on top of one another. When her father was alive he used the place to catch birds in nets, and kept little cages of lures hidden in the foliage of the surrounding hornbeam. At night the male members of the family put straw mattresses on the kitchen floor and the girls and Lodovico slept with her in the one room upstairs. In the summer Giacomo preferred sleeping in the woodshed, and in the winter he slept on the hay in the shed to keep company with Filippa, their only cow. They were forced to sell the others, along with the pig.

Life was much harder here than when they lived in town. The biggest, never-ending chore was hauling water from the brook; it was worse in the winter because a layer of ice had to be broken first, and the snow on the frozen path made it easy to slip with pails full of water. The older boys milked and took care of Filippa, while the younger ones took her to pasture and gave her water, cut firewood in the chestnut woods, spread manure in the meadow, cut the grass from spring through summer, and when it was dry enough, stacked it in the shed for fodder during the long winter months. They hoed the fields, sowed and harvested the corn, and hung it up to dry. Adele and Lodovico even ground up the corn in the coffee grinder. When they had had four cows they separated the milk and made butter to sell, which brought in a little money. But now Filippa barely provided enough milk for the family, with a little left over for stracchino. And without the pig there was no bacon or pig fat so they had to buy that.

When they had had a nice hen house, the money from selling eggs, geese, turkeys, and chickens was used to buy what the children needed, and once in awhile they could permit themselves the luxury of wringing a chicken's neck for Sunday dinner. Now only six chickens were left, and the smallest children got the eggs to help them grow.

The rocky patch cleared from the woods produced a poor crop of corn, and the harvest had been meager, so they had to buy flour for polenta—not the best, that costs too much, but the kind mixed with bran. There were plenty of chestnuts that autumn. Some they roasted in the fireplace, others they dried, ground, and used to boil in soups or to fry. The potatoes had been coming along well, but shortly before the harvest a night frost had clawed deep into the ground. Half of the potatoes were rotten and those that seemed sound had a heart as hard as stone. The vegetable garden, on a small square of flat land, was now bare as always in winter. But poorer people than they were lived on isolated farms in the mountains, people who had nothing to eat but polenta. First pellagra would make them itch and then it would drive them crazy.

Winter was the hardest season to get through. The food supply was gone and new harvests were a long way off. They didn't exactly live in abject poverty, but close to it. There were certain things they had to buy: sugar, salt, oil for the lamps, matches, candles, and soap that she had previously made from bones and pig fat.

Times had been hardest right after the disaster. The grocer hadn't wanted to give her credit. She had cried desperately at night because she didn't have enough money even for salt: not for herself—she could put up with anything—but for her innocent children. She felt sorry for them. Not that they had been rolling in money before. Of course not. But, in spite of what little they had, the children had all gone to school, including the girls. And so they all knew how to read, write, and do arithmetic. And she had to thank the Lord for all that.

She remembered how desperate she had been in those first years of marriage, when the two babies, still breast-fed, had died one after the other! She had been very young and inexperienced then, and it was certainly her fault they got sick with a diarrhea that turned them into skin and bones in a few days and carried them off to the tomb. How she had suffered from the loss of those innocent babes, and from the terror of not even being able to keep alive even those coming afterwards, and also for the three that, between two living children, she had lost before they were born.

When angels took the little ones to heaven and her milk ran like a fountain, she started nursing the babies of unfortunate women who didn't have any milk, and she continued doing it as soon as she weaned one of her own. It was a responsibility and hard work to raise other people's children, but she was paid well, and she missed that money now. Now she was old and tired and her bones ached. Her hands were deformed by arthritis, her knuckles had stabbing pains like hot needles, and the nightmare of creditors poisoned her days and nights.

As if the debts they already had weren't enough, her husband had had to borrow more money to pay for the trip to America, and it hadn't been easy. No one wanted to take the risk. In the end, after much dithering and insistence, he got half the amount he needed from a usurer in Albino, to be repaid with a staggering amount of interest within a year; and another had demanded money in advance, docking it from the money he had lent. Pigheaded and boastful as always, her husband was sure that over there he could start over as a road contractor, and while others earned a pittance by slaving away to make their employers rich, he would immediately get well-paid contracts for road maintenance. It was all a matter of being clever, knowing the right people, and asserting himself. As soon as Lorenzo came back at the end of the year, and Giacomo was finished with the army, the four of them would make money hand over fist. He figured they would stay five or six years at the most, like many others did, just the time necessary to pay off their debts and save what was needed to buy a house, land, and livestock. Maybe even the same house and the same land they had lost. A few years in America would be enough for them to live well for the rest of their lives. It made her tremble to hear him talk like that.

In the meanwhile a great deal of the money had already gone for the passport. Don't even think of emigrating to America illegally, like going to Switzerland: revenue stamps, good conduct and penal certificates, medical check-ups, vaccinations, visas and a slew of devilries enough to drive a person crazy. How much more would have to be spent for the trip and for expenses until they could begin earning over there? Her heart ached with worry.

When she heard her husband's harsh voice outside scolding one of the children, she turned the steaming polenta onto the cutting board. Next to it she put the pan of cabbage and the slices of stracchino. She poured a glass of red wine for him, put the rabbit thigh on his plate, and scrapped the burnt crust from the pot for herself. Then she went to the door and called them in to eat.

2

The old men had long memories and told the young ones wanting to go to America about various con artists in the past. Up until ten years ago in the town piazzas, markets, and fairs, representatives of various American companies tried to sell the men on the idea of leaving with slick talk that made their heads swim. They were well dressed and better fed, with gold watch chains on their vests. They said they represented important American businesses that had given them the responsibility of recruiting men willing to move over there. Like blood hounds sniffing the ground for wild game, more numerous in the winter when poverty bit hardest, they had the oily, friendly, smooth-talking manners of someone trained to bamboozle: shrewd and patient, they planted in the gullible peasants' heads the idea of an easy and prosperous future overseas. With the skills of hustlers they embroidered their fables with tempting particulars made entirely out of whole cloth, and slyly waited for the seeds they had planted to sprout and bear fruit. They often encouraged them to sell their houses, furniture, and land to get the money necessary for the voyage. Or else to take out loans that would be easily repaid with their first rich earnings. They didn't have contracts for them to sign, since they said that was prohibited in America, but they promised jobs on arrival, boatloads of money, deluxe lodging, and work so easy that even a child could do it. They said that the ship owners in America were Italians who had made a fortune and would treat them like brothers. They exhibited the credentials of the businesses they represented, and enthusiastic letters from emigrants who had worked for those companies for years. Some offered a free voyage to their destination, to be repaid easily once they arrived. As intermediaries they received high commissions from their American employers while, according to them, they asked the emigrants a mere trifle in exchange for help with the complicated practical details required before the departure, during the voyage, and after disembarking. The old men told about a man from Fiobbio who had written his wife that none of those promises had been kept. From the beginning they had been left to their own resources. Yes, there was work, but it was backbreaking and poorly paid, and they lived in hovels that by comparison made cowsheds seem like princely drawing rooms. This fellow had advised his wife not to say anything in town, not only because he was ashamed of having let himself be fooled, but also because he was afraid of being fired if his employer got wind of it.

The Italian government passed a law that got rid of those dishonest middlemen who had grown rich by taking advantage of poor ignorant people in need—a vile, contemptible business like slavery; after that, in place of the representatives sent by American entrepreneurs, the agents of Italian and foreign shipping companies popped up, vying to steal customers away from each other. In some cases the hucksters switched company allegiances. Every ship carried more than a thousand third-class passengers, so it was an extraordinary moneymaking opportunity.

Beginning in the autumn of 1909, notices began to appear in the more populated villages of the valley. And young boys handed out printed sheets of information at the weekly market in the piazzas of Nembro, Albino, and Gandino, at the livestock market on the edge of town, and at the patron saint's fairs or on the church square after high mass. It didn't matter whether they were young or old; the ship owners wanted them to be distributed to everyone, even to women and illiterates, expecting that each one would be given to a relative or an acquaintance. Later on posters went up in Abbazzia, even though it was a hamlet of only a few hundred souls. Posters were put on the tavern door, on the shop door, and even on the bridge over the Luio. With surprising audacity, given that everyone knew how the parish priest, Don Raimondo, had always been against emigration, they even stuck one on the church door. When thick envelopes full of information arrived from the shipping companies, the same as those sent to the diocese and town officials, he tossed them straight into the fire without opening them.

That poster on the door he had angrily torn into shreds before burning, and for many Sundays he had lashed out furiously against that mania for going to America, a hemorrhage of people who de-populated the countryside and the house of God and let the un-cultivated fields go to seed. They were foolish people who mort-gaged their homes and farms, or went into debt up to their necks with loan sharks to pay for their voyage, when they didn't sell what little they had for less than it was worth. Men left their wives to manage the best they could alone with small children. The holy sacrament of matrimony that commanded the couple to live toge-ther went to the devil, and the husbands, lost and alone in those distant foreign wastelands, were exposed to the most evil tempta-tions. They put themselves at risk in a country of Protestant here-tics, traitors to the true faith, an immoral and corrupt country where they were in peril of losing their integrity and decency and falling victim to vice. Why? Because of an unwholesome desire for adventure, a craving to see new places, the mirage of easy wealth, the sinful adoration of the money god. Then they ended up spending everything they earned, because everyone knows how expensive life is in American.

How many lonely and helpless men had been lost in that alien land, without the help and comfort of their family? A land where a different language is spoken that they don't understand, and where Italians were ostracized and looked down upon. How did they end up? They probably died from starvation and nothing more was heard of them. And how many, after becoming sick or injured in their dangerous occupations, without anyone to nurse and help them, had lost their jobs, were left without a cent, suffered the most dreadful hunger, and in the end were left with no choice but to return home poorer than before? And what about those who out of exhaustion, solitude, hostility of the people, and the tremendous effort to adapt to those places, had lost their wits and gone mad? What sorrow, what unhappiness, just to follow a vain illusion! There are children who have never known their fathers, wives who can't even remember what their husbands looked like, old people who despair of ever seeing their children before they die, families destroyed when their sons leave, and those who live in the hope of joining their husbands over there but instead never leave.

The men, stock-still in the back benches, listened to the sermon with hat in hand, eyes on the ceiling, and gnawing in their stomachs: it was easy for the priest to talk, seeing that he had his stipend, a cozy parsonage with a housekeeper always at his service, and a table loaded with all kinds of good food. The more shrewd among them knew that those words echoed the angry complaints of the valley's rich land owners, Counts Fogaccia, the Salvi, the Spini, the Suardi, accustomed to exploiting the woodsmen who cut wood for their personal use or for selling in the city, exploiting the farm hands and shepherds who cultivated their fields and tended their herds. If woodsmen, farm hands, and herdsmen emigrated, who could they get to work on their land for a pittance, as they always had in the past?

At first colored posters of the La Veloce shipping line appeared, with the imposing silhouette of a ship viewed from below, the prow as sleek as a shark's fin, the huge anchor lodged in its place, the single tall smokestack with a swirling tail of black smoke. On the ship's side was the name of the company in block letters.

In the cluster of men around the poster, those who didn't know how to read (and there were many) depended on the labored reading aloud of someone who had been to school. The black letters boasted of their steamers' absolute modernity and the safety of the crossing. It claimed they had every comfort, from splendid dining halls with dining tables to comfortable cabins, from electric lights to sanitary facilities. High quality meals cooked by outstanding chefs who consider the tastes and preferences of the passengers, a doctor and infirmary on board, moderate tickets, the continual assistance of an emigration inspector, as provided by law. Departure from the nearby port of Genoa, food and lodging at the company's expense while waiting to sail, and the same provision for transporting luggage and handling the practical details at embarkation and debarkation: a gentleman's vacation of clean air, sun, and a guaranteed welcome upon arrival at the port of New York.

Shortly afterwards posters appeared of the Anchor Line, a foreign company whose ships also left from Genoa: a gigantic steamship was reproduced with three smokestacks tall as towers, hundreds of portholes, four decks with elegant passengers, including a woman dressed in red holding a parasol, the prow slicing the sea into two wings of white foam.

The La Veloce representative was the first to arrive in the village, a plump middle-aged man with fat red cheeks who, with a handful of coins, got some youngsters to go from house to house to inform those interested that there would be a meeting at the tavern after sunset.

On his way home from work, Giacomo passed by just as a crowd was beginning to gather there on the street. Curious, he decided to stop. A dozen men of different ages, with hat in hand and the self-conscious manner of shy peasants in the presence of a stranger, were hesitantly entering the tavern. The representative welcomed them cordially, and making every attempt to put them at ease, invited them to sit down at a table. He ordered two liters of red wine, filled the glasses, and offered snuff and Tuscan cigars to each man. One of them took time to deeply inhale the fragrance of his cigar, turning it gently in his fingers, before beginning to enjoy every puff of that pleasure made for gentlemen. When the representative noticed three men sitting a few feet away furtively observing the unusual assembly, he invited them to join their company. One of the three, shaking his head sadly, took off his cap and showed his baldhead to indicate that he was too old to emigrate. But the representative insisted that in America there was a place for everyone, the young and the not-so young; and anyway, America or not, they should drink a glass to their health. They let themselves be persuaded and the owner brought more chairs.

The fact that the representative spoke their dialect, was friendly, and didn't put on airs immediately put the men at ease. Giving them time to empty their glass, put a pinch of tobacco in their nose, or enjoy their cigar to the end, he introduced himself: Bortolo Cortinovis, from Clusone, a retired carabinieri marshal. To reassure them about the legitimacy and correctness of his activity, he showed them his government-issued license as carrier representative. Everyone craned his neck as the document was passed around, even to those who didn't know how to read. The ancient, rooted, and justified suspicion of peasants toward strangers was for the moment placated and the man suddenly rose in their estimation. To ward off any suspicion from himself, he hastened to warn them to be on their guard because charlatans were going around tricking people into thinking they were someone they were not.

The marshal pointed out, with self-satisfied pride, that only twenty Italian and foreign shipping companies, selected and controlled by the relevant authorities, were authorized to use representatives to speak to those interested in emigrating. With such guarantees they had nothing to fear. Everything took place in the light of day, with great openness and honesty. As a representative of the La Veloce Company, he was known and esteemed in the whole of Val Seriana. They could ask anyone. His only task was to provide the necessary information about the voyage. Those who had already gone had done so with the security of having a relative, a countryman, or an acquaintance waiting for them who would tell them where there was work, what the accommodations were, and how much they would earn.

Everyone nodded. That's the way it was. The man's straightforward talk had placated the anxieties and worries they had dragged around for months. His background as retired marshal, his air of prosperity, his simple and friendly manner, his calm and unassuming way, his experience and know-how in that business had reassured them. He seemed to know what he was talking about, and they waited trustfully to learn the rest.

The representative poured more wine, passed around more cigars and tobacco, and sang the praises of his shipping company, which boasted a long tradition of overseas voyages with great steamships that were fast and trustworthy. Experience is the best guarantee. If in the past the crossing to America took forty days, it now took only ten to reach the New York port. Tone popped up to say that some people from Gandino left several months ago and it had taken twenty days and not ten, as the representative said, but someone nudged him to keep quiet and listen instead of interrupting with useless objections. The representative was not flustered in the least, and patiently explained that it depended on the ship: some were hundred-year-old asthmatic tramps that miraculously stayed afloat, and when a wave rippled them they struggled to keep upright, tossing passengers here and there like sacks of corn. On the other hand, the vessels owned by his employer, a gentleman from Genoa who wasn't interested in making money because he already had so much, were brand new, so fast they cut the voyage in half. They were furnished with the latest and most powerful boilers, so that tons and tons of coal were loaded at the embarkation point, as they could see for themselves when they got on. Not only that, but the ships were absolutely safe, the most important thing of all. Life jackets and lifeboats were on board for everyone, not like some junk heaps that were not in compliance with the law, and if anything happened it would be "Every man for himself!"

And besides, in the old steamships the third class dormitories were in the hold—cold, pitch dark and unventilated. In the modern ones even third class passengers slept in bright, warm cabins, with two berths—three at the most. All had windows to let in fresh air and light with an ocean view, and a safe place to stow luggage. And what's more, there was running water, sinks, and clean and disinfected lavatories, as prescribed by law.

The men around the table were as tense as slingshots, almost as if the marshal was telling the story of their destiny and knew in advance how it would end. The endless discussions with family members, relatives, and villagers, always a bit unrealistic, were based on the scanty information of those already emigrated. They hadn't been given details about the departure, the sea voyage, the arrival, their treatment, and the actual expenses.

There was plenty of excellent food on the ship, Cortinovis went on, his voice growing louder with excitement. There was fresh-baked bread every day, meat for lunch and dinner, pastries or fruit on Sunday, as much wine as you like, and he could confidently guarantee, or swear, if they wished, that never in their life would they eat so well or so plentifully. The thought of the bread, meat, and pastries, made eyes shine and mouths water. The tavern owner sidled up to the table and nodded enthusiastically at every word.

Still to mention was the recreation provided to make the time pass more quickly on shipboard: card games, raffles, sack races, parties on the promenade deck, a small orchestra playing under the stars from sunset 'til late at night, or in the ballroom in case of bad weather. And all these conveniences—let's call them luxuries

—were offered at more than reasonable—actually exceptional—prices, because there was a special fare for emigrants. As perhaps they already knew, the train trip to the port at Genoa, for at least ten emigrants, was estimated at outstanding reductions; therefore it paid to leave together. And as for dealing with the practical matters, once they made up their minds to go they would be assisted and accompanied as far as their destination. And for those who had to travel further in America, the company would also take care of up to half the expenses for the train ticket from New York. Not to mention the cost of food and lodging at Genoa while waiting for the ship to sail, depending on the weather, which was also at the expense of the shipping company. What more could they want?

The representative was very eloquent in describing the safety, comfort, and amenities of the voyage, as well as in giving instructions about how to proceed. He had convinced them that he was there for their interests rather than those of the ship owner, as if he were a friend or a relative. Everything seemed simpler and easier than they had imagined. They felt encouraged and enthusiastic, and they desired—and at the same time feared—to venture into that unknown country on the other side of the world had acquired a concrete, friendly aspect.

Giacomo, elbows on the table and head on fire from the wine, stared at him, mesmerized: that ocean that he had never seen, that ship so modern, that land overflowing with promises of prosperity and abundance, rekindled his desire to marry Ninetta at the end of his military service and go there with her. They had talked about getting married for a year, but her parents were opposed: he had three more years in the army, and as an unskilled worker he would earn very little; he hadn't saved a red cent, and moreover the ruinous breath of his father's creditors was blowing on his neck. Whatever gave him the idea he could support a family? He argued that Ninetta could also work over there instead of staying here to earn a pittance at the spinning mill. But her parents would not listen to reason, almost as though they expected their daughter to stay home and play the lady once she was married. His father was in Switzerland and would surely be opposed to the wedding for the same reasons, and his mother's opinion didn't count. But at the right time, as soon as he was discharged from the army, he would fight like a tiger and win.

As the representative talked, Giacomo imagined himself standing on the ship deck contemplating the vast ocean with Ninetta snuggled up to him. The wind was blowing her skirt and she laughed and laughed as she tried in vain to hold it down and hang on to her shawl that risked flying into the sea. He even seemed to hear the panting of the boilers, as powerful as a dragon breathing, and the crash of waves as they broke against the keel, and he felt drunk with happiness, like someone about to enter the gates of paradise. And suddenly on the horizon appeared something that at first seemed like a low cloud, but sharpening his gaze and shading his eyes from the blinding light, he understood that it was a strip of land. That strip of land was America. Ninetta, touched by the moment, looked into this face, and he felt a lump in his throat; he held her to him and caressed her arm, her slender waist, her round hips. Giacomo gasped for breath and his blood roared in his ears.

He came to his senses when Cortinovis filled their glasses again. The marshal waited for everyone to drink before he pulled a letter from his pocket. It was from someone from Val di Scalve, he explained, a certain Giovanni Crotti, who left for America the previous year on one of the La Veloce ships. He now worked in a coal mine in Oregon—a state in the north ten times bigger than Lombardy—whose owner was from Piedmont. He read in a loud voice, emphasizing each word as though reciting: he said that the trip had been excellent, with a calm sea and bright sun. He had rested and eaten so much on the ship that he even gained weight. The work in the mine was easy, and he earned three dollars a day, which would buy all kinds of good things in Italy. The owner was a good man and treated them like his sons. He lived in a nice little house with a yard and in his spare time he tended his garden and raised chickens. The representative passed around two photos that Crotti had included in his letter: in the first, indicated by a red dot over his head, he sat at a café table with three very cheerful friends raising full glasses of wine. The proprietor stood behind the polished wood counter in a white jacket and bow tie next to a forest of bottles, glasses, cups, and an imposing cash register. Behind him a large mirror took up almost the whole wall. Tucked in the frame was the photo of a young woman dressed in white, her beautiful face shaded by the brim of a straw hat, a parasol in her gloved hands. A crystal chandelier hung from the ceiling. On the left wall was a pendulum clock next to a picture of a snowy mountain scene, perhaps the Alps. There was also a wide shelf with boxes of cookies, chocolate bars, and mysterious little glass vases. A rug with floral designs could be seen in a corner.

The representative called attention to the healthy appearance of the quartet, their contented air, the elegance of the locale illuminated by electricity, the appropriateness of the proprietor's clothes —he, too, from Lombardy. He turned the photograph over. The café was called the Alpino, and was in Portland, a big city in Oregon.

In the second snapshot was a group of musicians, with guitar, accordion, and clarinet, along with Crotti who plucked a mandolin. Underneath was written: FESTIVAL OF THE PATRON SAINT. It was a shame they couldn't hear the music, lamented the marshal. The letter and photos were proof that the emigrants had a beautiful life in America, or rather, a grand life such they had never dreamed of here and, as could be seen, they continued to celebrate the same festivities and special days of their villages and church. The men passed around the photos of that fellow from Val di Scalve, greedily scrutinizing every detail, almost as if that single instant fixed on the paper could reveal every detail of his days over there. Corinovis declared that if he weren't too old, he would leave without giving it a second thought.

For some time now Gioanì had been acting like a tarantula had bitten him. He squirmed in his chair, fiddled with his glass, moving it here and there, scratched his head, made faces, and bared his teeth as though he had a stomachache. He was forty years old and had worn himself out in French coal mines for twelve long years before deciding to return home as destitute as when he had left. Now that two of his sons were adolescents he got the idea in his head to go with them to America where he hoped to make his fortune. After restraining himself for so long he finally exploded: that sea voyage seemed just like paradise and he couldn't wait to get on the ship. However, he didn't know how much money he needed for such a heaven on earth, and then he wondered if he would be able to understand anything of that English language, and how he would be received and treated there, if better or worse than France, and how he could support himself before he began earning something, and if the Americans wanted older men like him, who didn't even know how to read and write, and furthermore, had a miner's bad lungs.

Caught off-guard, Cortinovis hesitated a moment, then he conjured up his most captivating smile and said that shortly he would tell them the price of the tickets, fixed by the emigration commissioner, and in the meantime he assured them that the language was nothing to worry about because they would have very little to do with Americans; they would be dealing mostly with northern Italians. He repeated that young or old, illiterate or not, they needed men so badly over there who could work hard that they didn't care about age or education; and he skipped over the subject of Gioanì's lungs. That wasn't his department; it was something for the health officials to handle.

As he had already explained, Cortinovis went on patiently, he was there to deal with details of the trip, while it was their business, before leaving, to find work in America through a relative, a villager, a friend, and ask him for information about what to do. And that same person, whose address they must show to the American officials on arrival, must guarantee to be their sponsor in the beginning. Because the biggest fear over there was having to support the emigrants at public expense. Therefore it was mandatory upon arrival to show they had fifty dollars, that is, tangible material evidence that they were able to reach their final destination by their own means. An enormous sum, it seemed to the group; there arose a murmur of concern very close to fear, and the burning question: How many lire equal fifty dollars?

The representative firmly restored calm. This is a subject he would deal with later. More important than anything else now was for them to know that they should not for any reason — for any reason! he repeated — leave with a work contract already signed, because that was absolutely prohibited by the authorities, and if it was discovered at the other end they would be rejected. Too many emigrants in the past had signed contracts, and then discovered they had been tricked, victimized by the boss, fired after fifteen days without a cent, and forced to rely on public assistance or actually beg to keep from dying of hunger. That was why the Americans had severely prohibited contracts.

Cortinovis wanted to delay the thorny subject of cost. He knew from experience how delicate the matter was for those who had the cash and for those who had none at all, and he was very reluctant to face their reactions. The ignorant peasants seemed to expect the trip to be practically cost free, and except for those who had already gone, they had never stuck their nose outside their isolated valley. Accustomed to measuring distance by their stride, they were incapable of understanding how far away America was. Now was the time to bring out the sheet of paper with the La Veloce letterhead and the picture of a beautiful steamship, on which was listed the ships' names, dates of departure, the tonnage of each, the hourly speed in miles, and the number of days for the voyage. They should understand that it takes at least a month to get all the necessary documents ready for expatriation, and so they needed to get started right away.

The men passed around the printed sheet with little curiosity: Cortinovis knew very well that the minor details didn't interest them. Their thoughts were fixed on the cost of the voyage, and he was waiting for them to ask. As they soon did, in fact; but the question went unanswered, because Gioanì, over the voices of his companions, nagged by those fifty dollars that he would have to take with him, dug in his heels and wanted to know first of all how many lire were equivalent to a dollar. Cortinovis was forced to reply: Keep in mind the value can rise or fall. One dollar is equal to five lire. Deathly silence. The representative waited in that silence for someone to laboriously make the calculation, waited until someone, beside himself, shouted: Two hundred fifty lire! Pandemonium broke out that seemed like a political insurrection. Gioanì shouted louder than everyone else, with such pain in his voice that even the marshal was moved, though accustomed for some time to a feeling of indifference that verged on cynicism. But there are three of us! Gioanì shouted, close to tears, there are three of us! as if that deserved a discount.

After that outburst the men were struck dumb, overpowered by dizziness at the edge of the abyss that separated their pitiful possessions from that vast sum.

Cortinovis thought it to his advantage to be silent and wait for them to calm down before speaking about the price of the ship ticket. It was the right moment to fill their glasses again. He signaled to the innkeeper who, as soon as he brought the wine, launched into an extemporaneous lecture about their exaggerated fears: No use making a mountain out of a molehill. You'll find the money. What the devil, there was always a friend or a relative to help out who wouldn't even ask for interest but would be happy with a small return or a gift from America. And if you really can't find a friend or relative, you can borrow the money or mortgage your house, and then when you get to where you can earn a lot of ready cash you can pay it back without getting an ulcer.

The innkeeper's tirade (who had known his chickens from the day they were hatched) was the result of the representative's hefty tip as well as a subtle way to suggest himself as a financial backer of the emigrant villagers, and it had the expected calming effect. So at that point Cortinovis could announce the ticket price, more or less, calculated on the duration, from ten to eighteen days, depending on the ship's speed, as he had already explained. For third class train tickets to Genoa, fixed by law, there was a thirty percent reduction for emigrants if they traveled in groups of ten. The prices didn't provoke sparks of revolt, but only a downcast, devastated, mute meditation.

The representative was winding up his evening's work and was exhausted by the effort. He only had to wait for the seeds he had planted to germinate. He knew those men had no way out of poverty and therefore had no choice. Beaten, discouraged, shilly-shallying, and tempted to sidestep such a serious decision, it was up to him to prop them up and give them a shove. He smiled kindly, and with his paternal, polite, and persuasive manner, he comforted and exhorted them not to let themselves be tormented by doubts or frightened by that leap into the unknown. Prosperity such as they had never even been able to imagine was waiting for them in America. The difficulties that they feared would melt like snow in the spring, and for the rest of their lives they would thank him for encouraging them to get out of a dead-end existence. And finally he invited them to raise their glasses in a toast to the health and good fortune of them all. He recommended they take all the time they needed to think about it, and as soon as they made up their minds to tell the innkeeper who knew where to find him.

And in the meantime, he cautioned, don't be hoodwinked by un-qualified and unauthorized individuals, untrustworthy riff-raff, who try to hook the unsuspecting with lies.

Ernesto Bertocchi, representative for the Anchor Line, came from Nembro in a gig one Sunday morning in December. He hitched his horse outside the tavern, went in rubbing his benumbed hands, and ordered bread, salami, and a glass of wine from the curious innkeeper. While Bertocchi ate and drank, he made some casual comments about the worst weather on record, and asked about the village. The innkeeper, as suspicious and guarded as all the valley residents, didn't open up right away, but as soon as he be-came better acquainted and saw there was something in it for him he began to chat.

In order to entice passengers for his company's ships, Bertoc-chi didn't assemble likely customers in the tavern, but adopted pro-cedures and strategies that, in his opinion, saved time and money, with the same results. He was a clever young man, with a cock-sure and no-nonsense manner. He had switched from being a live-stock middleman to working as an intermediate for the shipping company, firmly convinced he was dealing with the same kind of merchandise. He didn't frequent fairs and markets, didn't stop at church squares to snare emigrants or distribute illustrated pam-phlets, but limited himself to a practice he himself defined as "snif-fing out poverty," which consisted of gathering information in places where he could find valuable and furtive collaboration, al-lowing him to strike with confidence. Therefore he moseyed around registry offices and land offices, waiting rooms of notaries who took care of mortgage transcriptions and judges' offices where financial failures were recorded, pawn shops and offices with the lists of conscripts; in other words, places where the misfortunes of the poor were documented in black and white. That wasn't all. He wormed his way in everywhere he went and was skilled at getting people to talk. He collected and sifted through the gossip, slander or vilification fomented by old grudges. In this way he got to know about the quarrels or lawsuits over money between relatives or villagers, the disputes between in-laws over brides' dowries, the expirations of rentals or contracts of tenant farmers, the debts assumed with usurers, and with this list in his pocket he plunged like a vulture straight into their kitchens.

Leaving the tavern and the impressed innkeeper, he climbed up the frozen path that led to the bird-catcher house, already knowing that in that hovel on the side of the mountain there were four pigeons to catch with one bean: the head of the family, financially ruined and in debt up to his eyeballs, who for that reason had gone with his son to Switzerland, another son in the army and close to being discharged, and a third about to be called up. Actually, his bean was tailored to fit the specific situation of each one of them.

He found the bustling activity of a bee hive: an elderly mother working in the kitchen, a couple of boys shoveling snow from the yard, another one breaking the ice in the chickens' water pan, one going and coming from the brook with pails of water, another stacking wood to dry next to the fireplace, and still another sweeping the uneven floor and using the broom to chase away two chickens in search of warmth and crumbs. The mother, gripped by the uneasiness that simple and unlettered people feel at the unexpected arrival of a stranger in city clothes, had him sit in a rickety chair, and looking around helplessly, she stammered an apology for not having anything to offer him.

The representative took pains to calm the woman's discomfort, and at the same time looked around to take stock of the destitution in which that family lived (calculating she was easy prey for his flattery): the dark, narrow, crumbling, smoke-blackened room where they lived on top of one another, their patched and mended clothes which barely protected the children from the pungent cold, the numbing air, their frostbitten hands, the hollow-faced mother who busied about the fireplace mixing the eternal polenta of the poor. There was real hunger here.

Congratulating himself for the shrewdness with which he had sniffed out their miserable poverty, he introduced himself as the representative of the shipping company Anchor Line, a foreign company much more honest and trustworthy than those home-grown scoundrels who are good about making promises they do not keep. The Anchor Line steamships left every week from Genoa for America; they were brand spanking new, modern, fast, safe and powerful, furnished with every comfort, and he talked at length in praise of all the good qualities and advantages.

Mario and Egidio stood riveted to the wall, open-mouthed. Bertocchi was thinking that even the two minors could emigrate if accompanied by their father, and he figured on putting them in his game-bag. Giacomo was sitting in front of him, and just to let him know that he was informed, and therefore able to make a comparison, he mentioned the meeting in the tavern with the La Veloce representative. At once Bertocchi, aware of his rival's in-cursion, parried the blow, shook his head, and affably advised him not to trust too much in the first comer. You had to listen carefully to distinguish between those who were honest and those who were swindlers who would even bamboozle the devil. It was not a question of rivalry, he assured them, because in this activity there was room for everyone's business. He just felt it was his duty to warn the unsuspecting about the dangers they ran without realizing it.

I know, he continued, lowering his voice, that certain shipping companies, besides boasting of good qualities often invented out of whole cloth, behaved in ways absolutely prohibited by the au-thorities in order to attract emigrants to their ships. They commit real crimes, like paying Italians already working in America to write letters full of lies about their lives over there, about their good salaries, treatment, work, house, and they send photos with everyone looking rich, fat, and happy. Some of the companies pay the bosses directly to blackmail their employees, making them tell lies in order to sway other emigrants, that is, other third-class passengers such as have filled their ships and coffers. That wasn't the case with his company, which was not only of proven honesty, but as its offices were abroad, it wasn't in the position to do such shenanigans even if it wanted to.

He advised them to always trust in the straight facts from relatives and acquaintances who had already emigrated rather than believe the letters bandied about by representatives. He knew of colossal frauds by companies that put the lives of unfortunate people at risk: for example, the trick one company, which he did not want to name, played on some men from southern Italy leaving on a ship from Naples. A ship in a manner of speaking, because it was old and dilapidated, and they took advantage of the ignorance of those day laborers by making them think that a tramp like that could cross the ocean. The poor devils had paid a lot for their tickets, and after several days on the high seas the ship drew near the shore, and they were told that that was America. They argued that they wanted to get off at a port, as they had been promised, not on a lonely beach they didn't even know where. Then they were threatened with clubs and knives and had to jump in the water where they couldn't even touch bottom, so that those who didn't know how to swim risked drowning. Well, guess what. That wasn't America. It was the coast of Tuscany! See how they were swindled? And when, half drowned and soaking wet, they ran into a fisherman who spoke his own dialect, they did not understand a word and thought he was speaking English. That's the kind of disaster you could run into by trusting certain companies.

Though thinking that this guy was out for himself, just like Cortinovis, Giacomo hung on his words, drawn into a new, exciting world of dangerous adventure, far from the stagnant pond of the valley where nothing ever happened, and where destinies were fixed from the day they were born. Every time the talk turned to emigration—and at the tavern for an entire evening after Corinovis' visit the villagers had discussed it heatedly—his imagination had reared and pawed like a restless colt, to then collapse in the sad reality of his impending military service. And just at that point, as though guessing his thoughts, the representative made a brusque right turn and began belittling the obligatory military service instituted at the time Italy was unified, which however, let's be honest, only the sons of poor people had to take part, especially those in Sicily or Sardinia, while rich men paid a fortune to keep their sons home. It was a downright shame, because for three long years families had to go without their indispensable help, and so they became poorer than ever. And what did the government give in exchange? That sorry bit of soldier's pay, disgusting rations, and all the crabs and lice they could ever want. One son in the service is bearable, but when two have to go, or even three, it smacks of real injustice, and at times real tragedy. But there was a way to avoid it.

Bertocchi was pleased to see how Giacomo's eyes lit up with interest, and how even his mother, who up to now had been silently puttering around the fireplace, suddenly stopped to listen, drying her hands on her apron and sidling up to the table. He assumed a conspiratorial air, made a slight gesture of caution in the direction of the young boys, lowered his voice and said that since it was a very delicate business it was better that they speak privately as adults. Giacomo rose and escorted his brothers out of the kitchen.

All you have to do is pass the Italian border illegally, he said in a guarded tone, and go to a nearby French port—Marseilles, for instance—and get on a ship. Of course, this sort of thing costs a lot. It's dangerous for the guides, and no one does anything for nothing. But you have to figure you're ahead in the end, because instead of staying here to rot in the king's barracks for three years, you can be raking in money to pay off all your debts quickly, and what's left over you can stash under your mattress.

Bertocchi, shrewd character that he was, played both ends against the middle: for the Anchor Line he did everything aboveboard and earned his pay; for the illegal expatriate, who was the source of high commissions from opportunistic shipping companies, a percentage from the smugglers, and a fee from the fugitives themselves, he tried hard not to give his game away. And anyway he only made his appearance in the first phase of the operation, to give information about crossing the border; then different actors entered the scene, and he disappeared without leaving a trace.

He was careful not to bring to Giacomo's attention the fact that not only did he risk going to prison for desertion if they caught him at the border, but that when he was extradited back to Italy he could be imprisoned for five, ten, even twenty years. In short, he wouldn't be able to set foot in his village again until he was an old man. But that was something one should know anyway, and if that young man didn't know it, too bad for him.

He noticed a look of dismay on the mother's face, and on her son's face a perplexity very close to panic. A long silence followed which Bertocchi respected. They were simple and naïve people, and whether or not they were informed about the serious consequences, he decided that this was not the time to persist: once he had planted the temptation to escape in their heads he had to give them time to react. He was vague about prices when the mother asked in a faint voice what it would cost, and then, rapidly switching tack, he observed that frankly he couldn't understand why anyone would want to go to work in Switzerland where they had to break their backs for starvation wages and waste so much time and energy, when all they had to do was board a ship and their lives would change like day and night. If so many others had done it and hadn't regretted it—otherwise they could have come back, wouldn't they?—it meant it was worth the effort. He returned to the painful subject of the debts by telling them he knew many men who had gone to America with his company and in a short time not only had they been able to pay off their debts to the last lira, but they had been able to save enough to buy back their house and land and let their families live in prosperity.

Bertocchi had cast all his bait and was about to leave, but he couldn't go without launching one last lure, considering that the fraud was lucrative and so well conceived that it wouldn't be discovered until they reached their destination, and the poor deceived devils wouldn't have any breath left to protest. (Though few had snapped at it, because the narrow-minded valley inhabitants were suspicious of anything new and different.) He said that no matter what they decided to do, emigrate, or stay home, he felt duty bound to inform all the respectable people he had anything to do with of the risk they ran with the doctors' examination after reaching the port of New York. They could be rejected for any stupid thing, even a swollen eye, an infection, or a contagious illness picked up on the ship. To be rejected was a disaster, a tragedy, a disappointment that could drive you out of your mind: just think of the money spent for the trip, the expenses for eating and sleeping from the time they got off one ship and on to another, and on top of that, they had to pay for the return trip on ship and train out of their own pocket. Such a calamity could drive a man to desperation. But luckily there was a way out, a very modern invention and totally legal, which has finally come here — because we are always the last to get anything — that is, a special insurance covering the expense of such a misfortune. It cost something, true enough, but this was a sure way of being reimbursed to the last red cent.

Bertocchi rose to leave. He had concluded the most important part of his work and there was nothing left to do but wait for the results.

3

Too young to have memories of their father and brother, Adele and Lodovico had hidden behind their mother's skirts, and from that safe place cast furtive, frightened glances at the two strangers. Lodovico, the smallest, was forcefully torn from his maternal stronghold by the dust-covered intruder, a bear with a thundering voice who held him in his arms, tossed him into the air and caught him as he fell. The little boy had broken into sobs so that his father, put off by that hostile behavior, snorted and put him down at once. Adele, because of what happened, was saved, but her little brother's fright convinced her to run and hide in the woodshed for safety's sake.

Even the older children had had the anxious air of not knowing which way to turn. There was no joy or festivity in the reunion. Their difficult and isolated life had continued without their father; they had become accustomed to his absence and had managed by themselves. The small amount of money received and immediately turned over to the creditors, the rare, curt letters that seemed to come from another world, had built a wall of indifference, along with a great deal of resentment. His years away had given the children time to observe how his presence had been a source of tension and bad humor and how, on the other hand, without him their mother had dealt with everyday life with the necessary firmness and understanding to create a relaxed atmosphere in spite of the hardships and privations. His return brought back memories of the previous tyrannical regime and threatened their fragile tranquility. It aroused a tenacious resistance to making room for him, and to giving him back the baton of command he seemed to expect. Their mother's hesitation and alarmed expression seemed to mirror their own fears.

Still clinging to his mother's skirts, while she stroked his head to calm him, Lodovico continued to cry without let up. Mucous dripped from his nose into his open mouth, and a thread of drool dribbled from his mouth to his chin. Cipriano, offended by the reaction of his youngest child and by his daughter's quick exit, shouted for him to shut up, which only provoked a new attack of convulsive sobbing. By now on the verge of losing his temper, he ordered his wife to make him stop or he would teach that spoiled crybaby a lesson. When he started to unbuckle his belt, Maddalena took her little brother by the hand and led him screaming out of the kitchen.

A frozen silence filled the room. Pulling a long face, their father began fumbling with his gear, untying the strings of a hemp sack that resembled an enormous sausage. He opened it, looked around, and not finding what he was looking for, began to throw the contents on the floor: a pair of rolled up work pants incrusted with mortar, two long johns out at the knees, some faded, sweat-stained wool sweaters, a pair of nail boots covered with dried mud some socks with holes in the toes and heels, two torn shirts without collars, a piece of laundry soap, a razor. The children followed his actions, increasingly more disheartened by those pathetic belongings spread out on the floor. Finally, from the bottom of the sack he drew a newspaper-wrapped bundle that he unfolded to reveal a Swiss chocolate bar. On the return trip it had been so thoroughly smashed that not one square remained intact. Mario ran off with a little piece for Lodovico, who gobbled it down and finally quit sniveling. None of them had ever seen or much less tasted chocolate. It was so good that Egidio took some of the foil and licked it until not a trace was left. Attilio snatched it from him, stuck a piece on his teeth, and smiled a horrible metallic smile. Mario put his head in the sack in the hopes of finding another one, but that was the only gift. However, the little present had sweet-

ened mouths, loosened the tension and tongues, so that they all began to talk at once. Their father said he had meant to bring a piece
of Gruyère, too, a delicious Swiss cheese with holes, so different
from stracchino, but he hadn't had time to buy it. He went to find
Adele in the woodshed, handed her a smidgen of the chocolate
she had been waiting for, and peace seemed made.

From a distance Gildo watched his siblings, disconcerted by
the fact that they had grown so much he hardly recognized them,
and he was trying to assign the right name to each. He anxiously
scrutinized his mother's toothless mouth, the blue shadows under
her eyes, her ashen color and sunken cheeks, and he was astonished how much she had aged, and even shrunk over those few
years. He had envied those at home, including her, but those signs
on her face and body indicated a suffering and exhaustion equal
to his, and he reproached himself for not being able to imagine
that. Except for his mother, who in her watchful and silent way
had always protected him, he felt like an uncomfortable stranger.
The only connection during those years away from home had
been Giacomo's few letters, always the same depressing refrain
about their health, (including the cow's), debts, the short supply of
money, work, the harvest.

Naturally reserved and uneasy around people, Gildo had quickly adjusted to the separation from his family, which the presence
of his father did little to compensate for. It didn't take long before
he accepted his solitary life made up of incessant work, a few
words exchanged with fellow workers, an occasional smile, a joking remark, a clap on the back. He didn't miss the absence of affectionate gestures and words, because he had never experienced
them, did not expect them, and was incapable of them himself.
The country people's habitual lack of sociability, their modesty
and natural reticence, checked every impulse; and the relentless
hardships did not just inhibit the expression of feelings, it
annulled them. He had never met anyone who didn't grind away

like he did between difficulties and anxieties; he felt certain that no one was spared the harshness and bleakness of existence, and that the absence of any solace whatever was an inevitable part of it. There was no time or desire for sentiment or affection; everyone struggled desperately for pure survival. Everyone kept his pain to himself, out of sight, like a sin.

Only with children did Gildo not feel afraid or shy. Taking advantage of the confusion, he slipped out the door unnoticed and went to find Adele, still holed up in the woodshed, with traces of chocolate still on her pouting lips. He sat beside his little sister, smiled at her, ruffled her hair, and hugged her to him. At first she resisted, then she leaned against his leg, smiled back at him, and suddenly Gildo felt revived.

After lunch came the time to speak of practical matters. Giacomo told his father what he had learned from the two ships' representatives, including the possibility suggested by Bertocchi to emigrate illegally in order to avoid military service. When they went to Switzerland, and Giacomo was already on the list of recruits, he had argued long and hard, as stubborn as a goat, to cross the border secretly, even knowing that he risked arrest and years of prison. At that time Cipriano had been definitely opposed, and now, astonished, he listened to that knucklehead starting all over again. Mounting anger fogged his vision: already resentful about his children's hostility, a gang of lazy snails who had grown impudent and defiant during his absence, forgetting who was in command, Giacomo's affront to his authority was intolerable, a slap in the face. He had returned, even though for a short time, and he would get it into that blockhead that he was boss. He was beside himself. He cursed the saints and the dead, while his wife, dismayed by that blasphemous outburst, made the sign of the cross. He pounded on the table, kicked a chair, rushed at Giacomo with hands outstretched, and Maddalena, terrified, quickly stepped between them. Lodovico began his uncontrollable sobbing again, the young children, frightened by their father's violence that they had had time to forget, ran off as fast as their legs would carry them. Gildo, flat against the wall, grew white as a sheet. Their father shouted until he was hoarse, Never never never would he allow Giacomo to ruin his life and that of the whole family. It was one thing to cross the frontier illegally, as they had done, where the most you risked was being sent back after a few days of jail; it was another thing to cross it as a deserter, to end up in prison for years and to have a criminal record for the rest of your life. In fact, if you ask him, they shoot deserters.

As soon as he calmed down a bit, Giacomo, who was as pig-headed as his father, and on top of that rash enough to challenge his fury, told him about the insurance against the risk of being turned back at the New York port that Bertocchi had proposed, a modern invention that, after payment of a modest sum, allowed one to recover the expense of the entire trip. Another outburst was expected, but instead his father replied that it wasn't a bad idea. In Switzerland many people were insured for all kinds of things. It was something to think about. The fear of being refused entry because of age had been gnawing at him for some time now, and the chance of getting back all the money he had put out appeared like an unexpected solution.

At the tavern he talked to villagers he hadn't seen for several years. Their cordiality comforted him after his children's cold welcome. Many had decided to emigrate. Five of them had decided to join Tranquillo in Washington State. Some had already begun the process for the passport; one had chosen Corinovis to take care of things for him, another one had been swayed by Bertocchi and lined up with him. They spoke again about the two representatives and their offers that were more or less the same. Between one glass and another they spent hours figuring how much money they would need for the trip. The innkeeper offered to finance only those who could mortgage their house and their land, so it was clear that those who had already lost their house and land would have to turn elsewhere. It wasn't at all easy to get a loan from the usurers. To be eligible for the train reduction, they still lacked three men, but after spreading the word through the villages, they were soon joined by a young man from Fiobbio and two from Bondo Petello.

Someone must have whispered something about Ninetta in his father's ear, because another avalanche of abuse fell on Giacomo. His father accused him of wanting to desert in order to hook up with that girl he didn't even know, and if Giacomo had done that he would be the first to turn him in. He should get the idea of marriage out of his dumb head. How could Giacomo dare think about such things while he had been in Switzerland breaking his back to keep the family afloat? Young people today were spoiled and thought of nothing but themselves. He should first do his duty as soldier, and then he could go break his back in America.

In the commune of Albino, the town hall secretary charged with the issuing of passports told him briefly and on the sly that he needed to talk to him in private about something important, and to wait for him on the corner around noon. When they met the man glanced around as though afraid of being seen, and pulling Cipriano to a more secluded spot, he recommended the greatest discretion, considering his delicate position in the local government, and asked him if he would be interested in saving a nice hunk of money on the trip to America. Damn! What a question! Cipriano replied. Because there was a way. Get onboard a ship in France, at the port of Le Havre, with a French shipping company. From there the voyage to New York was much shorter, it took just a week, and that means a cheaper ticket. It's one thing to be on a ship for twenty days, and another to be on one for seven. Even a child could figure that out. Many emigrants had chosen that way, and if so many had done it that meant it was good.

Cipriano didn't have the foggiest notion where Le Havre was

or how to get there, and the secretary explained that it was a city in the north of France, easy to get to, just take a train from Milan, get off at Paris, change trains and in two or three hours they were there. He had to consider one big advantage: you could sleep on the train without paying any extra. They could bring food from home, and this also meant a big savings over leaving from Genoa. Because it's not just the cost of the transportation, the crossing, but people have to eat and sleep. A ship is like a hotel that moves, and you know that the food and lodging is a big part of the price. He advised bringing food Italians liked, which they wouldn't find on shipboard, and sell it to them for double the price. Many did that, and in this way they paid for part of the trip. And because foreign companies didn't have to respect tariffs fixed by the government like we did, you could bargain for the price of the passage and save even more. Everyone knows that foreigners are more honest, upright, and dependable than Italians, including the shipping companies. He knew about some tricks played on emigrates that were so disgusting he wouldn't even mention them.

The secretary glanced at the gray-haired man standing in front of him. He imagined that he was worried about his age, and so he claimed that by going to America from France, you didn't risk being rejected because you were too old to work. Not only that: except for contagious illnesses like trachoma, conjunctivitis, or tuberculosis, you could disembark even if you were blind, crippled, or hunchbacked. In short, the agreements between America and France were very different from those with Italy. But the most important and advantageous thing of all, he added, lowering his voice, a real gift from the company, was that the tariff also included the train trip from New York to the final destination. Where exactly did he and his companions want to go in America? To Renton, in the state of Washington? Fine! There was nothing to worry about. They could set their minds at ease. That ticket would be in their hands several days before leaving; a big help, because then all they had to do in New York was go to the train station and get on the first train. Everything was arranged beforehand and paid in advance.

Admiring the efficiency of the secretary, who really seemed to have thought of everything, Cipriano brought up the question of the insurance that guaranteed reimbursement of the trip's expenses, over and back, should they have the misfortune of being rejected at the port of New York. For a moment the secretary seemed puzzled. He had Cipriano repeat the question and then his face lit up. He said that he had forgotten to mention that to him. He had too many other things to think about. It was a good thing that he remembered. You could see he was an expert traveler. Right! A great way to keep from losing all their money. He would get the paper work done at once, and in the meantime Cipriano could get busy and talk the others into buying this insurance plan. He didn't yet know what it would cost, but certainly very little.

There was one last stumbling block. How could they make themselves understood with those people who spoke French? Cipriano asked. The other one laughed and explained that at the Modane station, on the other side of the border, an Italian who would accompany them to Le Havre would meet them, and so there would be no language problem.

The secretary handed Cipriano a leaflet that described a steamship and all the services on board, but gave no list of prices or hours of departure. He would get those to him as soon as possible. In fact, he would make an appointment with him at the same place on Thursday, and he would bring everything then. In the meantime Cipriano should spread the word about the offer — without mentioning his name, of course — and try to convince the others. Never never mention my name to strangers, he repeated before leaving; Be careful not to talk about this private business. If the discounts this company made got around, the other companies could cause a lot of trouble out of jealousy. He was careful not to inform Cipriano that there was a law against illegal, unlicensed recruiters like himself, and against people who encouraged emigrants to leave from foreign ports.

The leaflet, without any specific letterhead, promised a comfortable voyage on a luxurious steamship, cabins with two or four beds, wonderful dining rooms, separate smoking rooms, waiters, incomparable service, a different menu every day of the week.

Actually, the fare offered by the secretary of the commune, whose name, as agreed, was never mentioned even at home, was quite a bargain compared to what Cortinovis and Bertocchi had to offer, so it was not difficult to convince the others. On the other hand it was harder to explain the advantages of the insurance, an innovation not easy to grasp. Gioanì was a help—he who dreaded being rejected for his weakened miner's lungs. Gasping for breath, he got so worked up in the discussion that in the end he won the group over. Young and healthy men were excluded, as they ran no danger of being rejected. Bigio, who was forty years old and nearly bald and toothless, decided to take the insurance, as did Gioanì and Cipriano. Bigio and Gioanì didn't know how to write, so they made a crooked cross at the bottom of the document.

Everything went as smooth as oil, except when the secretary asked sharply for an unexpected commission of ten lire a head, otherwise no tickets. When Cipriano relayed this to the others they revolted: no one had said anything about a commission; it was up to the ship company to pay the intermediaries, and not them. The men who had selected Cortinovis or Bertocchi had already left, and they hadn't forked over a cent of commission. Why hadn't Cipriano told them earlier, considering he had been the one to recommend that bandit and had dealt with him from the first? And he had even bragged about it with an arrogance that sometimes got on their nerves. Since he had been such a sucker, he could just pay for them all; they wouldn't dream of coming up with that amount. A violent quarrel broke out and stopped just short of fisticuffs. When they had calmed down, Leone asked why in the world the secretary didn't want anyone to know his name. There was certainly something fishy behind it. How could he have two jobs? They had to meet him face-to-face, demand an explanation, and threaten to report him.

Great! Bigio observed. This way no one gets to go, and we start all over from the beginning, and who knows how much time that'll take. And besides that they were in it up to their necks; they should know what kind of trap they were in. If it was outside the law, then they were too. Now that they were involved they had to go through with it. That argument worked and they calmed down. Gioanì remarked that those prices were better than the other offers. Finally, with a resigned sigh, Leone said that they were hooked and might as well hand over the ten lire and be done with it.

A few days before their scheduled departure an employee of the shipping company delivered the tickets for the steamship Chicago, leaving from Le Havre for New York—weather permitting—on February 7, 1910 at 10 P.M., third class passengers to start boarding at 3 in the afternoon. He also gave them an unsigned leaflet with instructions for the entire trip, not to be shown to a soul for any reason in the world. It cautioned against speaking with anyone, including the casual trip companion, until reaching the train station across the border. And if the police asked who furnished the company's instructions, to mention no name but only say that a relative in America had told them. The leaflet advised bringing a folding stool for comfort on the ship, to dress properly, and to take suitcases instead of sacks or bundles in order to make a good impression upon arrival: useless advice considering the reality of the situation. No one could afford new clothes or appropriate luggage, not to mention the luxury of a folding stool. He gave them a blue sticker to put on their caps as soon as they got off the train at Modane, so the person who was to meet them would recognize them, and he gave them tickets for the various segments of the train trip. He told them to be careful to get on the right train, because as emigrants having the legal right for a discount, they could only travel on the local, slow trains, and only in third class—otherwise they would have to pay the difference along with a heavy fine. When they got the train ticket for the trip from New York to Renton, no one was surprised that it was written in Italian.

In pitch-black darkness of four in the morning, they met at the bridge over the Luio, at the intersection of the road to Albino. The torrent roared in the indistinct darkness below them. They walked quickly, one behind the other, bent under the weight their baggage. No one spoke. There were fourteen kilometers to the train station at Bergamo, and it was better to save their breath. An accumulation of snow from previous days was piled at the edge of the dirt road. A cold night breeze sliced into their faces, ears, and hands. Gioanì had wrapped a tattered scarf around his neck and from time to time was racked by fits of coughing.

Gildo carried a sack filled to bursting on his shoulders, and under his arms a heavy bundle wrapped in an old sheet and tied with a cord. It contained food to resell once they arrived: corn flour, stracchino, salami, bacon, and borlotti beans. The stink of the cheese wafted through the cloth and choked their breath. His father had sworn that the emigrants from Bergamo, yearning for familiar food would snap it up fast, so that they would make back all the expenses of the trip and maybe even something extra.

Leone had a round bulging sack with him that looked like an immense bologna. Bigio was carrying his old accordion on his shoulders like a large breadbasket; and his arms ached from carrying a large wooden crate and an enormous package tied with a rope. Gildo was the last in line. In the darkness he could barely see the thin lanky shape of Luigino, Gioanì's oldest son who was ahead, and he was guided by the sound of their footsteps. From time to time Gildo had to stop to put his bundle down and straighten the sack that kept sliding off his shoulders, and then hurry to rejoin the others. They had nearly three hours to walk, and already his back and neck were aching. At the last moment, the night before, Giacomo had given him an old pair of shoes to wear in place of his worn out pair. But they rubbed his heels and he was afraid they would make blisters on the long walk. He should have wrapped some cotton over his feet, but he hadn't thought of it.

Not a crack of light shone from the sparsely scattered houses along the road; everyone was asleep at that hour. Behind the barred doors someone was snoring, a horse pawed and scraped the ground, a cow snorted. The roar of the Luio just below the escarpment accompanied their walk; the dark shadow of Monte Misma loomed ahead. Many years ago Gildo had climbed to the top. From there you could see the whole Serio valley and, mixed with fog, the outskirts of Bergamo. Behind him were Monte Altino and the sanctuary in the middle of chestnut woods. As an altar boy in surplice and censer in hand he had followed the procession of the Corpus Domini. He could still remember the aroma of incense that filled the air. A little below the sanctuary was the small church of Dossello. In good weather on Sundays he preferred going up there for mass instead of the parish church because of the nice view. He looked in the direction of the mountain slope where their house was, but it was useless, you couldn't see three feet in front of you. It was better that way. Better to forget the house. Anyway who knows how many years before he would come back? Maybe never. To leave the house he had had to step over his brothers who were sleeping on straw mats on the floor. In spite of the commotion they didn't wake up, but it wasn't important to tell them goodbye. Who knows if he would ever see them again? And even if he did he probably wouldn't recognize them, and they certainly wouldn't know what to say to each other. Sometimes they are brothers in name only. He would have liked to have given Adele a kiss. He would miss her, but he didn't want to wake her at that ungodly hour. She had been so happy with the rag doll that he had sewn and stuffed for her, the first doll of her life. For eyes he had attached two buttons and had embroidered a mouth with wool thread. He had learned to sew in Switzerland and attach buttons, but he had never been able to manage a thimble. He could still see the image of his little sister cuddling that cloth doll like it was a real baby.

His mother had uncovered some still glowing embers from the ashes in the fireplace and had heated up a pot of chicory. When he went outside Filippa, frightened by the unusual nighttime noises, had started to moo. In the dark his mother had come up to him, brushed his face with two fingers and handed him a slice of cold polenta, which he put in his jacket pocket. She told him to be good and to remember to go to church and made the sign of the cross on his forehead while whispering a blessing. Barely able to make out her face in the dark, he bent to give her a quick kiss on the cheek, his heart beating wildly.

Giacomo, still half asleep and disheveled, had come out of the cowshed where he slept at night. He had helped lift the sack onto his shoulders and had walked with him as far as the bridge over the Luio with the rest of his baggage. As a way of saying goodbye he had dealt a cuff on his shaved head, told him to be careful and not get lice on the ship and to send money home as soon as possible. It was clear he would have liked to be in his place, and Gildo would have willingly given it to him.

Hoisting the sack on his other shoulder, he passed the bundle under his left arm and started walking faster. He couldn't wait to get on the train and take off his shoes. His stomach was already grumbling from hunger. His father was carrying the sack with provisions for the trip, together with a bag filled with bottles of red wine and a bottle of Fernet for seasickness. They had to carefully ration their food, he said, or there wouldn't be enough. They would eat breakfast when they reached the city. The slice of polenta in his pocket was tempting him: in the dark no one would notice him chewing, but he resisted the urge. His heart skipped a beat when he remembered the money in his jacket, along with his brand new passport. The terror of losing it all made him break out in a sweat. With a trembling hand he felt the small bulge inside his jacket and was reassured. His father had given him only thirty-five of the fifty dollars he had to show when reaching New York, with the excuse that he might lose it with his head always in the clouds. Since he was head of the family he would keep the remainder with the other dollars he had exchanged, which added up to one hundred and thirty. They were all in one-dollar bills — crackling green bills of strong paper that radiated wealth. Who knows where the others hid their money? Maybe in their shoes, socks, the cuff of their trousers, in their underwear. Gioanì had kept his sons' fifty dollars in spite of their protests, and he didn't want to say where he had stashed it, along with his own fifty. He heard about someone who had folded several bank notes one by one lengthwise, putting them under his hat ribbon. He thought he was being very clever, but then he left his hat on the train.

At the junction for Fiobbio a lantern flashed in the dark. Pino Carminati joined the group, followed by his wife who, it was said, had been pregnant when they got married. Shouts and greetings were exchanged, a few racy jokes about eating sweets before dinner, and some sly laughter. Pino bent down to put his lantern at the edge of the road and straightened up with tired slowness, breathed a deep sigh, and turned suddenly to his young wife. He took a step with his arms outspread and with a vigorous motion and a harsh sound like the moan of a wounded animal, he grabbed her and held her tightly, his face hidden in the hollow of her neck. The men were suddenly silent, holding their breath, dumbfounded by the audacity, the vehemence, and the desperate urgency of that embrace, and in the silence they heard him whisper something in his wife's ear. The woman clung to his neck, choking with sobs. In the weak lantern light the two shapes were so tightly joined that it seemed impossible to separate them without ripping their flesh to shreds. The young man picked his wife off her feet, bent her back in such a way that her body seemed to sink into his, and in the brusque movement a comb fell from her hair, loosening it in waves around her face. Hidden by that trembling curtain, they exchanged a long kiss.

Then Pino abruptly put his wife down, and roughly pulled her arms from around his neck. He made a sound like a stifled scream, and as she sobbed and called his name, he resolutely turned his back, frantically seized his baggage, and without a word was swallowed up by the group. The men started walking again in silence, enveloped in darkness; the woman's heart-rending cry accompanying them for a way, growing ever weaker. Gildo found himself next to Carminati. He heard him grinding his teeth and swearing softly to himself. But he didn't turn around once.

Confused and troubled, Gildo had witnessed the exhibition of amorous passion with dry mouth and trembling hands. When Pino had wrenched himself free from his wife's arms with such a violent gesture, he felt he was the spectator of a brutal separation that left both of them wounded and bloody. He hadn't even suspected the existence of the fire that was in their bodies, and thinking it over, he blushed with embarrassment, as though it were something improper and scandalous. He had never seen a married couple embrace and kiss in public, and except for this, even touch or walk arm in arm. The husband usually walked ten feet ahead of his wife without saying a word to her, as if he didn't know her or was ashamed of her. His father and mother had never touched each other in front of the children, and he was sure they didn't do so when alone. That thing that husband and wife did in secret was only for bringing children into the world. It lasted half a minute at the most, like the animals, and it happened in the dark because it was a sin to see each other. The husband ordered his wife: come here I want to use you, so a friend had explained to him with a snicker. The wife obeyed even if she didn't want to. She raised her skirts, and lowered them again when he finished. That was it. He had felt a powerful aversion to the idea that his parents did that animal act, and he drove it out of his mind with disgust. How was such an intimacy possible between them if an insurmountable distance separated them, a kind of shared scorn and hostility that confined them to two different levels that never met? His mother, as a sign of respect and submission, used the polite form of "you" with his father, as his children did, and he called them with the familiar form used with underlings. He never called her by her name, Lucia; he only addressed her with a grunt or an angry gesture. He repeatedly said: Women aren't people, and, offended, she would lower her eyes. When he had saluted her before leaving he hadn't even embraced her, he had only muttered: Take care, old woman. And he left. At the table, when he wanted something, he pointed to it like a king, without wasting a word. He expected her to read his mind and rush to serve him and became enraged if she hesitated or made a mistake. She never sat with them, but ate the leftovers standing, leaning against the wall, ready to obey his commands.

Gildo had never imagined that such understanding, such harmony and abandon, could exist between a man and a woman. The vision of the young wife clinging to her husband in that shameless way, instead of drawing back and shying away as women were supposed to do, that passionate kiss in front of so many men that she made no effort to avoid, the long hair falling over her face, upset him and at the same time stirred his blood. A woman should respect her husband and not throw herself at him. Wavering between condemnation and envy, the intolerance of his age and experience was set against the vision of the ardent merging of the bodies he had witnessed, an unexpected revelation of what love could be between a man and a woman. He would never know it, and while he walked on, bent and tired, he was tortured by the melancholy of the disinherited, forcefully banished and exiled in everlasting solitude.

At Albino they met up with Serafì and Bortolo, two adolescents from Bondo Petello who joined the brigade after a tired exchange of greetings. After walking for a while, to lighten the march, Bigio started singing *Quel mazzolin di fiori* on the wrong note. A pair of voices joined in, growing more off tune with each stanza. That ramshackle choir provoked in Gildo, gifted with a superfine ear, unbearable pain, and an urgent desire to start the song over again on the right key. The sour notes caused him real agony. Was it possible that they didn't know they were singing out of tune? He was just about to start it over, but it wasn't necessary; the song broke off, silence returned and everyone continued walking lost in his own thoughts.

The eastern sky was slowly growing lighter. From a distant church steeple came the peel of morning bells and some made the sign of the cross. Those silvery sounds reminded Gildo of the big celebration in October 1905, with the first bell concert of the Abbazzia parish church. The priest had the five existing bells recast and added three others, all eight with little hammers. They had made a wonderful concert like no other church around. After sunset on the night of the celebration, the whole county turned as bright as day with bonfires in the surrounding mountains, fireworks and firecrackers in the church square, and candles everywhere. Every Sunday morning the sexton, carried away by enthusiasm, played the entire repertory of church songs with the bells, and the echoes went as far as the most remote farmhouse. There had been no more celebrations or music for Gildo after he went to Switzerland — only work, work, very hard work.

One after the other the sleeping villages in Serio valley that ran alongside the road—Pradalunga, Nembro, Alzano Lombardo, Torre Boldone —were waking up, lapped by the first tongues of light. At the city gates peasants were already climbing up steep paths to cut wood, axes and saws on their shoulders. They turned in amazement to see the line of men on the road laden with sacks and bundles. They greeted the departing emigrants with arms raised, shouting: Take care! Greetings to 'Merica! The little children, behind the bigger ones carrying baskets on their backs, were open-mouthed at their sight; infrequent carts loaded with wood or hay went along beside them for a ways and offered to carry the men's bundles.

Gildo remembered an old man telling him that the year before, when thirty men from Pradalunga left for America, half the village, at four in the morning, accompanied them as far as the church piazza at Nembro to say goodbye, along with a band playing happy marching songs. No one had come to see them off.

They reached the outskirts of Bergamo exhausted and walked on to the train station in a stinging sleet. Soaked and chilled, they took shelter under the platform roof to wait for the train to Milan. Apart from those who had already emigrated, the others had never seen trains or train stations. They had only heard about them from those who had traveled, and everyone had imagined them in his own way. However, they had never envisaged such a mighty engine, powerful and impressive as that moving back and forth, whistling and clanking, on the third track, or the enormous plume of dense and foul-smelling black smoke that the stack spit out. Accustomed from birth to the slow and tranquil pace of their legs and carts, they stared bewildered and frightened by the puffing monster guided and controlled by others. They were anxious about their own country awkwardness and the judgment of those who might notice. They pretended indifference, but their dilated and wary eyes betrayed their apprehension. To ward it off they ate the meager food brought from home, huddling next to one another, exposed to the freezing wind that blew blasts of sleet under the platform roof. Gildo devoured the piece of polenta that had filled his pocket with crumbs, and thought it would be the last for many years, because they wouldn't know what polenta was in the land of plenty. Who knows what they ate over there? From what he had heard, even poor people ate meat every day in America, and soft white bread that melted in their mouth.

The train arrived from Brescia enveloped in a cloud of steam, and they recoiled in fright at the great commotion of pistons and wheels. Gripped by the anxiety of missing the train, and goaded by the engine's whistle, they rushed to the doors, hoisted themselves up the steps, and frantically pushed their baggage inside; as soon as they were in the train started moving. To go the fifty kilometers from Bergamo to Milan took more than two hours. Gildo collapsed on a wooden bench, removed his wet jacket and spread it out to dry, took off his shoes, stretched out his legs, and immediately fell asleep.

4

At the Milan train station, a gloomy cavern as smoky and noisy as a forge, they clustered on the platform. In order to keep an eye on their baggage, they piled it in a pyramid and sat around it while waiting for the local train to Modane. The hurried crowds regarded them with annoyance, as if they obstructed their pressing affairs. Some looked at them with the open disgust that people of a more elevated state bestow on manual laborers, skirting around them as one does beggars, and moving on with the decisive, rapid pace of someone who knows where he is going. Further ahead other groups of men were bivouacked in the same miserable condition: clothes patched and shabby, eyes shadowed with weariness, faces unshaven, all with the lost and frightened expression of someone leaving home for the first time. They were emigrants, too, Gildo decided, maybe going to French mines, or perhaps to Le Havre to get on a ship for America. He listened carefully, watching them out of the corner of his eye. They were speaking in a dialect he understood, softer than his, maybe from Brianza. A little further away other men speaking a Veneto dialect were having a lively conversation between loud bursts of laughter and generous gulps from a bottle of grappa being passed around. It must burn their throats and make holes in their stomachs, but at least it made them happy. The platform was swarming with people: men mostly, with a few women in black dresses and head scarves, with skinny, tearful brats hanging on their skirts. This meant that peasants were emigrating from all over the northern countryside, motivated by the same hunger, the same poverty, and the same hopes.

A direct train for Florence was on the track near to them. Well-dressed men sat at the windows of the first class coaches—men in felt hats, jackets, vests and ties. Distinguished women in travel suits, gloves and veils. Inside the compartments one could see elegant leather suitcases, traveling bags, and hatboxes. Some passengers waiting on the platform were chatting with relatives who had come to keep them company, and they wrinkled their noses at the scattered bands of shabby men that spoiled the view and made it reek. Gildo could smell himself and understood that the refined nostrils of city folks must be offended by the stable odor that saturated their clothes, and the stale sweat and grime of their unwashed bodies after the long walk. He felt embarrassed. He looked surreptitiously at a girl his age who still wore her hair loose on her shoulders and moved restlessly between a couple, perhaps her parents. She questioned them continuously and impatiently, jiggling the purse over her arm and shaking her brown mane like a colt. Every action released the delicate perfume of violets in the air.

The local train for Modane was nowhere to be seen. They had an urgent need to urinate, but no one had the courage to go looking for a lavatory, which had to be somewhere around there, for fear of getting lost in that gigantic, echoing labyrinth; but most of all they were afraid of missing the train if it should arrive in the meantime. Bortolo couldn't hold it any longer. He swore, fidgeted, jumped around, and searched desperately for an isolated corner that wasn't there. Suddenly he dashed down the platform to get away from the people waiting to leave and, overcome by need, went up to the wheels unbuttoning his trousers. Serafi had shouted for him to stop, and when he got no response, had followed Bortolo until he got hold of his jacket tail. There was a brief scuffle: Bortolo waved his arms to free himself and dealt his companion a few weak blows. The other yanked him and shouted not to behave like a pig, goddamn it. Don't let everyone know them for the country bumpkins they were; they weren't in a pasture or behind a stable, stupid fool, customs were different in the city; they didn't piss in the first corner they saw. Bortolo wrenched free and swore even more furiously, but Serafì didn't give up. In the end the desperate man surrendered and buttoned his fly.

The stationmaster appeared in his braided cap, signal in hand, and shouted: "All aboard!" The travelers to Florence said goodbye to their relatives and hurried to get on. The girl went quickly up the steps with another shake of her long hair. The stationmaster, making sure the windows were well shut, gave an energetic blast on his whistle, and the train slowly began to move. Gildo followed it with his eyes until the track curved and the last coach disappeared from view.

Suddenly his heart skipped a beat. He had been distracted and so for a long while had forgotten to check his money and passport. He patted the bulge on his chest, sighed with relief, and promised himself to pay more attention.

A cold wind gusted under the vaulted roof, stung their skin, and penetrated to the bone. Gildo's teeth chattered in the numbing cold. He walked up and down the platform stamping his feet to warm them, his hands in his trouser pockets, his cap pulled down over his ears. Cold, cold, cold, he had suffered from the cold everywhere. His hands, ears, a knee, and his toes were swollen from frost—painful bluish lumps where his blood stagnated. Every time he had taken up a pick or shovel he had had to bite his lip to keep from howling. The wait was growing longer; he yearned for a bowl of hot soup and a warm, sheltered place.

He cast a glance at Pino sitting on his sack, elbows on his knees and face in his hands. He hadn't once looked up, spoken a single word, or touched his food. When someone said something to him he looked at them like he hadn't heard. Most certainly he was missing his young wife and the child he wouldn't see born. Pino had even turned down the bottle of wine Gildo's father had pulled out of his knapsack and passed around. Bigio stamped his feet on the floor to warm himself, Serafì walked back and forth with his hands under his armpits, Leone adjusted large bundles on his shoulders and thighs; Gioanì, bent double, coughed as much as is possible for a person to cough. They were all exhausted and chilled, and the train had still not arrived.

Finally an engine appeared at the end of the track, and all at once a great commotion broke out on the platform. Dozens of shouting men jumped to their feet and struggled to fish their baggage out of the pile. In the feverish excitement they bumped into each other and one man was knocked flat on his back. Anxious voices in that pandemonium called out to friends in fear of losing them. Some counted the members of their own group to be sure no one was missing, and others ran up and down the platform in search of friends. They jostled furiously to get on the train first. Baggage was piled in a heap and blocked the long passageway. They argued over seats and roughly pushed intruders away because everyone wanted to be with his friends. Soon the train was in open country and the arguments continued in a variety of dialects.

Bortolo was the first to make a beeline for the toilet that stank bad enough to turn his stomach, a Turkish-type hole in the floor incrusted with layers of old crap, a foul smelling, filthy stagnant mixture under the metal grate on the floor. There was no water in the tank and not a drop came from the tap for washing his face and hands.

On the uncomfortable wooden benches that tortured their gaunt bodies some men fell asleep immediately, some pulled out their supply of food, others shouted with an excitement that bordered on desperation. In the stuffy air, along with the stink of the toilet, wafted the odor of country salami, and over it all hung the wild odor of poverty, exhaustion, and feet finally liberated from shoes.

Outside the breath-steamed windows flowed the monotonous Lombard plain. They passed fields with random patches of snow interrupted by irrigation ditches and rows of mulberry trees. In the background rose formations of bare popular trees; remote farmhouses appeared and disappeared between banks of hanging fog, a bell tower barely poked through the mist. Peasants bent over the furrows pulling up dry corn stalks. As the train passed they straightened up to look at it as though it were a phantasm. Some leaned on their hoe handle and waved a greeting.

It was growing dark when they reached Modane. The train had stopped many times on the secondary tracks of many little isolated stations in order to give precedence to faster trains that shattered the air and the silence like meteors. Other stops without apparent reason had relegated them to the quiet deserted countryside. Many had tried unsuccessfully to sleep, stiff and numb in their corner, their knees bumping against each other because of the narrow quarters, their bones aching, joints painful, and legs numb. One exhausted man stretched out on the floor between the seats, using his bundle as a pillow, but was constantly disturbed by those going to the toilet. At the Turin station more people got on, making it even more crowded. It was worse than a military troop train, Leone commented, reminded of his service in far off Sicily. As they approached the Alps the temperature in the car fell. To protect himself from the biting cold Gioanì put on everything he had. When the train entered the Fréjus tunnel, which seemed endless, the deafening roar awoke those who were sleeping. Without an outlet smoke filled the car, poisoning the air and blackening their faces.

After arriving, during passport control, they all held their breath, fearful and nervous. The guards questioned them about their final destination, they wanted to see their ship tickets and doggedly demanded to know who had told them about the shipping company. A relative in America, Cipriano replied, and luckily that satisfied them. The French gendarmes put on haughty airs. They mispronounced the names they read aloud from the passports, tossing scornful glances at their haggard, dirty faces and beggar-like bundles, and returned the document with a brusqueness tantamount to an insult. Each whispered to the other, with a disdainful sneer: macaroni. Gioanì, who had boasted of his knowledge of French during the trip, repeating voilà, and bon every three words, shrank mutely into a corner, terrified in the presence of the gendarmes. Later he confessed he had never learned French while working in France, because the emigrants always kept to themselves and no one ever said a word to them, as if they didn't exist. Once he had hurt his arm in the mine because he hadn't understood an order from the Frenchman in charge and had moved a cart in the wrong direction.

Before getting off the train, according to instructions, they had fixed the blue identification symbol on their caps and berets. Those from Brinzio, heading for the rocky caves of the Jura, had orange stickers; green for those from the Veneto on their way to Le Havre and California. Hundreds of men poured out of the train onto the platforms, every group with its colored identification. They wandered around the station in a daze, dragging their bulky luggage — and some even with wives and small children — in search of the person supposed to meet them. No one came forward, so little by little that sea of ragged individuals, confused and dead tired, poured out again into the piazza, a few with arms raised to call attention to their colored stickers. Finally some well-dressed gentlemen pushed through the crowd with identifying placards on display. Introducing themselves, they grouped the emigrants according to their colors.

The representative for the French line regretfully explained to the Abbazzia group that because their train was late they had missed the local for Paris, and unfortunately there wouldn't be another one until the next day. But they needn't worry, he would take them to a boarding house nearby, highly recommended and cheap, where they would have warm food, a good wash, a nice rest in a comfortable bed, and leave re-energized tomorrow. Despite the man's reassuring smile and friendly manner they were silent, dismayed by the unexpected setback. Cipriano tried to object, but the representative replied glibly that on such a long trip many unexpected things could happen. Anyway, a stopover was useful for renewing their strength and energy. It didn't pay to reach their destination in a state of exhaustion. They had plenty of time before the ship sailed from Le Havre, so they didn't need to be anxious.

The boarding house wasn't nearby at all, and Gioanì coughed desperately all the way. When they arrived wheezing and dog-tired from the weight of their sacks, bags, and bundles, they discovered that it was a filthy, moldy shack, and the old woman who greeted them didn't speak a word of Italian. She made them understand that there was no place for them to hang around during the day, so they left their baggage and wandered around the city streets in a daze. The supper was so disgusting that in spite of their hunger they left most of it on their plates. Shortly afterward the representative reappeared, and with the same show of regret and a cast-iron smile he announced that they wouldn't be leaving even the next day, but the day after, because the train was packed. There were too many people traveling, and on French trains, unlike Italian trains, you couldn't get on if there weren't enough seats. This time they protested vigorously in chorus, but the man remained imperturbable: it wasn't his fault, he had done everything possible to get them seats, but the French wouldn't budge. He was so convincing that they didn't know what to say.

The toilet in the courtyard was even more rank and foul smelling than the one on the train. That night they slept in a frigid room, packed two by two on wobbly, creaky cots with lumpy mattresses, raggedy blankets, grimy gray sheets. Before lying down they inspected the beds for bedbugs and hid their money and passports under their pillows. Gioanì kept his in his underpants. They had a restless night: the beds were too narrow for two men, the blankets too light for the icy night. Some of them woke up numb with cold and were forced to put all their clothes back on before going back to sleep.

Early in the morning the landlady woke them by knocking loudly on the door. She shouted and gesticulated: Deòr, sorté! but no one understood what she wanted. They were standing around in bewilderment consulting with each other when some dirty, shabbily dressed men appeared in the doorway. Manual laborers, apparently. And Italians. One of them from the province of Varese explained that they worked the nightshift in a nearby factory and during the day slept in those same beds, so the travelers were obliged to dress in a hurry. The landlady brought two pitchers of water for all ten of them, and pretended not to understand when they asked her for more. They had to wash in the each other's dirty water and no one was able to have a proper shave.

All morning long they wandered around aimlessly and without rest through slippery and treacherous streets swept by winds off the mountains. When they collapsed in exhaustion on the benches of a public garden a gendarme approached them and shouted angrily until they understood from his excited gestures that they had to leave. Then they took shelter in a church, sitting on the benches and obstinately ignoring the scowling priest who walked back and forth with his breviary in hand shooting fiery glances their way. Luigino whispered that maybe he was afraid they would rob the alms box.

After checking to see how much money they had left, they went to an inn for lunch and devoured a tasty stew with great delight. They wiped up every drop of sauce on their plates with bread, and Gildo licked his plate surreptitiously. Not knowing where to go and reluctant to leave the warmth of the sputtering stove for the intense cold of the street, they hung around until the host began to turn up the chairs on the tables and sweep the floor under their feet, and so they had to leave. In search of some shelter, they dragged themselves through the nearly deserted streets whipped by the biting wind and went to the railroad station waiting room. Shortly after they sat down a uniformed man came up to them and rudely demanded to see their tickets. When they complied he shouted that only passengers waiting to leave had the right to sit there, not just any foreign homeless vagrant. It was just too convenient not to pay a cent of taxes and to dirty public places at the French citizens' expense. With furious gestures he told them to clear off before he called the gendarmes.

They returned to the same inn for supper, and to save money they settled for vegetable soup with black bread and a glass of wine. Back at the boarding house the landlady presented them with a stiff bill, to be paid on the spot, which — they managed with difficulty to understand — included the meals they hadn't eaten. A furious quarrel broke out with insults flying back and forth, until the man from Varese, about to leave for his nightshift, explained that the woman hadn't been told that they would eat out. Therefore she had cooked just the same and now they had to resign themselves to paying. Not having foreseen the stopover, and much less the extra expenditures, they hadn't exchanged enough francs, and the woman absolutely refused to accept lire, with snorts and loud clicks of disgust. Suddenly, after much dithering, almost as though reciting a part, she changed her mind and was disposed to accepting the Italian money. She set about making furious calculations on a piece of paper, showed them a figure without explaining how she reached it, or informing them of the exchange, or giving them time to check it, and almost snatched the bills out of their hands. It had all happened in such an agitated and confused way that, dumbfounded by the sudden about-face and inhibited by their ignorance of the language, they hadn't dared demand an explanation. For some time now they had been humiliated by their inability to face the unexpected and the arrogance of others:

too many new things, too much they didn't know or understand, too many dangers laying in wait at every turn.

In the morning they set off with long faces for the station, their feet aching and their legs shattered by fatigue. Gildo limped from the blisters on his heels. The man from the ship company was waiting for them in the square, as affable and smiling as always, who, according to the agreement, would accompany them to Le Havre. They complained to him about the treatment they had received at the boarding house, but he replied coolly that those were French ways and the woman was honest and upright.

When their train pulled out of the station the man had disappeared. Gildo and Luigino, with the blue tags on their caps well in sight, looked for him everywhere, going as far as the first car in case he had made a mistake, but the man was not to be found. It was clear the bastard had tricked them, and not just once, but three times: the first with the lie about the train that had just left, the second about the lack of seats, and the third with his disappearance. They had been blindly trusting, like dumb fools, when they should have checked the schedule for departing trains. They had let themselves be hoodwinked real good, and so had tossed a lot of money to the winds for two useless nights in the hovel of a lying thieving old witch, and for disgusting food a pig wouldn't eat. It wasn't as though they had money to spare. It's a cinch that that bastard was in cahoots with the boarding house owner and made money out of the deal: he brought the clients and she gave him so much for each sucker he was able to bamboozle. Ten suckers, ten commissions, and now they were both laughing behind their backs.

Luigino realized that he hadn't seen any of the men from the Veneto, also going to Le Havre. That must mean that they had taken the train two days earlier. Bigio observed that when they arrived at Modane the local train for Paris must have been on another track, and they hadn't noticed. Leone said that it had seemed to him that their train hadn't been late at all, but at the time they hadn't paid attention. And he guessed that if instead of listening to the commune secretary, whose promises had turned out to be lies, they had signed up with Cortinovis and left on La Veloce out of Genoa ... Cipriano's withering look kept him from finishing.

They sank into discouraged silence, obliged to take a hard look at reality: no one had any compassion for poor people. Far from it! Everyone was on the lookout like bloodthirsty beasts, ready to take advantage of their ignorance and inexperience of the world, with a ferocity that shocked them. It wasn't easy to spot the traps lurking behind so many fine words, and much less to defend themselves from them: to be trusting and trustworthy came naturally in their desperate need to have faith in their fellow man.

After a while Cipriano took the last fiasco of wine from his knapsack, a light, sparkling wine made in their region. The bottle passed from hand to hand, and their spirits grew lighter. The bottle of Fernet was to be saved for the ship in case someone got seasick. Bigio, encouraged by a couple of big gulps, took his accordion from the heap of bundles. Slipping the straps over his shoulders, he played a few chords and started singing: "La Mariana la va in campagna fin che il sole tramonterà," and someone joined off-tune. Controlling his uneasiness over that painful rendition, Gildo closely observed the fingers of Bigio's right hand that ran up and down the keyboard, and those on the left hand that pressed the chords of accompaniment on the row of buttons: every white key a note, every black key a half note. Too bad Bigio so often pressed the wrong key, and didn't respect the rhythm, but lengthened or shortened the notes and pauses any way he pleased. Gildo corrected the tone in his head and scanned the beat as his ear suggested, and was amazed that Bigio was so deaf to the rhythm. He loved music; it calmed him and at the same time exalted him in a mysterious way. He didn't know how to play an instrument, and admired and envied anyone who did. However, as a child he had learned to whistle perfectly. It was enough for him to hear a tune one time for him to repeat it without mistaking a single note.

The train proceeded slowly on the iron tracks covered with fresh snow. One curve after another through a narrow valley between steep mountains thick with fir trees. At the station in Chambéry it stopped to fill the water tank in each car from a tank at the side of the track, and to empty the toilets. Afterwards a thick, rusty liquid that smelled like sewer water came from the sink faucets. Gildo, dazed, stressed, and famished, watched the coming and going of the people on the platform, and the rail workers busy refilling the water and talking loudly in their rapid and nervous language.

Vendors appeared on the scene with heaping baskets of bread. To tempt the customers they waved golden, oven-fresh baguettes and shouted in Italian: Pane! Pane! That word drew them all to the windows to stare with longing at the slender loaves with brown and crunchy crusts that made their mouths water. The aroma of the bread just out of the oven reminded many of them of country festivals, of their teeth sinking greedily in the supreme, rare gluttony of a soft warm hunk. Only the well-off gentlemen could afford it; they had to be content with the cold and by now rancid polenta brought from home. After the fleecing at the boarding house in Modane, they had to economize for fear of being left with no money in case of other unexpected expenses. They were already resigned to not having the fresh bread, when Cipriano impulsively leaned out, motioned to the vendor, and bought two baguettes. Gioanì objected to that waste of money, but Cipriano magnanimously replied he was paying. He divided them into ten pieces and handed them around. Each man ate in religious silence, taking small bites, savoring every mouthful and chewing slowly to make it last.

Gildo didn't dare refuse the piece that was his due, but it renewed his resentment of his father's squandering, a vice he would never overcome, like his drinking: it was his fault they had set off on this journey, and in spite of the pile of debts, he continued to waste money. Playing the big spender was his typically foolish way of disarming hostility, a hostility that he typically provoked by his irritating arrogance. During the trip Gildo had kept his distance, using his friends as a barrier, and the two had hardly spoken a word to each other.

At the station in Lyons many of the travelers jumped off with empty bottles and ran to the drinking fountain, but the line was so long that when the train whistled, most of them hadn't had their turn.

Now the train was moving through a wide valley along a winding river. Someone at the back of the car said it was the Rhone, but someone else contradicted him, certain it was the Saône, as he had made that trip three times. As night approached the light slowly faded, and the men silently ate the last of the rancid polenta and the leftover cheese. A nauseating odor spread through the car from the accumulation of dirt, disorder, and garbage. Greasy paper, newspapers, cheese crusts, salami skins, spit, wine spills, ashes and cigar butts, empty bottles were scattered haphazardly over the floor. The water in the lavatory was soon gone and was not refilled.

In Paris they got off at Gare de Lyon and looked around in alarm. Where in the world was the train for Le Havre? Pino roused himself from his silence and offered to go find out. Luigino followed him and together they wandered around the station without knowing whom to ask. They couldn't muster the courage to face the long lines at the ticket booths. Not knowing a word of French, what would they ask when it came their turn? They went searching for the posted schedules like those they saw in the Milan station, but couldn't find them. When they ran into a uniformed station employee they screwed up their courage and asked him, after politely removing their caps, where was the train to Le

Havre? They pronounced it several times: Le Havre, Le Havre! He looked the Italians up and down, so ignorant they couldn't even pronounce the name of a great French city correctly, and pointing toward the exit he said, emphasizing each syllable: Gar sèn Lazàr! Delotr coté de la vil! And he went on his way.

Not understanding a word, they follow the direction indicated and walked around in the lobby. Nothing that they saw appeared connected with Le Havre in any way. Finally, in the farthest corner, near the window that looked onto the square, they saw a book of train schedules attached to a wooden pole and ran to consult it. There were schedules for trains for Italy, Switzerland, and the south of France, but not one mention of Le Havre. Now truly alarmed, while returning to their companions empty handed, and cursing through gritted teeth the bastard who had left them to their own devices, they recognized the speech of some countrymen heading for the exit. They were from Piedmont, headed for Metz, in Lorraine, to get to the iron mines at Thionville, and they were leaving from Gare de l'Est. One of them explained that Paris had several train stations — in France "station" was called "gare" — and trains went in different directions from each one. For Le Havre you left from Gare Saint Lazare, north of the city. Go straight along the river and you can't miss it, half an hour of fast walking, no more. If they preferred, they could take the tram in front of the station, he added, and went away with a salute.

They tried to get on the vehicle without success: instead of moving aside to make room, people formed a wall, grumbling and complaining. They could wait for the next tram or rent a horse cab instead of annoying respectable people who had no time to lose. How did so many of them expect to get on, and with all that baggage? There were private services for travelers in large groups. But that costs money, and it wasn't likely that those good-for-nothings had any. That bunch of macaronis halfway up the steps were keeping the tram from leaving. The conductor should come to settle the question, or better still, a gendarme if one could be found. The conductor rushed over, and shoving them rudely, told them to get off, they were blocking the tram. He returned to his place cursing that plague of emigrants who, instead of staying home where they belong, come to take bread out of the mouths of honest French citizens.

The walk along the Seine, plowed by barges and boats launching loud sirens, was a topic of conversation and celebration for a long time—for the magnificence of the city, the well-tended gardens that even bloomed in the winter, the wide tree-lined avenues, the island in the middle of the river, the enormous building with high windows that seemed like a royal palace, the coming and going of automobiles, carriages, trams, the well-dressed people, the elegant houses, the luxury stores blazing with lights, the great cathedrals, the monuments. They had never seen such wealth, sumptuousness, and elegance. But it was also remembered for the grueling march under the weight of bags and sacks, for the melancholy light in the daytime, the wind that whipped their faces and froze their bare hands, the continuous pelting rain, their soaked clothes, ruined feet, and the hunger that gnawed at their stomachs.

Oh, certainly! Half an hour of fast walking! It took an hour and a half after getting lost several times as soon as they left the river bank, retracing their footsteps, timidly asking the way from passersby who gave them nasty looks. Finally, in the center of a wide square appeared the station of Saint Lazare, its windows as grand as a church's, a clock on the front, slopping slate roofs, the long illuminated platform, the vehicles, the porters with numbers on their caps and carts laden with luggage, the bustling crowd. The familiar iron odor of train stations greeted them: a mixture of locomotive smoke, of oily lubricants and dirty sediment, and overall the usual permeating stench of latrines.

A train left for Le Havre in half an hour, just enough time to buy two baguettes and a piece of cheese. Don't even think about wine. It was expensive enough to give you a heart attack.

They would reach their destination that evening, and they hoped to get on shipboard immediately so they could sleep in their assigned cabins. That way they could avoid the expense of a bed in an inn. The next day the steamship Chicago — a name that made them laugh like crazy — would lift anchor.

5

It didn't go as they imagined. When they reached the port a multitude of emigrants were crowding around the ticket office of the French Line, pushing and shoving as if a riot had just broken out. Fists were in the air, shouts, oaths, blasphemies, threats, in the accents and dialects of people from the north, from Brescia, Padova, Verona, Vicenza, Belluno, crossed with those dissonant accents of the Sardinians and Abruzzesi. There were Frenchmen from Normandy and large groups of foreigners from Poland, Russia, Slovenia, whose shouts were incomprehensible. A Babel of languages that hurt the ears and confused the brain.

From what they were able to make out, the first reaction of these people was civilized. They were worn out by their long, exhausting travels across half of Europe, and began to murmur the moment the clerk announced with the greatest indifference that the steamship Chicago was not in port and no one knew when it would arrive. The reason given was the violent storm at sea that had raged in the Atlantic for days, and they would have to wait until it calmed down. Many had protested loudly, waving their tickets dated February 7, but the clerk had coldly advised them to read the boarding card carefully where it was written in clear letters that the departure would take place "weather permitting." No, he had replied scornfully to a question, if the ship was not in port it was obvious they couldn't get on board. They should look for lodging nearby and wait for information.

The insurrection exploded when they asked for confirmation that the expense for food and lodging for the days they had to wait would be paid by the company, as they had been told, and the man had answered in an irritated tone that allowed no argument that they had dreamt it. The company is responsible only in case it defaults, not when it is a matter of a greater power, such as a storm at sea. If they didn't understand the difference, too bad for them. At that point he had rudely slammed the window and disappeared.

That was when a platoon of gendarmes armed with billy clubs, standing in a threatening semicircle a short distance away, started to move up one by one.

The men stood still, disconcerted, undecided what to do, talking it over excitedly in groups without finding a solution. That unexpected delay with no predictable end in sight, along with the added expense involved, was a serious setback. They felt victims of an injustice, or still worse, victims of a swindle, because each of them had been promised that the company would provide lodging and support no matter what happened. Some were quiet, worried about how they would pay for a prolonged stay, others cursed their bad luck and the heavenly father responsible for hurricanes, and others, much more numerous, overcome by bad temper and rage, suspected bad faith on the part of the French Line. The company, they said, was a gang of crooks, conspiring with the local inns to extract money from poor people who were forced to put up with every kind of banditry.

Take it or leave it. The way they saw it, the departure date on their ticket was an obvious sham. An earlier date had been written deliberately to oblige them to stay in Le Havre for who knows how long at their own expense. It followed that even the excuse of the stormy sea was a lie. In fact, from the port where they were, that is, from the deep estuary of the lower Seine, it was impossible to know if there was a storm on the Atlantic or not. Although it was cold as hell, there wasn't a breath of wind, and the water was so still that the moored sailing masts seemed planted in solid ground. If the open sea weren't visible from there they would tell all the lies they wanted and say it was due to causes beyond their control.

As soon as the clerk had slammed the window some unkempt

and sinister figures appeared who, with big smiles and persuasive words in terrible Italian, tried to snag customers for a boarding house just a few yards away. Persistent, obstinate, aggressive, compensated with a fee for every customer they nabbed, forced to battle tooth and nail against fierce competition, they worked hard to get everyone they could, touting nonexistent comforts and knockdown prices.

The more mistrustful groups stayed clear of the middlemen and huddled in deep conversation on the pier. In the end they had to give up, and slowly and reluctantly disperse through the streets near the port in search of accommodations for the rapidly approaching night. So also did the ten men from Bergamo, scarred by their experience in Modane and bitterly convinced of being once again deceived; and on their way, bent under the weight of their baggage, they ran into those men from the Veneto who had left on the right train from Modane three days earlier, and they all ended up in the same boarding house to share the same grimy beds.

Every morning, doggedly and full of hope, they appeared in a group at the French Line looking for news, each morning less belligerent, more dejected, and finally passive. There was no shelter or waiting room—and only one lavatory—and not knowing where to go, continually more exhausted, dirty, and run down as the days went by, they camped on the bare stones of the pier, sometimes in an icy downpour. Those who didn't find a place along the pier stationed themselves in streets surrounding the port. Muffled in their rags, livid with cold, they ate their paltry meals in the open, in the frigid northern winter. The port watchmen tried in vain to chase them away. At sunset, after slowly dispersing to return to their hovels—where the large part slept on filthy mats in rooms without windows—a troop of street cleaners collected the garbage, tossed water on the stones fouled with spit, feces, and urine, and spread lime from big canisters.

They waited for nine days. On the morning of February 16, the steamship Chicago was there, docked at the wharf, engines running and stacks smoking. The one thousand two hundred fifty third-class passengers were ordered to deposit their baggage in a large room to be disinfected. Gildo, after trying to hang on to the food he had wrapped in paper, fearful that it would be ruined by the disinfectant, had to turn it over. This practice was carried out by port employees: some of them, claiming that the baggage would be opened and that the disinfectant would ruin the contents, extorted a tip to guarantee they would stay shut. Once the operation was completed, the contents of the carts were carelessly overturned in a huge malodorous heap, covered with the fine gray dust left by the formalin fumes.

In the meantime the men were ordered to line up at the clinic. As soon as they entered two gendarmes searched them to make sure they had no knives or other weapons. They commandeered the jack-knife Leone used for cutting bread, and a penknife Luigino used to clean his fingernails. Gioanì nearly passed out when they announced the doctor's checkup: white as a rag, unsteady on his feet, he swallowed convulsively, his terrified eyes staring into space. One of his sons held him up, his friends tried to give him encouragement. Cipriano kept saying that the secretary of the commune had been absolutely certain he wouldn't be turned back at Le Havre. The check up was only a formality; there was nothing to worry about. As a matter of fact the two doctors in white coats merely glanced at his open mouth and turned back his eyelids. That was all there was to it. Gioanì suddenly seemed to revive.

Meanwhile the dock swarmed with activity and illegal business deals, tolerated by the port authorities that got their cut. Among the masses waiting to board were vendors selling all kinds of high-priced merchandise: cigars, tobacco, soap, razors, towels, scarves, hats, stockings, wine, absinth, pastis, cookies, fruit, footstools. One of the men from the Veneto bought a footstool and two lemons; he had heard about the risk of getting scurvy on the voyage.

As they came out of the clinic the travelers were ordered to take from their baggage whatever was necessary for the crossing; the rest would be locked up and returned to the owner upon arrival. In great confusion each one fished his things out from the gigantic pile, and those who hadn't planned ahead because no one had told them, had to open their sacks and bags, scatter the contents on the dirty ground, and cram their everyday necessities into a sack.

Gildo, according to the instructions he had received in time, had already taken out a good shirt to wear after the ship arrived, in addition to some underwear for the trip. He also kept his food with him in fear that someone might appropriate it from the storage area.

On the dock feverish preparations for the departure were underway: tanks were filled with potable water, porters brought carts of provisions to be hoisted up on pulleys: sacks of flour, rice, and dry beans; canned food, cases of wine, beer and liquors, chicken and turkey coops, pigeon and rabbit cages, mountains of coal, barrels of lubricants. Secured by cinches, cows, pigs, and sheep were lifted bellowing, squealing, and bleating with terror, thrashing their legs in the air. The sight cheered some of the men because they thought that meant there would be fresh meat to eat, but one man who had made the crossing before, advised them not to get their hopes up: Don't forget there are gentlemen travelers in first class.

The third-class passengers were allowed on in the afternoon. The pandemonium, which went on for several hours, was beyond description. In the crush of people and the small space on dock those close to the side of the ship, pushed by the multitude thronging the gangplank, risked ending up in the water. They yelled in fear and grabbed at the person closest to them. The protective chains placed along the dock were not strong enough for the press, and some in the crowd were knocked violently against the supporting posts. Furious fights broke out for precedence. The more robust men pushed and elbowed their way in. Some came to blows. Swept away, kicked and torn by force from their mothers who yelled at the top of their lungs, the children cried in terror. Some gendarmes tried without effect to bring order, shouting insults and threats, swinging their billy-clubs over heads, hacking away at random. The narrow passage leading to the gangplank, flanked by ropes, a lethal bottleneck where one risked being crushed, was made even more difficult by all the baggage each person had in tow.

On the bridge the ship personnel took what was to be locked up in the storage area and handed out receipts for retrieving their belongings after the crossing, along with a berth number. The purser kept their passports and suggested they deposit any money and valuables they had in the safe, with a regular receipt, but they had no confidence in such an idea. The men were separated from the women and children and sent in different directions, bringing about an anguished exchange of farewells, blessings, and advice.

The ship shuddered convulsively from the din and racket of the motors. From the bulwarks a wide vista opened on the river Seine that was chock-a-block with warehouses, shipyards, dry docks, boathouses, smokestacks. On the river an incessant coming and going of small boats, flatboats, barges, tugboats that plowed wakes of foam on the yellowish water. Toward the north was the faint glow of the open sea.

From the bridge they descended down through a labyrinth of ladders, corridors, niches, walls, cubbyholes, small doors, illuminated by flickering lamps; an interminable descent into the bowls of the ship smelling of coal tar, disinfectant, grease (It's just like the mine, Gioanì whispered), until the man they were following threw open a door. In the darkness they could barely make out a dormitory in which a hundred iron berths, stacked three deep, formed walls to the low, arched ceiling. There were no windows. The large room must be in the hold, under the waterline, and considering the hammer-like racket over their heads, they must be right under the machine room. The stench of old filth, excrement, and disinfectant filled the stagnant air; along the walls spread great rust-colored trails made from water dripping over time; everything was covered with a grayish mildew that seemed like a malevolent excretion. There was no heat. A little air came from a hatch in the corridor. A clammy cold penetrated their bones. Each numbered bunk, narrow as a casket, was provided with sheets, pillow, and blankets.

The men from Bergamo looked around in confusion: where were the cabins with two beds — three at the most? But they didn't even try to protest, so accustomed they were to broken promises, aware of the futility of argument, resigned to what they found. Out of the corner of his eye Gildo noticed something run along the floor and disappear in a dark corner. A rat?

Before leaving the man informed them that the toilets and sinks were on the upper levels. They had fifteen minutes to get settled, as the purser expected them on deck for instructions pertaining to the voyage. Cipriano and Gioanì exchanged with their sons the uncomfortable third level bunks they had been assigned.

Printed instructions in different languages were distributed on the bridge concerning the ship's rules: after the morning wake-up call at seven and washing up, they had to leave the dormitories so they could be cleaned, and go to the forward deck for breakfast. They were not to return to their rooms until after sunset. At no time during the night and day were men permitted to go to the women's rooms, even if related. The bell for silence rang at 10:30. They were forbidden to sing, play instruments, make noise, or play cards. Meal times were to be strictly adhered to. Late arrivals were out of luck. Every group of six should choose someone to get the food. The members of each group would take turns washing the dirty dishes and utensils. Drinking water was in tanks on the deck. They must not throw anything from the bridge. Clothes should be washed in specially provided sinks. A doctor and nurse were on board who could be seen at specified times of day if needed. The greatest personal and environmental hygiene was required in order to avoid the spread of dangerous diseases. Severe penalties would be imposed for gambling and drinking. Only one glass of wine was allowed at every meal.

Six of the Bergamo group chose Cipriano as their representative. The remaining four, including Gildo, hurriedly enlisted two men from the Veneto group who also were too many. Each group of six signed a receipt for mess tins, eating utensils and aluminum cups, a ladle, a container for food rations, a sack for bread and a can for wine, all to be returned at the end of the crossing in the same condition in which they were distributed. Any damage would have to be paid for.

The first supper on board was chaotic, that is to say catastrophic. The men came on the forward deck at the same time as the women and children. The captains formed a long line in front of the kitchens, and when they handed out the rations of stew in which minuscule bits of meat floated, furious squabbles broke out over the injustices each one felt at such treatment. The two dining rooms were too small for the number of passengers; therefore, a great many were forced to eat on the cold deck barely lit by a few lamps and lights coming from the riverbank. They bunched together, some standing, some squatting, some sitting with the mess kit between their knees, pieces of bread and a cup of dreadful wine at their feet. The stool that the man from the Veneto had bought, and of which he was very proud, shattered as soon as he sat down, sending him flying backwards.

There was not even room for everyone on the deck. Many ended up perching on the steps, and ship personnel rudely turned away those who got the idea of going down to the dormitories to sit on their bunks. The thirsty besieged the two concrete storage tanks of drinking water. The water had a nauseating metallic taste, so that many children, when lifted by parents to drink from the spigots, spit it out in disgust and burst into tears. A little three-year-old boy with sores on his mouth sucked on the spigot and soon other children became infected.

On that first evening Gildo offered to wash his group's dishes. The noisy lines at the sinks were very long and he had to be careful where he stood in order not to be pushed aside, and not to dirty his clothes with sauce and fat drippings. When it was his turn at the sink, Gildo discovered that the soap had disappeared, there was no more soda, and not even a rag to wipe his greasy hands, or any room in the cabinet to store the dishes.

At ten o'clock with all lights blazing, the engines revved up to a loud roar, the gleaming ship moved slowly away from the dock, accompanied by the siren's hoarse scream.

They spent a very restless night. There were no closets for their things, and few racks on which to hang their clothes, so they ended up hanging their clothes on the frames of their bunks. The room soon began to take on the appearance of a tramp's campground. No one felt safe leaving his baggage unattended, so each kept it in sight and within reach; therefore they put the smaller things on the bunks while the larger ones stayed on the floor. Bigio wanted to keep his accordion next to him, but he had to move it in order to stretch out his legs. In the dim room barely lit by two bluish lanterns, the men tripped over the heaps of baggage as they groped their way through the narrow passage between bunks, causing loud curses and arguments that lasted deep into the night.

Gildo arranged his bundle under his head, along with his jacket and money, and next to his feet (because of the stench), the package of food. His shirt would get wrinkled, but before they reached the port in America he would hang it out to air. Like many of the others in that room, he didn't sleep a wink—not only because of the bother of his cumbrous things in the short narrow bunk, but because of the commotion from swarms of rats that squealed and scurried over the floor, even running over the beds. The ship was infested with legions of rats that hid in the false bottom of the hold, in the storage rooms, in the kitchens, in the dormitories, in the beams that supported the decks from one side to the other. The repugnance he felt and the fear that the rodents might smell the stracchino and clamber over him, added to the piercing cold unmitigated by one blanket, the loud snoring of so many sleeping men, and Gioani's incessant coughing, kept him staring into the darkness. Armies of rats had galloped around the shed in Switzerland too, and he had never gotten over his disgust of them.

Later someone woke up scratching furiously and shouted that the mattress was full of bedbugs or lice, or both. He was shushed by a singsong Veneto voice that jeered: What did you expect, fool?

In the dead of night there was a sudden bustle and confusion and stifled profanities when those who had climbed down from their bunks once more stumbled over the clutter on the floor. Searching for the toilet, they got lost in the maze of passages, stairs and corridors without finding it, and ended by urinating wherever they happened to be. One man, unable to hold it, relieved himself right there in the dormitory, and the mephitic emanations of the urine, along with the water vapor, the lack of oxygen, the aroma of unwashed bodies, poisoned the closed room and made the air stuffy and oppressive.

By now the ship was on open sea. That was clear from the sound of the waves breaking against the keel. The engines roared at full speed just above the ceiling. Gildo finally managed to fall asleep toward morning, only to be rudely wakened by a booming voice that ordered the floor cleared of baggage and arranged on the bunks to allow for cleaning. After washing at the sinks situated on upper levels, they were to get dressed and go up on deck.

There were only two filthy squat toilets with shit-encrusted walls for a hundred men. They stank to high heaven, and only a provident few came prepared with sheets of newspaper. Only one bucket was provided for throwing water down the hole. At the four sinks stood a long line of foul-smelling men trembling with cold, each with a piece of soap, a razor, a towel, suspenders dangling, woolen sweaters patched and out at the elbows, buttons missing, stained with under-arm sweat, bare feet in unlaced shoes.

Gildo waited patiently for his turn, surreptitiously observing his neighbors and he found there the same humiliation that he felt: disheveled, dirty, prostrated by fatigue and dejection, treated like cattle being led to slaughter in spite of having paid for a regular ticket, chased from one place to another as if they belonged no where and were always in the way, denied the smallest comforts. That first night had been enough to break them. An unnatural silence reigned over the men in line, almost as though the effort to speak would cost them too much. From the hatch drifted the fragrance of cake just taken from the oven, but no one allowed himself any joy, knowing well that it was destined for the invisible rich gentry in another part of the ship. With the bitter resignation of those predestined to bad luck, they submitted without murmur to the inhuman rules of that concentration camp atmosphere. They expected mistreatment, injustice, suffering, and deprivation, and accepted it without a flicker of rebellion, almost as though they thought they deserved it. Many of them were now scratching the bedbug and lice bites they got overnight, and Gildo instinctively moved away.

The English Channel was the color of molten lead. The wind swept the prow, black soot from the stacks whirled in the air: it landed everywhere and blinded the passengers huddled over planks still wet from the washing down. Those who had managed to eat hurriedly and messily in the dining rooms had been urged to join the others in the open. After every meal, the dining rooms were cleaned and then locked to keep them from getting dirty again. Those who had been decisively sent away found shelter downwind in the spaces between bollards where the cables were wrapped, or between the curled rope, under a meager canopy or against the rails, muffled up to their ears, caps pulled down, huddling close as sardines. Blankets were not to be taken outside the bunkrooms, the steerage officer had told them, emphasizing each word. The poop deck was swarming with people. There wasn't a chair to sit on or even space to walk or stretch their legs. As soon as one stood up another took his place immediately. The man from the Veneto had repaired his stool and took it everywhere with him, afraid that someone might steal it. Some ventured outside the assigned area to the covered promenade deck, only to be sent back where they came from.

A kitchen assistant, recruited by the chief cook, picked his way with difficulty among the passenger's feet to sell the officially prohibited alcoholic drinks at three times the price: wine, beer, cognac, liqueurs, vodka for the Russians and Poles, and bitters to ward off seasickness. Cipriano bought a bottle of terrible wine. The assistant also peddled slices of cake just out of the oven, white bread, Alsatian sausages, sugar of which there was not a trace in the morning watery coffee and milk; Périgord apples, Spanish lemons, cigars, tobacco, shoe laces and every kind of goods. A nurse flogged medicines stolen from the clinic: purgatives, eye antiseptics, cough syrup. The purser deliberately turned a blind eye.

When the occupants entered their dormitories at sunset, they were struck in the face by the acrid blast of burnt sulfur, along with chloride of lime and carbolic acid. The floor was covered with a layer of damp white powder that gave off suffocating miasmas, exhalations that closed their throat and provoked furious fits of coughing. The planks, wet from scrubbing, oozed a deadly dampness.

The difficulty in orienting oneself at night in the ship's incomprehensible maze when searching for a toilet, the unbearable stench and filth of the latrines from intensive use, the sharp contrast of the outside cold with the tepid warmth of the room, reduced many men to the barbarous practice of relieving themselves of minor and major needs in the corners, like wild animals. There were others who didn't want to be inconvenienced, and relieved themselves directly from their bunk onto the floor, and others who dumped on it every sort of trash. The loud protests did little good, except to encourage some men to get empty cans from the kitchen — for a price, of course — to use as chamber pots. When many men, thanks to a meal of dried pea soup and spoiled tuna, got diarrhea, they felt absolved of sin when they did it in the corridor because of the urgency of their need and the distance from a more suitable place. Many got intestinal disturbances from the rusty, putrid water they drank from the tanks that also contained grains of crumbling concrete. As the ship advanced the dormitory became like a filthy menagerie, communal life degenerated, and bitter fights broke out over the least trifle.

The entire crew, from the officers to the hired personnel, became progressively more hostile and brutal to that horde of tramps that made such messes. Particularly toward the Italians, known to be dirty, uncouth, and ignorant, since most of them could not read or write, and even had problems understanding each other because of their different dialects. In fact, like the Poles, Russians, and Slovenians — justified, however, by their different national origins — they formed in groups according to the region they came from, especially those from Sardinia and Abruzzi. The hired hands complained everyday to the steerage officer; they went into the dormitories holding their noses, disgusted by the stench, the spit, the trash, the excrement. It wasn't worth the bother to put spittoons in the rooms. Those pigs would find it more convenient to continue dirtying the floor.

On the deck the two thousand one hundred and fifty beggars stacked on top of each other left the same repugnant pile of filth, not even bothering to throw it into the ocean. As a matter of fact they didn't even look at the ocean, although most of those country bumpkins were seeing it for the first time. It was as though it terrorized them and they preferred to ignore it. Not one of them leaned over the railing to admire the dolphins that leaped so gracefully alongside the ship; not one watched the flight of gulls following the wake in search of food, or looked at another ship that appeared in the distance. Nothing aroused their curiosity. They stayed hunkered for hours, in a stupefied, inert, vacant state. At the most they sat in a circle and played morra, briscola, or scopa. They smelled like wet dogs and had primitive, cavemen habits. Without a doubt they wore goatskin for clothes in the countries they came from. They blew their nose between their fingers, chewed tobacco, and smeared the deck with sickening brownish spit. They didn't know how to use a knife and fork and ate with their hands. They chewed on the bread instead of breaking it; they licked the mess kit, and gobbled down even the most revolting food. On deck the mothers deloused their children, crushing the nits between their fingernails. The men rummaged around their clothes in search of lice. When animals were being butchered in an area under the deck some of the Italians, attracted by the bellowing and bleating, stood staring impassibly, as though they were watching a stage play.

After a few days they crowded around the sinks to wash their underwear; one man put his handkerchiefs to soak in the mess kit he used to eat his soup. They hung their miserable rags to dry on the deck wherever they could find a place: undershirts and underpants tied by the arms and legs, like the flying bunting of the homeless.

According to regulations, the crew had demonstrated rescue operations, which only resulted in painful confusion; although an interpreter translated the instructions given in French, no one understood a thing, not even how to put on a life belt, tie a life jacket, or get into a lifeboat. It was fervently hoped that there would be no need for them, or everyone would surely drown.

One late afternoon the festive notes of a waltz flew on the wind's wings from the first class salons to the third-class deck. Bigio, who took his accordion everywhere with him, even to the toilet, jumped up and shouted: It's the *Blue Danube*! And while everyone listened intently and smiles blossomed, he put on his instrument and triumphantly, laughing open-mouthed, played the same waltz several times from beginning to end, and then *The Merry Widow* and *Southern Rose*. A crowd gathered around him beating their hands and feet, swaying in rhythm to the music, overcome by irresistible joy. Two adolescents from Brescia, with the burning faces and embarrassed gestures of country lads, clumsily joined arms and spun like tops in the space that opened up for them, and with the enthusiastic incitement of the spectators, stamped their feet in turn and constantly risked loosing their balance, until they collapsed breathless, their heads spinning.

Many requested favorite songs and Bigio, proud of such success, played those he knew. During a pause, they noticed that there was no sound coming from the first class salons, as if the little orchestra of the rich was silent, overwhelmed by the brashness and exultation of Bigio's accordion. It was truly a great satisfaction. Obviously even the gentry traveling in luxury, someone observed, were listening to the music of the poor devils in third class.

It was a wonderful evening. When the time came to leave, Bigio continued to play for the entire circuitous and disconnected walk back to the dormitory. He sat on his bunk and continued playing ever more boldly, as though he had drunk a whole fiasco of wine. The room, shot through with the blast of familiar music, seemed almost welcoming. The men, even melancholy Pino, sang at the top of their lungs, arms around shoulders. And suddenly unprecedented goodwill and common compassion united them, and each felt pierced to the core by nostalgia for all they had left behind.

That is, until a furious bulldog materialized who ordered them to stop. It was severely prohibited to play, sing, and make a racket in the dormitory. While Gildo undressed, carefully folding his clothes before climbing up on his bunk, he whistled every note of the waltz he had just heard for the first time, and thought how nice it would be to know how to play—especially if, unlike Bigio, you played all the right notes—and how he would love to learn, because music softens the heart and brings joy to the listener and to the one playing.

6

We've been traveling a lot more than the one week the damned secretary of the commune talked about, Leon began furiously, and not a sign of the end. And then someone needs to explain where the hell was the advantage in taking the ship from Le Havre instead of Genoa, like those did who have brains in their heads instead of sawdust. The rip- offs of the trip by land and by sea never end. We've thrown away money, time, and effort, eaten worse than criminals, slept with rats and bedbugs, for what? I think the cows, sheep, and pigs in the hold — not a bit of which we have tasted — have it better than we do. The others did not dare contradict him.

A few days later, after some warning signs — the quickly darkening sky, the suddenly frigid wind driving flocks of large clouds resembling molten lead — a storm broke out. During the night the sea swelled, the waves slapping the keel grew louder until, toward morning, it became a great din. To the uninterrupted cracks of thunder was added the fierce lash of torrential rain and the roar of wind that seemed to savage the ship. The vessel creaked and groaned like a gigantic animal under torture. The joints screeched as though about to split apart and the entire framework about to break into a thousand pieces. Pitching and rolling, dipping from one side to the other, the ship seemed about to turn over or sink into the depths to be swallowed and regurgitated. Precipitous plunging into empty space followed by surging upward emptied many a stomach. Crashing, pelting, splashing sounds were heard, and within that racket, the intermittent throb of the engines, the sudden and prolonged pauses, seemed final and made hearts stop. The strained propellers screeched furiously when spinning outside the water until a violent jolt of the prow plunged them down again. The ship seemed out of control, kicked and punched by savage conflicting forces that no one could restrain. The men, still lying in their bunk beds, awake for some time and terrified, felt wrenched from their beds, and they hung on to the bed frames with both hands to avoid being bounced on the floor or hurled against the ceiling. The great dance they had feared so much without talking about it had begun.

Accustomed to country sounds and familiar with animals, they were more than ever affected by the mooing cows and the bleating sheep, imprisoned as they all were in the ship's hold. Animals sense imminent disaster before men do, and this was a sinister omen.

Many men began to vomit from their bunks, and those underneath began to swear. All bedlam broke loose. The dormitory reverberated with yells, invocations, stifled lamentations, prayers, curses, violent retching that seemed ripped from their guts. Many made the sign of the cross and recommended their souls to God and all the saints. The baggage and shoes left on the planks were scattered in every direction by the brusque movements of the ship. The tin cans used as chamber pots and filled during the night were overturned and clanked as they rolled around. The bundles kept in the bunks shot around like missiles and ended up in a tangled heap on the filthy floor. Bigio hugged his accordion tightly to his chest, which an iron claw tried to wrench from him. An abrupt slip and slide ripped from Bortolo's hand a piece of bread he had kept aside. Those who tried to get out of their beds to save themselves from the overhead showers ended up on the floor along with the vomit and urine, and they cursed as never before. One man hit his head against a bed frame and was bleeding, another one caught a flying bundle full in the face, and someone dislocated his shoulder in a violent jostle. Cipriano, undone by retching, groped in his bag for the Fernet bottle, but as soon as he had it by the neck, a great jolt snatched it from his hand and it broke against the ceiling.

Gildo and Luigino, miraculously free from sea sickness, if not from fear, and spurred on by the indomitable curiosity of adolescents, wanted to see the storm with their own eyes, at whatever cost. They climbed down from their bunks, grabbed their clothes and shoes, providentially tied to their bunks by the laces, and staggering and reeling made their way through corridors and up stairs, trying to dress the best they could. Bashed against the walls by the loud slapping of the waves, jerked in every direction, torn violently from the handrails, they were thrown to the floor many times. When the pitch raised the ship's prow, they tumbled backwards for yards, and forward when the stern rose in the air; bruised and sore, they were forced to go on all fours and climb the stairs like four-legged animals.

On the deck, in the dreadful crash of waves, they could make out excited voices, shouted commands, the creak of pulleys, the thud of hurried footsteps, doors slamming. They looked on open-mouthed. The harried sailors rushed past, protected by slickers and knee-high boots. One of the sailors stopped when he saw Gildo and Luigino, and shouting something they didn't understand, pushed them roughly aside, closed the watertight door, and gave them a hard push toward the kitchens. Bent under the lash of the wind, they crossed the bridge, and before being hit by a wave that soaked them from head to foot, they had time to look around. That was the storm: gigantic, pitch-black waves edged with foam accompanied by black, dense clouds pierced by flashing arrows and rent by thunder. The planks were swept by torrents of water that formed eddies. The wind whistled angrily between the masts and the rigging. It seemed like the end of the world, the apocalypse, the Universal Judgment, just as the priest had described them in Sunday sermons.

The kitchen was in turmoil: chairs and stools streaked across the floor and bumped into the furniture, the walls, the legs of the personnel; cabinet doors slammed and glass shattered. Pots and pans, casseroles and even knives flew everywhere. Barrels of wine rolled on the floor, and jars and bottles fell from the shelves and smashed. The floor was covered with pieces of glass, crockery and a mixture of flour, oil, lard, sugar and other things. One of the cooks, glassy eyed, twisted with nausea and vomited into the sink. Helpers, assistant chefs and dish washers struggled to gather up the things and put out the coal fire in the oven out of fear it might start a bigger conflagration, and they emptied pans of boiling water that threatened to overturn. A kitchen helper cried out in pain waving a burned hand. The skin had turned scarlet and a blister was swelling before his eyes. They dragged him to the infirmary that was in the same pandemonium as everywhere else.

Children with festering sores who had drunk from the water spigot occupied bunk beds against the walls; they screamed as if they were being slaughtered and vomited continually. Their pale-faced mothers, with stomachs as upset as their little ones, weakly tried to calm them. An emaciated old woman, sick with pneumonia, murmured prayers from her cot, her breath labored. An elderly man, lying immobile with eyes closed, seemed dead. A sailor who had been thrown against the wall by a wave was nursing a bleeding gash on his forehead. To a nurse one man credited a watery eye blinded by trachoma to sleepless nights on the long voyage and to soot from the stacks. Others in the room, bleeding from head injuries, held dirty handkerchiefs to their wounds. This floor was also filthy from the contents of overturned pans and chamber pots. The awful stench was mixed with the stink of chlorine and tincture of iodine. The nurse, in a bloodstained shirt, and barely able to keep his balance, medicated the diseased eye, disinfected wounds, bandaged them the best he could, and tried to get the crying children to swallow some medicine. On the kitchen helper's burn he applied a yellowish salve.

After three days and three nights of hell, the storm slowly subsided, and the exhausted crew worked long hours repairing the damage on the deck. The passengers in steerage left their dormitories where a revolting stench of vomit was stagnating, and went up to breathe the fresh air.

Gioanì seemed to be paler and sicker, tried by the fury of the hurricane, racked by continual coughing, exhausted and without appetite. He followed his sons reluctantly to the infirmary where the ship's doctor listened to his chest and shook his head in wonder, and the nurse gave him some cough syrup. Gildo noticed that neither the old man who had seemed to be dead already nor the old woman who had had a hard time breathing were there any longer, and he wondered what had become of them. Luigino, troubled, whispered that maybe they had died, and the dead were thrown into the sea at night when everyone was asleep and would not see. He sighed and added: Let's hope dad makes it to America.

One morning America finally appeared on the horizon, wrapped in fog. At first the land looked like a bizarre jagged cloud sitting on the water. Someone looked over the ship's side, cupped his hand over his eyes, and shouted to his neighbors. Hundreds of eyes scoured that oblong shape with blurred and ragged edges. The sea was calm, the sun high and bright. In the distance a ship advanced in the same direction leaving behind a plume of smoke. Then something shone from afar, in the middle of that feathery cloud, as when a sunray strikes a mirror or glass window. Suddenly restless, everyone wanted to see and pushed each other against the rails.

There were no cries of joy. The great moment had finally arrived, but in sight of the goal the passengers felt the oppressing weight of the fierce accumulated tiredness — the cold, the discomforts, the privations that were nestled in their muscles and bones. The terror suffered in the course of the storm and not yet dissipated had worn down their strength and resistance. In the long eventful journey by train and during the weeks of the crossing, they had had to bend to the will and rules of others. The waiting in a forced passivity had produced a sort of dullness of conscience, an inert resignation, a paralysis of the will that left them mute and stunned.

Intact, if not reinforced, was their anguish over the unknown that awaited them on the tongue of land that became sharper as they approached. Confusion over the loss of their old and reassuring habits grew stronger. Bewilderment over the too imminent challenges to be faced intensified by the moment. Each kept his fears to himself. The future was there, but it was a nebulous future, of intruders who knocked at the doors of an unknown and strange country, uncertain whether to be welcomed or rejected. The last miles that the ship covered brought them to the desired, but at the same time greatly feared, end.

The few who had already made that voyage had held forth for days with stories about very rigid inspections, interminable interrogations, obligatory showers, disinfectants, doctors' check-ups, baggage rifled, objects confiscated, body searches, unexpected taxes, expenses and duty, rejection for silly reasons. They had planted seeds of panic. Some were only embellishing their previous experience, but most of their listeners had believed it and squirmed with anxiety. They were especially worried about how to answer the officials' questions. They didn't know if they should admit they had no job promised by a relative or an acquaintance. Wasn't it better for the American authorities to know they had employment, and therefore were able to provide for themselves? And those whose voyage was paid for them didn't understand why they had to declare they had bought the ticket themselves. Didn't that mean they had someone there to vouch for them? They were unable to follow such a line of reasoning that left them confused and bewildered.

In the morning the purser appeared on the quarterdeck to announce that they would be arriving at the New York port in the afternoon. They should gather up their personal effects and take them out of the dormitories, being careful not to forget anything, and go to the line in front of the office to get their passports. The luggage kept in the hold would be unloaded by the porters and returned to the owners on shore.

Early in the morning Gildo had already laid his clean shirt on the bed to smooth out the wrinkles. He spot-cleaned his jacket and trousers he had worn for the whole voyage – all he owned – washed his neck, ears, feet, armpits, shaved his scant beard and combed with water his hair that was beginning to grow back. He was pleased he hadn't picked up any lice, unlike his father who had scratched the whole time and now, along with some others similarly infested, soaked his head in gasoline bought at a dear price on the ship and raked it with a fine-tooth comb.

One man with a dampened handkerchief attempted to remove some grease stains and traces of vomit from his clothes. Another reattached a loose button with needle and thread. One darned a hole in his sock, another pared his black-fringed fingernails, and still another shined his shoes with spit. A large crowd at the sinks removed the crusts of dirt and rancid odor of sweat. The women soaped and scrubbed their screaming children, loosened their hair, untangled and gathered it up in an orderly knot, mended the tears in their dresses, and sewed up unstitched hems. Everywhere preparations for landing were in full swing, as if getting ready for a merciless court sentencing.

That afternoon the ship passed through the strait that fed into the bay without docking. A boat came alongside and an official jumped on board. When he left the purser announced that that day there were more than five thousand emigrants disembarking, and Ellis Island was so congested it would be necessary to wait until the next morning. The Chicago dropped its anchors in sight of two strips of land, Brooklyn and Staten Island. In the distant background, like an apparition against the low sunset, a gray forest of tower-high buildings was silhouetted. Gildo asked himself in amazement how people made it to the top floors. To the right of the enormous city, there where a wide river penetrated into the interior, one could see part of a spectacular bridge that seemed suspended in air. Awe struck, Gildo thought how immense and boundless everything was in America: the dome of the sky with high-sailing clouds, the coastal bay fringed by deep inlets and tongues of land leaning into the sea; everything, the animated landscape of green hills and steep banks, the dizzying barge traffic, small boats, ferries, and everywhere houses, houses and more houses, in which a multitude of honest, conscientious, and hard-working people live in peace and plenty. A boundless space. This was why there was room and work for everyone, and America opened its arms and offered hope to everyone.

In the darkness the city, the suburbs, and the riverbanks glittered with lights. A spotlight illuminated the sky all night. No one on board could sleep. At dawn on March 3, 1910, preceded by a tugboat that whistled to open the way, the ship advanced slowly, sirens blasting, in the wind-raked bay. It glided close by the gigantic Statue of Liberty that was holding something in her hand no one could make out — some said a sword, some a lantern, some the Bible — and it continued until it reached the port of Manhattan. Two inspectors came on board, who disappeared into first class where the comfortably seated passengers were waiting.

The third-class passengers stood crammed together on the deck in anxious silence. They were given numbered cards to pin on their collars along with the train ticket for their final destination. They went by groups on boats shuttling back and forth between the dock and Ellis Island. On the sides of the little steamboats was written: U.S. Immigration Service, Department of Commerce and Labor, and this startled Gildo. The meaning was very clear to him, so that meant English was easy, almost like Italian. Reassured, he told himself that the devil is never as black as he is painted. On the island were some redbrick buildings surrounded by a high chain fence. In the center was a particularly imposing building with four towers and iron bars on the windows that made it look like a gloomy prison.

As the boat drew up to the wharf, another one was leaving, full of emigrants heading toward the mainland, who leaned over and waved to the new arrivals. They were guided through a canopy that led to the baggage deposit, and up a stairway to a large reception hall: high, almost up to the ceiling, ran a long balcony festooned with large American flags. Against the wall a dozen dour policemen stood with their hands behind their backs. At a certain point in the obligatory routine, two officials with the help of an interpreter separated the immigrants who were staying in New York from those who were going on to other destinations. And so the men from Bergamo were put with those from the Veneto, all of whom were going to California.

In the huge hall, such as no one had seen before, stood an enormous metal cage like an immense chicken coop, divided into sections, with two long facing benches in each. The men from Veneto and Bergamo sat with their baggage at their feet in a nerve-wracking wait to be called. At least in here no one dies from the cold, Bortolo whispered.

At a table sat the stern immigration inspectors registering new arrivals. Further on, in a corner, were the navy doctors in blue uniforms and insignia charged with giving physical examinations. The large room was a bedlam: dozens of languages and dialects criss-crossed, incomprehensible orders were yelled hysterically into megaphones, the hubbub echoed and was amplified as though in a cavern. Waves of exhausted emigrants, hungry and dazed, followed each other dragging their things, stepping on each others' heels like a herd of sheep, urged in a rude and no-nonsense manner to move faster, almost as if there was not a moment to lose; in the end they were pushed brusquely into the cages that were closed with a clang. All that's missing is the whip, hissed Leone.

Those who had been separated by the crowd from relatives or friends hung back looking for them, calling them loudly and blocking the way. They tried their best to stay together, their only safeguard against the confusion. Children, dragged by the hand, and jerked around crossly, were crying. One man, burdened as a mule, lost pieces of baggage and fumbled to retrieve it; others, convinced that in the confusion their wallet or bundle had been stolen, when instead it had been handed over to a relative, screamed like the possessed and didn't shut up until it was back in their possession. Some tried to make their way by pushing and elbowing, and some bumped suitcases against the legs of the person ahead, who expressed his resentment loudly. Exhaustion and extreme tension set the stage for quarrels and someone even raised his fists. The officials were in a great hurry to get through the paperwork of this newly arrived river of emigrants in order to make way for others coming from the port. They worked for days on end without rest, growing ever more grim and exasperated by that massive invasion of shabby foreigners.

From the cages large groups were led to the showers, where the hot water ran in torrents and the soap smelled like sulfur. Prodded to move faster by the irritable attendants, covered by vapors of disinfectant, drying themselves in rough towels and putting on their clothes again in a great rush, they returned to their places, and then the doctors began their work. A great silence suddenly fell. It seemed that they were holding their breath in desperate attention. This would determine the fortune or ruin of each. Gildo sniffed the disgusting odor of sulfur that remained on his skin. His heart was pounding in his chest and saliva filled his mouth. He was distraught by the thought that his thirty-five dollars might be judged insufficient and he would be sent back where he came from. He fingered the bills nervously, felt the number twenty-three pinned to his collar, rubbed a spot on his trousers that didn't want to go away. His father rested his elbows on his knees and held his head in his hands, almost as though wanting to hide his gray hair that he feared might disqualify him. Suddenly Gildo felt sorry for him. Luigino pressed against him with fear in his wide eyes and gnawed on his fingernails. Bigio opened and closed his toothless mouth, almost breathless, and he tortured his accordion case. Bortolo cracked his knuckles and massaged his hands until they turned white. Gioanì, paler than ever, closed his eyes and turned his head as if not wanting to see or hear anything. His son Giusepì, bursting with tension, scratched an ear until it bled. Even the men from Veneto, usually great talkers, kept a frowning silence and stared into space. Behind them a child cried and his father covered his mouth with his hand.

The entry procedures lasted for hours. The emigrants, waiting helplessly for the judgment of a malevolent and despotic power, were plunged into apathy. What could they do except wait, resigned and inert, for a sentence they could in no way avoid? Those who were called rose at once, gripped by panic as if going to their execution by firing squad; stumbling, they walked blindly across the others' feet, and staggering, headed toward the group of doctors, followed by a multitude of frightened eyes.

The organization was practical and efficient: the doctor's examination was the first step in determining their state of health, which made the successive interrogations and formalities superfluous, a waste of time, and everyone knows that time is money. A group of twenty emigrants at a time were directed toward the navy doctors, and assisted by interpreters. And there, on their feet, their eyelids were raised with instruments to check for trachoma. Those affected were isolated and CT was written in chalk on the back of their jackets. This was the fate of the man Gildo had encountered in the ship's infirmary. Here, as there, he tried to tell the doctor through the interpreter about his insomnia during the trip, about how the train smoke and soot from the stacks had made his eyes water. After he was relegated to a corner, with the white initials scratched on his back, he continued to tug on the sleeve of the indifferent interpreter, repeating his justifications endlessly, until the interpreter lost his patience, and shaking him loose, pushed him rudely against the wall. Only then did he seem to realize the consequences of that verdict. He begged for pity, jumbling together in a hasty and confused discourse the reasons he absolutely could not return to his country, but it aroused nothing but ill-concealed annoyance. No one was listening to him, and when at last he realized the sentence was irrevocable, he gave a cry of desperation and collapsed like an inanimate puppet on the floor. No one paid any attention to him.

After the eye exam, the men stripped to the waist and the doctors palpitated their necks to locate goiters, listened to their hearts and lungs, looked at their teeth and throat. They had the men take a few steps to check for those who limped, were crippled, or suffered some foot defect. The men bent over to reveal any impediment of their backs, were questioned to verify their mental state. All at the disconcerting speed of an assembly line.

When Gioanì heard his name called he shook himself from his lethargy and jumped to his feet as through bitten by a tarantula, and went out quickly from the enclosure. He pushed his way through the line, and brandishing his dollars, ran toward the astonished doctors, waving them under their noses. Everything was in order, he shouted. He had worked in France, was in good health, and had enough to provide for himself in America. At that moment he was wracked by a coughing fit that bent him double. And while Luigino held him by the shoulders and Giusepì slapped him on the back, the interpreter ordered him to strip to his waist. The doctor listened carefully to his chest, shoulders, and back, asked him to breathe deeply, to cough, and to spit in a basin.

He was told to put his shirt back on, and a very pale Gioanì obeyed with trembling fingers, a string of saliva dripping from his mouth. On the back of his jacket they wrote P, and he was isolated in a corner. He then realized that what he had been so afraid would happen had happened. In America they didn't want a wreck like him. He did not protest or beg; not a word came from his mouth. He gave his dumbstruck sons the dollars he had managed to put together with such pain and effort, turned to the wall as though to hide his shame, took his face in his hands and broke into sobs that seemed like the gasps of a dying animal. Unfazed, the doctors and interpreters continued to work. Over time they had become callously indifferent to such scenes of suffering.

Bigio was afraid of being rejected because of his lack of teeth, although he kept repeating like a litany that whether he could chew or not was his business and of no importance to the Americans. They took their time looking into his open mouth, but accepted him in the end.

A family from Friula—father, mother, two thin, rickety, bundled-up children, and a third still in diapers—was rejected because they didn't have the required amount of dollars. The man, as though struck by lightning, staggered under the blow, and rubbed his face while he looked around stunned, almost not believing his ears, looking elsewhere for his salvation. His desperate eyes turned back to the faces of stone that stood before him, and he picked up his dollars from the table as if he were about to leave. But he suddenly straightened up and with a voice cracking with tension, protested that he had a contract for work in a mine in Wisconsin, and therefore was able to start earning as soon as he reached his destination. The poor man didn't understand why that guarantee, instead of opening doors, worked against him. Convinced that there was a misunderstanding, he insisted on explaining, begged and implored until the interpreter grew impatient and roughly told him to leave. Gildo watched him walk away unsteadily, the two little children grasping at his pants' leg, his dazed wife following with the little one in her arms. The miserable family seemed to him like a picture of the cruelest despair.

When, after the summary medical examination, it was Gildo's turn to be interrogated by a brusque and frowning inspector, in addition to the generalities such as questions about where he came from, he heard the interpreter ask who had paid for his passage. Without hesitation he replied that he had paid for it himself, just as he did not hesitate to furnish the name and address of the countryman in Renton. Fine. Was he already in possession of the train ticket for that destination? Certainly, he answered with the surety of one who knows he had done things properly, and he displayed it pinned to his collar as required. The inspector examined it, turning it every way, and handed it to the interpreter to show him something. He turned it over in the same way, shook his head, mumbled something in English and threw it on the table: it was false. That piece of paper was worthless. Who did he think he was dealing with? Gildo blushed as if they had called him a thief. Stammering, he tried to explain how he had paid for it fairly and squarely, but he was cut short: don't give us the usual Italian bullshit. In the lobby there was a ticket office where he could buy a real one. Point blank he was asked if he had a work contract at Renton. Confused and intimidated he was about to say yes, but bit his tongue and said no. With his heart in his mouth he displayed his thirty-five dollars, the requisite amount—but five was taken for the entrance fee. He heard his name mispronounced, but he didn't dare correct them. And then, to his great surprise, he heard them ask if he were polygamous or an anarchist, and that left him open-mouthed because he didn't know what they meant. They asked him to add two and two and to reconstruct a ship puzzle, so easy that a five-year-old could do it with his eyes closed. They looked into the bundle he had with him, and confiscated the stracchino, salami, lard, and borlotti beans without any explanation.

His father came next, without his customary arrogance: Gildo saw the tangled gray hair on his bare chest, his suspenders dangling, his wide-open mouth and extended tongue. He watched him, meek and humble, show the inspector the one hundred thirty-five dollars, heard him heatedly defend himself at the sharp reprimand for buying a fake railroad ticket, and watched him retreat backward with a series of obsequious bows, knock over a chair and make elaborate apologies that no one listened to.

They were admitted to America. He should have been ecstatic, but instead Gildo felt like he had a nail in his chest. For the first time he had tasted America's hardness, revulsion, and hostility. He had thought there was room for everyone in that immense country; he was young, honest, he had strong arms and the will to work. Wasn't that what the Americans wanted? Then why did they treat them with contempt and dislike, as though they were lice-ridden beggars looking for a handout?

The group from Bergamo gathered around Gioanì in dismay. Cipriano, after first bemoaning the steep price of the entrance fee, swearing about the train ticket swindle (just one more of the many), and about Gildo letting them confiscate the food, remembered that luckily Gioanì, just as he, had taken out insurance for reimbursement of the trip expenses in case he was refused entrance. So he could get his money back at least. Better than nothing.

Leone and Luigino, documents in hand, went to the window of the Society for Italian Immigrants, in the building's central lobby, where a clerk, after reading and rereading them declared they were as false as counterfeit money. That insurance company didn't even exist. Unfortunately frauds like that happened all the time. They weren't the first and wouldn't be the last to fall for them.

They talked it over for a while, and not finding the courage to tell Gioanì that they had been tricked once again, they plotted to tell him that it was a long and complicated process to handle once he returned, because the money would be sent to Italy. They collected a few dollars, which they finally persuaded him to take.

A well-dressed man approached, and in halting Italian declared he was a lawyer and in the position to take legal action for the unjust expulsion of an Italian citizen, and to win it, naturally. He identified a sheaf of papers in his hand as copies of the positive judgments he had already attained, bragged about his long experience in this field, and informed them that they would have nothing to pay but a small advance for the initial expenses. The rest the federal government would pay, because the court would certainly agree. They couldn't treat an honest man like that who had merely asked to work.

Overcome with anger, they told him to beat it. The man tipped his hat, bowed, and moved away to make the same proposal to a group of men from Como gathered around a companion who had been rejected on the basis of age — he was little more than fifty years old — wearing the letter S on his back.

Bortolo, in an attempt to console Gioanì, kept repeating that when he got well in Italy he could join them the following year. But Gioanì shook his head in despair. The disappointment of being rejected after that long trip was too strong: all his hopes had crumbled with that refusal, and he wondered how he could pay off the debts he had run up in his town and how he could face the shame of the failure everyone would know about. He hadn't much longer to live, he was thinking, no longer any strength to work. He was finished, a wreck, useless to others and to himself, and the disgrace of unemployment was ahead. And when he thought of the trouble and of the long return voyage on the Chicago — even though at the expense of the shipping company — and the train trip from Le Havre to Italy, he hoped he would die before left.

His sons weren't resigned to leaving him. Luigino was afraid that he might do something desperate, like jump into the sea and drown, or hang himself. They wanted to go back with him, not leave him alone, but they didn't have the money for the trip. Now it became even more necessary for them to work and get some money. Their father was ashamed to return to his town, but the shame would be tripled if they all returned together. They wrung their hands in despair.

The leave-taking was excruciating. Gioanì, like the other rejected emigrants, was sent to a place nearby to wait for the departing ship. One after the other embraced him, stammering words of comfort, and looking at him miserably until he was nearly out of the port. Pa, Luigino called him at the last moment, Pa, as soon as you get to Abbazzia have the priest write a letter. Let us know how it went, and he repeated Tranquillo's address in Renton several times, emphasizing each syllable. Their father turned, nodded yes and with a disheartened gesture disappeared. Luigino's eyes filled with tears.

They had lunch in a huge dining hall, the men again separate from the women and children. Dazed by the noise and confusion, they paid out of their own pockets for the revolting, colorless, gooey pap: a slice of stale rye bread, a bowl of cooked prunes. No wine or beer, not even glasses. Reluctantly they forked over more dollars for the train ticket, picked up their baggage once again stinking of disinfectant, and got on the boat that took them to the mainland. The emigrants going to other destinations by train were not allowed to stop in the city, but had to go directly to the train station.

On Battery Square a large crowd was waiting for friends or relatives. Some held signs above their heads with the name of the person they were meeting. Shouts, calls, happy greetings intersected; hugs, handshakes, and loud slaps on the back were exchanged.

The men from Bergamo were assailed by swarms of all manner of salesmen — shysters offering to send telegrams or buy train tickets, hawkers from boarding houses or restaurants trying to snag customers, lawyers ready to resolve every problem, intermediaries offering well-paid jobs in the vicinity, money changers holding up signs in six languages, porters, beggars—but by now wise from experience and angry, they made short shrift of them.

7

Except for two narrow openings in the ceiling, the bunkhouse had no windows. The alarm went off at 5:30, even before the pale dawn light filtered through the disjointed siding. Gildo, eyes opened wide in the dark, watched the day arrive. Anxiety gnawed at him even in his sleep, as if it moved the hands of a clock lodged in his chest. Lying on the straw mattress, he wondered apprehensively what the weather was like. Not that knowing changed anything. You worked in good weather or bad, even in the rain if not a downright flood; knowing was useful only for determining how hard a day it would be.

Fifty men slept in cots in a row: those from the Piedmont, Brescia, Valtellin, and Friuli areas, managed to understand each other's dialects, while the Abruzzesi—who tried to explain how the mildew years before had destroyed the grape vines and that was why they had to emigrate—were kept at a distance and derided for their ridiculous and incomprehensible dialect and for the pervasive aroma of goat. Africa! Bortolo yelled after them, roaring with laughter. Leone made jokes and launched insults at the southerners, any place from Florence on down. He called them lazy onion eaters, and boasted of the superior northern civilization. He disapproved of the unification of Italy that had unjustly given equal rights both to savage shepherds who lived in caves, and to advanced people like they were who deserved respect.

Gildo listened to the breathing of his sleeping comrades, the deep breathing of worn out men, the discordant timbre of suddenly interrupted snoring, the deep sighs, the coughing, the grunts of suspended breathing, the groaning and mumbling. Luigino, who slept next to him, sometimes whimpered like a child looking for his mother. From outside came the unfamiliar songs of night birds and animal cries never heard before. They said black bears wandered around in the dark looking for food. No one had seen them, but anyone who went out at night did so in fear of that mysterious beast that rummaged in the bushes.

They locked the door at night against the bats' nocturnal carousel that caught in their hair and brought bad luck. From cracks in the walls cold drafts of wind came in. In the course of the night the air grew warm, but it became thick and poisoned by the heavy breathing, the stench of bare feet and cloth stretched out to dry, the odor emanating from dirty bodies and clothes, the smell of stagnant tobacco smoke and the nauseating stink of kerosene lamps. To Gildo the stable at home seemed sweeter than that stinking hovel, and he missed the cows' tranquil ruminating and their loud vaporous snorts. When it rained water came up through the planks and soaked the floor that sometimes became a muddy pond. Dampness sank into their faces, hair, clothes, mattresses, and continued doggedly up as far as their clothes hanging on nails on walls. The older men complained of aching bones. They got up stiffly in the morning, their joints creaking; they straightened their backs painfully, and cursed all the saints of the calendar. They had asked their foreman for a stove to dry the unhealthy humidity in the bunkhouse, but his answer had been that if they wanted such extravagances they would have to buy a stove at the company store. They all pitched in to buy one, and put it in the center of the room where it wouldn't catch the wooden wall on fire. A long pipe ran straight up and out a hole in the roof. The morning began with the stars and finished with the stars, as Bigio observed, so they lit the stove when they came back numb from work and found the bunkhouse as frozen as the North Pole. They gathered firewood in the forest, but often it was damp and produced more smoke than heat.

There were no toilets. Each man had to shift for himself around the yard, behind a tree or bush, a practice that caused angry outbursts when someone stepped in it. They washed outside in metal buckets filled with river water they bought at the company store. Some mornings they had to break an ice crust with a hammer. Spring was having a hard time getting there. The buds seemed frozen on the trees, and a north wind chapped their faces. Sometimes a stinging sleet swirled around them all day long.

As soon as the train left New York to enter the still snowy countryside, they had noticed that winter hung on longer in America than where they came from. Bortolo was certain that since they were heading west, where the sun set, it would certainly be warmer there. However, he was badly mistaken: they were going northwest, toward a very different climate. In fact, as the train made its way, the woods seemed as bare as in the depths of winter. The sparse prairie grass was burned by the cold, the wheat fields dry and yellowed. The roofs of the occasional farmhouses lost in the nothingness were still white with snow and the chimneys smoked furiously.

Heated and interminable comparisons were made between the country they had left and the one they were in: the immensity of that land, the vastness of the horizons, the expanse of forests, cultivated fields, and prairies. The enormity of the distances made them feel as small and lost as ants.

Gripped by amazement, for a while they had been anxious to defend their country: the little towns where everyone knew each other and everything was close at hand, the church, the store, the tavern on the piazza, the fields a stone's throw away, the distances measured by foot, but then they had been seized by curiosity. How did the farmers manage to cultivate all by themselves those endless fields with the newly sprouted wheat, rye, corn, where it would take all day just to cross? They were astonished by certain strange machines that clanked back and forth tilling, plowing, spreading manure, transporting loads of firewood or hay. That was certainly a convenience, but Pino commented that it would be funny with their handkerchief-size plots of land where such machines couldn't even enter. And how could they take care of huge herds of cows like those that looked up at the passing train and stared stupidly? Who fed them, who milked them? And the horses, sheep, goats, pigs? Who saw to it that the animals didn't climb up the train embankment and get killed? Was it to keep the livestock away that the locomotive kept blowing its whistle, so loudly that it made them leap in the air?

In the endless prairies, where there wasn't even a house for miles, men on horseback galloped alongside the train for a while, and in an immense forest of very high fur trees they passed through for hours, they had seen groups of woodsmen armed with ax and saw, busily cutting trees and sectioning the trunks. Where did they live? How did they get there in such bad weather? Did they have families or live alone? Where did they buy food and everything else they needed, if there was nothing to see in any direction? And where did they go to mass on Sunday, since there were no bell towers on the horizon? And those who lived in isolated houses, a day's walk from one to the other, how did they make it without neighbors to exchange a few words, drink a glass together, and give each other a hand when necessary? And where were the women? They had seen one in the distance, standing in the doorway of a rustic farmhouse, children attached to her skirt watching the train, and chickens, geese, turkeys pecking in the farmyard.

As a matter of fact, the comparisons between Italy and America had begun even before they left New York, when at the station Gildo was amazed to see a black man, a porter loaded with luggage, and had nudged Luigino, as surprised as he by the sight, because there were no Africans in Italy. And they were amazed by the food in the store they bought for the trip: slices of bland, yellowish cheese that tasted like cardboard; a weird square-shaped bread, as white as rich folks', but with no flavor, like a sponge that stuck to the roof of your mouth. After frantic calculations they realized they had spent four times more than they would have in Italy. Bigio commented that if the prices were so high, it meant that in America people made heaps of money, and that surely would be the case with them. So there was nothing to worry about. Actually, Leone objected, they didn't know how much they would earn. Tranquillo had never said exactly. They had trusted him because he was a fellow countryman and certainly wouldn't cheat them.

They didn't know anything about the trip or about the geography of the continent, except that the state of Washington was the farthest state away. But how many miles away was it, and how many days did it take to get there? Some said one thousand, some said two, some said one week, some said three days, some fifteen like the ship — an exaggeration. In any case, the distance was certainly greater than from the Alps to Sicily, or rather, from Sicily to Le Havre.

It was in the New York train station store that they realized they had now truly set foot in America: no one understood them. There were no interpreters and they had to get by on their own. If words were useless, they used gestures: a finger pointed toward the thing they wanted, fingers open to indicate the amount. They got the idea at once that it was good to show their money in order to make the storekeeper's face turn from suspicious and grim to well disposed. Only then, face to face with the Americans, did they realize how immediately recognizable they were by their features, manner, dress, language as Italian emigrants; and how this difference was met with unexpected suspicion, immediate dislike, and sometimes the cruel desire to take advantage of them.

The wine story, for example. At the station store they had paid an arm and a leg for six bottles of wine, but when they got on the train a conductor stopped them and talked himself hoarse explaining that alcoholic beverages were not allowed on the train. It had taken some time to understand what the devil he wanted, but when they finally caught on they were dumbfounded. Why in heaven's name couldn't they drink a sip of wine to keep their spirits up? In Italy, and in France also, you could do it, so why not here? That American rule was hard to swallow. They were forced to take the bottles back to the store, but in spite of all their gesturing attempts to explain their situation, the owner wouldn't give them their money back. Furious, Cipriano had grabbed one of the bottles from the shopkeeper's hand and downed it right then and there. And already a little tipsy, he inveighed against the damned American laws and the damned American shopkeepers that pretend not to understand. They knew very well wine couldn't be taken on the train, but they sold it anyway, robbing the poor devils of their money. He was desperate at the prospect of not having even a drop to drink for who knows how many days, unless the train stopped at other stations long enough to buy a bottle and gulp it down on the platform.

But what if the train goes directly to Renton? Serafì wondered. Then, in addition to having no wine we'll be sure to die of hunger.

In Chicago they changed to the Great Northern line that went to their destination. The train stopped many times and for long periods on dead-end tracks in desolate and deserted places where they didn't see a live soul, and the silence roared in their ears, in order to allow a train to pass that was in a hurry, or to wait for one coming in the opposite direction. At such times they got off to stretch their legs and urinate with pleasure out in the open instead of in the filthy toilets onboard. Or the train stopped to hand over mailbags to a fellow standing next to a little wooden shed on stilts, his horse tied to tree. Not a building or fence or sign of cultivation or life on the horizon. Or it stopped to refill the steam engine and carriages with water from red tanks raised on a high steel structure on wheels, and to check and oil the pistons. And it stopped in other deserted places where, next to the rails were gigantic pyramids of coal that the stoker and two assistants shoveled vigorously for more than an hour, first loading it on the rusty carts parked on a service side track, then in the tender attached to the steam engine. Gildo and Luigino offered to lend a hand, proud to show the Americans their willingness to work and the strength of their arms. But no one seemed to notice, and no one would have dreamed to thank them.

One day, after a big rain and traveling miles without passing a village or even a farm, the train stopped at an isolated little station, and the machinist, concerned about landslides or flooding, got out to ask about the condition of the tracks. Since the guard merely shrugged his shoulders, the machinist was obliged to ask that the tracks be inspected for a distance with a trolley, and if there was no trolley, he could telegraph the request for one to be sent from the last or next station. After a couple of hours of inconclusive telegraphic negotiations, the machinist decided to go ahead; and at a snail's pace, with the greatest care, the driver leaning out the cab to check the tracks yard by yard, the train entered a valley flooded by a raging river. In places the water almost reached the top of the railroad embankment. Miraculously there had been no landslides. Gildo leaned out of the window also to watch the vast muddy lake in which were reflected dark violet clouds blown by a furious wind that shook the fir trees at the edge of the valley like twigs. In those unprotected spaces nature was going on a rampage with unheard of violence, and Gildo remembered with a kind of tenderness the harmless way the Luio overflowed its banks and the mild torrents that ran through the small and familiar Abbazzia valley.

When their provisions had been gone for some time and their stomachs rumbled with hunger, Leone and Gildo were motivated to timidly explore the train as far as the restaurant car and came back dispirited. Dinner cost an astronomical figure, seven dollars. Rich and well-dressed gentlemen sat at the dining tables. The odor of expensive cigars floated in the air, and the waiters had looked them over with a scornful condescension reserved for beggars. Luckily the train had stopped half an hour in different stations — Minneapolis, then Fargo and Minot, and the final one, Spokane — just enough time to run to the store where they sold everything from shoes to food. Gildo, Pino, and Luigino stood at the end of a long line of impatient travelers who spoke English, and therefore were served first; and as if that were not enough, they shoved them aside roughly in an arrogant manner that was hard to take. Each customer had premised the request with the same word: "pliis," and after a while Gildo guessed that it meant "per favore," and unaccustomed to such polite ways, blushing with embarrassment, he said it himself, happy about that first victory with the American language. Someone in the line had said the word "dego," which seemed addressed to them. And although Gildo thought it over carefully, he couldn't figure out what it meant.

They bought the usual gummy bread, a little cheese, and few very long sausages that made their mouth water just looking at them, but the taste was so different from their country sausages that they had trouble swallowing them. Bigio launched into a passionate celebration of the taste and smell of the Abbazzia salami and tears came to his eyes. The long train made brief stops in dusty little nondescript towns, made up of a few dilapidated houses with an air of impermanence: Barnesville, Larimore, Gulbertson, Nashua, Saco, Chester, Libby, Bonners Ferry and many others, with abandoned passenger coaches and old wooden steam engines parked on dead-end tracks. Usually they couldn't even see the station, because only the head of the train, with the first class Pullman cars, reached the platform. The other cars remained so far back that it was necessary to take off at break-neck speed, and run through heaps of rotting ties, scrap, and pieces of rusty track. Just time enough to fill bottles with drinking water and rinse their faces—don't even dream of having time to buy something to eat, so that they truly suffered from hunger—and climb back on while the engine was whistling and puffing. Only in some small stations had they been able to buy some sandwiches filled with fried meat and onions from a street-merchant's cart. Wine cost a fortune, so Cipriano would linger on the sidewalk to drink a couple of beers and risk being left behind.

During the stops they had glanced surreptitiously and with amazement through the curtained windows of the luxurious Pullman cars: a sumptuous sitting room, an elegant room for smokers, compartments with red velvet divans and head rests of white lace, mahogany walls and tables, lamps with rose lighting, beds with immaculate sheets. In this world there are winners and losers, Bigio said, spitting on the ground, some eat meat and some suck on the bones. While stopped in the stations a couple of policeman would unobtrusively plant themselves in the way of the third-class passengers so the wealthy would not be annoyed by the curiosity of such poor people. Bortolo cursed as he squirmed on the wooden bench that made his backside sore, wondering how much in the world it cost to ride in one of those luxury cars that even King Vittorio Emanuele was not privileged to have, and resentfully reminded the others, in case they had forgotten, that they had decided against the couchette to save two and a half dollars.

Many people got on and off even in the little stations lost in uncultivated and uninhabited places, and who knows where they came from and where they were going and for what reason. Men alone or entire families, some getting off at the next stop, like a tram in the city. For days that single track cut a straight path, as if drawn with a ruler, through yellowish, dry prairies, dark coniferous forests, thick woods of maple and beech trees, flat and fertile black fields freshly plowed, stretches of parched clayey land,

and low swampy areas where herds of buffalo bathed. The monotonous chug of the wheels, the rhythmic reverberation of the axles, the uniform clang of the connecting rods under the floor, in addition to exhaustion and hunger, produced a heavy drowsiness in the travelers, brutally interrupted from time to time by the engine's shriek.

The train track formed wide curves when it began to follow the winding course of the Missouri River, the contours of small lakes or the capricious sharp bends of the valleys between low and wooded hills. Then, for an entire day, they went through endless undulating pastures where herds of wild horses galloped, frightened by the train's racket, and when they least expected it mountains appeared: high snow-covered peaks, rocky walls, jagged crests, perpendicular towers of pink stone as far as they could see. The Rocky Mountain chain. The train slowed to a walking pace, almost as though looking for an impossible passage in that barrier. It went ahead cautiously through rugged winding valleys embedded between steep barren slopes. It entered long, dark, dripping tunnels, until, between brusque curves and jagged slopes, it climbed panting along side snow-covered mountains. Going even slower it crossed bridges of dizzying height that seemed built of reeds and they passed over rapidly flowing rivers, little streams, giddy precipices, bottomless ravines. At every crossing over those fragile arches, the passengers held their breath in terror of ending down below, and Luigino shut his eyes to the view. Yes, America was beautiful, he whispered, but also a little scary. His fear also included poor pa, all alone, lost and sick on that sad island; he wondered if pa was already on the ship, how he would be treated at home, and if the country air would cure him. Broken hearted, he sighed and renewed his promise to send him the first money he and Giusepì earned, as soon as possible, and maybe that would be a little consolation for the painful disgrace.

After seven days of travel they finally reached Renton. For some time they had been on the alert for fear of missing their stop or not being able to get off in time. The train usually remained outside the station and they couldn't read the name of place or even understand what the stationmaster was yelling from the far platform. The conductor had come through to announce the next station in a grave and serious manner, but they hadn't caught the name; and if it hadn't been for an American pushing them toward the door, who knows where they might have ended up. They got off at the last moment, so frantic and agitated that they were left exhausted and upset, and dragging their baggage, they walked long and far along symmetrical streets looking for Tranquillo's house at Post Box 45. But they couldn't find it. Even this was an American oddity that they couldn't understand, because in Italy an address consisted of a street name and house number. They wandered around for more than an hour and finally, dead tired, they turned to a merchant sitting on the porch of his shop on the main street, showed him the address and the man directed them to the post office.

The clerk, a large woman with a brusque manner, impatient because they didn't understand her, led them to the rows of boxes on the wall and knocked her knuckles against one of them, Post Box 45. In this way they learned that Tranquillo didn't live in town, but worked fifteen miles away and came to Renton occasionally to get his mail. There was nothing to do but wait for him and hope he came soon.

They took a room in a miserable boarding house, the cheapest one they could find, and everyday took turns going to the post office to wait for Tranquillo. Finally one Saturday afternoon he arrived.

That evening in a tavern, to welcome his dear countrymen to America, he offered a lavish supper, generously sprinkled with many bottles of wine. Even Gildo, who avoided alcohol as a protest against his father's immoderate use of it, was encouraged by his friends to drink a few glasses, deriving from it a childish euphoria and an irrepressible, silly fit of giggles. Bigio hoisted his accordion onto his shoulders, and already tipsy, passionately played familiar tunes far into the night, until Tranquillo, nearly moved to tears, invoked his old mother back in the home country, named his relatives, friends and acquaintances in Abbazzia one by one, and even felt nostalgia for the priest and his fiery sermons. With shining eyes and blurry speech, Cipriano shouted: Bend your elbow and you'll live to eighty. A colossal drunken evening, which at that moment was seen as an epic event, to celebrate the beginning of their new life in America, the promised land of wealth and abundance. While the very next day it took on quite a different aspect.

Gildo slipped quietly out of the bunkhouse to wash in peace before the others crowded the washtubs. He trembled from the cold gusts coming off the mountains and the thick fog that had settled in the valley; and as he liked to do when alone, he was whistling a tune, and thinking again about that first Sunday morning in which, dazed and confused after the big drinking party the night before, they had left Renton for the roadwork site. And he was thinking about that first incident that had taken them by surprise, a hint of what was to come, which at the time they had not considered in its full and alarming significance.

His father, Bortolo, Leone, and Pino sat in Tranquillo's buggy. The other five rented another buggy, settling on the price of two and a half dollars a head. Too much, but the driver was stubborn: it was a holiday, they were going a long way and the road was in bad condition, the return trip the next day was a loss, and moreover he had to spend the night at the work site. Tranquillo had acted as an intermediary in the negotiations and assured them the price was fair. Perhaps they didn't know that fifteen miles was almost twice fifteen kilometers.

Outside Renton, after going over a stretch of decent road, they turned onto a bumpy, muddy trail full of potholes, which entered a wooded valley and ran alongside a quiet, clear river, the Cedar River. They had to make frequent stops to let their panting, sweating, foaming horses catch their breath. At the worst sections the wheels sank into the mud, and to dislodge them the passengers had to get into the muck, push hard on the spokes, and pull the bridles of the stubborn animals. The sludge raised by the wheels splattered in their eyes and hair, splashed onto their clothes, and nearly ruined their shoes. Tranquillo swore and intoned a refrain that certainly sounded like an accusation: the horses were overloaded; they were too many in the buggy, and they had too much luggage; it had never happened to him before, although he went over that road every two weeks; there was a danger that they would break the wheel hubs or the buggy would sink down—and who would pay for it? He went on and on while they sat in guilty silence.

After a wide curve in the valley, the trail became a veritable swamp from the roadwork underway; in some areas it was three feet under water. To make it worse it had begun to rain, and when they finally reached their lodging they were soaked to the skin. And there, while they were unloading the baggage, the first red flag was raised: Tranquillo, with a hard look, had demanded two and a half dollars a head at once from the four who had traveled in his buggy, the same price the driver had asked. Stunned, they stood looking at each other, but no one dared object, including Leone who couldn't bear injustice and abuse of power. They talked it over that evening: Tranquillo had had to come to the site anyway, why the hell did he expect to be paid? And furthermore, how much did it cost the driver, an American who does it for a living, to eat and sleep there that night and take the empty buggy back to Renton the next day? Tranquillo was a crook and a cheat, ready to take advantage of his own countrymen and fill his pockets with their last bit of cash even before they begin to earn anything. Bortolo pointed out how that welcoming supper, offered in apparent generosity and received with enthusiastic gratitude, had soon been repaid by the dollars Tranquillo had pocketed.

That same evening Leone had asked him about the terms of the agreement between the company and the workers, the conditions of work, their hours, and the amount of the daily wage. Work began at 6:30 in the morning and ended at 5:30 in the evening, an hour for lunch, Work stopped Saturday at 3:00 in the afternoon. Ten hours a day, more with the time of travel to and from work. Food and lodging cost fifty cents a day, ten cents a week for the drinking water that the boy the company hired took from the spring on the hill and carried back on his shoulders to the work teams. Wine and beer was extra at the midday meal, to be consumed at the work place. Each man bought what he needed to eat from the company store. Prospero, Tranquillo's distant relative from Val Brembana, cooked supper. The pay was $1.50 a day for working days. Overtime due to emergencies was not paid. A late arrival of two minutes would cost an hour's pay.

After washing up, Gildo looked at the stars growing pale in the clear sky, forecasting a sunny day, and he thought back over that long evening. Though worn out by the trip, they had been lost in the complicated calculations of the Italian lire in relation to $9.00 a week, of the amount that they would be able to save to send home in a month or two, minus the necessary expenses. Feeling weak in the knees about the puny amount, their resentment was rekindled over the incredible dishonesty of Tranquillo, who had taken almost two days' pay for the trip in his buggy. To their rage against that bloodsucker was added the discomfort, sadness, and sense of abandonment of someone who is forced to realize he cannot trust anyone, not even a fellow countryman.

The company store, for example, was run by a certain Modesto Agazzi from Brescia, apparently a good friend of Tranquillo's; he was hard as granite, with a brusque and no-nonsense manner, and he charged exorbitant prices. In a ledger that they had to buy, he wrote down the amount of each purchase without specifying the item and collected it at the end of the month. Bigio, who didn't know how to read, was forced to pay an astronomical amount which he didn't understand; Bortolo meticulously checking each figure one by one, discovered that in front of a three, with a different pencil, a five was added. The trick worked just fine with the illiterate. It was difficult to determine and even more difficult to prove, so that when Bigio confronted Agazzi, backed up by Bortolo, that barefaced thief and liar denied it and threatened to report him for slander.

From Agazzi they had to buy tools for work: a pick, a shovel, a wheelbarrow. They could have rented them for so much a day, but in the end it wasn't worth it. And also a pair of knee-high rubber boots, indispensable for walking in the swampy work site. A hooded oilcloth slicker for protection during storms, bed covers — they renounced the use of sheets — a couple of towels, a piece of soap, and an aluminum food container. The roadwork site was so far from any kind of habitation that it wasn't possible to go anywhere else for their daily needs: the company store was a gold mine. Every day the workers bought food for lunch, bread and sometimes moldy cheese, sausages spoiled or filled with disgusting things, rancid bacon and lard, beans, cans of tuna or meat in which they found revolting things, damp and stale cigars and tobacco. The socks they had to buy were of the poorest quality, and turned into rags after a few days, even though they protected them with strips of cloth wrapped around their feet; the flannel shirts were of such poor quality that they soon became smooth and worn and of no use. They bought needles and thread for mending, attaching buttons and reinforcing trousers with patches on the back side and knees, soap for washing underwear, nails for mending shoes, leather to resole them, and even disinfectant for little wounds and cuts, seeing that the company didn't even put tincture of iodine at their disposal.

Leone tried to reason with Agazzi about the stratospheric prices and the poor quality of merchandise: if they had to spend so much of their pay just to survive they wouldn't be able to send much home to their families. They might as well have stayed in Italy. So why not go back? Agazzi had replied, stony-faced, and they nearly came to blows.

The foreman, an American by the name of Fred, called deferentially the "bosso," a stocky man of middle age with a ruddy complexion, was seen only rarely. He spoke English with Tranquillo, who translated his orders to the team leaders in charge of a group of workers, all Italians except an Irish group for which no love was lost. They had the reputation of being big beer drinkers, quick-tempered and quarrelsome when drunk. They openly showed their contempt for the Italians, accusing them of unfair competition because they worked too hard and under the worst conditions. They accused them not being good Catholics and of taking the name of God in vain, blaming them even for the breach of Porta Pia and the pope's humiliation.

The work extended for several miles. The valley looked as though shaken by a typhoon that had battered the woods, uprooted trees, turned the ground upside down, eradicated and scattered underbrush everywhere, smashed rocks, tore apart hills with dirt and stone quarries—a chaotic disorder in which a battalion of men labored in frantic activity. Supervisors on horseback, leather whips in hand, made certain that not a moment of time was lost, and anyone needing to find a place to relieve himself had to ask permission.

And finally the bitter surprise: at the end of the first week they collected their pay, and from the nine dollars each one was expecting, three had been deducted. It was Fred's commission, Tranquillo explained, since thanks to him they had their jobs. And ten cents for the drinking water. They had better play by the rules, he admonished; those who didn't have the will to work would earn little and would land in trouble. If they misbehaved or got sick too often they could be fired on the spot without warning. There was an economic crisis and a sea of unemployed men waiting impatiently to take their place whatever the conditions, even starvation wages. They had fair warning. . .

Bortolo hazarded a guess that a portion of the three dollars turned over to the American boss went into Tranquillo's pocket. It was a well-founded suspicion, and Bigio had concluded sadly that to be taken advantage of by a countryman was much worse than being taken advantage of by an American. Leone furiously declared that they should rebel, they shouldn't let anyone take advantage of them, they should work honestly, of course, but not let themselves be skinned by corrupt individuals. But, Pino objected, they were completely powerless; those who made the decisions set the conditions. If they were fired, how would they find new work, seeing that they didn't know anyone in America? And where would they go without any money? Who knows how long they would be unemployed — and that would be a real tragedy. The only thing to do was spend as little as possible at the store, be happy with a little bread and something to go with it for lunch, get their water at the river themselves to save ten cents a week. It wasn't much, but better than nothing.

At that point Luigino spoke up: he had learned from the water boy that he earned five dollars a week. So if each one of hundred fifty workers paid ten cents a piece that added up to fifteen dollars, if he wasn't mistaken. That meant that the company kept the difference of ten dollars, or more likely, Fred took it and divided it with Tranquillo. And then, he added in a whisper, the bicycle, that one in the photograph they had seen in Abbazzia. Tranquillo didn't have one. Who knows who it belonged to. Even that had been a trick.

8

Woodcutters cleared a wide strip from the thick forest of ash, hornbeam and scattered patches of fir, and a thick maple tree woods for a road in an area aptly called Maple Valley. The company store sold tins of syrup taken from those trees—maple syrup, an amber honey, stringy and very sweet, which big spenders had learned to spread on bread for breakfast.

The valley echoed with axe blows, grinding saws, warning shouts, and the crash and thunder of trees falling heavily to the ground. Other teams stripped branches from the trunks, and with pickaxes uprooted stumps and eradicated roots down to the finest strand. They ripped shrubs and bushes from the ground and dug deeply to get rid of every kind of vegetation. The road, at first summarily marked by stakes, began to take shape. In the thick bright grass of the meadow appeared a slice of bare red land resembling a bloody wound.

Gildo, Luigino and Giusepì, after digging up the vegetation with picks, loaded it on the wheelbarrow and rushed off at breakneck speed to a distant place to dump it. The supervisor harshly reprimanded Giusepì because his wheelbarrow wasn't full enough, and Gildo, on the spot, as if the reprimand were for him, overloaded his wheelbarrow with an incredible amount. He had a painful need to be appreciated, and he didn't feel he had any quality or value other than physical strength. Sometimes, in his vigorous activity, he barely escaped fallen logs rolling down the hillside. The straight and regular logs, compact and sturdy, were left alongside the dirt road to reinforce it at vulnerable points—to brace the steep escarpments, buttress little bridges over narrow ditches and keep the drainage canals from caving in.

They labored incessantly under the now burning sun, suffocated by a thick reddish cloud of dust and persecuted by swarms of voracious mosquitoes. They gulped down the water brought by the water boy who ran without pause from one to the other; and as soon as they drank they were thirstier than ever. The supervisors kept an eye on them so make sure they didn't waste a second more than necessary.

The rock outcrops had to be broken up by sledgehammers and chisels, or dug out by pickaxes and set aside for the roadbed. A team specialized in the use of dynamite, and paid two dollars a day, blew up the massive boulders that blocked the way and those that loomed from above or from the escarpment threatening to fall. The boom of explosions, preceded by wild shouts of warning and headlong dashes to safety, echoed throughout the valley, redoubled by the echo bouncing off the slopes. It sounded like two armies exchanging cannon fire.

The excavated dirt cleared of debris, in addition to what came from a nearby open quarry, transported with Decauville railcars pushed by hand on provisional tracks, was dumped on the road to fill in depressions and form a raised embankment of several yards. In many of the swampy and soft areas they laid down bundles of branches and logs to keep the roadway from sinking. Four of the strongest men were charged with moving the logs cut several weeks ago and left to season, sometimes so heavy they couldn't be budged. In such cases they would call others to give a hand, but the team leader would object: it was a waste, four men were more than enough, but it was just his hard luck to have chicken-livered slackers who didn't want to bend their backs. They had better get it into their heads that they were paid to work, not to stand around or blow their noses, and if they didn't like that work they could leave whenever they wanted. Pietro, one of the Bresciani, in attempting to move a gigantic log had torn a biceps, and another fellow dared suggest that they use one of the horses for that backbreaking and dangerous work. There was always the danger of dropping a heavy log and breaking a leg. Their only response was the threat of dismissal. Jackasses, pigs, the men whispered between their teeth, treated worse than slaves.

More dirt was dumped on top of the bundles and logs, first dampened and then compressed with road rollers dragged by hand, and then the rock specialists came into the picture. That was a particular art that required a good eye, precision, and skill: they chipped the rocks taken from a nearby open quarry to make them the exact shape, and then placed them one by one by hand over a surface wider than the dirt. Next they filled the cracks between rocks with smaller stones and drove them in with loud and powerful blows of the sledgehammer. On top of the solid rock roadbed the unskilled laborers scattered wheelbarrows of stone crushed in the quarry, and at last put down macadam, which they sprinkled liberally with river water and tamped down with pestles and heavy road compressors pulled by hand.

Gildo was dog-tired, but he gave it all he had: after spitting on his raw hands to protect them from contact with the tool handle, he dug, shoveled, ran like crazy, almost as though he were being chased by a slave driver, pushing the wheelbarrow heavier than a boulder, sweating like a sponge under the searing sun, his head burning, his eyes glazed, his mouth dry from unquenched thirst, his muscles stiff and sore. And going through his mind were blind and disconnected thoughts, unrelenting worries, anxiety, grief as though over a death. He was worth nothing, he didn't exist for anyone, he was useful only for being taken for a fool and squeezed to the last drop. And what if he couldn't keep up that exhausting rhythm anymore? What if he should collapse, then what would become of him? Was this America, was this the Promised Land?

Reluctant to shut themselves up inside the foul, suffocating hovel — more distressing than the day's work — the men would sit around an open fire in the evening. It was the end of April, the sun was scorching during the day, but at dusk a cutting wind came down from the mountains, almost as though the winter blizzards were still swirling up there. On Saturdays they hung around late, passionately talking over the little they had seen of America: the customs, the people, the food, the cost of living. Someone asked if there were women in America, as they had never seen one in those parts, and they elaborated on the subject, concealing their longing for the female body with vulgar comments and laughter. It made Gildo angry to hear that kind of talk, and he hung his head in shame, hoping that the dark would hide his red face from his comrades who were always ready to poke fun at him for his shyness.

Bigio played his accordion around the fire. Others sang and everyone drank. Although wine and beer at the store was very expensive and bad, no one gave up the opportunity to raise his spirits with a glass or two. Already tipsy, Leone sang in his baritone voice:

> Everyone says I am pale
> but I'm consumed by love.
> On the day I become a bride
> My colors will then rebloom…

Bortolo, who nursed a great rage over his disappointed hopes, the tricks and the wrongs done to him, the slim pay and the back-breaking work, laughed at himself and his illusions with bitter irony and sang at the top of his lungs:

> America, America, America,
> in America I want to go,
> even astride a crab louse
> in America I want to go.

Perhaps because he had bent his elbow once too often, Vincenzo, one of those from Brescia, his eyes shining and tongue loosened by the dark beer, told about some workers from a town near Cremona, who, from what he had heard, were hired a few weeks before they were and let go just before they arrived. Leone perked up his ears and wanted to know more. What did that mean? Gildo listened silently, apart from the others, and caught the alarmed looks the Brescians had exchanged and then focused on Vincenzo, as if warning him to shut up, and Gildo wondered why. In fact, after that mute, mutual interrogation, Vincenzo had hesitated before continuing, as though weighing the effect of his words only at that moment. But Leone, with growing suspicion, insisted on knowing, and Bortolo, Cipriano, and Pino chimed in so insistently that in the end Vincenzo had to give in. Avoiding the faces of his fellow townsmen and lowering his voice to a whisper, he said that at the construction site, like everywhere else emigrants worked, it was common practice to fire a certain number of workers after a few days, weeks, or even a couple of months, to take on new ones. It happened suddenly, overnight, when you least expected it, and they disappeared very quietly.

Well, Leone interrupted, by now seething: How the devil did it help the company to send away those who had some work experience and take others on with no experience, if the pay was the same for all? Gildo noticed Vincenzo had looked up again at his townsmen at that question, almost as though asking permission to go on, and was once more struck by their looks that ordered him to keep silent. Torn between their intimidation and Leone's stubborn insistence, and perhaps emboldened by the effects of alcohol, he finally decided to go on, and he explained that Fred and Tranquillo (as they must have already figured out) divided the three dollars of commission taken from the first week's wages—and sometimes when the notion strikes them, they also deduct it from the second and third week's pay. Therefore those two bandits were in the habit of assuming new workers in order to extort money, and letting go those they have already robbed. It was an illegal practice, real thievery, although a common practice in all the work sites where no one kept an eye on what was going on, and so the foremen were free to empty the pockets of fools like them. No one knew how to protect himself from their schemes. One man had tried, by refusing to pay, and was fired on the spot.

The Bergamo cronies sat in stunned silence. After a long while Pietro, a beanpole with a big nose and protruding ears, seeing that the cat was out of the bag, after looking around for fear that someone might be listening in the shadows, explained that it was a profitable deal because that one—and by a motion of his chin it was understood he was alluding to Tranquillo—wrote letters in Italian to relatives, acquaintances, and shipping company representatives to convince men to leave. Just as had happened with them, Gildo thought. Fresh merchandise, inexperienced, ignorant of those tricks, who paid up without a word. Tranquillo was involved with other work sites in the state of Washington and with employment agencies in America run by Italians: from the Renton post office he telegraphed the boss or representative to make his deals, and in fact every once in awhile he received a nice money order for his part.

On the evening they arrived, Vincenzo continued, they had seen those down-and-outers walking along the valley in the dark. There were twenty of them, young and old, pushing carts loaded with their few things—tools and all the rest they had to buy at the company store and that Agazzi had refused to buy back. A silent row of poor devils alone, beaten, and dejected who didn't know where to go, with only the little money from the last weeks' work in their pockets.

I still remember the sound of the wind that night, Vincenzo whispered, a sound we don't have in our part of the world, like wild beasts howling, ferocious wolves, that makes you sad, torments you, breaks your heart. Like a wind of the dead. Only later did I understand what had happened. From then on I've been afraid it could happen to us, too.

So how do they decide which workers to let go? Leone asked in a quavering voice. Vincenzo shrugged as if to say he didn't know, but after a pause and a look of consultation with his companions, Pietro said they fired those who got drunk, or those too old to work hard, but even those on the ball who argued or those they considered shirkers because they had to be prodded to work, or because they took a piss too often, or those who weren't too enthusiastic about working overtime without pay. In this way the bosses got two birds with one stone: eliminating those that gave them trouble and keeping the more compliant men who never complained and slogged away like mules. The roadwork moved along smoothly on schedule, and everyone was too afraid to slip up. In the meantime those two criminals filled their pockets.

Gildo now understood why the Brescians were reluctant to talk: they were afraid of being fired, and if the others were kept in the dark about who was eliminated and why, there was a greater possibility that it would happen to those uninformed rather than to them.

Around the fire silence had fallen. Now it was clear that that work they had counted on lasting for months, until the road was finished, could end from one moment to another. And if the will to work, to toe the line, not to cause trouble worked in their favor, they just had to accept the greediness and ruthlessness of those two with all the power.

Everyday more concerned, Luigino wondered if his father had made it to Abbazzia and why he hadn't sent word. Tranquillo picked up the mail when he went to Renton, or the driver of the team of four horses brought it when he came every two weeks with store supplies. But more than two months had gone by and they had received no letter from pa. The brothers stewed over that incomprehensible silence: was pa waiting for them to send some money before having the priest write a letter? He was right, but they had put aside so little, in spite of severe economizing, that they were ashamed to send it to him. And even more ashamed to write without sending money. Every time Luigino mentioned pa Giusepi's face grew dark and gloomy. He hunched his shoulders and wouldn't say anything, as though brooding over his ever-present remorse as well as his heartfelt sorrow.

At the end of May a letter arrived from their mother, the envelope addressed to the three of them in the priest's sharp and unmistakable hand. Disconcerted, Luigino opened it, and from the opening: "Dear husband," he understood that his father had never arrived. His mother went on at length about news of the town, the relatives, the smaller children, the animals, inquired about his health and that of the boys, and asked the Lord to protect them. She complained that they had not yet written or even sent a little bit of money, and implored them to send something as soon as possible. Even a little bit would help because she didn't know how they could keep going.

He was stunned. What could have happened to pa? Why didn't he get on the ship? And if for some reason he hadn't been able to, why didn't he have someone write home for him? And let them know, too? Maybe he stayed in New York with someone's help, maybe a lawyer who had presented an appeal against expulsion, and maybe he even found work there. But if that's what happened, there was even more reason to let them know.

Luigino and Giusepì, anxious about their father, talked over with their friends what they should do. The only thing was to write to their mother to explain that pa had been refused entrance, and therefore should have already returned. However, this bolt out of the blue would plunge the poor women into despair, and she couldn't do a thing about it, seeing that it was certainly more difficult to search for the missing person from there in Abbazzia than in America. Who to turn to? And where? Leone said the Italian consulate, who must exist somewhere, maybe in Seattle, a modern city, from what he had heard, thirty miles from Renton. But how could they go so far if they never had a day off except Sunday?

They decided to talk to Tranquillo about it, who they didn't trust, but who certainly knew more than they did. He advised them to take it by steps: to write their mother telling her some lie so as not to alarm her while waiting to learn what really happened. And in the meantime to send her a little money in order to calm her. Be careful about putting cash in a letter. There was the risk, as had already happened, that in the passage from one post office to another someone might steal it. A more sure way would be to send it through a Piedmontese in Renton who functioned as a bank for the Italians, and who he (Tranquillo) would swear on a stack of Bibles was honest. In the meantime this same guy could be given the task of searching for Gioanì.

Gildo had sent word to his mother a few days after he reached the road works. Giacomo had written back asking for details about America, the place, the work, the weather, the pay, the cost of living—a sign he was still thinking about leaving with Ninetta after his military service. Gildo hadn't replied: what could he say except that it was backbreaking drudgework, and they were just as poor as ever? For some time now he had had the uncomfortable feeling he had come that far for nothing, just to be crushed by inhuman work and earn pennies. In Switzerland the pay was less, that's true, but the cost of living was lower, so the game's not worth the candle.

Now it became imperative to send his mother the little bit of money he had saved, so she could begin to pay off the debts to the loan sharks. In spite of the fact that they had fetched their own water from the river, Tranquillo had deducted ten cents from their weekly pay. At their objections he flew into a rage, shouting that they paid the water boy for this service, and if some ignorant fools got the notion not to pay, the deal would be ruined, and they could just get that out of their heads, goddamit. Rules were rules. And also he had something to say about their spending so little at the company store. What was that he heard about stale bread for lunch and supper with little or nothing to go with it? They should either buy a certain amount of food each month or be charged for it anyway. And if they didn't like that, confound it, they could pull up stakes whenever they liked.

Gildo doubted that his father had put any money aside, what with his getting drunk so often, but he didn't dare ask. In the beginning, Cipriano, glorifying his own past and his past experience as road maintenance contractor, had tried to get Tranquillo to name him group boss, with the secret intention of raising his standing gradually to suggest himself as Tranquillo's sidekick and even to take over his job. At such presumption Tranquillo had looked at him in amazement, making fun of him and advising him not to get such big ideas. And so Cipriano stayed in his place as manual laborer, which was no sure thing itself.

The three left for Renton on foot at daybreak on a Saturday they wouldn't be paid for. Gildo put thirty dollars in the inside pocket Maddalena had sewn for him, together with another ten that his father had given him at the last minute.

The sun had not yet risen over the hills. Dewdrops covered the trees and meadows as after a cloudburst. Frayed patches of fog hung in the valley. The path that had been a swamp when they arrived had dried with good weather, and the landscape that had then seemed gloomy and oppressive, now appeared green and lush. The three walked briskly, joyful because of a day of freedom all to themselves, a freedom dreamed for and denied for such a long time, which loosened muscles and made their bodies light with forgotten energy. Sundays at the work site was anything but festive: they did their laundry and hung it to dry, mended the tears in their work clothes and holes in their shoes, straightened and cleaned the room, washed the wash tubs, shaved, deloused themselves, cut each other's hair. The accumulated tiredness of the week was such that they had no desire for anything. They threw themselves down under a tree and slept like rocks. Toward evening some played at bocce on a flat level, but reluctantly, just to pass the time together. Or they played card games like scopa or briscola. Agazzi had barrels of beer delivered and insisted in a threatening tone that the workers drink and spend as much as possible. Any dissenter was picked on, pestered, teased, and provoked until he gave up. Tranquillo had prohibited morra, on Fred's orders: it was a gambling game, money was staked, and it caused endless fights.

This day, however, was a real vacation, everything to enjoy, including lungs full of good air. They were masters of their time, no one to prod them in the ribs, and even the worries that had tormented them in the past days, as they walked and sunshine flooded the valley, grew lighter until they vanished, conquered by the boldness of youth.

They crossed woods of monumental Douglas firs so tall they seemed to touch the sky, so thick that the sunrays barely filtered through the trees. When they came to the little wooden bridge that crossed Green River, they stopped to watch a curious herd of gigantic sheep with large horns graze on the thick grass. In the clear current flashed silver fish, from time to time leaping in the air and diving back in. On a small island a big tawny beaver was busy building a dam with willow branches. A blue jay swept from one tree to another and seemed to be following them. After Maple Valley the path skirted the railroad tracks for a while, but there was no train. They were enchanted by the discovery of so many new things impossible to see in the valley wrecked by the teeming road works, where they were always head down digging and shoveling.

The troops of motionless crows in the meadows, their cawing as they passed overhead, were like those at Abbazzia, as was the bird warbling in the thick woods.

A few miles from Renton the path followed the placid course of Cedar River and they couldn't resist the temptation to jump in the transparent water shimmering in the sun. Because of their modesty of country adolescents, unchanged in spite of their oppressive close living quarters, they undressed behind the shrubs and kept on their long shapeless flannel underwear. The water was frigid, and clear enough to count the rocks at the bottom. After some inexpert strokes, accustomed to the familiar pools of the Luio, joyful feelings took over. They splashed each other, laughing like children, and swallowed great gulps where they had just urinated. Stretching out on the grass to dry in the sun and contemplate the clouds shoved across the horizon by the wind, they gustily devoured the bread and cheese they had brought.

On the outskirts of Renton they walked alongside a vast orchard with trees laden with small, very green apples, pears, and plums — the unripe kind that pucker your mouth. They hadn't eaten fruit since last summer and just looking at it made their mouth water. Look and don't touch Luigino admonished severely.

In town they mailed the letters and went in search of the man Tranquillo suggested, who gave them a receipt for the dollars he would send, after the payment of a rather stiff commission, and he took down information regarding Gioanì, the name of the ship and the day of his arrival in New York. He would go to the Italian consulate in Renton to see what he could find out. He asked for a down payment to cover expenses, the remainder to be settled after the mission was completed.

They wandered around the town's dusty streets for a long time;

they went as far as the shore of Lake Washington, and walked alongside the Black River and Cedar River littered with huge piles of coal and sawmills with stacks of logs and beams. Barges loaded with lumber and coal moved down the river towed by tugboats whistling to clear the way. Clouds of smoke, black dust and sawdust swirled in the air that rose from the various accumulated piles at each gust of wind and drew yellowish streaks in the sky. Further down a brick and tile factory stood next to a glassworks.

In the streets animated by a busy crowd, they admired the arrogant, well-dressed men going about their business, and they felt ashamed of their unstylish, threadbare cloth jackets, and their worn-out boots that made them immediately recognizable. Luigino said that they had to learn to appear casual, to dress and wear their hair like Americans, so people wouldn't look at them like they did — somewhere between mockery and disgust, in a way that hurt and humiliated them and made them feel as stupid as young calves.

An ice cream salesman with a brightly colored cart recognized them as compatriots at first glance and called to them. He spoke a pure dialect that they barely understood; he had come from Sorrento four years earlier, shipping out from the Naples' pier Immacolatella Vecchia. After sweating blood for two years as a stonebreaker he had set himself up and now had a very good business, since the Americans ate anything they could get their hands on. He gave each of the young fellows a delicious chocolate and vanilla cone, and advised them to forget manual labor that just made the owners rich, and find a good paying business, maybe when they were a little older.

On the main street, along with carts and gigs, a trolley rattled and clanked, and dazzling automobiles tooted and honked. The three looked at them with enchanted eyes, as if contemplating a magnificent object impossible even to desire; though in time it might be possible to own a bicycle such as darted through the traffic. Through the open doors of a row of saloons they noticed noisy groups of men leaning against the counter tossing down alcohol like it was water. They were impressed by the scarcity of women. Those few who circulated in the streets moved very quickly, looking straight ahead.

An American flag hoisted on a mast flapped on the front of a building. Advertising posters were everywhere, on the walls of buildings and on tubular structures fixed on the sidewalks. The words were incomprehensible, but the images were clear: foaming dark beer overflowing a pitcher, the silhouette of an elegant lady in gloves and hat, boxes of cigars and cigarettes, a bottle of whisky, a Winchester rifle.

They were astonished by the difference of food prices they saw in shop windows compared to those exorbitant prices in the company store—a true and continuous thievery impossible to get free of. They passed by a school, a bank, a cigar and tobacco shop, they stopped to look at the façade of the Saint Anthony catholic church that seemed brand new. Inside, the nave was a copy of an Italian church, lavishly decorated with gold, statues and pictures of saints and the Madonna, the altar covered with linen and lace, silver candles, a great crucifix on the wall. They quickly genuflected, made the sign of the cross, and left. Down the street was another church with a bare-bones exterior: entering hesitantly, they were amazed at the plainness, the bare stone walls, the absence of any portrayal of Jesus, the Madonna and the Saints. That church must belong to a religion different from theirs, but they didn't know what.

They bought an Italian newspaper. Sitting on a low wall, Gildo read the news aloud. It said that in America, among the Italian immigrants, there was an oversupply of barbers, and that more than eight thousand Italian immigrants lived in Portland, Oregon. There were six societies of mutual help and a Jesuit school that was part of the San Michele Catholic church. One article in particular caught their attention: the writer accused the Americans of prejudice toward the immigrants, especially the pick and shovel workers — crassly exploited and underpaid, forced to live in terrible conditions, accused of being dirty and poorly dressed, of strict economizing in order to pay off debts to their home-town loan sharks.

The journalist commented: "Poor people. How can we expect that in such financial straits and moral torment, with an almost absolute lack of time, they could live in comfortable houses and go through each day with ironed shirt and collar and clean-shaven face? Americans think that life in the immigrants' country must be unspeakably atrocious if they can so readily adapt to such miserable conditions in America, and therefore it would be foolish to pay a normal salary to those who can live on so little and who are hardened by so much resignation. To Americans, the Italians were a nation of beggars and organ grinders. They called them hordes, disorderly meddlers, pests, and they harbor 'a racial aversion' toward them. They call loudly for restrictions on immigration, forgetting the immense services rendered, the great public works they have produced."

Another article explained that American workers dislike Italians — just as they do immigrants from other countries — because, by accepting low pay, they make unfair competition and change the dynamics of the labor market. In fact, an American worker is paid two dollars a day, an Irishman, Russian, and German one dollar and seventy-five cents, an Italian one-fifty, and as our own are capable, strong, untiring, and sober, who wouldn't prefer them? Only blacks are paid less, but they are unreliable, lazy, lethargic, and of little account.

The three remained silent for a while. The Americans' offensive opinions, though already noticed and experienced on various occasions, took their breath away. Downcast and humiliated, once more they saw themselves through the pitiless eyes of others: they were poor and misfortunate but honest, hard-working, undertaking the most difficult jobs, those that the others refused. Was it possible that they were considered the worst, the poorest, and the scum of the earth?

Luigino was the first to react. He stood up and angrily snatched the paper from Gildo's hands and threw it in a trashcan. Giving Giusepì a clap on the back, he shouted: Who cares what the Americans think! And he dragged them away. They resumed their walk, slowly, listlessly, and unhappily, until they found themselves in from of a photography shop exhibiting portraits of charming and elegant young women, babies, children, and mustached men in straw hats. Giusepì cheered up and suggested they have a photo made to send home. Their families would be happy to have a picture of them. Even all three of them together. And they'd save money that way. Gildo argued that since the clothes they were wearing were the same they left in, the Abbazzia townspeople would know that they were still as poor as before, and he could just hear their spiteful remarks. Luigino said they should comb their hair well and have just their heads photographed so no one would have anything to say.

They mustered up courage to go in, pushing each other along. With gestures and stammers they explained what they wanted and the photographer understood at once. Accustomed to the emigrants' hesitations and squirming, he greeted them with exuberant cordiality and led them into a big room at the back of the shop. Hanging on the walls were some elegant scenes, each at a different price: luxuriant palm gardens, sumptuous brocade and Damascus tapestries, frescoed walls, and in front of them vases of evergreens, a stuffed armchair and a carved console table with curved legs, and finally the prospective of a city square with café, bank, and theater signs. The three stared in amazement at that unheard-of extravagance and consulted with each other in low voices. One of those photographs would cost an arm and a leg, and they absolutely could not afford it. Gildo, nonplussed, repeated that no one in Abbazzia would fall for a picture of them against those elaborate backdrops as badly dressed as they were, and they would laugh their heads off.

The photographer watched them from the corner of his eye, and grasped the problem at once. It was nothing new for him, and he hastened to show an assortment of suits of different sizes to rent for the occasion at very reasonable prices: well-cut trousers and jackets of good material, complete with a white handkerchief in the breast pocket; plain or embroidered vests, shirts with starched collars and removable cuffs, plain-colored, flowered, and bright striped wide ties complete with tie clasp, or bow ties, as they preferred, felt or straw hats, large pocket watches, a chain fastened to the vest buttonhole to form a perfect arc on the stomach. They made a deal with the photographer that they wear their stained and tattered trousers, and he make a half-length portrait of them.

So the first photograph of their young lives showed three elegant young fellows in front of a white wall, each with a different kind of tie, their hair parted perfectly, goggle-eyed from the unexpected magnesium flare.

9

At the end of May the work site was moved toward the south-west: after a few miles of road were completed it became less efficient to walk and transport the materials, and so the bunk-houses, the company store, the kitchen, the dining hall, the store-houses, the tracks for moving the carts, were all dismounted and reconstructed further along. The move involved all the workmen for many days, and at last they moved their tools and personal items to the new camp by wheelbarrow.

They had just begun to clear a row of trees to make way for the new section of road when a violent storm broke out and a tor-rential rain poured on the valley for an entire day. The workers crowded in the bunkhouses, watching the water rise on the floor before their eyes, in the nerve-wracking wait for the rain to end. That forced leisure weighed on them heavily because, as it dealt with circumstances beyond human control, they would not be paid.

The cloud burst didn't play itself out until late afternoon, and it was then that a supervisor, sent out to inspect the road con-structed as far as Green River, returned at a gallop to report that the river had overflowed the banks at certain places, the valley was flooded and in one section the roadbed had given way. It was an emergency, swore Tranquillo beside himself, a serious emer-gency. Everyone had to get to work, put on boots and raincoats in case it rained again, gather up their tools, get some lanterns for the night that was coming on and follow the supervisor to repair the road as soon as possible. The damage could be irreparable if the storm started up again.

A long line of men quickly headed out, the dark sky hanging low over the valley. In the leaden dusk Leone pushed a wheelbarrow through the mud loaded with clanking tools, and he angrily grit his teeth over Tranquillo's damned rules about no overtime pay when the work was due to emergencies. A whole day's work had been wasted and now it was up to them to dig and shovel all night for nothing, for that cheating rat-faced Tranquillo and the shit-faced American boss. With his own ears he had heard Tranquillo grumbling that the road wouldn't have caved in if they had done a better job. As if the rain coming down in buckets and the river overflowing had nothing to do with it. The workers always got short changed while the business didn't lose a cent. Bosses were tightfisted and always in the right, as they said in Abbazzia.

They worked for a good part of the night reinforcing the road in places where it had collapsed. In the lantern light, under a heavy rain that had started up again, they sloshed around in water up to their knees, while the noise of the river grew louder, increasing their fear that a surge of water might knock them down in the dark. They returned to the campsite in stark darkness exhausted, covered with mud up their eyes. They collapsed on their cots and were awakened by knocks on the door a few hours later: the sky had cleared, a new day had begun.

The day they were unable to work because of the rain was deducted from their wages paid on Saturday, and not a penny was added for the night spent repairing the road. Leone protested, backed up by Bortolo and Pino. Tranquillo did not reply, but limited himself to giving each one a fiery look that shut them up.

It was a Saturday afternoon when a wagon pulled by two horses appeared in the valley. One man curiously watching saw it wasn't the usual wagon that restocked the store, which didn't come on Saturday anyway, and from a distance it seemed to be carrying a gaily-colored and restless cargo. When it drew closer to the site, the man on the lookout noticed that it was full of women and, suddenly enlightened, he called to his companions. A crowd of excited men ran to him shouting at the top of their lungs, laughing, tossing their caps in the air and catching them as they fell.

A dozen young women and some more mature, skirts flapping, with dizzying low-cut bodices and painted mouths, stepped down from the wagon, aided by the men's sweaty, trembling hands. Their greetings were friendly—Oh, darling! they chirped. They were lavish with their smiles, tossed kisses from the tips of their fingers, and thrilled the crowd of men with their calculated coquetry, waving little handkerchiefs perfumed with carnation and rose water.

The men were beside themselves and immediately went on the rowdy and boisterous offensive to compete for the prettiest women. One man had already grabbed a pretty one and held her tight as others, with a mix of insults and protests, fiercely tried to snatch her from his arms. Others were setting the price and still others were impatiently dragging off the first one they found, wondering where to go for some privacy. Someone suggested the woods as the only possible place, another decided to shut himself up in the dormitory and threatened anyone who dared open the door. There were also those who were dazed by the free for all, paralyzed by timidity or by the embarrassment of choice. It was a fracas in which the women protected themselves as well as they could from the male horde, determinedly removing rapacious hands, wriggling free from too violent embraces, straightening their mussed dresses and hairdos, dispensing pacifying pats to encourage calm. There was enough for everyone; the party hadn't even begun. Better to enjoy small sips instead of choking. Up close some of the women revealed tired faces, rings around their eyes, wrinkled skin, and flabby bodies. Behind their simpering ways, forced smiles, and artificial professional gestures, the younger women had difficulty hiding their fear and repugnance for that troop of ill-mannered, stinking boors.

Shocked, with his heart racing, Gildo observed the scene, while

he quietly retreated to a safe corner in the fear that one of the prostitutes might grab him and force him to follow her. He had never
imagined anything like this: a group of women available to so
many men, women to touch, smell, use for their own pleasure. He
didn't even know how a woman was made. He felt attracted and
upset by the incredibility of it all, it took his breath away; but the
prospect of close contact with a female threw him into an uncontrollable panic that made him want to run and hide.

With shock and a burning sense of shame, he saw Pino going
into the thick woods toward the hill, furiously dragging without
the slightest regard a pale young woman with red hair who was
trying to get him to slow down. He remembered Pino embracing
his young wife with such passion at the Fiobbio junction; he remembered how that sight had perturbed him, like when you
discover something you didn't even suspect existed. And how for
such a long time during the trip Pino had kept to himself, mute and
sad, sunk into inconsolable grief. Gildo had attributed that silence
to Pino's painful yearning for the wife he had left and the child he
wouldn't see born. Flabbergasted, Gildo was pondering how, without thinking twice, Pino was ready to betray his wife and console
himself with the first comer, and in his naïve inexperience of
sixteen years he was surprised that the love and memory for one's
own woman didn't have the power to save a man from temptation. At that moment he saw his father going toward the woods,
arm in arm with a woman with rouged cheeks. He felt a sense of
repulsion toward his father who never denied himself anything.
He gorged himself with food, he drank like a fish, he smoked cigars, chewed tobacco and paid prostitutes as if his debts to the
town were of no concern to him. While Gildo followed him with
looks of disapproval and disgust, he saw Luigino and Giusepì,
also visibly disturbed, watching the scene from behind the bushes.

He expected the men to spend hours with those women, to enjoy them for as long as possible, to touch them, squeeze them, em-

brace them and be embraced. Instead, after a few minutes, those who had gone into the woods came out buttoning their trousers followed by the women straightening their bodices, and shaking grass, dried leaves, and sticks from their skirts. They approached the men waiting their turn, went with them into the woods, and reappeared in the blink of an eye. Gildo was horrified by that swift coming and going that upset his vague notions about love between men and women. So he didn't notice the woman approaching him as she tidied her hair after a turn in the woods until she stood before him, smiling invitingly and caressing his arm. He jumped back as though burned by a red-hot iron, and quickly walked away.

Bigio injured his left hand badly while stripping the trunk of an oak with an ax. The wet and slippery ax handle slipped in his hand as he was striking a hard downward blow, and the blade cut the back of his hand between his thumb and index finger. He compressed the gushing wound with a filthy handkerchief he found in his pocket and tried to go on working, but the bleeding wouldn't stop and became progressively more painful. The group leader came to see what was going on and decided that the cut wasn't anything serious, it was his left hand so he could go on working and take care of it at the end of the day.

By evening it was as swollen as a sausage. Bigio washed it in the tub, trying to remove the blood clotted on the wound. He dabbed it with tincture of iodine and bandaged it the best he could. The next day it was even more swollen and painful. His arm was numb and the infection pulsed under the tight, bluish skin.

Bigio was moved to an easier job, at least according to the supervisor. He made a sling for his arm and managed to pick up stone with his good hand to load on Bortolo's wheelbarrow. The wound began to fester. It took two weeks to heal and when it did he had trouble moving his thumb and index finger, as if the joint was damaged. Because the accident was due solely to distraction and incompetence, that dumbass Tranquillo declared, the company wasn't required to compensate him. It's just too bad if someone goes around blind as a bat.

Bigio struggled along as best he could. His grip was weak, but he tried to compensate for it with his other hand.

The first evening he took up his accordion to play a little tune, he discovered that his thumb and index finger didn't respond as they should and he wasn't as quick with the finger buttons as he once was. He tried again and again, convinced that the repeated exercise would do the trick, as his companions assured him it would, but in the end he had to admit that he had lost the mobility of his hand forever. He would never be able to play again. He wasn't a great musician, and he knew it, but it was enough just to squeak out a song to feel better, and sometimes even happy. Silently he caressed his accordion, as if leaving a faithful friend who had been with him for many years and through many hard times. He closed it up in the old battered case, pushed it under his cot, and turned away to hid his tears.

The Piedmont man in Renton sent word that he had received news about Gioanì and waited for his sons next Saturday to inform them in person. Luigino and Giusepì didn't feel like losing another day of pay, so they started off at three in the afternoon, along with Gildo, as soon as they finished work, and they walked quickly without stopping, anxious to learn what happened to pa.

He had them sit down in his cramped and dusty office. He offered them a glass of water, put on his glasses, rummaged through a pile of papers, carefully studied a sheet as if reading it for the first time or as if biding his time, while the three squirmed in their chairs. He began by saying that the investigation had been long and complicated. The New York consulate didn't know anything and had to get information from Ellis Island where every day so many people pass through that no one knows where to begin. At first it seems that their father had taken a ship for Italy, but they couldn't say when or on what ship. On further investigation, however, a different version came to light.

The man paused and sank his face in the heap of papers. The brothers, becoming more agitated, twisted in their chairs and wrung their hands until they were white. Gildo wondered if the Piedmontese was stretching it out to get more money, or if he couldn't find the courage to communicate bad news. Finally the man looked up, stared into space as though he couldn't bear to look at his interlocutors. He said they should be strong and show they are adults. The misfortunes in life are many for everyone and one must face them with courage and not be broken by adversity. By God's grace they were young, strong and healthy and had all their life ahead. Youth rightly looks to the future and soon forgets the past. If only he were their age, the age of energy, faith, plans for the future. And he would have gone on for some time in his alarming preamble if Luigino, exasperated, had not brusquely interrupted, shouting in a broken voice: What happened to pa?

It so happened, the man murmured, stammering, it so happened that the day after you left the island to continue your journey, he jumped into the bay and drowned. They don't know if he was trying to swim to the New Jersey shore, as many rejected emigrants do, or if he wanted to put an end to that tremendous disappointment that had destroyed all his hopes.

Pa didn't know how to swim! Giusepì shouted in a tearful voice. He was scared to death of water, so he jumped in to die, not to save himself!

The two brothers broke into sobs. Gildo would have liked to comfort them by putting an arm around their shoulders, but he didn't dare, and so he sat as still as a block of wood. The Piedmontese, eyes down, cleaned his glasses with a handkerchief.

After a short while Luigino raised his head, dried his tears on his sleeve, and asked where pa was buried. The man hadn't the courage to tell him that after the body had been fished out it had ended in a common grave, so he lied: he didn't know yet, but he would tell them as soon as he received word.

Because pa, Luigino went on, would want to be buried in his village cemetery, not in a strange land that isn't even catholic. So our mother can cry and pray over his tomb. When we can put aside the money we want to send him home. At least in the Abbazzia cemetery he can look at his mountains and get a little consolation.

Sorry and embarrassed, the Piedmontese hunched over and fiddled with his glasses some more. Then not knowing what to say or do, he began to straighten his papers. Shortly afterward Luigino stood up, sniffled, and with a voice still tense, asked how much they owed him. Nothing, the man replied, shaking his head and staring at his fingernails, absolutely nothing.

Gildo often ran his eyes over that dark shape that he could see under Bigio's cot, and fearing that in the next rain, when the water flooded the floor, the accordion might get soaked and ruined, he suggested hanging it on a nail in the wall. Bigio shrugged as if nothing was important any more. He, who usually enjoyed talking and liked company, had become glum and sat around in discouraged silence since the accident. Bortolo said he was depressed. The supervisor stayed on him all the time and pestered him continually with comments and reprimands. Bigio felt persecuted. He was convinced that they intended to sack him because of inefficiency, and that the supervisor had the job of provoking a reaction they could use as a pretext. So he just took it, kept his mouth shut, and worked as best he could.

The rumor was going around that after the next, final move of the building site to the southeast, a certain number of workers would be eliminated and fresh hands would replace them. Some time ago the Irish had come to a bad end: not only did they cost more than the Italians, they were often drunk and caused endless problems, including that final one, when, angry about the exorbitant prices, they had beat up Agazzi and destroyed his store with their picks. The incident was not reported: the prices really were thievery, and it was better not to have the authorities sticking their noses in the road construction business.

The Brescians grumbled that Fred and Tranquillo's pockets were empty and they intended to fill them in the usual way. The men pretended to be indifferent, but they were worried, and even more so after Serafì overheard Agazzi order a number of wheelbarrows, picks, and shovels from the supplier: all things they had bought in the beginning, so that meant new customers were on the way.

Finally Bigio noticed Gildo looking longingly at the accordion peeping out from under the cot. They didn't say anything; there was only an exchange of meaningful looks. Bigio pulled it out, dusted off the case with his hand, fingered the peeling leather for a long time. He took out the instrument, removed the little hooks that kept the accordion closed at the top and bottom, and put it on his shoulder. It's the last time, he declared, and Gildo felt a blow to his chest. He opened the bellows wide and with his right hand played some chords on the black and white keys, suggesting the beginning of a melody, but without accompanying it with his left hand. He bid a sad farewell to this longtime companion, caressing the casing and the yellowed keys. He closed the hooks, and handed it to Gildo, who took it cautiously, as if it were made of glass.

When I started playing, he said softly, I was just sixteen years old, like you, and it took me months before I could play a song from start to finish. I was really happy when I could finally do it. Don't get discouraged if it's hard, you just have to keep at it, keep trying until you can do it. Learning how to play is worth the trouble because it's such satisfaction, it lifts your spirits, and makes you feel happier than you ever thought you could be. He sighed, scratched his nose, and left the bunkhouse.

Gildo learned in just a week: every evening, after washing up, in perfect peace and quiet, he sat on a pile of planks at the edge of the site, adjusted the shoulder straps, opened and closed the bellows slowly while pressing one key at a time, from the highest note to the lowest, gradually picking up speed to make his fingers more limber. The instrument seemed to breathe deeply, the breath of a living creature. As soon as he realized that his hands, callused from the pick and shovel, were under control and docilely complied to this much more delicate action, he started to play the musical scale over and over, searching by ear the keys corresponding to the buttons. It was a question of method, he told himself, with a heart heavy from waiting. He had to take it step by step, familiarize himself with the instrument, know its power and versatility. To him the sound of the accordion resembled the church organ at Abbazzia, a powerful, solemn sound that he felt deep inside.

On the third evening, thanks to repeated practice, his right hand and left had become independent, and his stiff, wooden fingers had become agile and loose, almost as if they had never done anything else. They flew up and down the keys like butterflies. His fine ear controlled and guided the tempos and sound. On the fourth evening he began to play a familiar melody, accompanying it with chords—all done with an excitement that cancelled the fatigue of his arduous days and sleepiness at night. At sunset on the seventh day he played perfectly from beginning to end one of the songs that Bigio had played clumsily with wrong notes. Gildo's heart sang from a sense of triumph.

Someone attracted by the music would look into the corner from time to time, watch a moment in silence, and then go away, taken by a kind of respect, almost of awe, because it was clear the boy was playing for himself and not for the others. Absorbed as he was, Gildo didn't even look up, hardly noticing the furtive visits, immersed and submerged in the musical universe he was producing. During the day he worked without let up, almost as though wanting to be worthy of that evening gift. That was all he thought about, and he believed that by killing himself with fatigue he brought the evening musical encounter closer: dominated by his obsession, he looked forward to it while he dug, shoveled, and raced pell-mell to dump the brimming wheelbarrow.

When the heat became insufferable, the cook quit making polenta that everyone liked—the men from Piedmont and Brescia, Valtellina and Friuli, and above all those from the Bergamo area—because the odor and the taste took them straight back to their lost and regretted valleys. Once he had put a polenta on the table made with a different cheese and flour, but it had been a disappointment. The cheese was a long way from what they were used to and the sage seasoning wasn't right. And then the American corn flour left a lot to be desired: it wasn't the large grain like in their areas; it was gluey and bland, but they had to make do with what they had.

Now Prospero's suppers consisted of revolting greasy and watery stew, stewed sausage, indigestible casseroles, tripe, entrails. Many evenings in a row he had served mutton, which he had bought in great quantity with a significant discount. Some suspected that the animals had died in an epidemic. In the summer heat it had begun to decay and gave off a putrid smell. The workers complained about the smell and the disgusting taste, but they were hungry and ate it just the same, until those with more delicate stomachs began to get sick. After a few days most of the men had raging diarrhea and all hell broke loose. They writhed with stomach pain, ran like the dickens to take shelter in the woods; they came out pulling up their trousers, only to have to return to the woods again. There were no newspapers, so they cleaned themselves with leaves. Sometimes they couldn't make it in time and their clothes stank with the foul odor for days.

That continual coming and going infuriated the supervisors, who no one bothered to ask permission to leave during this emergency. They shouted themselves hoarse for the men to get back to work, threatening to dock their wages. One of them went so far as to accuse his crew of doing it on purpose, as if dysentery were an invention to get out of work. The usual fast pace completely broke down and the roadwork fell into confusion. Because the various work phases had to be coordinated, the interruptions and absences in one crew backfired on the other crews, so little work was being accomplished. Some men grew sicker, with bleeding and high fever, until they didn't have the strength to lift a shovel.

Heated arguments broke out. The workers blamed the kitchen for poisoning them with bad meat. Tranquillo intervened with his usual impudence, denying them pay for the time they couldn't work, threatening to sack them all. He ordered Prospero to give them nothing but boiled potatoes until the little sissies' guts were in better shape, and he forbade wine and beer, even though the store receipts suffered from it, as did he.

Gradually the men started feeling better. Pale, haggard, dehydrated, subject to dizziness, they moved stiffly, and although they drank quarts of water they were always thirsty. On Saturday the usual charge of fifty cents a day for board and room was deducted, which brought on loud protests: not only had they eaten disgusting stuff that even pigs wouldn't eat, but for a week they had eaten only potatoes that cost much less than meat—even less than that rotten stuff. They stubbornly refused to eat it any more, so it was replaced with slices of wafer-thin cheese, and again they questioned why they weren't given even a penny discount. Also those who preferred sleeping out in the open instead of in the oven-hot bunkhouse were charged full room and board.

It was the beginning of July. A growing discontent was spreading among the workers, like a lighted fuse underground, but the fear of losing their jobs forced them to keep their mouths shut.

Luigino could think of nothing else but pa drowning in the New York port. He imagined him wandering around alone, miserable, and lost, with that tremendous weight on his heart, in the middle of strangers like him, cruelly rejected, maybe even mistreated that last day on the island where someone, even without knowing what he was doing, could have given him the final blow. He could imagine him bent over, skin and bones, racked by coughs, sneaking around the guards to find a way out, reaching the shore, jumping into the much feared and detested water, wearing his only suit, worn out by use, and moving out into the hostile sea until it swallowed him up. His death must have been atrocious. The thought was so unbearable he couldn't picture the whole story clearly. He couldn't stop blaming himself for not waiting until pa got on shipboard, in spite of his having a suspicion of pa's desperate intention at the moment they said goodbye on Ellis Island. Maybe that wouldn't have been enough to save him; it would be even easier to jump off the ship to put an end to it. At the time it had seemed impossible to return to Italy with him, with that nightmarish debt for the trip and no money for a return ticket. Now, bitterly, he had to realize that if he had returned to Abbazzia with his father and brother he would most likely have talked all his life about the American earthly paradise and would never have known personally the cruel harshness of that land.

Bortolo tried to comfort him in his own way, shaking his head sorrowfully, deploring the sad end of Gioanì who he had known forever, an honest, hard-working man, if only they were all like him: too bad that he was such an unlucky person, and the unlucky will find bones even in their polenta.

Luigino informed his mother of pa's death. As a little consolation for this dreadful loss, he had included in the letter the photograph made in Renton, in which they appeared healthy, clean, and elegant. His mother replied through the priest asking for details of that terrible misfortune and begging them to return. All alone she felt lost and needed their help and support for the younger children. They could find work at home. Their sending such a little amount of money from America meant that they might as well have stayed home, that at least they would all be together and could help each other.

The two brothers didn't know what to do. They talked it over at length with the men from the Bergamo and Brescia areas. Some advised them to go back to help their mother, but more suggested they should stay, that there was more poverty there than here, otherwise why did they come? It was easy to understand a mother wanting her older sons with her, but to find work in Val Seriana was like going to the moon. Most of those who returned had empty pockets. What kind of impression did that make? Wasn't it better to send her a few dollars, to write that they were thinking about it and were taking some time to make a decision?

And what if that idea of returning was the priest's and not their mother's? Leone ventured. If she didn't know how to read or write, how would she know what he wrote? They knew very well what he thought about emigration: everyone should be working the landowners' fields and dying of hunger.

Luigino didn't feel like talking to the banker in Renton again, he was sure he would never learn the truth about where pa was buried from him; and besides, even if he found out they wouldn't be able to get the money together to have his remains sent back to Abbazzia. So the two brothers gave Tranquillo, who was going to town, the few dollars they'd saved for the Piedmontese to send to their mother.

The question of whether to leave or stay was resolved a few weeks later when Tranquillo announced to his fellow countrymen that they could take to their heels and find other work. They were fired. Luigino, Giusepì, Gildo and Serafì were kept on — that is, the youngest, strongest, and least combative—and the whole Abruzzi bunch who worked like mules and never complained. The road was nearly finished, went the excuse. Only a few miles left, so the work was slowing down and they didn't need so many on the job.

It wasn't exactly unexpected. The signs had been there, and yet it was hard to take. They supposed Bigio had been eliminated because of his disabled hand, Cipriano because of his age—but only he knew about his ridiculous discussion with Tranquillo—Bortolo and Leone because of their aggravating complaining. Sometimes Pino had come to work late—and for a few minutes he would be docked an hour's wages—because he was obsessively neat, and before leaving the bunkhouse had to be sure his cot and few rags were in perfect order. Other crews were also drastically cut with apparently similar criteria, such as those from Bresia, Friuli, Piedmont, Valtellina. But everyone suspected the real reason lay in Tranquillo's and Fred's inexhaustible hunger for money —two more ruthless men never lived.

Luigino and Giusepì interpreted that decision as a sign of fate: if others were fired and they were not, it meant they didn't have to go back to Italy. How could they throw away a sure job when their companions were out of work?

Leone and Bortolo exploded in anger. No one knew what to do, where to go, to whom to turn. They were afraid of being unemployed for any length of time, the money would be gone in a flash, and if they were no longer able to take care of themselves, they would be sent back to Italy. If there was one thing that made the Americans furious it was emigrants on public assistance. Bigio, desperate, contemplated his injured hand and wondered how he could hide the handicap if and when he got another job.

They all walked away together at daybreak one Sunday morning, pushing wheelbarrows full of their tools and miserable belongings. As was his custom, Agazzi had firmly refused to buy back the tools unless they would be happy with a tenth of what they had paid for them. What would they do with them if they had to take a train? They certainly wouldn't be allowed to take them onboard and so would have to leave them behind.

Those who were remaining came out to tell those leaving goodbye. Tranquillo prudently made himself scarce. Leone had sworn that if that louse showed up he would smash his face. Gildo stood waiting until his father left. Cipriano launched a collective salute —Take care! He took a few steps, then turned, and giving his son a stern look told him to behave, not to waste time playing the accordion that would never bring in a red cent, to write his mother and send her money as soon as possible. He would let him know his new address as soon as he found work. He walked away stumbling on the stones, while Gildo asked himself if he was sorry he was leaving and the answer was no. From the time he was a child his father had been a stranger and often an enemy. He felt indifference alternating with dull animosity for him, and the distaste expressed about the accordion, which renewed his resentment, had added a pinch of bitterness: his father did not wish a better future for him. He preferred that he continue with his present life, without hope, without dreams, without liberation.

Bigio seemed to be at the end of his rope. He took Gildo's arm, pressed his face against his chest and told him to keep on playing, he was good, much better than he, and someday he would be able to earn his living with the music and quit breaking his bones with that awful work. We just have one life, he murmured, and these damned men want to take it from us.

The next day Tranquillo went to Renton. Toward evening he returned with fifteen new arrivals, some in his carriage, others in two rented carriages. All Italians from the northern provinces.

10

The roadwork was finished by the end of October. The work site was dismantled and the workers prepared to scatter in every direction in the search of new employment. As they had nothing to lose, they decided to settle the score with Tranquillo and Agazzi; Fred, the invisible and all-powerful boss, responsible for the cruel regulations that governed the camp, would have been dealt with too if he hadn't wisely cleared out in time. They would have beaten him with pleasure and for good reason, though with some anxiety, because the laws favored an American citizen over a foreigner, and such an assault could have been risky. From the rumors going around, they knew that emigrates got the worst of it in a trial, because they didn't speak English and so couldn't defend themselves and justify their actions.

Two groups of men jumped on Agazzi and Tranquillo separately, and while one of them held their arms, the others punched them in the face. The vengeance ceremony took place in absolute silence. Neither party spoke a word. Nothing was heard but the sound of dull thuds. Those hitting and those being hit knew what it was all about. Gildo observed the scene from a distance. He shared the rightful anger of his companions, but violence was foreign to his character and it repelled him.

Immediately afterwards they took a shortcut through the valley, already covered by a soft carpet of golden and purple leaves, very satisfied with the results of their action and at the same time very worried about their immediate future. It was almost winter, which came early in those parts. Work in the open had been suspended everywhere. Unemployment was widespread and crowds of emigrants like them flocked to the cities where they felt more protected during the winter. Some thought of going to Seattle for the mild climate and nearness to the sea, where they thought it would be easy to find work; others thought about going south, to California — the Italian-sounding name was comforting — to join a fellow countryman or relative they had vague knowledge of and no exact address.

Since the man from Piedmont also served as an employment agent, Gildo, Luigino, Giusepì, and Serafì, frightened by the prospect of being out of work for any length of time, went to him with the hopes of finding something to do.

The man was sorry not to have any work right at the moment. This was the most difficult time of year. Work would start up again and help would be recruited closer to spring. The suspension of road and railroad work because of the oncoming bad weather provoked a chain reaction with many other activities where lumber was needed in large quantities. In fact, now would be the right time for cutting trees in the nearby forests of oak, poplar, alder, Douglas and Canadian fir, where they grow thick as hair on a dog's hind end. However, because of such a backlog of lumber stacked in the warehouses for seasoning, the huge sawmills along the river were in serious trouble, and many workers had been let go. The lumber used for shoring up the mines in the area was small potatoes compared to the enormous amount needed for railroad ties; that's why workers weren't needed in the winter. Perhaps they could load the coal deposited alongside the river onto barges, those piles of coal that on windy days made whirlwinds of black dust mixed with sawdust. Surely they had noticed the dark yellowish clouds that often darkened the city, making it difficult to breathe.

He would find out if the coal mines in the district of Newcastle or Coal Creek, or in places nearer to Renton were hiring workers, but only for work above-ground, because he really didn't feel like sending kids their age to bury themselves in those rat holes, the tombs of thousands of poor devils. And besides the pay was miserable. Not only did the dust in the tunnels ruin lungs, but also there was the risk of being blown up in a gas explosion, or drowned from a sudden flood from an underground river or lake, or crushed under a collapsing tunnel. Not to mention the accidental explosion of cases of dynamite or buried mines, or the accidental breaking of an elevator cable coming up or going down to the bowels of the earth. That's the way it is with mines: some find wealth, others death, and the one who gets rich is most often the owner.

As was his way, the Piedmontese went on at length. He pitied those lonely, defenseless, lost adolescents. He said that in American fifty thousand men died each year in the mines, all emigrants, many very young, as they were. They died in Primero, Colorado; in Peoria, Illinois; in Earness, Pennsylvania. All the papers had reported the story about the mine tragedy last year in Cherry, Illinois, where three hundred miners—all Italians—were asphyxiated and burned to death: a carbide lamp had set fire to the bales of hay that someone had imprudently taken into the tunnel as fodder for the mules living there. Poor devils, to end up like that after so much sacrifice and hope. No, he didn't have the heart to advise them to take such risky work. If something happened to them he would never forgive himself. Better to tighten their belts and go hungry than to throw themselves into a hole underground and never know if they would come up that evening dead or alive.

Unless they moved south, to California, he continued, where thanks to the mild climate one could still work in the fields for a couple of months. But was it worth spending the money for a long train ride for such a short time? No, it wasn't worth it. To start with, he concluded, they would do well to find lodging with a couple he knew from Piedmont, and he gave them their address on the edge of town.

The house was more ramshackle than the bunkhouse. There were eight people in a filthy basement room, the cots on top of each other, and the walls dripping with humidity. Gildo kept his accordion in his bed to protect it from mildew; and before going out for the day he wrapped it in blankets, like something alive; and so no one would steal it, he fastened it to the bed with a chain and lock. He didn't play it anymore. The basement was too inhospitable, dark, crowded with people, and he had nowhere else to go.

They scoured the local Italian newspaper for job notices, but offers for manual labor had disappeared. Only nursemaids, cleaning women, seamstresses, experienced cobblers and hatters, expert butchers for the slaughterhouses. In the morning, soon after dawn, on a pre-ordained corner, groups of chilled emigrants congregated to beg a day's or few hours' work. A "foreman" would come, choose someone by feeling his muscles, for raking leaves, cutting wood, delivering coal to private homes, moving furniture or delivering, without setting the pay, hours, duration of job, certain that those ragged, haggard men, driven by need, would accept whatever they were offered. Most of them were left empty handed. With hopes vanished in the waiting, they went away disappointed, weary, head down, hands deep in their pockets, with no idea how or where to spend the long hours until evening.

The costs for room and board threatened to rapidly deplete what little money the boys had left after the last, hard earned amount sent to their families. To economize they ate only supper, and settled for a skimpy sandwich for lunch. The Piedmontese got them ten days of work picking apples from the same orchard they had passed the first time they had come to town. They earned only 90 cents a day, from which he deducted his commission. To make up for it the owner gave them two cases of good smelling, tart and tasty Canadian Rennets, which they devoured with pleasure and ate for breakfast and lunch for several days.

For another ten days they were hired to take rocks and pile them at the edge of a field to be plowed. They expected a couple of oxen to pull the plow, but instead a farm machine went noisily back and forth spitting black smoke. The work stretched out for a few more days while they dug holes on the land of the same proprietor for planting fruit trees, then they had nothing to do. The Piedmontese shrugged unhappily: unfortunately there was no work to be had anywhere, and more men were available than were needed.

That town on the plain near the ocean was not too cold, but for weeks it rained heavily and continually and the four friends had no place to take shelter. Even when it stopped raining a ray of sunshine rarely pierced the clouds. A thick gray fog hung low and dampness seeped into their bones.

At the end of November the temperature suddenly dropped. The sky grew leaden, gusts of cold wind swept through the city until a powerful storm was set loose such as had not been seen in a hundred years, so they said. For one day and night without pause snow was dumped on the city. The four friends, who were desperate by now, were hired by the day to shovel snow, along with a swarm of emigrants of various nationalities, at a reduced wage because of the high number of unemployed. They worked like slaves in the blinding white flakes whirling in the air, caps pulled down to their eyes, wool rags protecting their mouths. From Lake Washington, toward the north, a stone-cracking wind blew that cut their faces and sliced their ears, and covered their bare hands immediately with frostbite. On the shovel handles a crust of ice formed that stuck to the skin of their palms. The snow penetrated their shoes, soaked their socks that froze and became harder than frozen codfish. And yet, in spite of their fatigue and pain, they heartily hoped it would continue snowing until spring.

The city clanged with the sound of many shovels removing snow from the streets. They piled it up at the edge of the roads, scrapped down to the pavement in the fear that it would freeze at night, and when the piles blocked the houses and traffic they loaded it onto wheelbarrows and dumped it in fields outside town. Some homeowners hired the four, just because they were young and agile, to climb up on the roofs to remove the heavy weight that threatened to collapse them.

After the great snowfall work continued for a while longer, fortunately, to repair some damaged city streets, but that didn't last long; therefore a job as dishwasher in a dinette proposed by the Piedmontese was welcome. They drew straws and Serafi won. The pay was miserable, but there was the advantage of being warm and dry in the kitchen and of taking home leftovers everyday. It was a godsend for hungry teenagers.

They weren't able to save even a dollar to send home. Because their clothes weren't enough protection from the cold and continual rain, they had to buy some second hand jackets. They would have liked to buy some new boots to replace their broken down ones, but they didn't have enough money. Except for Serafi, they didn't know what to do with their days. When it rained from morning to night they took shelter in their beds, but not even there did they find peace. The forced inactivity got them down. They felt useless, failures, incapable of taking care of themselves, and a relentless sadness devoured them and made them silent. They breathed the hostility of people around them. Customers in a grocery store where Gildo and Luigino went to buy bread looked scornfully at their worn out boots and burst out laughing. Someone spoke a word they had already heard, dago, and another word new to them, wop, both incomprehensible. When it came their turn the owner had refused to sell them the bread. He yelled at them rudely to leave. Was it because they spent so little? Or because he recognized they were Italians? Or simply because they looked poor? Hurt and bewildered, they left the store in silence, and the painful sting of being refused and insulted unjustly tormented them for days.

They lived in the middle of the natives, but no one spoke or looked at them; it was as if they didn't exist. They bore a mark that isolated them in intense, ferocious solitude. They were not accepted or appreciated, in spite of their managing on their own. And they took whatever work was available, even the dirtiest and most difficult, and they did it with great care and even with dedication, including that of cleaning the outside drains of latrines and emptying cesspools.

When they lived in the city they made themselves follow the American rules of good conduct, even though they found certain habits of the locals objectionable, such as continually masticating chewing gum like a cow, and spitting it on the ground to end up sticking to their shoes. Or drinking to the point of passing out in the street, until a policeman came to put the drunk on his feet and take him home. They stayed sober, even though a drop of alcohol would have comforted them and warmed their stomachs. Not only because they didn't have the money to waste, but also out of principle, so they wouldn't be criticized. They had learned to give women precedence and to take off their caps when they went into a building; they had added some English words to their vocabulary and knew how to say ies, ellò, gummonning, gunnait, gubbai, pliis, olrait, tenchiù at the appropriate time and sometimes at the wrong time. As soon as they opened their mouths, Luigino commented sadly, everyone knew they were foreigners. The four were deferential, stood in line, spoke softly, didn't spit on the floor as they did in their own town, didn't toss leftovers and paper just anywhere. At a suitable distance they observed with curiosity and horror the busy traffic coming and going from a brothel in a sordid back alley: they still had their fear of women, to which was joined the fear of catching syphilis or clap, and the lack of money put an end to any temptation. They had never stolen anything, not even when they were ferociously hungry and had the opportunity. They behaved like exemplary citizens as far as they understood American ways. Even so, gruff and scowling policemen had stopped them many times to check their documents and make them empty their pockets to see if they were hiding knives or other weapons. They always felt guilty, awkward, slow, unsure, and the shame they felt about themselves and their origins escalated.

The man from Piedmont explained that Italians were disparaged everywhere. They were called garlic-reeking ditch diggers. People made fun of them: they were the targets of jokes and abuse if not of beatings. Americans were convinced that they were so poor because they were worthless; they were an inferior race, so stupid they couldn't even learn English; lazy and without initiative—otherwise they would get rich in a hurry, wouldn't they? And if they tolerated the poverty, exploitation, and oppression, it meant that they had been worse off in their own country, and so it wasn't wrong to treat them that way. Every time anything serious happened, a theft or a crime, the newspapers wrote that it was an Italian, even though there wasn't a scrap of evidence, but they found witnesses ready to swear they saw them with their own eyes. Only later would the police discover that American citizens had committed the crimes.

All Italians, including the most destitute that got along by the skin of their teeth, were accused of belonging to the Black Hand, a criminal organization that was said to be everywhere in America. But he, who met many different people in his business, had never known anyone who was a part of it. He had lived in Renton for years and spoke English, but at times he wished he didn't because he had frequently heard himself addressed as scoundrel, spaghetti, black face, and once someone had shouted: Go back where you came from, filthy Italian! It's enough to make your skin crawl. Better to resign yourself, to pretend not to hear, don't take it seriously; sooner or later they will understand that without them no buildings, streets, bridges, tunnels, railroads, subways would have been built, under the worst conditions and with the lowest wages that no American would have accepted. They were even accused of accepting low pay in order to take work from American citizens who had a legitimate right to it. A colossal lie because those citizens avoided dirtying their hands in shameful, low work. They wanted dignity and respectability. America is a pitiless country, the Piedmontese concluded sadly, it's not the country where milk and honey flowed, as they had been told. According to him, instead of honey, it was bitter gall that flowed.

Christmas was just around the corner. Gildo received a general delivery letter from Giacomo: everyone at home was well, and he hoped he was the same. Lorenzo would decide when to join them in America after he came back from the army. He (Giacomo) would be leaving for the army in May. He still didn't know where they would send him. They hadn't heard anything from their father since he left the road works. Where was he now? The families of Bortolo, Leone, Bigio hadn't heard anything either. And why, dear brother, have you sent so little money? Hurry up and send some because the loan shark from Albino was on the devil of a rampage. The photo had arrived and was very much appreciated. Everyone had noticed how neat and clean and well fed they looked, and admired their new suits and elegant ties—a sign they were doing all right, like someone from Nembro had said who just returned from America. He said that over there life was one big party and the dollars came thick and fast. All you had to do was hold out your hat and it would be filled at once.

Gildo could not send a red cent, and he hadn't heard from his father, so he didn't answer the letter. Work had been sporadic for some time. For several days the three of them had a job collecting garbage. The "foreman," after fruitlessly looking for experienced Russian workers, hired a dozen men to cut the ice on a frozen lake in the interior, in the mountains, but they had been sacked because they were too young and inexperienced for the dangerous work that required a good eye, skill, and know-how, not only to select the right thickness to cut, but to get out the slabs and transport them. With a horse-drawn plow a rectangular mark was made on the ice, the block was sawed by hand, then tied with a rope to ferry it on the water and load it on a cart to be deposited underground at the edge of the city. If you didn't stay very alert, the ice could collapse and you could end up in the water. At that temperature a minute was enough to send you to the other world. The three of them worked a few days unloading the carts with heavy blocks wrapped in jute bags and stored them, one on top of the other, to be kept until summer when they would be sold at a dear price for iceboxes. Then no more work.

One dismal day, after wandering around aimlessly, tired and numb and not knowing where to go, Gildo, Luigino, and Giusepì sought shelter in a protestant church that they had already visited once, the only place warm and free in the city. Saint Anthony Catholic church reminded them of the glacial temperature of the parish church in Abbazzia; there the faithful muffled up their eyes, were convinced by the priest that the cold in the house of God was just punishment for their sins. Why weren't the Protestants punished like that? Was their God kinder and more indulgent? They sat silently on a bench in the deserted nave, near a large iron stove that gleamed in the shadows and radiated benevolent warmth that melted the ice in their veins, relaxed their limbs and pleasantly fogged their thoughts.

A middle-aged woman came up to greet them with a nice smile. From the cascade of words that issued from her mouth they understood little, but her gestures inviting them to follow her were eloquent. She led them, red as turkeys and paralyzed with embarrassment, to a large room and had them sit at a table next to some Italians and Irish, who looked as down-and-out as they did. Two young women served the guests a smoking bowl of tasty stew with potatoes and a pitcher of dark beer crowned with foam. Luigino, between mouthfuls, whispered to Gildo that he didn't understand a thing: this was a Protestant church and gave food to the Catholics, while the Catholic Church wouldn't dream of it? What did that mean? That they were good Samaritans who didn't care what church they belonged to, but only wanted to lighten the suffering of the emigrants in that dark and gloomy winter? He had never understood the difference between Catholics and Protestants, but they were certainly both Christian.

At the end of the meal the woman came back, and with her kind smile assured them that they could come to eat whenever they wanted. They would always be welcome. In case they didn't know how the spend the rest of the day, they could stay there to keep out of the rain. At five o'clock they would be served a good hot tea with fresh bread and butter. She added that she would be pleased with their participation in the religious ceremonies and the Sunday services. And if they wanted to they could learn the words of their hymns, in a little book beside everyone's plate, and sing in the choir with the church members, as a sign of gratitude for the Lord's goodness. An Italian who spoke some broken English translated the woman's words.

From that day on their wretched existence improved. They had a friendly place to go, warm meals, appetizing snacks and nice people who took care of them. They learned the hymns parrot-like and sing them loudly, mispronouncing the incomprehensible words. Never mind. In the church in Abbazzia they sang in Latin and didn't understand a bit of that either. In addition, by hearing themselves addressed in English, they began to understand something, and it was like a small light in the dark. It wasn't important that those good people expected regular attendance in exchange for food. No one does anything for nothing: it's a hard law of life. They hadn't been asked to convert to their religion, but if it should happen, it wouldn't be so bad, seeing that it was a matter of the same Jesus, and if the saints and Madonna were missing in the church, that wasn't so bad, either. They had gone to the parish church for as long as they had lived in Italy, and hadn't even known other religions existed, except for Jews, damned for eternity because they nailed Jesus on the cross. Now uprooted from their homeland and customs, the memory of religious ceremonies had become vague and unreal. In the hell of the work site they had neglected their prayers, forgotten even to make the sign of the cross, and heard only curses against that cruel life. In time that was replaced by indifference that in turn was transformed into skepticism and then into mistrust toward any religious practice and belief. Now it seemed to them that all religions were alike, but if one offered them help, and the other offered nothing, you might as well take advantage of it. They were always welcome provided they attended the services. They sang hymns with them, and listened to the pastor's sermons, understanding not one iota.

On Christmas there was a solemn ceremony that was nothing at all like mass. A group of pretty girls in small hats sang a sweet Christmas song accompanied by the harmonium. That chorus of heavenly female voices made shivers run up and down Gildo's back. He was mesmerized by the fresh, young strawberry mouths, the little white teeth and rosy tongues that appeared between their open lips while singing, dazzled by the white palpitating throats, disturbed by the blooming breasts that swelled under their bodices and by their gentle respiration. Luigino's elbow in his ribs brought him back to earth, and he sang loudly with the congregation crowding the benches:

> Sailen nait, oli nait,
> ol is calm, ol is brait…

At lunch the emigrants, more numerous and hungrier than usual, were served an enormous roasted turkey stuffed with chestnuts and garnished with cranberries, sweet potatoes, and applesauce: another American oddity, but they had to say it was truly good. They were also served a sweet desert made with raisins. Under a pine tree sparkling with lights were presents for everyone: socks, gloves, and soft wool scarves.

The remaining winter months were much easier than the former, thanks to the kindness of the Protestants. The regular meals had reinvigorated them and they put on lost weight.

The Piedmontese came up with some temporary little jobs just to make ends meet while waiting for the work sites to reopen. They started reading newspaper job announcements that became more frequent and diversified as the days went by. In February appeared a rectangle in bold print: in the state of Oregon, in the county of Deschutes, James Hill, president of the Great Northern Railway Company, was looking for qualified, general manpower for the construction of a railway from Chemult to Bend, to continue to the boarder of Washington state. The work was assured until the end of October, pay and work conditions excellent, cost of trip at the company's expense, comfortable lodging and good food served at the camp, foreigners welcome. Those interested should talk to a company representative who would supply the address.

The Piedmontese made a face when they went to talk to him about it. That seemed like pure propaganda to him. As usual the company exaggerated the benefits, and even emphasized the beautiful scenery, with the aim of attracting the gullible, who once they were hired and went to the place, didn't know how to get out of it. They found themselves in a hell hole, in some out-of-the way, god-forsaken place in the middle of the mountains and in the end either had to like it or lump it. Some of the sad stories he had heard about emigrants came to mind, but didn't want to discourage them.

They conferred among themselves what they should do, and lacking an alternative, decided to go there. Oregon wasn't too far away, and if by chance it didn't work out, they could always come back to Renton. Serafì elected to stay at the restaurant, as he was working his way up. From dishwasher he had been promoted to kitchen helper. He pealed potatoes for frying, ground meat for hamburgers, beat eggs, sliced cheese, bread, and bacon, and though the pay was low, he had had a raise.

11

With tickets paid by the company, Gildo, Luigino and Giusepì left by train in February, along with fifty other Italians who had just barely made it through the winter at Renton, Seattle, and Tacoma. First they went to Portland, then to Eugene where they joined up with a large group of various nationalities coming from the south. They waited in Eugene for a wagon caravan to take them along the Willamette river to Chemult, a dusty village of few houses, piles of coal, stacks of railroad material, heaps of debris and rubbish, from which began a short section of already constructed tracks. Then they climbed up on open wagons of a service train loaded with railroad tracks and ties that went into a cold and windy valley between high, snow-covered mountains.

The work camp was crowded with hundreds of men. The three friends didn't know, because no one told them, that here the workers were paid by the job: the more they worked the more they earned. On the surface, compared to a fixed daily rate, it seemed an advantage because it allowed for personal dedication, ability, strength, resistance, desire to compete and be assertive. After the financial straits and discomfort of the hard winter, they felt reassured and trustful: the work would last for months and their salary would depend on their will.

Before leaving the city they said goodbye to and thanked the good people at the Protestant church who had been so kind to them. Now that their horizon appeared brighter and Gildo was convinced he was leaving deprivation and suffering behind, he was ashamed of how he had been reduced to begging for a charitable meal and a warm corner, just like a tramp, and he promised himself never to do that again, or to die trying. Without realizing it, hard-pressed by need, he had fallen into the category so abhorred by Americans, that of the poor, starving emigrant living off public charity, or in his case, private charity. He must learn to save during the good season in order to face the winter unemployment, which at that northern latitude seemed inevitable. He must take care of himself no matter what, even in the worst circumstances, he stubbornly told himself over and over. It went along with pride and respect for oneself.

The three of them worked like the possessed from dawn to dusk, without slowing down even a moment to rest, except for the half hour lunch break. Daylight and darkness marked the beginning and the end of the workdays, but often, in order to earn more, they continued to wield the pick ax even in the dark, by the light of lanterns or bonfires, in the biting cold. Giusepì and Luigino, who were worried about their family, sometimes worked on Sundays when the pay was almost double. Gildo, oppressed by a sense of guilt, didn't want to miss any opportunity. The pay-by-the-hour system generated constant tension, a perverse anxiety that gripped their stomachs. Anxiety about what they would find in their pay envelope made them work until exhausted.

According to the management that kind of arrangement was a two-fold advantage: to the company, because it hastened the construction of the railroad, and to the workers who gave their all to put as much cash as possible in their pockets. The company supervisors counted on another advantage: the great distance from Bend, the only inhabited center a good sixty miles from the work camp, with its attractions, distractions, temptations, stores, saloons, alcohol, brothels, to keep the men from concentrating on their work. In a place so remote from the world there was nothing to do but work like slaves and sleep.

Sixty men slept in the bunkhouse. Gildo chained his accordion to the cot. Even though anyone who might steal it would not get far in that out-of-the way valley, it was better to be prudent. He didn't have the time or the energy to play it. Evenings he fell like a dead man on his bed, his hands massacred by the pick and shovel, and his bones aching as though broken. The muscles of his arms, neck, and back, pulled and twisted like ropes, didn't relax even in sleep. His swollen feet burned from bloody scratches and cuts. He cast a discouraged eye on the neglected instrument and hoped that as the days passed his body would become accustomed to the debilitating fatigue and the tiredness would disappear. He had to be careful not to injure his hands; Bigio's accident was still fresh in his mind. Others owned musical instruments, but they collapsed at night also and no one played.

At the work camp there was no factotum like Tranquillo—a despot, cheat and thief like no one else. Supervisors, technicians, and engineers supervised the work in addition to many energetic crew captains and overseers. The company store was a place of profiteering, cheating, intimidation, and bullying also, with no way to defend oneself. By now the three were well acquainted with the rules that govern the remote work sites in which there was a monopoly of consumer goods and outrageous prices bit deeply into their pay, an extortion tantamount to a survival tax.

The only consolations were food, tobacco, an occasional pitcher of beer, and prostitutes that arrived by train on Saturdays. At first there had been a cook who cooked only fat indigestible meat, and beans that moved the guts. Then he was transferred to Portland and replaced by an angry Japanese who spoke only his own language. He would gesticulate like a madman and in the beginning had wanted to serve exotic Japanese dishes. However, due to a lack of basic ingredients, he soon converted to local tastes.

A short distance from the camp was a fenced enclosure for the cows, sheep, pigs, which were butchered from time to time. So there was no lack of fresh meat. But vegetables were rarely served and the bread had the usual rubbery consistency. The men yearned for fresh salads seasoned with oil and vinegar and loaves of crunchy bread to cut with a knife. Provisions arrived every two weeks with a four-horse team, and every once in a while the driver brought a sack of mail. They rushed at him in a frenzy, grabbed their letters, and after laboriously spelling out their contents, each one curled up glum and sad in a corner, mulling over the curse of being cast from house and country, separated from family and friends. Everyone was consumed by a sense of loss and abandonment, feelings magnified by the enormous distance and by their isolation in that godforsaken valley. The little they had left behind become as precious as pure gold in their memory. Lives shattered, irreconcilable with the new country, strangers to its people, language, customs, humiliated, sore and aching, confused.

News circulated the camp that the financier James Hill had won a million dollar battle against his rival Harriman to be the first to put a track through the endless forests of Douglas firs, the precious and costly wood for construction, until now out of reach. Once the railroad was finished, the thousands of trees cut down would be loaded on freight cars and unloaded at the sawmills in Bend which were going up like mushrooms on the banks of the river Deschutes. From there the logs would be transported on the new tracks as far as the mouth of the river Columbia, where the railway connected with a branch of the Union Pacific, already in use for years. The work had also started at the other end, and the two sections had to join halfway. In this way the lumber would quickly reach every locality of the region in frantic development, to be sold at a good profit. A colossal business in which there were staggering capital investments, a business to be carried out with the greatest urgency so that they made their money back as quickly as possible, multiplied by enormous profits. A part of which would come to them, the workers trusted.

The valley was uninhabited and wild, without roads, boxed in by steep, majestic snow-covered mountains, dominated by the two thousand four hundred meter Paulina Peak. For months the topographers had the maps drawn up and the way of the tracks marked off. They camped and decamped, gradually advancing on horseback, making their way through the tangled vegetation. With the help of instruments they carefully chose the most solid and level terrain, calculated the correct incline and appropriate curves for the smooth transit of the trains where a straight line was impractical, and chose possible alternative routes to avoid the long and costly excavation of tunnels. Whenever possible, they followed waterways, an indispensable element for running steam engines and necessary for men and animals.

The three friends and a slew of unskilled workers were given the job of excavating a large area of ground already cleared by the woodcutters, for the construction of a solid roadbed for the tracks; they attacked the soil with furious blows of pickaxes, moved tons of earth with wheelbarrows, piled it on the plotted course, smoothed and spread it out evenly, leveling and compressing it according to instructions. On the compact embankment where the tracks and ties would go, they overturned gravel and small stones transported by wagons or brought from quarries, broken with hammers and then crushed by machines. In certain tracts where it was anticipated that the tracks would run along deep trenches, they excavated entire hillsides and large slices of mountain spurs. At the same time, at the edge of the plotted course, other workers dug holes, planted poles for hanging cables and insulators for the telegraph line connecting the work site with the rudimentary station at Chemult. The railroad ripped, gashed, and slashed the remote valley landscape.

When the roadbed was ready for the tracks, a long convoy of locomotive-hauled platforms, weighted with the necessary materials, proceeded along the tracks already constructed. Expert trackmen, paid two dollars a day, lived on and moved with the train.

One car was set up as a dormitory and a second as a kitchen and dining room. They worked at a fast pace, in a tempo that was coordinated and synchronized with invariable precision, punctuated by the brisk orders of the technicians and by the counterpoint of warning shouts to the other workers. The orchestrated activity worked like well-oiled gears. In the shortest time possible the ties were placed on the roadbed of gravel and stone, and the heavy tracks were removed by tongs from the platforms and lined up. And after carefully measuring the gauge, they were fastened to the ties with steel spikes, and the latter bolted with fish joints. Once they finished a section, the convoy moved on. Two miles a day were programmed. That meant the workers had to be squeezed like lemons, but they couldn't always keep to the schedule. It was rumored around camp that the company took in fifty thousand dollars a mile from the government and only spent twenty thousand.

One morning the frenetic rhythm of track laying hit a snag. Lengths of track had been unloaded from the platforms of the service trains and aligned on the roadbed. Two workers with pincers had picked up the extreme rear of the track, weighing more than two hundred pounds, while two others did the same at the front; and without missing a beat, at the proper signal, the four moved to place it on the ties. Just as they were ready to launch it one of them slipped on a rock, and as he was about to fall he lost his hold on the track, which fell on the leg of the man next to him. The man began to bleed profusely and howl in pain. With no wheelbarrow around for them to use, his companions carried him as quickly as they could to the camp infirmary some distance away.

The person in charge (an old hand at this business, who managed the best he could), after medicating it perfunctorily, made a splint for his broken leg with two wooden boards. The injured man stayed on his cot for more than a month. The wound healed but the bones mended poorly, and when he finally tried to get up he couldn't take a step or even stand. He was badly crippled and couldn't walk without a crutch, dragging his useless leg. His companions kept encouraging him to walk to strengthen his muscles. As the days went by he stopped talking, sunk in grim desperation.

The company kept him on the payroll and didn't deduct his daily expenses from his pay, but they refused to give him workman's compensation; the insurance company had invoked the clause "fellow servant rule," where compensation could not be paid when an accident was caused by an employee's negligence, and not directly attributed to the company owner. It was obvious that the incident had been caused by the distraction or incompetence of a fellow worker, if not of the worker himself; therefore, the company had no responsibility.

The supervisors seemed to be in a great hurry to get rid of him and sent him back to Chemult with the service train; now he was an invalid and would have to manage for himself, those were the rules. Before he left, his friends took up a small collection and had to work hard to get him to accept it. It was some time later when the news reached the camp: the man, gripping his crutch, had leaped to his death in front of the train as it was pulling out of Chemult.

The first time the foreman measured the cubic meters of soil they had excavated and removed and made a note of it in his little book, they had carefully followed the operation, but without much understanding. The amount due would be figured at the end of the week. On Saturday, when they were paid, they were in a quandary. Was it a lot? Was it too little? They compared it with their previous job paid by the day. That was less for sure, but it seemed to them that they had worked three times harder here. Observing their puzzled looks someone sneeringly commented that the worker always feels underpaid, while the owner is always convinced they were paid too much.

Often it was the weather that determined the compensation:

the night frost hardened the soil and early in the day the pickaxes barely dented the surface, torrential rains stopped all activity, and when a blizzard plunged the valley into such darkness that they couldn't see a few feet ahead, the work would be necessarily suspended for a couple of days and the workers paid by the hour wouldn't earn a cent. While preparing to shovel after a snowstorm, a freeze might unexpectedly arrive. In spite of bonfires set up along the plotted course, the ice- covered ground remained hard as marble and resisted every effort. Pick handles broke into pieces and earnings fell to zero.

Then came the accident. During the thaw, while teams worked at freeing the ties deeply embedded in mud, and copious streams caroled down mountainsides, they heard a crack of thunder that seemed to come from the peak of the mountain range. The men who were shoveling in a section alongside a steep mountain looked up in amazement at the sight of a dazzling blue sky, and muttered about the strangeness of American storms. Contrary to what was expected, that roaring sound, so like a rockslide, grew in intensity instead of fading. Then someone in the crew sensed the danger and gave a shout of alarm. A shout stifled by terror. Instantly panic spread among the men who dropped their tools and dashed madly toward the center of the valley. Too late: a second later the avalanche fell with a deafening roar. It followed them like a hungry beast, grabbing and clawing at them as they ran at breakneck speed toward salvation only to be buried under an enormous mass of snow. Dozens of workers, in spite of the risk of being crushed by a second slide, began to dig furiously. In the terrified silence nothing could be heard but panting and grunting, and excited shouts when a shovel hit a body. On their knees, clawing frantically with their hands and fingernails they would free their snow-buried companion, brush it off his face so he could breathe, pick him up by the shoulders and feet and run to lay him on the grass at a little distance; they would shake him, call his name, slap him to come to, press an ear to his chest to hear his heart and breathing. Angry curses accompanied each recovered body. One after another, twelve dead men were dug up.

All work stopped as the workers gathered, in tormented silence, around the cadavers lying on the grass. The supervisors and foremen nervously consulted among themselves in low voices: there was no time to lose, they had to arrange the funerals as soon as possible, that very evening, in order not to let the men be overwhelmed by anguish and to get the work back on schedule; at the same time they must be very careful not to offend those who had lost friends, above all the Italians who were very close. They knew from experience that the slightest thing could set off a conflagration.

Augusto, a laborer from the province of Cremona who had lost three fellow villagers in the avalanche, was given the responsibility, along with members of his team, to dig twelve ditches in a forest clearing. By dusk the workers stood bareheaded to assist at their unfortunate companions' last rites. Augusto read a requiem aloud while they all grieved. Someone sobbed without restraint. The supervisors and foremen attended the funeral services, standing contritely in the rear. The corpses, recomposed, cleaned and combed, dressed in the only suits they possessed, laid beside their tombs and were lowered by rope into the fresh earth. At the head of every grave they placed a cross made from stripped pine branches, with the last name in white paint.

Work had slowed down by the effects of the incident on the men. They were in a bad mood, discouraged, depressed, and could not stop talking about their friends' death. They were worried about their own safety and afraid of further catastrophes, even of a different nature since the weather had made a turn for the better and spring was on its way. They wondered if one of them should write the families in Italy about those unfortunate men, or if it was up to the company that was obliged to send them the men's last week's pay. Some of those men's compatriots offered to go to Bend and send their families the money the poor fellows had hidden away in places known to them. The Italians were anxious to know if there was personal accident insurance, or if the company hoped to get away with a wooden cross over the graves and best wishes.

As the workers' representative, Augusto went to speak with the head engineer, who assured him that he had already ordered his employees to inform the dead men's families and at the same time to send them their final week's pay. The company had insured all its employees collectively, and the insurance company would handle the compensation. It was only a matter of time and patience. August understood the need of the dead men's families, and he was determined to follow the progress of the insurance company, pestering the engineer every other day to know how it was proceeding. The engineer soon had enough of that pain in the neck who could stammer only a few English words, so he turned him over to a book-keeper, a friendly man but cautious, faithful to instructions received. At first he had been reassuring: they mustn't worry, everything would work out as it should, the insurance company was honest and trustworthy, there was a lot of paperwork that can't be hurried.

After a while, at Augusto's impatient insistence, the man began to rummage through a pile of papers and showed him a 1908 law according to which the owner was directly responsible for the accidents only if the workers were in the service of the federal government, which was not their case. Therefore, he was guessing, the company's responsibility in the accident must be proved, otherwise they wouldn't be covered. It's difficult to prove the avalanche was the company's fault. No one can be held responsible for such a catastrophe. Let's wait and see, he summed up, let's not rush things.

Furthermore, he regretted not yet having received any communication from the insurance company. Unfortunately this business could be long and laborious. In the meantime he was beginning to wonder if the Oregon law (as in other federal states, for example Pennsylvania and Wisconsin) recognized the right of compensation for the heirs of an accidental death if they did not reside in the state in which the death took place. He needed to look into that; he would find out from the insurance company's legal office, which would be dealing directly with the interested parties. It needed patience. Just think of the distance between Italy and America in order to understand how the process could go on for a good while.

Actually, the insurance company's legal office had every interest in dragging it out as long as possible, trusting in the inaccessibility of the Italian consulate with its legal offices, unreachable for good or bad because of the long distance; and trusting in the discouragement of the families in Italy, too naïve, poor and ignorant to get a lawyer in America to represent them. They also figured that the companions of the dead men, so surly and insistent, would be dispersed to the four winds in a few months, after the work was finished, and the matter would be resolved by itself. And so it happened, and not one of the twelve families ever saw a penny.

In the days following the catastrophe, teams of hourly workers were given the job of removing the debris that obstructed the section of track work, including Gildo, Luigino, and Giusepì who also shoveled vigorously. The supervisors ordered a shelter built to protect the trains in the future against possible massive snow slides — a long, solid building made with logs from fir trees, with a slanting roof.

On Saturday the workers discovered that the labor of freeing their companions buried in the snow and digging the twelve graves was not calculated in their pay. They talked it over for a long time. Some of them, including Gildo, would have been ashamed to receive money for the rescue attempt that proved useless after all, and for burying the unfortunate men. Who wouldn't have done it spontaneously, for nothing, wherever and for whatever reason? It was a case of worker solidarity, pure and simple. On the other hand, others wondered why the workers should be penalized instead of the company that made so much money. Being exploited like that didn't set well with them. Emergencies and the unexpected were part of the railroad owners' economic risks, particularly when it was such a ridiculous amount for a company with enormous capital, truly a financial giant. And they didn't understand why removing the snow from the tracks was paid, while the desperate efforts to save those who had been buried in it and digging those graves was not.

The second party won. A representative was sent to express the collective complaints to the bookkeeper, who prevaricated at first, and then, with his back against the wall, said the company could not afford that extra expense. An ill-considered reply that had the disastrous effect of lighting a fuse: it released a rebellion that even the tracklayers joined in sympathetic support. Outraged, the men protested loudly that they wanted the wages they had earned. With insults and threats flying, the bookkeeper locked himself in his office while the men outside kicked the door. Foremen arrived with rifles leveled and positioned themselves behind the furious crowd.

This warlike deployment worsened the situation. Angry shouts and upraised fists forced the head engineer to leave his chalet and face the rebellious workers. He took off his hat and with conciliatory gestures and measured words urged everyone to be calm, there was no reason to be upset, better to talk and work out a mutual agreement. Which they did. The management, frightened by the insurrection and the negative effect on the work and good disposition of the workers, quickly decided that it was better to avoid conflict and they agreed, though reluctantly, to pay what the men demanded.

Those who were opposed being paid didn't stop brooding over what seemed to them a demeaning settlement: compensation for the death of their unfortunate companions and for their row of graves in the clearing. The unskilled laborers leapt at the opportunity to haggle over the way the hourly wage was calculated, which did not please them at all: if at first the bosses paid according to what they actually observed and noted, afterwards they paid according to approximate calculations that seemed dishonest. The rebellion brought the original system back, the men calmed down, and they made more money.

Gradually spring worked its way through the valley haze and the days grew longer; work hours were also longer. The camp was moved a few miles and now the tracks passed near the winding Little Deschutes, a tributary of the larger river. It was hot. The men worked close to a swampy area and day and night were attacked by clouds of mosquitoes. After weeks of grueling work without respite, they were exhausted, haggard, and thin and had become lackadaisical, worn out by the long hours under a burning sun. The work proceeded slowly while the company, in a rush to collect the government subsidy, wanted it to move faster. To get it going they decided to increase the pay.

After the incident, to avoid responsibility, the supervisors put signs along the work course advising: "Danger!" But not many understood English, and it was doubly difficult for the illiterate. Some accidents happened just because the workers did not understand the orders shouted in English. Therefore mishaps of various degrees of gravity were the result: a water tank for replenishing the locomotives, built on piles of fir logs and coated with tar, had been filled by wagon barrels supplied by river water. When the workers filled the tank to the top, the piles suddenly gave way. The tank collapsed and broke in a thousand pieces. A torrent of water knocked the men down and the nail-riveted logs struck them on the head, back or legs. Luckily no one was seriously injured. The carpenters who built it were at fault. The nails were too short, and the braces not strong enough. The company would not take responsibility, and so the men could do nothing but quarrel among themselves.

A few days later rocks fell from the mountainside onto the tracks, destroying a long section that had to be rebuilt. Luckily it happened at night, when the place was deserted, but it still upset the workers who felt exposed to constant and unforeseeable danger. They moved around gingerly, as though it was in their power to prevent such accidents.

No one could have predicted what happened the next week. As the service train moved along the tracks, a spark from the steam engine stove started a fire at the edge of the woods. The strong wind, the underbrush, and the tree resin stimulated the flames. In an instant they enveloped the locomotive and burned the stoker and some workers. Buckets of river water from the wagon tanks were thrown on the flames, but the fire snuffed out in one spot broke out in another. It took three days to put it out, and in the meantime work came to a halt.

But that wasn't all. One afternoon, while the machinist was taking a necessary break the locomotive, detached from the wagons in order to clean the boiler and grease the joints, began to move on the slight decline. At first it moved so slowly that no one noticed. The engine, imprudently abandoned without securing the breaks, slowly slipped along the track, and gradually, pulled by its own weight, began to gather speed. The machinist was just returning from the woods all refreshed, whistling to himself as he buttoned up his trousers, when he found himself face to face with that astonishing spectacle. Standing petrified, open-mouthed, for a few seconds, he suddenly came to life and letting out an inhuman cry, ran in hot pursuit after the creature entrusted to his care and thoughtlessly neglected. As fast as he ran he could not reach it in time to stop it, so the locomotive moved steadily toward the end of the track where men were buttressing the ties with stones. Because of the racket their tools made they didn't hear the engine until it was almost upon them. Terrified, they shot off in all directions and their quickness saved them. The derailed beast continued its blind dash, its wheels plowing the ground and raising a storm of red dust. Finally it crashed into a barrier of fir trees, snapped them like twigs and ended up on its side, its snout flattened by the collision, headlights and windows shattered, panel instruments in pieces, pistons and wheels bent, paint scraped. A wreck. At the crash echoing through the valley, the supervisors came running, afraid of another massive slide, or an eruption of the centuries-long extinct volcano above Sunriver. They were petrified by amazement. The irresponsible machinist, a middle-aged American, was sacked on the spot, and as soon as the engineers were at a distance, the workers soundly thrashed him for taking his ill-advised leak. Because of that they had risked their necks.

Different teams worked for days to lift the engine out of the crater it had dug. The mechanics tries in vain to repair it. Before laying the tracks they had to wait until another engine was available at Chemult that could come to the work site. The interruption of the work schedule infuriated the supervisors, and consequently the workers, as the delay in payment of the expected funds meant no one was paid for two weeks.

At the end of June Gildo received a letter from Giacomo, forwarded from Renton and now old news. He wrote from Salerno, where he was doing his military service in an infantry regiment. After the customary preliminaries and many complaints about interminable marches up and down the coast with backpack and rifle, awful rations, and the miserable seventy cents a day soldiers were paid, he informed him that he had grown a mustache to make himself look older, and hoped Ninetta would like it. He added that Lorenzo was back home and working for a locksmith at Albino but earned almost nothing. Therefore he wouldn't be able to join him in America if Gildo didn't send him money for the passage. Given their father's reputation and the slow pace of debt repayment, no one around there would lend a lira to his son, because like father like son, as the proverb goes. For months they hadn't heard a word from him. He was beginning to think that their father was dead or off enjoying himself somewhere, as usual. Then, in an off-hand manner he mentioned that Ninetta was pregnant. He had obtained leave to marry her at the beginning of July. Then he would return to the barracks, but he expected to be discharged when the baby was born, that is, around November. And as soon as possible he would come join him with his wife and child. Therefore he was counting on the dollars that his dear brother would send.

Gildo was filled with anger. It seemed like the whole world was on his back, a crushing weight he would never be free from. Everyone, but most of all his older brothers, who rightfully should be the pillars of the family, took it for granted that his earnings belonged to them, and they weren't in the least concerned about the grueling daily work that broke his bones and fogged his brain or about the risks he ran every day, and much less about the solitary life he led in a foreign country hard as granite, where he had ended up by chance. He felt bitter resentment toward his brother who, like a brainless half-wit, had made his girlfriend pregnant, and now was planning to come to America at his expense, with two obstacles like a wife and newborn child, when it was hard enough for one person alone to get by. Who would pay their expenses until Giacomo began to earn something? Who would continue paying off their father's debts? And in case his brother didn't get his discharge and was kept for the two full years of military service, who would provide for his wife and baby? Whenever he thought about the suffering and deprivation of the winter in Renton he renewed his vow to save everything he could to tide him over the winter lay-off, which he could just forget if they came.

Gildo was nearly choked by fury. Giacomo's letter was the last straw; transforming his naturally mild manner into furious rage. He was beside himself, as though possessed. He rebelled against a burning injustice too long endured: without even asking they had always treated him however they pleased. He had been forced to bow down humbly, and before his eyes he had had only dirt and rocks, dirt and rocks to dig and move. That's all there was for him, and sometimes he felt like he would lose his mind. He seemed to be living in a dark hole, like a mole, without horizons, without air to breathe, without even a glimmer of light: He staggered around like a blind man feeling his way, pursued by anguish. Beasts of burden, slaves to be exploited to their last gasp, until they spit blood, was what they thought of the manual laborers in the camp. No recognition for their work: what merit is there, what value, what skill, to wield a pickaxe, to shovel, to load and push a wheel-barrow? Any idiot could do it, it didn't take a brain, it only took muscle. If he thought he'd be a manual laborer all his life he'd go crazy.

Gildo had tried to get ahead, but couldn't make it. Getting up his courage he, along with Luigino and Giusepì, who were just as dead tired, had asked to be transferred to help the tracklayers, mostly Americans. But they were told that was specialists' work, and they weren't trained. As if they couldn't learn. That meant they intended to use the emigrants only as low-level laborers, while the Americans kept the more skilled and better paid jobs for them-selves. He would never get out of that position with the barriers set against him. That was his place and he couldn't aspire to any-thing else. It made him want to laugh when he thought of Giaco-mo's illusions about America, and at the same time it made him so mad he wanted to break something.

To be honest he had to recognize that in the poisonous anger strangling him, ran a corrosive vein of envy for his brother and the wife he hardly knew: he envied the intimacy and the sweetness that they had enjoyed and would enjoy, while for him he could only see desolate and lonely years stretched out endlessly before him. A poor fool without prospects and without a future. No sensible woman would ever bother to look at him. He envied his brother having married, with a baby on the way, an anchor to cling to, a help to count on, a hearth to warm yourself by. Instead, he blundered around in uncertainty, drifted without a goal, his youth swamped by confusion, crushed by brute fatigue, annihilated by fear. Nothing except confusion, fatigue, fear, utterly without affection.

He looked at his swollen, calloused, cracked, hands—ruined from rough and brutal use, the veins on the backs ready to burst. In the crevices that tools had cut into his skin, just as under and around his fingernails, red dirt was incrusted like cement and wouldn't go away in spite of repeated washing. That hard dirt was like an indelible brand on his body. His fingers were nicked and covered with scabs, his fingernails split. A piece of his thumbnail stuck out like a splinter.

He couldn't bear the sweaty smell in the rags he wore (and rarely washed because of fatigue and lack of time), the parasites that infested his body, the dirty stink of his skin, the dust that had worked into his hair, filled his ears, nose and eyes. His arms, neck, face were marred by mosquito bites. Swollen red boils itched day and night, which he scratched furiously until his skin bled. He was disgusted with what he had become. When he had the opportunity he observed the head engineer—neat, elegant, well combed, clean white hands, and the polite ways of civil people. He would like to be like that, educated and well mannered, casual and sure of himself, with clean clothes and body.

He sighed sadly and shook off his gloomy thoughts. It was a clear, bright Sunday afternoon. Putting Giacomo's letter under his pillow, he went outside. The men were lounging around in groups, talking, smoking, some drinking, some playing tressette. He avoided them. He didn't want to talk to anyone; he knew all their dull talk by heart, always the same subjects. Slowly he walked away from the camp, heading toward the river. He walked through trees to the riverbank and sat down on a smooth round boulder warmed by the sun; he sat there in a daze for a long time contemplating the eddies and rapids. The water was deep but so clear that he could watch the fish against the smooth, clear sand on the bottom — disciplined flotillas that suddenly changed route as though obeying the leader's command. He tossed in some pebbles and the school darted to safety among the rocks.

Gildo stood up and looked into the water. He thought that if he filled his pockets with rocks and jumped headfirst into the deep part, the weight would drag him to the bottom and in a minute it would all be over. It would be enough to stay still with his face under water, keep from paddling instinctively, let his arms and legs hang inert. Only a minute, and it would be over. Who knows when they would notice his absence? Maybe Luigino and Giusepì would look for him but wouldn't be able to find him. The river was flowing northward and the current would take his body away from the camp. It would be nice to disappear into nothing. It seemed like a sort of revenge, a way to hurt the others. Or maybe not. That wouldn't be enough, because the sons of poor Gioanì, drowned in the port of New York, didn't mention him anymore, as if they had finally turned their backs on his death as just a sad interlude that had lost its importance in time.

And his mother, when she learned of it, would she be grief-stricken? Perhaps, but only for a short time because for those still living life goes on, grief doesn't last and the memory fades. He imagined her in the kitchen, bent over the polenta, her gaunt face, her faded blue eyes, her sunken toothless mouth, her bony body, her timid, wary, frightened ways of a hunted and mistreated animal that lives in fear of being beaten. His heart ached.

He had to find the courage to put an end to it, just as Gioanì did, and the man who threw himself in front of a train in Chemult. He remembered the twelve workers buried in the distant clearing that they had turned their backs on for some time, on their unadorned graves that no one visited, buried like common, unlamented animals, junk thrown in a corner and forgotten, almost as though they never existed. Miserable, worthless lives discarded like garbage by a cruel country that destroyed every hope for a better future. There had been no future for them, just as there was none for him. He might as well look things in the face, snuff out every remaining illusion and say that's enough forever. He sighed broken heartedly, and head down, walked along the grassy edge of the river.

Suddenly, over the roar of the water he seemed to hear music coming and going, as though carried by gusts of wind. At first it seemed like the delusion of his incoherent brain. He stopped and listened carefully. No, it wasn't a hallucination. Somewhere someone was playing a lively tune, a flood of notes that sounded vaguely like a polka. Who was playing? It sounded like a little orchestra. He distinguished a saxophone, a violin, perhaps a guitar and in the background the rhythmic beat of a drum. The sudden rising of the music was followed by bursts of excited shouts, and in the background a dull stomping sound, which he soon realized was the sound of feet keeping time.

What was going on? Prodded by curiosity, he turned and ran back toward the camp. In front of the engineer's chalet he saw a cluster of men and for a second was afraid something serious had happened. But they were happy, laughing, slapping each other on the back, clapping their hands and stamping their feet, and at the end of the tune all shouted: olé! The music that set their veins on fire and got their legs going came from the head engineer's chalet. Were real flesh and bones people playing? Who were they and where did they come from?

Gildo pushed through the group that blocked his view and craned his neck: in front of the open door was a gramophone sitting on a table, a black, bright disk turning slowly. The needle swished in the grooves of the record, the sun glistened on the copper trumpet, and from that golden corolla burst forth and carried into the air the excited rhythm of the one step, the latest dance craze in big American cities. Gildo, speechless, gaped at the magic music machine.

Luigino came over and told him that as soon as the music had begun some workers had gathered to listen by the chalet's closed door, and a crowd gradually grew. At that point the engineer came out and told them to come inside to hear it better, but the room wasn't big enough to hold them so the gramophone was set outside. You had to turn the crank every time the sound wound down with a groan, and they had taken turns winding it up. But only the engineer touched the records because they were very fragile and could easily break or be damaged.

The concert lasted for a long time. Many tunes were played, one after the other: waltzes, tangos, mazurkas, and even the cancan, the newest fox trot, and finally *Oh, Susanna*, accompanied by a ragtag choir. No one left even though it was suppertime. The sun set and twilight shadows enveloped the valley. The workers lingered a long time chatting, ignoring their hunger pains, reluctant to separate in order to prolong a shared pleasure. Some hummed a tune just heard, a laborer from Aversa, off-tune enough to hurt your teeth, sang *Marechiaro*, and everyone joined in.

His gloomy thoughts forgotten, excited by that musical torrent, electrified by the melodies that were stacked in his memory, Gildo yearned to run to get his accordion and play it there in front of everyone to surprise them. He didn't dare do it, because his timidity paralyzed him and kept him from showing off, but he could imagine it: he imagined taking up his instrument, opening the bellows, improvising chords like a fanfare and then playing the songs he had just heard one after the other. He fantasized that his calloused, tough fingers became magically agile and flew over the keyboard. He followed them in his imagination as though those fingers belonged to someone else. The triumphant and irresistible music rose to the night sky, expanded, woke every living thing. He played filled with gratitude for that prodigious gift he couldn't understand, which indelibly incised every single note in his memory and transferred each to his fingers, which through a process equally mysterious, he reproduced one by one with amazing precision. He imagined that his companions, stunned, euphoric, exalted by his music, forgot their unhappy situation. He fantasized his own triumph, the delirious applause, the shouts, the hugs, the smiles, the cordial handshakes of the engineer congratulating him for his skill and artistry, his exceptional talent, his extraordinary ear, and warmly inviting him to play any time he wanted. Because music calms the mind, cheers the spirit, and sweetens existence.

A full moon came up behind the mountain hump and illuminated the ground like daylight. Gildo shook himself out of his reveries and promised himself to play his accordion every evening after work, even with his arms broken by fatigue and his fingers cut and painful.

12

In November a son was born, whom they called Daniele. After the forced wedding in May, the scandal in the village died down, and Ninetta raised the boy in her parents' house. That birth, which everyone thought the fruit both of irresponsibility and guilty passion, had really been calculated and pursued with persistence and enthusiasm in woods and haystacks, with the dual aim of presenting the accomplished fact to her family, opposed to the union with a young man without a future, and to get his release from military service in order to emigrate to America. But the country was disposed otherwise, and in early October Giacomo was sent to the Libyan front with his regiment.

The soldiers were informed by their superiors that Italy had declared war on Turkey, whose empire included Libya, for irrefutable reasons: the continual injustices of the Ottomans against Italian citizens residing there, and France and Germany's threat to occupy that land whose immeasurable riches tempted them both, as the disembarkation of the French army at Fez, and the two German warships anchored in Moroccan waters attested. Another reason was the lack of any real resistance to the conquest, which was seen as an easy military walk since the Turks were few, poorly armed, and notoriously unwarlike, and the Arabs were only waiting for the moment to free themselves from the Ottoman oppression and would welcome the Italians with open arms. And finally, occupation of the very fertile Tripolitania area and the Cyrenaica plateau, a genuine "promised land," had solved the age-old problem of southern poverty and emigration. Down there was room for thousands of Italian colonies that would work hard for themselves and their country.

Giacomo embarked at the port of Naples on October 9, 1911, with the first echelon of the expedition corps. To salute the infantry in grey-green uniforms and sun helmets for protection from the torrid African sun, was King Victor Emanuel III, and in his presence the commander of the expedition, the elderly Lieutenant General Caneva, gave an impassioned speech about love of country. He dwelt at length on the appropriate behavior of the army toward the Libyan population, to which Italy was ready to bring civilization and wellbeing: total respect for the sentiments and practices of the Muslim religion, respect and deference toward women and the family, humanity, correctness and moderation, protection of private property, greatest fairness and impartial justice. Behavior that would arouse nothing but reciprocal respect and even devotion on part of the indigents toward the Italian military.

On the transport ships, in addition to the infantrymen destined to substitute the marines already disembarked at Tripoli a few days earlier, were about a thousand horses and mules, fodder for weeks, wagons, rifles, ammunition, cannons, machine guns, tents, lumber, furniture, tools and hardware for the battalion of the Engineer Corps' sappers, containers of water, food supplies in abundance and all the necessities for a modern army. It was rigorously mandated that the soldiers' rations should be of the best quality, and in addition to bread, rice, pasta, and plentiful rations of meat daily, there was wine, cigars, tobacco, coffee and even lemons to combat scurvy.

Giacomo was very excited, like the rest of his comrades-in-arms: that expedition seemed like a wonderful adventure, and at the same time a risk-free skirmish that would be over in no time at all. Numerous ardent and passionate articles in Italian newspapers praising the undertaking, including illustrations in the *Domenica del Corriere*, were passed around among the soldiers, and Giacomo and the others quivered with impatience to see that legendary, wild and primitive country, populated by poor, docile, submissive and ignorant dark-skinned people, and by ragged and happy children, living along the coast among palm groves, sweet date trees, vineyards, olive and orange groves, and flowering expanses of pomegranate. The immense desert of the interior inflamed their curiosity most of all, from stories they heard about the fierce Bedouin nomads who lived in tents and continually moved with their herds, flocks and families in search of pastures and wells, and about the picturesque camel caravans loaded with exotic merchandise that plowed the sandy dunes from one oasis to another. After they won the war, it was worth giving a thought to staying there rather than immigrating to America. In the first place their grateful government might give land to the valiant combatants and veterans for farming and money to build a house. He dreamed about a house facing the sea, shaded by palm trees and he could already see Ninetta busy cultivating a vegetable garden and raising chickens and rabbits for the family's needs.

The convoy of transport ships was mustered in August, in southern Sicily, and from there, escorted by around twenty war ships, it sailed toward Africa. At daybreak two days later it was in sight of the Libyan coast and landed at the port of Tripoli, where disembarking operations began. They were in a chaotic and tumultuous state, because of the confusion of orders and the narrow space that made it impossible to find a place for the overflowing mass of transported materials. Contrary to every prediction and expectation, and to the commanders' great surprise, instead of welcoming the Italians with open arms and collaborating, the natives refused to help unload the ships. It became immediately obvious that the military could never do the unloading alone, and much less free the docks of that inordinate clutter. Therefore they turned to an Italian who had lived there for years and had at his service armed Arabian camel-drivers who rounded up about a hundred reluctant men in the desert near Tripoli, and with rifles leveled had forced them to work. The few men who dared to rebel were shot on the spot.

Only after the unloading did they learn of a serious, unexpected calamity: the cholera epidemic that had infested Tripoli for several months, and was transmitted, or so it seemed, by contaminated well water and dates in the oasis. Several officers and soldiers died within the first few days, and numerous others in the ensuing weeks.

Aside from that inconvenient setback, the war really seemed like a tranquil walk in the park. Everything was peaceful and quiet. Not a shot was fired. The infantry had nothing more to do than dig trenches around the city, fill thousands of sacks with sand to fortify them, eat, drink, and sleep. The population kept a respectful distance. Not a shadow of a Turk. The Italians began to think that, like clever cowards, the Turks had run away.

Toward the end of September, after being mustered out of the army for a few months, Lorenzo was recalled to service, and mid-October was sent overseas to Bengasi. For the duration of the war the two brothers never met or had news of each other. Lorenzo fought with bayonets against the Turks and the Arabs who, despite every prediction, fought beside them, and after the fort was stormed and the enemy resistance moved to the edge of the city, he witnessed the useless naval bombardment of Bengasi. Among the ruins of the city were countless cannon-smashed bodies reduced to strips of bloody flesh and scattered limbs in the dust. He shuddered at the moans of the dying and was choked by the stench of the dead.

The destruction and massacres caused by the unnecessary naval bombardments of the costal cities—Tripoli, Homs, Derna, Bengasi—the pitiless shootings, the careless persecution of women by the shameless and fatuous members of the rifle regiment, the Bersagliere, had encouraged the Arabs everywhere to switch *en masse* to the Turkish side. Without the Italians' knowledge, on the night of

October 23, the oasis of Tripoli was surrounded and attacked. The next morning all the troops everywhere were attacked. Crouched in the trenches between the wells of Bu Meliana and Fort Messri, his rifle aimed through a peep hole, Giacomo, stunned and terrified, observed in the furious assault how, in addition to the Turks that they had assumed to be in flight, and the Arabs on foot or on horseback, the whole enraged population of the desert and part of Tripoli was engaged in the fight: women, the elderly, the young, and even children in the front line. He discovered that he felt good about firing into that scruffy crowd, the way he had aimed his slingshot at birds when a boy. He didn't feel like he was shooting at human beings at all, but black savage beasts with no life in their eyes. He talked about it with the other infantrymen, and one of them admitted that when he kills one of those monkeys, their faces wild with rage, it seems like smashing a cockroach or fly.

The Bersaglieri of the 11th regiment who protected the position of Sciara Sciat, in the heart of the desert, were the most exposed. Only when the fighting was over did they learn how awful a tragedy it was, leaving very few survivors. The screaming, vicious Arabs galloped at full speed, shooting with both hands weapons taken from the dead. They waved clubs and daggers, threw themselves like bloodthirsty beasts at the terrorized soldiers, and cut them down one by one. They took no prisoners, but dragged the living and wounded into Muslim cemeteries or into nearby gardens and massacred them. They were found decapitated, impaled, crucified on palm trees, quartered, emasculated, eyes dug from their sockets or eyelids sewn with string, guts torn from bellies, buried up to their eyes in sand, tossed alive into wells with ankles tied. A massacre.

The Arabs removed the Italians' last misguided illusion about their welcome with open arms when they killed Italians randomly with knives or rifle fire from balconies and windows, right in the middle of Tripoli; and even the merchants knifed soldiers unwise enough to shop in their stores. As soon as the curfew went into effect reprisals broke out: poison gas grenades were unloaded from boats that could wipe out the armed Bedouins in the desert, but the command declined to use them. Instead the desert was searched inch by inch and the inhabitants arrested in mass, taken to the castle, and the next day great numbers picked at random to be shot or hung. Four hundred women and four thousand men were killed, including a number of children. Another thousand were deported to the islands of Tremiti, Ustica, Ponza, Gaeta, Favignana where many died from illness, hunger, or hardships due to inhuman treatment.

Giacomo, along with his fellow infantrymen and the Bersaglieri who survived the massacre, inflamed by hatred for what the command defined as the Arabs' betrayal, came out of the trenches, and armed to the teeth, beating the desert day after day, stumbling over putrefied cadavers that stank unbearably, jumping at every sound they heard: the braying of a donkey left unguarded, the whimper of a stray dog, the bleat of a kid goat, the stamp of a horse's hoofs wandering lost among the low walls and paths. Fearing an ambush, they even jumped at the wind rustling the palm branches and at the soft gurgling sound of running water in the irrigation canals. Panic gripped them even more with noises at night. The meow of a cat in love or a white rag in the dark was enough to set off their gunfire, and in the thick darkness they were likely to shoot at one another. The tacit order was not to take prisoners. The treacherous Arabs were shot on the spot, while the Turks, the belligerent enemy, had to be treated with respect. Glowering, resentful, frightened, the soldiers talked of nothing but hangings, firing squads, destruction, and they yearned for the complete extermination of that miserable population.

On November 5, 1911, the Giolitti government issued a decree establishing Italian sovereignty over Tripolitania and the Cyrenaica. The news circulated through the troops that Commander Caneva, in addition to refusing to use poison gases, had refused to set fire to the oasis, so as not to transform it into a burned desert, which would keep anyone from living there, and Giacomo, his anger now cooled, was pleased with that wise decision. In spite of the horror of what had happened, he continued to think that once the indigenous people were subdued and the country pacified, he would like to have land and a house right there, in that fertile and shady place, where grapes, pomegranates, apricots, figs, plums flourished under palm trees, and luxuriant green grew in the dark, cool soil.

He replied enthusiastically to Ninetta's letter that announced the birth of a beautiful, strong baby boy, hungry as a wolf, the picture of his beloved father so far away. He described that enchanting place where he dreamed of setting himself up in the future with his wife and son, and she replied adoringly that she was ready to follow him wherever he wished to go.

It was now the middle of November, and while the chestnut woods of Abbazzia had certainly lost their leaves and were prepared for their winter lethargy, everything here was blooming like the middle of spring, the air was mild and the rain that fell during the day was warm and sweet. It washed the ground polluted by the dead, renewing it and preparing it for the March planting.

Everything seemed to have stopped the end of that year. Nothing was going on in the fixed costal positions. Penetration into the interior of the country had been postponed: it had been limited to attacking a desert village ten miles from Tripoli, where Arabs and Turks had congregated and supplied the fighters around the oasis. The retaliation, however, went on without let up. In the city's bread market, on a moonlit night, fourteen locals who had participated in the assault of Sciara Sciat were hung. At Bengasi nine Arabs were hung in the public square, and all the men of one nearby village deported to Italy. The inhabitants were distressed and unable to work. For a week they locked the doors of their shops:

poisoned by bitterness toward the gun-happy occupiers, they were preparing guerrilla retaliation. Even 1912 seemed to begin in the calm boredom of monotonous days, except for some incursions against convoys coming from Tunisia to refurnish the Turks with weapons and provisions, immediately compensated for by using a trail further south.

There was no end in sight of that war that was supposed to last a few weeks. In February the men were still encamped on the Mediterranean shores, and from the trenches they could hear the booming surf. Before advancing into the heart of the country they waited for the Eritrean askari, much more adept than the Italians for going into the unknown, hostile, frightening desert. And when they marched through the streets of Tripoli singing, the people were astonished by those dark-skinned warriors, Muslims like they, ready to fight and die in the service of the white invaders.

In the fiery heat of late spring, the soldiers were by now tired, unhappy, and discouraged. Most of all those who, like Lorenzo, had three years of military service behind them, in addition to seven months in the Libyan trenches. That endless time was also time wasted. The families at home, deprived of their sons' help in the fields, sank into poverty and suffered from famine, especially those who felt the bitter injustice of two sons under arms. Their morale low, the young men wanted to be discharged and sent home, not only because of homesickness, but also because of the urgent need for them. Those few who objected were arrested and referred to a military court, some getting a seven-year prison sentence.

At home, their mother was alone and weary. She didn't know how to feed her hungry children. Who knows when the older boys would return from Libya? Gildo rarely wrote from America and even more rarely sent money. For almost a year there had been no news of their father. Maddalena and Carolina worked in the silk mill and came home occasionally to turn over the few, hard-earned savings that ended up in the hands of the creditors. The boys earned a little at Nembro and Albino. The little ones helped as they could. Disconsolate, she begged the Lord to protect her sons in war and bring them home soon. She knew she would never be able to count on Giacomo, because of that youthful mistake that the whole town had talked about for months. He would have his problems taking care of his wife and child, and he couldn't wait until he could leave for America. And Lorenzo would do the same, so she would be alone and more exhausted and lost than ever.

In October Gildo received a letter from Carolina informing him that their brothers were fighting in Libya. She also wrote how their mother worried about the risks her older sons were facing, about how the younger ones didn't have enough to eat, about the debts not yet paid off, about how terribly poor they had become. Even though she didn't mention it openly, Gildo understood that once again he was being asked to make sacrifices. He thought about those sisters and brothers whose faces he could barely remember, except for Adele's pouting face, who he should take care of in the name of their blood ties that his prolonged absence from home had made tenuous; just like the ties of affection from sharing a common childhood had been worn down by neglect, dissolved by time and distance. A family is like the fingers of a hand, according to an old saying, but in his case the fingers had been amputated.

The construction site closed at the end of the month. The railroad had gone beyond Bend and was ready to be joined to the section starting alongside the Columbia River. One Sunday at daybreak Gildo and others walked back from one tie to the other on the track that crossed the forest. They proceeded silently, alert, listening hard for the rumble of the trains that sometimes, even during holidays, tested the alignment of the tracks.

At Bend they found frantic commotion: in a few months, in

view of the construction of the railroad line and the activities related to it, the population had doubled, and houses, stores, saloons, restaurants, hotels, ballrooms, offices, ice factories had shot up. Sawmills along the Deschutes, waiting for the convoys of timber soon to come, had enlarged and multiplied.

Some of the Italian workers entrusted the savings they put aside for sending to their families to the companies they worked for. Recently several emigrants turned to a man from the Veneto, newly established in town, who kept his store open on Sundays for them. They avoided the local banks because of the impossible hours for someone who worked all week, and because of their difficulty in understanding the mumbled English; but also because they were ashamed of their shabby appearance, with unkempt beards, dirty and ragged clothes, mud-encrusted boots, and the arrogant, brusque ways and the unfailingly haughty condescension of the stiff-collared clerks who took their frugal savings with open scorn, counted the dollars with their fingertips, making a face like the money was filthy or contaminated. They seemed to believe that foreigners should feel a debt of gratitude toward Americans for the opportunities they were offered and did not deserve, and they considered it an affront to send abroad the money made by the emigrants, because in that way they impoverished the country that so generously gave them hospitality.

In spite of repeated disappointments, the Italians clung to the dangerous habit of considering every compatriot a friend, including the shopkeeper at Bend. He had opened a small grocery store and in addition to selling various items, he sent their money back home, charging the exaggerated commission of twelve percent so that he made a lot of money with no risk. On top of that, he sent the money to an accomplice in Italy who, before turning it over to the receiver, sliced off another hunk of commission. Only after many months did the sender learn from his family the extent of the cut, usually too late to object because in the meantime he had been transferred elsewhere for new work. The dishonest intermediaries counted on getting away with it because the emigrants continually changed residence. So it happened to Gildo: he had already left Bend and did not receive Carolina's letter about the theft, which was returned to the sender.

The Burlington Northern railroad was inaugurated on schedule, at the end of October 1911. The financier James Hill, proud of the accomplishment, organized a big party on the grounds where the station would be built, and he had on exhibition for public viewing two of the latest locomotives, decorated with ribbons and American flags, several first class passenger cars with a restaurant car, and a superbly elegant Pullman. Freight cars for carrying logs were on a lateral track. Everything was displayed to satisfy the specific interest of every visitor.

Mr. Hill greeted the guests. He had invited the best known personalities of the political and financial world, competent professionals, journalists from the most influential newspapers of the region who would recount his triumph, and photographers to illustrate it; businessmen and speculators, timber merchants and sawmill owners (certain to become customers of the railroad), shop owners, sheriffs and policemen, pastors of different protestant churches, beautiful, refined and elegant women and a platoon of smiling local young women.

Wanting to immortalize the occasion, Mr. Hill invited everyone, guests and employees, to gather around the two brand-new locomotives, a huge crowd that the photographer wasn't able to capture in one picture. Taking the situation in hand, Mr. Hill ordered the workers to climb on the powerful back of the iron horses. And once positioned, to make the scene more dramatic, he suggested some embrace the smokestacks as if they were the ample hips of a beautiful woman, and others hold open the flags and those remaining raise their arms in a gesture of victory. The two engine drivers were balanced on the front of the steam engines facing each other, and while the one on the right held a bottle of champagne, the other held out a glass. The guests and the engineers mixed cordially with the workers remaining on the ground, and they formed two wings, with Mr. Hill and the head engineer in the middle. Standing immobile, with their eyes fixed on the lens, they shook hands for an interminable length of time. The workers were wearing their best for the occasion, but compared to the distinguished company their best seemed like rags.

The hundreds of people coming to the inauguration were offered a sumptuous open-air banquet. Mr. Hill had spared no expense. Arriving by train, under ice, was the magnificent salmon caught at The Dalles, a town on the Columbia River, which was roasted over a fire of good-smelling juniper and fir by a battalion of cooks. A big deer hunt, in which Mr. Hill had taken part several days previously, provided succulent roasts and stews, in addition to fragrant pheasants in Madera sauce, crisp musk duck, and for desert, golden apple crumble with cinnamon, covered with cream. The food was washed down with an endless number of bottles of authentic French champagne ordered from Portland, and kept on ice in large silver buckets. In the joyfully unrestrained atmosphere profitable business deals were put together.

As soon as darkness fell torches and lanterns illuminated the area. For hours the sky was filled with garlands of fireworks—a first class pyrotechnical spectacle that excited the men and wrung cries of admiration from the women. Later, to the music of a brass and woodwind orchestra, the dancing began. The dancers twirled and stamped until it was nearly dawn and at last, exhausted and dust-covered, they climbed on the train that took them back to town.

For the workers, sitting at a table apart, far from the guests, a banquet had been prepared more in keeping with their simple tastes: gigantic beefsteaks, lamb chops and sweet potatoes roasted on coals, red wine, smoked fritters, baskets of apples, oranges, and walnuts from California. They ate grudgingly, exchanging few words, weary and apathetic, superfluous to that party that was not for them. The enormous project they had worked on so hard for months belonged to the owners, their earnings had been ridiculous, worse than pathetic, in respect to the colossal earnings for the company and the others who were eating a discrete distance away from their table. The supervisors, technicians, and engineers they had worked with paid no attention to them, and much less thanked them for the finished job. They felt marginalized, excluded. Never in their lives had they seen a gathering of such rich and well-dressed people a thousand miles away from the problems that concerned them: winter that was coming on, work they didn't have yet, the little savings that in the blink of an eye could vanish and plunge them once more into poverty.

On October 18, 1812, a cease-fire in Libya was decreed. For months there had been inconclusive negotiations between the Sublime Door and the Italian government to resolve the conflict, and they would have gone on forever if at the end of September Bulgaria, Greece, Serbia, and Montenegro hadn't mobilized their armies to liberate themselves once and for all from the centuries-old Turkish domination.

In the meantime Italy occupied the Dodecanese islands and had immediately taken advantage of the Balkan situation to launch an ultimatum to the Ottomans, threatening to attack Smyrna and to cut off an essential railway junction that connected Constantinople with Salonika. The Turkish Empire caved in and signed a peace treaty.

The military march, costing a fortune and thousands of deaths, ended, and the soldiers in the trenches shouted their joy at the top of their lungs: they could finally go home. Giacomo wrote Ninetta that he would be back very soon, he couldn't wait to hold her again and get acquainted with his son. For some time he had not said any more about his plan to settle in Tripolitania. It had become clear that the state-owned lots available for emigrants were few and not very fertile. The Tripolitan oasis where he would have liked to live, with its tiny plots of soft brown soil had from time immemorial belonged to generations of indigenes who would never have agreed to share it with the colonists. Returning to their walled gardens, Giacomo watched them climb barefooted up the palm trees, agile as cats and skinny as rails in their rags, to gather dates.

Deeper into the interior, beyond those thickly cultivated regions with cool fountains, extended olive groves and fields of grain. But the land was arid and rocky, hard work to cultivate, water only the little that fell from the sky, periodic droughts, atrocious heat in the summer, frequent locust infestations that destroyed the meager harvests and all vegetation. The thought of Ninetta and the baby in these unsafe places was frightening because of the never-ending hostility of the Arabs, the never-crushed guerilla warfare that flared up occasionally, the raids, pillage, robberies, destruction. It wouldn't be worth it. At the time it had been a big disappointment, but soon Giacomo put it behind him and returned to his earlier plan of going to America. He wouldn't be the only one emigrating, because between 1912 and 1913 a million and a half Italians left their homeland, a few for Libya, the majority for Europe and the two Americas.

Lorenzo also wrote his mother that he would be back soon. He was dead tired of the war that had dragged on for a year, and he was anxiously waiting to be discharged so he could finally take off his uniform and think about the future. He hoped to find temporary work in the valley in order to scrape together enough cash for the trip to America.

The longed-for discharge was late in arriving. The soldiers itched with impatience while their superiors labored to assure them it would only be another month or so, that some important questions had to be resolved first. Fresh troops arrived to substitute those gradually being sent home, but they were drafted recruits without experience, ignorant about the region, the customs, the unstable mood of the locals, and it took some time to train them about the place so they wouldn't go around letting themselves get shot like fools. The first battalion of Libyans independent of Italian command was also formed, but not yet in sufficient numbers. In short, the country still had need of its brave, heroic, faithful soldiers.

The situation in the immense territory was tense, complicated, difficult to manage and control. Many Arab leaders were submissive, thanks to the lavish stipends handed out by the commanders. The farmers from the costal strip had gone back to their fields and the merchants had reopened their shops, but everywhere the people remained hostile and unfriendly. And although they were bedeviled by extreme poverty, as soon as they heard the army was coming, they would evacuate their villages, dragging their poor belongings behind them. From Tripoli, because of the astronomical prices due to greed and speculation of businessmen running like jackals from the mother country, many people immigrated toward Ottoman Syria where the Turks promised land and money.

After a year of war, because the fields had been left uncultivated, the stored grain destroyed by liquid incendiary bombs or explosives, the stocks exhausted, the camel caravans bringing new provisions raided repeatedly, the wells dry, the pastures burned, the animals dead from hunger and thirst, famine reached out its long arm, and hunger weakened the people who became ill with typhus, small pox, and cholera.

Rebellion spread in every direction. Arabs, Bedouins, Berbers, and Senussi united against the invaders. They set up new camps where they could enlist volunteers, roved undisturbed over the high plains, attacked the garrisons, laid traps, made incursions, broke up communication lines, shot, killed, and flew swift as the wind on their lively mounts.

To the occupiers inability to understand the popular and religious nature of the revolt, their errors of strategy, summary firing squads and hangings out of ignorance, insensitivity, arrogance, was added their colossal stupidity, which irritated the population even more. In order to lay out an unnecessary road they wrecked the tombs of an Arab cemetery; they went in to look around the mosques without any respect for the Moslem faithful in prayer and without taking off their shoes; they peeped inside houses and courtyards from terraces; the doctors went without hesitation into the houses to tend to sick women, while their fathers, husbands, brothers bristled, horrified by the idea that they were touched by the infidels' impure hands. Some thoughtless officers even, adopted an abandoned dog (an unclean animal to the Muslims), and called it Allah or Mahomet.

Lorenzo anxiously counted the days and hours, but instead of a discharge the order arrived to send a mixed column of Italian and Libyan soldiers to comb an area south of Benghazi, where the Senussi practiced banditry and smuggled provisions and arms. In a bitter shoot out with a mounted band, two companions were killed, and as the rebels had rapidly vanished, the commander ordered that five Bedouins suspected of coexistence be hung in revenge. The Libyans refused to put their brothers to death so, as was the custom, the officer suggested the soldiers volunteer their services for financial reward. It was a tense and dramatic moment. Lorenzo grew stiff, sweat ran down his forehead, and his heart beat crazily while he tried to control his disgust for that barbarous practice of butchering the natives like animals. He would never, for any amount of money, do such a thing, but he knew that one of his poorer companions enticed by the reward, or perverted by that filthy and bloodthirsty war would accept. In fact, some of them offered to do the awful job. They wrapped ropes around the necks of the thin, ragged men, their arms tied behind their backs, and in absolute and ominous silence took them one by one to the telegraph poles and hanged them. Not a shout, a moan, a plea was heard. Lorenzo turned away and vomited.

The column picked the two dead soldiers off ground and lined up to return when they were attacked from two sides by a horde of rebels coming out of nowhere. The surprise threw the platoon into confusion and they responded with scattered fire. The Senussi, who dashed like demons on their horses, captured Lorenzo and another soldier who were isolated from the others and took them away by force.

It was the end of October 1912. Lorenzo remained there for almost two years, when thanks to a prisoner exchange the Libyans and Italians were set free. While at first he had lived in fear of experiencing the same fate as the five Bedouins, he grew calmer in time: the Arabs, he observed, were more humane and civil than the Italians. They treated the prisoners decently, shared the little food at their disposal, and left them free to move around in their villages.

When he returned home in August 1914, the world war had already broken out in Europe.

13

Augusto relayed the information: the head engineer had informed him that to the south, not far from the Oregon and California border, a railroad company was recruiting workers for the construction of a tunnel on the line that would go from Klamath Falls to Chiloquin and from there, in the spring, it would go as far as Kirk and Chelmut to hook up with what had just been inaugurated. In the tunnels one was sheltered and could work in the winter. Therefore he advised those who hadn't already found something else to go there. From what he had been able to understand from the engineer's allusive words, the company had taken advantage of the absence of periodic inspections, and had had the section of tracks finished and postponed the tunnel, the usual expedient among entrepreneurs to collect government financing as quickly as possible. Taking into account how difficult it was to find work during the bad weather, Augusto considered it manna from heaven.

Getting off the train in Chemult, weighed down with baggage, tools and blankets, they marched south, following the muddy, scarcely marked tracks and paths in the valley at the foot of the Fremont Mountains. Their rough peasant hearts grew happy to find nature intact; farther north the railroad construction had devastated nature like a furious earthquake: vast woods, river beds, endless meadows of luxuriant grasses were destroyed, animals were deprived of pasture and forced to flee quickly and forever. The coming and going of men and convoys had driven the birds away, depriving the place of song and flights. They recognized with surprise and gratitude the same vegetation as in their land: just as in their valley autumn tinged the sumac with flame, the weeping willow branches were a brilliant orange, the juniper berries changed from green to blue, the oaks, elms, maples turned their golden leaves lightly in the wind, violet crocus and the last faded cyclamens peeped from the silver-streaked wild grass. Here, as in their thick woods, the solitary golden oriole piped, flocks of brightly colored kingfishers dived for insects, quails shrieked stridently from the thickets. Troops of roe, stags, and antelope, having become familiar when they lived in the heart of the continent, dashed off at the men's appearance. Just like the herds of wild horses with wide rumps, blond manes flowing like a thick head of hair, and robust hocks with tangled hairy socks.

They went around a wide swampy area raising a festive commotion from frogs, and big white birds with long legs, unknown in their parts, searching the muddy bottom with their beaks. The men looked around indecisively, disoriented. They retraced their steps until, almost by chance, they ran onto a rail track. They followed it for about ten miles until they came upon the construction site.

The camp was in the process of getting organized. The stokers, the carpenters and the miners from Friuli who had built other tunnels together had just arrived and were putting up the oilcloth tent they had brought with them. For a nighttime shelter the newcomers were shown a dilapidated bunkhouse used by the previous gang. They had to make the most of the interior blackened by smoke from a rickety, rusty stove, and the filthy and uneven floor covered with mildewed straw, which they replaced with dry leaves from the woods.

Two days later the Americans — three supervisors and Joe, the camp overseer — arrived with a convoy loaded with material, tools, sticks of dynamite, furniture, barrels for water and provisions. It was clear at once that coexistence would be difficult. Joe, a stocky man with little pig eyes, bad teeth, and an eternal cigar in his mouth, snarling like a bulldog, seemed to burn with hate for the

Italians, and most of all for the pick and shovel workers—those who didn't know how to do anything else and who were justifiably not allowed to do anything else. Possessed with a sadistic streak that seemed to grow stronger by the day, he harangued them daily, his harsh voice sharp as an axe, thundering orders seasoned with insults. He threatened to sack them at every turn with no cause. He badgered them to work faster, calculated the day's earnings as he pleased, and if someone objected, he waved a blackjack in his face. He seemed to be looking for a fight. A regime of terror was established at the site that kept everyone on tenterhooks. Anxiety, the fear of making a misstep, of being assaulted, punished or sacked, increased the confusion and uncertainty and raised dreaded visions of aimless vagrancy and dark months of hunger and unemployment.

Gildo was filled with anxiety every time he saw the overseer. His outbursts, his red-faced, senseless attacks of rage, the ill will that spewed out with every word and gesture terrified him. Giusepì and Luigino tried in every way to avoid him, and when they found themselves facing him they stiffened, frozen with fear. He showed some regard for the tunnel specialists, perhaps because he was afraid of losing them and being unable to replace them, while common laborers were a dime a dozen. Furthermore the camp food was awful, the deductions from their earnings higher than anywhere else, and they were heavily fined for the slightest error or delay. The men grumbled unhappily, but Augusto calmed them down by saying they would make up for it with the promised bonuses for job finished ahead of schedule.

The tunnel was going to be just large enough for the average-size locomotive on a single track. The unskilled laborers cleared the dirt and vegetation to make an opening for the workers and equipment. With hammers and chisels on bare rock the miners made a series of holes in which the firemen placed cartridges of dynamite and the detonators. Experts at their job, they went from the center to the exterior and staggered the explosions with fuses of different lengths. The shorter ones, placed in the pipes located in the center made the mines flash before those in the periphery, so that the force of the exploding gases projected the rocky material backwards in a well-calculated succession to obtain perfect results.

Gildo, along with squads of workers with spades in hand waiting to clear the debris, watched the first assault on the basalt wall. The supervisors watched over them like guard dogs to make sure they didn't lose even a minute. The firemen, before lighting the fuses had shouted at the top of their lungs, the agreed signal for everyone to move back a hundred yards, carrying with them whatever could be damaged. As soon as the fuses were lit it was their turn to run as fast as they could. And at the proper distance, in the deafening blast that shook the mountain and raised gigantic columns of dust, the firemen counted the explosions aloud with fingers over their heads to make sure they all detonated: an essential confirmation to avoid the risk of one exploding later on. When a stick of dynamite didn't detonate tension rose to the skies: the firemen broke into cold sweats and hesitated to enter the tunnel, waiting for the explosion with their hearts in their throat. And if it didn't come they embarked on the delicate search for the unexploded mine like a trip to the gallows. They told about working in another tunnel where an American foreman, impatient to go in, lost an eye from a delayed charge that blew up in his face. There was also the danger of cave ins. Fragments could easily break from the stones as well as boulders made unstable by the explosions. It had happened once, and some workers in too big a hurry had been struck.

Day after day the excavation went deeper into the bowels of the earth. Dozens of men worked elbow to elbow in the feeble carbide lamplight, in a convulsive, exhausting rhythm: with pick axes the manual laborers crushed the largest loose spurs, picked up the fallen rock with their torn and bloody bare hands, shoveled up the small debris and went back and forth pushing the loaded wagons. The carpenters hurried to put up reinforcement to avoid cave ins. It was a rough tunnel, a rocky cave bristling with sharp projections.

In the reverberating hell of the narrow, airless enclosure hung the acrid stench of sweat and the pestilential stink of excrement and urine, a by-product of the men's furtive visits to dark corners. As the tunnel grew longer the supervisors thought too much time was being wasted by going and coming, and besides the men took their time, so a system of fines was introduced and that put an end to going outside to satisfy their needs.

In that unventilated hell hole, saturated with suspended dust that often cut visibility to zero, the suffocating toxic fumes of the explosions also accumulated: irritating poisons that choked the breath, causing furious coughing fits and copious tearing. Using the shortness of the tunnel as excuse, the company had not installed a machine that pumped in fresh air from outside. What came in from the opening was insufficient; often someone would fall in a faint, and his companions would carry him hurriedly out into the open air. Sometimes it took so long for the man to come around that he was given up for dead.

Because of the gases Gildo often vomited all he had eaten. When the crew that had worked in the tunnel for the first eight hour shift was replaced, the workers left with broken backs, exhausted, pale, staggering with nausea and dizziness caused by the prolonged lack of oxygen and toxic vapors that poisoned their lungs. Dazed by the abrupt change from darkness to light, they shaded their eyes constantly inflamed from the dim lamplight, and with unsteady steps headed for their cots.

With the onset of winter the bustle of the construction began while it was still dark — and every shift ended in the cold and dark. Bundled up to their eyes, the men marched quickly through the silent countryside beaded with an opaque white flowering of frost. The thin layer of ice covering the earth crunched under their feet like shattered glass. Their gray breath-plumes condensed in icy drops around their lips and in their nostrils. Their caps, mustaches, eyebrows turned silver from the swirling sleet. Compared to the glacial cold outside, the jaws of the tunnel opening to swallow them seemed a desirable warm den, despite the polluted air and poisonous fumes. The snow, falling heavily and without let up, had to be shoveled off the tracks, but the mine cars got stuck on the caked snow and much time was spent scraping it off with chisels and picks. They frequently derailed, and so the rails outside had been substituted by rough sleds of planed beams to slide easily to the tunnel opening, where they were filled with excavation material from the trolleys used inside.

One day as soon as the mines went off the workers set about to break up the rocks and clear the accumulation of stones and dirt, while the carpenters brought in large fir beams to prop up the last section of the vault. One of them, Eusebio, bent to measure the logs and mark where they should be cut. He suddenly straightened up in alarm, turned to those around him and abruptly told them to be quiet. He thought he had heard the supports creak somewhere behind them. In absolute silence everyone listened closely and held their breath, but no one heard a thing. The wood is giving a warning, Augusto whispered, and someone else retorted: I'm as deaf as a bell or Eusebio is dreaming.

Not at all convinced, Eusebio took a lantern, and projecting the light on the ceiling, carefully explored the vault supports step by step. Then he inspected the props one by one, but his expert eye did not detect a sign of weakness. Everything seemed to be all right: if Eusebio had not been dreaming, it must the normal settling noise. Nevertheless the workers stood listening for a while longer, and then, reassured, went to work. But Eusebio still wasn't sure: long experience told him that if his ear had heard something in all that commotion it meant his fear was justified. Unwilling to let it ride, he retraced his steps and went to the last section of the tunnel, shining his light on every single bare stone, every fold, every crack in search of a tiny drop of water, small and therefore unnoticed, a sign unwise to neglect. He found no seepage; therefore, though not at all at ease, he went on measuring the fir logs lying on the ground. From time to time he straightened up, had them stop wielding the axes, picks and shovels, and in the silence he listened. There was no suspicious sound, and after a minute, with an open-armed gesture he calmed the agitation and work resumed.

Without warning the roof suddenly collapsed behind the workers with a terrifying roar. The supports splintered and crumbled like cookies. As though an enormous plug had been pulled, rocks, pebbles, dirt fell at the entrance, and then, with a cataclysmic roar a torrential flood of water poured down as if the cataracts of the universe had burst open. The water, impeded by piles of debris and rough terrain, quickly rose almost to their knees. Most of the lanterns were out and they couldn't see a foot ahead. They sloshed around blindly, shouting, calling out to each other in the dim light. Noise from the falling water smothered their voices. Some stumbling against rocks swore and complained; some invoked the Madonna. And still others cursed the Heavenly Father. Most of them had had it with America and its damned railroads. Eusebio angrily defended himself: I told you, I told you!

The tunnel was transformed into a swamp. Feet buried in the mud couldn't move. The cascade didn't seem to want to stop or even slow down. Water crashing to the ground made high waves that rose to the ceiling, completely soaking the men. Dust formed a thick fog in the air that prevented the weak light at the entrance to enter. Eusebio shouted like a mad man for them to get out quick. The hole might get wider or the ceiling might collapse there or somewhere else, and they'll all be buried or drowned.

The excavation must have punctured a soaked layer just above them, or tapped into a spring that could be big as Lake Garda, a gigantic weight pressing down that could shatter the whole mountain. The terrorized men, shouting and groaning, bumped into each other, slipped in the sticky muck, stumbled over the broken logs, fell, got back up dripping and covered with mud, and made their painfully slow way toward the entrance.

Gildo was frozen with fear. Smashed against a wall, his shoulder hurt from a rock that had fallen on him, blood ran down his forehead that he wiped away with one hand. It was pitch dark and he couldn't see a foot ahead. He thought that if he moved cautiously, keeping his back against the rock wall and feeling his way with his hands he could get to the entrance and tell someone there about the disaster. If no one could make it out of there they would be trapped until the next shift came on. It seemed to take forever to work his way to the entrance. The furious torrent of water and mud carried rocks, tools, and pieces of wood along that hit his legs and made him lose his balance. He struggled to hang on to the anchorage of the wall. The effort made him breathless and he felt his strength leave him. Finally he got out into the open, and panting for air, his heart pounding like a hammer, his legs soaked, he reached the camp. He stumbled upon a supervisor and tried to explain with gestures, repeating: Uoter daun, uoter daun. While the man could not understand, and reacted with his usual impatience, another overseer understood immediately and ran to get the next shift and his two colleagues. In high boots they ran to the tunnel entrance. The slime had begun to flow out and spread, dense and murky as soft tar.

Mud-covered to their hair, unrecognizable, the workers came out one by one, the uninjured carrying the wounded in their arms. The men were counted to make sure no one was left inside. A miracle that everyone survived. Eusebio came out alone, hobbling and bleeding from a leg lacerated by a sharp rock. Augusto had a wound on his back.

They treated each other's injuries as well as they could and had to wait some time for them to heal. It wasn't possible to go back into the tunnel, so work was suspended, and any hopes of a reward for finishing ahead of time were dashed. Water continued to flow into the tunnel and mud made working there impossible; otherwise the injured workers would have been replaced at once, and the scabs would have been in danger of beatings. The need for work was so critical it normally did away with ordinary regulations and contracts.

Though they had escaped a sewer rat's death, the men could not get over their fear and anguish. It affected their sleep and appetite, and fostered a great aversion for that treacherous, damned hellhole waiting for them. Aversion, fear, anguish that even had an effect on the second shift as they heard the stories of the survivors who couldn't stop talking about the catastrophe that could happen again. Gildo listened, shuddered, but didn't open his mouth.

The avalanche of water was inexhaustible. Technicians came from Chiloquin to consult with each other about what steps to take: to reinforce the vault, the flow of water had to be channeled in a large pipe that would empty outside into a deep trench quickly excavated for that purpose. It took many days to get rid of the tons of accumulated mud. The tracks were buried in the slime that covered a wide area around the entrance, and in place of mine cars they had to use wheelbarrows. The men slipped around in sludge up to their knees and had trouble keeping their balance. The cold froze their wet and muddy trousers, and their shoes disintegrated. In the evening the men hung their clothes to dry in the heat of the stove. In the morning, with no other clothes to change into, they put on their mud-incrusted things, stiff as dried cod. They tied what was left of their shoes to their feet. The tunnel had become a circle in hell. The supervisor sneered at the coming and going of the damned. To him they were stupid men with buffalo brains who deserved no better than the dirty work they were doing.

In a few days' time a small blue lake formed in the ditch. A cackling flock of wild ducks passing overhead eyed it and landed all together with wings spread, rippling the surface as they took possession. When the overseers and supervisor, with visions of roasting duck over the coals, began shooting at them they flew away.

The work finally came to an end, with only a thin layer of rock blocking the other side. A convoy of flatcars was already moving on the tracks, full of water, crushed stone, sledgehammers, joints, ties, and tracks. Tracklayers were expected any day. Crews of manual laborers carefully smoothed the inside of the tunnel, leveled declines, filled gaps and cracks, scraped away irregularities, packed down dirt and toted the leftover material outside.

Coming out of the perpetual catacomb-like gloom, Gildo, gasping for breath, pushed the overloaded mine car like a yoked ox. His pupils dilated, he tried to focus on the place, people and things. His sensitive and delicate blue eyes were burning as if his eyelids were stuffed with iron filings. For days his body had been covered with little whitish blisters, an itchy eruption that he scratched until his skin was raw. It must have been the fine gray powder of the excavated rock, or perhaps scabies from the parasites that infested the bunkhouse. There was no way he could protect himself from one or the other.

His shift was about over, the next to last of the day. A little behind him the mine car pushed by Luigino was clattering, and Gildo forced himself to maintain a distance between them; it was hard to keep such a heavy weight moving. Someone had already been run over and seriously hurt. He pushed on blindly, head down, frowning, eyelids shut tight over his red eyes, muscles contracted until they cramped, relying on the tracks that guided the trolley, longing with his whole being for an end to that daily torture.

Though his body was fully involved in the effort, his mind wandered freely. He began to forget the terror he had experienced in the tunnel, even if every time he entered it he was alert for any sound and eyed the ceiling for hints of a second disaster; and every time he went out he breathed a sigh of relief. He pushed the heavy trolley and the rhythmic squeak of the wheels reminded him of the exciting waltz of the *Merry Widow*, memorized long ago when Bigio had played it on the ship. He had not been able to find the time and energy to practice the accordion as he would have liked. He played it in his mind as he worked, and it really seemed like his fingers were running over the keyboard and music was flowing from the instrument. The impression was so strong that he felt the cool contact of his fingertips on the keys and pleasure ran though his veins to his face ending with an involuntary smile. Absorbed and forgetful of what he was doing, he moved on to thinking about the defects of Bigio's accordion: the plastic keys, the wheezy billows, the old cracked leather, some chords out-of-tune, a stuck button. Bigio had been too poor to buy an expensive instrument. He dreamed about the day he could buy a perfect accordion made from precious material, the bellows soft, white calf's leather, the case shining embossed silver, the ebony keys deep black and compact, the ivory keys luminously white, the valuable leather belts, a glittering jewel from which he would release wonderful harmonies.

Whoever was around, and most of all Luigino behind him, saw how Joe, the supervisor, had deliberately cut right in front of Gildo's mine car, cool as a cucumber. He would have to admit that if Joe hadn't jumped over the tracks to save himself, he would surely have been hit, injured, or perhaps killed. Once out of danger, he hurled himself at Gildo with bestial fury, and as he poured an avalanche of abuse over him, he began beating him with a club — the ferocious, brutal blows of one who has lost control, and swept away with hate, could even kill. Gildo slipped to the ground, trying to defend himself from the blows with his arms. A rivulet of blood ran from a wound on his forehead, streaking his face. Those present looked on in horror, but no one intervened. With growing anger, the supervisor began kicking Gildo wherever he could with his hobnail boots, and since Gildo, to protect himself had folded over with head and knees bent, Joe grabbed him by the scuff of his neck, pulled him to his feet and in that vulnerable position punched him repeatedly in the stomach. He fell again, lying in the dust contorted with pain, but unable even to moan. Augusto picked him up from the ground and wiped the blood from his forehead. With a swollen face and aching body covered with bruises, Gildo dragged himself to work for days like a sleepwalker and didn't say a word.

The day might yet come when Joe went beyond his habitual verbal violence and beat someone to death. Though the men were on his side, Luigino repeated the whole story in great detail and someone suggested Gildo go to the police, but he felt crushed by a sense of guilt. He knew that at that moment he hadn't been watching where he was going, he had been daydreaming, thinking about other things; he knew how often he was distracted and didn't pay attention to what he was doing, losing himself in the music that swirled in his head or immersing himself in his worries. As much as his companions defended him, he had to recognize that the supervisor's reaction, though excessive, was the result of accumulated exasperation over his repeated shortcomings, and Gildo had been in his sights for sometime. A churning antipathy took hold of Gildo; it lashed him with constant derision, dogged his heels with continual observations and rebukes, attacked him with those insults — dago, wop — which he did not yet fully understand. The reproaches, the insults, the disregard that dogged him, awakened echoes of paternal spite, and had humiliated and annihilated him in the same way, plunging him into a demoralizing sense of inadequacy and guilt.

It was he who was wrong, strange, different, incapable of making something of himself, of arousing sympathy and goodwill. Inept and clumsy, ill suited for that work, too timid and fearful, lost in his dreams, passions, and ambitions — ridiculous and unrealistic for someone in his situation. In short, he despondently convinced himself he was unfit for life.

The convoy, loaded with tanks of water, material and supplies for the camp, completed its second and last trip around six in the afternoon. An hour later, at the end of his shift, while the others were busy with their evening chores, Gildo went around the bunkhouse, crossed the yard, jumped over the wing rail switches that fed to the side rails and starting walking on the main track that after a short while cut through the woods in a straight line for more than half a mile. He walked quickly and resolutely, head down, the dull thuds of his steps on the wooden ties echoing in his ears. He counted each step mechanically every time he put a foot down. Piles of dry needles, transported by the wind to the middle of the tracks, squeaked under his shoes. The setting sun lit up the sky and announced the imminent dusk. From time to time, when the curtain of firs suddenly grew thinner, an oblique light sliced between the trees and glanced off the tracks blinding him. To shade his eyes he brought a hand to his forehead, and without meaning to brushed the damp scab forming on his wound. His face was still swollen and a big bruise on his right temple traveled down his cheek as far as his chin. He had repaired his boots by nailing the loose sole to the vamp, but the point of a nail was now pricking his heel. He rummaged in his pants pocket nervously feeling the hole in his pocket that was growing larger. From time to time he scratched his chest and nape of his neck that itched from the sores that never healed.

After a hundred yards he stopped to listen. The train must not be far away. In the valley where the tracks ran alongside the hills was a wide blind curve. Before going around it the engineer would give a powerful whistle blast to warn the imprudent who used the tracks as a road and to scare away animals that might be perching on the roadbed. It had happened before that at the last moment he had found a line of men or a herd of cows in front of him, and the abrupt stop he made to keep from hitting them had scattered parts of the load in the escarpment.

Gildo thought about the first time he had traveled on a train in America, and how impressed he had been with the powerful whistles: deep as a stag's bellow, fierce as the roar of a hungry beast, suitable for being heard in the great distances of those endless spaces that still amazed him. A great quiet reigned around him now, animated only by the light rustle of ferns in the evening breeze and by the subdued chatter of birds preparing for sleep. A wolf's sudden bark in the thicket startled him.

He walked faster, and arrived where the straight part of the tracks began the bend. He stopped and looked up: darkness was rapidly falling in the valley. The thick wall of firs was partly immersed in shadow. To the west the stripped magenta of the sunset hung on and the sky above was rose-colored. Now everything was quiet. He hunched over and rested the palm of his hand on the track to feel for vibrations: it was warm from the sun, but there were no reverberations.

All of a sudden he seemed to hear a muffled echo of steps behind him: he stood up and quickly turned, alarmed, but no one was there. The tracks were barely shining, as though the metal had captured the daylight and released its reflection in the evening shadows. He started walking rapidly again. After a few minutes he realized he was about to enter the long arc of the wide curve, but he decided it would be better to go as far as the blind point where the arc widened, reached the culmination of the ellipse, and began to curve again.

That was when he heard the first hint of the locomotive: from the distant sound and the muffled echo off the hills, he judged the convoy still to be far away. He had time. He stopped on a tie and looked around. In the dusk the trunks of the fir trees along the roadbed, now seemed like a barrier of gigantic knives stuck in the soft mossy ground. In the streak of open sky between the two flanks of the forest, the sunset slowly disappeared. Again he seemed to hear behind him a scurry of footsteps, as if someone were running and slipping, but he didn't see a thing. The train was approaching. Now he distinctly heard a thundering that made the ground tremble. He knew that the locomotive had entered the far part of the wide curve because an uninterrupted succession of powerful wails exploded — the engineer's habitual, peremptory preoccupation to clear the tracks.

Gildo sat down on a tie, turned, lay down, and rested his neck on the cold metal of a faintly trembling track. He straightened his legs and put one over the other, leaving his feet suspended in air and one hand on the ground. With eyes wide open he stared above him at the transparent cobalt strip of firmament in which twinkled a few pale stars. The train's roar rapidly increased in intensity. In the racket, pierced by the warning whistle, he began to distinguish the rhythmic chug of wheels, the regular clank of connecting rods and pistons, the resounding gusts of steam. At the beginning of the curve the yellow eye of the lantern appeared. In the dark and distance it seemed gigantic. A sulfurous light cut through the dark, and lit the curtain of trees from top to bottom, marking the route of the convoy in the forest.

Gildo lifted his head slightly from the track and turned toward the headlight. The train was coming at high speed, the engineer wouldn't see him and perhaps wouldn't even be aware of anything, only a little bump, practically unnoticed. And if he did see him he wouldn't have time to stop. The enormous weight would pass over him and in an instant it would be all over. The luminous eye of the lantern was now a hundred yards away. Gildo stiffened, closed his eyes, and made his mind go blank.

A shout. An unexpected human shout right above his head frightened him and made him sit up at once. He struggled to understand. In the dark Luigino fell on him heavily. He grabbed him by the arms and shoulders, tried with all his strength to pull him from the tracks. He shook him angrily, and when he couldn't get him to move, he buried his fingernails in the bare skin on his neck. He screamed, beside himself: You blockhead! You moron! Get up! What do you think you're doing, dammit all? Stupid ass, stupid ass, damn fool! Get up, stupid! He was blinded by rage. Gildo fought and flailed to find something to grab. Luigino, teeth clinched, panting from the effort, tugged at his shirt, belt, the cuff of his pants, without moving him an inch. Growing more furious, cursing like a madman, he grabbed him by the ankles, trying to take off his shoes and drag him away from the tracks, but Gildo fought him off, wiggled free, kicked and punched. Then, swearing like a demon, Luigino began to hit him wherever he could, a hail of blows, kicks, slaps to force him to move. Gildo held on to the tracks with both hands and wouldn't give up. Terrified by the noise of the train growing louder each second, Luigino wouldn't quit flailing at him until the other, letting go for an instant, boxed him in the face.

The scuffle was interrupted by the shrill scream of the locomotive now a few yards away: Gildo, caught by surprise, jumping in fear, let go of the track. Luigino, relentless and desperate, grabbed his feet again and pulled furiously with all his last remaining strength. By that extreme surge of concentrated effort, along with Gildo's unexpected pliability, Luigino lost his footing and tumbled backward, dragging Gildo along with him. Clinging to each other they rolled down the embankment. The train roared past.

Gildo lay on his back on the rocks, as inert as an empty sack, his arms stretched out in a gesture of surrender. Luigino, gasping for breath, threw himself across Gildo's chest and continued punching him weakly, driven by left over bitterness for that terrible attempt. Suddenly, exhausted from the fight and terror, he broke into sobs, and ran his hand over Gildo's clothes, neck, shoulders, arms, as though wanting to reassure himself he was all in one piece. The clatter of the train grew faint in the distance. The engineer probably hadn't notice anything. Gildo lay still, mute, eyes closed, overcome by tension, exhausted by a deathly weariness. He hardly noticed the hands that roamed over him and didn't react, as if his body were far away, lost in an endless distance from which he could not return. From time to time he opened his eyes, stared vacantly at the sky above him, and closed them again.

Luigino's sobs gradually became more intermittent, like the ocean surf. Gildo would start with fright and tremble from head to foot; his breath would falter, remain suspended, then return to its normal rhythm. From the body that stuck to his and weighed on him spread a feverish heat. Against his ribs pounded a heart, palpitating like a frightened chicken's. On his neck he felt his warm breath and a thread of saliva that dripped from his mouth. He had never realized how thin Luigino was, all bones. And yet, that unsubstantial weight and strength in comparison to his had defeated him. Guessing his intention, just as he had guessed his father's at Ellis Island, he must have followed him from a distance as soon as he left the camp. Luigino had never mentioned his father and Gildo had mistakenly believed he had recovered from that sorrow, just as everyone is eventually consoled for every human sorrow. The rage with which he had wrenched him from the tracks, his passionate determination, the doggedness that drove him to the end must have come from that tragedy: the same rage and determination he would have used to save his father if he could. The torment of his death had made him feel bitter and helpless, rebellious and obstinate in the refusal of other loses and other pain. With tender surprise and reluctant gratitude, Gildo felt the impulse to embrace him. He stretched out a hand, hesitated; modesty stopped him and his hand dropped.

Luigino was quiet now and seemed to be sleeping. In the darkness Gildo stretched out his arm again but again let it fall. Finally he got the courage to timidly pat him on his shaved head, to let his open hand rest on his burning forehead. He looked at the sky attentively. Let's go, he pleaded in a weak voice, let's go.

14

Giacomo arrived home on Christmas Eve of 1912. Little Daniele had just turned thirteen months and was staggering around on plump little legs. Faced with the mustached stranger that allowed himself extraordinary familiarities and expected to take him in his arms and even kiss him, he broke into a fit of sobbing that even his mother was unable to quell. Ninetta soon abandoned her wailing child to throw herself on her husband and kiss him passionately in the presence of her astonished old parents.

Both Ninetta and Giacomo were itching with impatience to leave, but the already dreadful obstacles had become more serious than ever. Gildo hadn't sent money for the voyage, and furthermore they had lost track of him and didn't know where to go to join him. The last letter sent from Carolina, in which he informed his brother of the exorbitant commission for sending money, and urgently begged the others to redeem his mother's necklace and earrings from the pawn shop, had wandered for months, as the addressee could not be found. It was returned to the sender when the time expired. They knew even less about their father who had been silent from the beginning.

Giacomo went around searching for news. At Luigino and Giusepi's house he found out that the boys had left Bend many months ago, and it seemed Gildo was still with them. And after finishing a railroad tunnel in some deserted place, they had gone elsewhere looking for work. As soon as they found it they would send their address. Neither had Bigio and Leone's family received any letters recently. Giacomo went as far as Bondo Petello and discovered that Bortolo had disappeared from there into nowhere, and that Serafi had written he was still working at an inn at Renton.

He hadn't dared go to see Pino's wife in Fiobbio because of the gossip going around the village: After the first few letters she had heard nothing from her husband. She seemed to have lost her mind and sat staring into space for hours without saying a word. From time to time she would erupt into furious fits, tear her hair, curse, scream like a stuck pig. She paid no attention to her baby: he had come into the world after a pregnancy of tears and desperation. The delivery had been difficult, and they almost had to pull him out feet first. She seemed to hate that little child who had kept her from following her husband. The little boy was delicate, sad, and sickly, and still didn't talk. He was being raised by his grandmother who was much attached to him.

Giacomo sought out a man in Nembro, a certain Callisto, who had returned from America before leaving for the army. He had never met him, only heard the villagers' gossip that he had made a fortune and talked about the marvels of the American continent. Life over there was paradise and dollars poured from the sky straight into your pockets without your moving a finger. Therefore Giacomo was surprised to find a man aged before his time, haggard, gray, dark circles around his eyes, racked with a dry cough, short of breath. He was sitting by the fireside, sipping from a glass of red wine as though it were medicine. He had a curious foreign accent, and inserted English words in his conversation. He said he had worked fifteen years for a cement factory in a little town in the state of Washington, in concrete, which in English really means cement. From the time they had quit constructing wooden houses that burned up like straw, they had produced enormous quantities of concrete that sold like bread. Buildings, bridges, ports, subterranean railroads. For years now over there they built with reinforced concrete, strong enough to last for centuries. Jobs ("giobba") were not hard to find, but you had to work hard for your dollars. You had to work "veri ard" everywhere in America, twelve hours a day in toxic and blinding dust that got in your throat and poisoned your lungs. In the town, that wasn't much to brag about, there were a few Italian boarding houses where it was possible to live without spending too much. A fit of coughing interrupted him, and when it had calmed down, he took another sip of wine. In answer to Giacomo's quizzical look, he said that in the cement plant he had contacted silicosis, an invalidating chronic illness that kept him from work. After a grueling life without a moment of rest, he murmured wearily, there had been nothing left for him to do but come home to die. You work and work and when you put something aside and hope to have a rest you find out that the only thing waiting for you is death.

If he hadn't found work, he had made a slow recovery, and here in this poverty there was nothing to do. He advised Giacomo to leave, work for some time in the cement factories, put away a little money and then look for a healthier livelihood. Otherwise sooner or later he would ruin himself and be good for nothing.

Giacomo's face reflected his great disappointment. The villagers had told a heap of lies. Who knows how they came up with them? Maybe they were an expression of their dreams, and anyway he had believed them and told them to others, because if you give up fantasizing about the world you don't know and projecting your own future there, you might as well put a bullet in your head or hang yourself. And then there are those who are born lucky and those for whom nothing goes right, and Callisto was in this second category. Like his brother Lorenzo, who instead of going to America was still a prisoner of those tar faces in Libya and who knows when he would come back?

Giacomo wanted to know what Callisto thought about his plan to take his wife and little boy with him. He said that over there the women could easily find work as maids, dishwashers, or seamstresses, earning little but that little was a big help. And then a wife makes life easier and relieves the solitude — an awful thing for anyone far from home. On the other hand he wouldn't risk taking the child. Americans don't want to have immigrant children under their feet, they don't earn anything, in fact they are a burden, an obstacle. Italians are accused of breeding like rabbits and then turning to public assistance, "to become a public charge," as they say, to feed and take care of their brats. And if it happens within a year after arrival there is the danger of being sent back. So, once you get there don't have any more kids that won't be appreciated. Instead think about getting settled first and in a few years you can send for the boy who will be old enough by that time. Laboriously, pausing to gather his thoughts, sucking the stub of a pencil, he wrote two lines on a piece of paper to give, once he reached Concrete, to a man from Brembate near Bergamo, a certain Terenzio Zanga, foreman at the Portland Cement Company, where, as was the use over there, he would have to pay a commission on his first pay day.

The hardest part was getting a loan for the trip. He asked the town innkeeper and was turned down because he had no mortgageable property. The bird catching house was practically worthless and that was all the family owned. Loan sharks in Albino and Nembro had turned up their noses. They had no faith in the son of a man who was ruined financially and still hadn't paid off his debts. When he didn't know where to turn, he was told to try a certain priest in the valley who lent money at exorbitant rates, and he lent the money to Giacomo, with the interest deducted.

Ninetta was distraught at having to leave little Daniele and wept endless tears. Her parents offered to take care of him, but they were old and in poor health, and she was afraid they were not strong enough. Her older sister Camilla, married for some years and unfortunately still childless, was happily disposed to taking that little chirping bird into her home to brighten her days. Her husband was reluctant. It seemed too heavy a responsibility, but she convinced him that that innocent little angel would bring them God's graces and the child they so desired would surely arrive.

They left from Genoa at the end of January 1913. That voyage by ship that Giacomo had so long dreamed of turned out to be a nightmare. Ninetta was seasick and vomited day and night. The steamer was overcrowded, men and women lived in separate quarters, the food was disgusting, the discomforts were too many to mention, and after fifteen days when the American coast appeared on the horizon, enthusiasm for reaching the Promised Land had vanished for some time.

After a week on the Great Northern train, they changed at Everett for Burlington, then for Sedro-Woolley, and two hours later got off at Concrete. On the outskirts of the town lying on the banks of the Baker River, an unusual sight to their unaccustomed eyes, appeared the gigantic silos of Washington Portland Cement Company on which were written in block letters: WELCOME TO CONCRETE. The main street was dominated by the severe Assembly of God Church next to the town hall, further down was the school, a couple of stores, a barber shop, a saloon, a row of houses. The whole area was covered with gray powder that swirled in the darkened air. Surrounding it were steep, snow-covered mountains, rocky peaks and thick conifer woods.

They found lodging in the basement of a house near the river. A couple from Varesotto rented two dark, dank rooms to Italians who worked in the factories, and eight men slept in each room. The latrine, a small wooden moldy structure that let in gusts of icy wind, not unlike the bird catching structure at home, was behind the house, next to the chicken coup and a little plot of turnips and cabbage with cold-blasted leaves between patches of dirty snow. Water was drawn from a hand pump on the street.

There was no bedroom for a couple—and if there had been they wouldn't have been able to afford it—so they were forced to live apart. Ninetta, the only female in the house besides the landlady, was relegated to a narrow, airless closet under the stairs. The cot was too long for the door to be closed. They both suffered from the compulsory separation, even more intolerable after the separation on shipboard, and even before that by the interminably long military service and war. They were both tormented by the lack of intimacy so long desired and so briefly enjoyed. They jumped if they happened to brush against each other, they launched meaningful looks across the room, and when they met at the door without witnesses they hugged each other so violently they couldn't breathe. The noise and crowd at the noon meal and when everyone came back from work in the evening were oppressive and upsetting. They yearned for the closeness and warmth of being together alone, and the impossibility to do so made them sad and nervous. Once in a while late at night when the lodgers were snoring so loud the house trembled on its foundations, Giacomo would go in his stocking feet to his wife's cot in the closet. Every night Ninetta would wait for him in trepidation, but in the often-disappointed wait she would fall asleep, and when he finally arrived he woke her by burying his face in her breast. She would be aroused immediately, smile in the dark and gather him into her arms with her heart pounding. She would grab him wildly by the hair, pull his head close to hers and bury her teeth in his neck. He would bite her mouth and hug her until it hurt. Greedily, frantically he would rummage under the covers, find her ear with his tongue, babble incoherently; and she, afraid that the others might hear, would stop his mouth with her hand. But the open door, the haste, the fear that someone would get up and pass by, inhibited them, interrupted the caresses. The ardor that consumed them ended in melancholy resignation. Giacomo, exhausted, would tear himself from her arms and return to bed in despair. Ninetta, tense as a bowstring, would toss sleeplessly on her cot, tormented by her craving for her beloved, the weight of his body on hers, his enflamed sex and burning tongue. Tormenting were her memories of holding her swollen breasts to his mouth, spreading her legs, arching her back and offering him her body blazing with unsatisfied desire. Then she would cover her face with her hands and weep softly.

Terenzio, around forty years old, a gruff man of few words, gave Giacomo the job of unloading clay and limestone from wagons and putting it in the containers to be poured into the mill and ground up. A job in the open air, a manual laborer, paid $1.50 a day. He hoped that as soon as he learned the ropes at the factory he could work in the silos or at the ovens — more qualified occupations and better paid, and best of all, inside work. Remembering Callisto's warning, he tied a handkerchief around his nose and mouth to protect his lungs from the powder.

Ninetta helped the landlady in the kitchen at mealtimes, cleaned the toilet, brought in buckets of water, washed clothes, took care of the chickens and rabbits in exchange for a free bed and the noon meal. She was pleased, but intended to find a better job as soon as possible. She didn't want to remain a servant in that segregated dump for long. When she became more familiar with her new surroundings and understood more, she would see what she could find. She was determined to learn English, but she would have to get out of there where everyone spoke their own dialect. She knew how to cut clothes from a pattern, sew, embroider, and also cook and clean, and she was sure someone would want to hire her.

Shortly afterward she was dismayed to learn she was pregnant. When she told Giacomo he turned pale, staggered as if about to fall, leaned on the wall, and stood mutely staring at her.

Most surprising in a city by the sea were the thick waves of velvety fog pushed by the northwest wind blowing off the Pacific. In the morning and late afternoon it crept in the narrow passage of the Golden Gate, invaded the bay and buried it under a blanket, extending its soft, white tongue as far as the interior valleys. The somber foghorns of invisible vessels blindly plowing the water from one shore to another frequently pierced the milky flood. Suddenly, as though a theater curtain lifting, the fog would dissolve, opening views of the splendid landscape, the brilliant midday sun making glimmering lights in the wakes of the clippers and the steamships.

One Sunday morning, standing on a deserted spot at the foot of Telegraph Hill, Gildo peered intently at the barren island of Alcatraz veiled in haze, rising up in the sea opposite him, less than a mile away. Blurred in the distance behind Alcatraz was Angel Island, where the immigrants from Asia, largely the Chinese, passed through on arrival, just as Ellis Island for the Europeans.

From that observation point he could not see the Alcatraz landing wharf, which was situated on the other side of the island. Only a smokestack, a water tank, and at the top of the rocky hill, the imposing military penitentiary of gray cement, surrounded by high walls dominated by massive watch towers. Beside it a searchlight pierced the sky. Every day a ship connected the island to the mainland, delivering to and from school the children of the military who lived there, or their wives who went to shop in the city. Barges lined up loaded with provisions and water unavailable on the island, and sometimes gigantic pyramids of dark soil and bundles of trees and bushes lying crosswise.

It was said that the soldiers condemned to forced labor had enlarged the prison and constructed new wings with dozens of cells protected by strong bars, whose walls and ceilings were completely isolated from the outside. The surveillance was pitiless and the walls insuperable, making any escape impossible from that little island that seemed so close, separated from the mainland by a thin arm of sea. When the work of expanding the prison was finished, the inmates enlarged the garden, created fifty years before the garrison soldiers and their families. Tons of fresh dirt was dumped on the rocky crust in a layer thick enough to plant trees and bushes. From there Gildo observed the growth with the passing of days. They said that from time to time a covered barge would cross the bay transporting new prisoners from land. It was recognized by the lugubrious laments of the foghorn, whether there was fog or not, that warned everyone to get out of their way. An anguished sound that made shivers run down your spine. But he had never heard it.

Gildo worked in an enormous quarry on the east side of Telegraph Hill, not far from where he had observed the bleak and inaccessible island in the middle of the wind-swept sea that Sunday. The rocky material excavated was used for lining one side the bay and to pave sidewalks and streets of some San Francisco districts. The thought of those men buried in Alcatraz morbidly attracted and repelled him. What crime were they guilty of? How were they treated? Were they beaten? Tortured? Had anyone ever tried to escape? Swarms of gulls circled the island. He imagined the prisoners in the courtyard watching the birds that hovered on the breeze, the only free creatures they were allowed to see.

For several months he had lived in a big American city for the first time. At the camp they had spent whole evenings talking about the big cities, and each one had his own opinion even if he had never been to one. It was one thing, someone reasoned, to live in a tumbledown shack, stuck in a hell hole not even on the map, miles from the nearest inhabited place, and another to live in a city with a roof over your head and all the comforts of gas, running water, electricity, paved streets, trolleys, automobiles, shops. Where they were, isolated and without contacts, which sometimes seemed to drive you crazy, they could count only on each other, which wasn't bad, but it certainly didn't broaden your mind or your understanding of the world. On the other hand, you met all kinds of people in a city, and between one conversation and another you could make helpful friendships and find opportunities you dreamed about. Not to mention that among a large number of people busy making deals from morning to evening you could surely find a variety of well-paid jobs. Therefore, you would feel more protected and you'd live better, be warm, clean, and able to dress decently. Augusto had sighed: he couldn't wait to read a newspaper and go to mass on Sunday in his best clothes with other good God-fearing people.

Some of the men, who had been peasants in their country, were afraid of the city and dreamed of work on a farm, good land to cultivate and a house to build with their own hands. They knew they would never be able to put aside enough capital to buy land, or even rent it. A "farma" cost at least five hundred dollars. On top of that you had to buy animals, a horse and cart, tools, and had to have some savings a to survive until the first harvests. They were just castles in the air, but they kept them in the world. Yet, others better informed objected. They had heard about Italians who had bought land—for example the Frasinettis, the Foppianos, the Martinis—in Napa Valley or Santa Rosa near San Francisco, and had planted vast, prosperous vineyards. They produced excellent wine and made money hand over fist. A man from Monferrato shook his head: true, those Italians had planted the vineyards before the end of the century, but then vine pest had destroyed them. They had sunk into poverty and had had to start from scratch. The risks were too high if you didn't have sound capital.

California was most often mentioned, as that Italian name sounded so familiar to their ears, one of the rare words in English that was written as it was pronounced. They talked about its mild climate thanks to which, as in Italy, vineyards and olive trees flourished, and even oranges in the south, and most importantly it was not far away, next to Oregon. Luigino burst out laughing at the mention of Sacramento, the state capital, because in their country it was one of the worst curses, and in confession the priest had made him say a whole rosary or twenty Our Father's and Hail Mary's for penance every time he said it.

After the tunnel was finished many of the men had been tempted to move to Sacramento to do railroad maintenance alongside the Columbia River in spite of those impassioned discussions. The fear of being unemployed was too strong. Augusto had heard about a big road job about to begin in Oregon and had convinced some of them to move there with him; others, such as Eusebio and his carpenter friends had left for British Columbia to work on a wooden bridge over a secondary river. The three boys, lured by the big city myth had decided to go to San Francisco.

Not far from the quarry where they worked was the Italian district of North Beach, next to Chinatown that was full of funny little Chinese men stacked on top of each other. The Italians, like the other immigrant groups, stayed together where they knew and understood each other, and could keep their old reassuring customs, read the newspapers in their language, shop in the stores, stalls and markets where they had the comfort of finding familiar food, such as real bread, olive oil, fresh vegetables. In the streets the smell of coffee mixed with that of loaves fresh out of the oven.

When they arrived the Catholic church of Saint Francis was still under reconstruction, the oldest church in the city, burned and destroyed in the earthquake of 1906. After that terrible tragedy, San Francisco had risen from the ruins, but then seemed in the grip of quartan fever. Construction sites were everywhere. New streets and squares and buildings were laid out, new gas, sewer and water works were installed in neighborhoods, and the port was expanded.

The boys hoped to work as masons, but everywhere they applied for work they were told that all the jobs were filled. They suspected that the building contractors avoided hiring Italians on the pretext that they weren't familiar with reinforced concrete, but only lime and bricks, now obsolete. As if they couldn't learn. However, they knew that the powerful American unions threatened and intimidated the business owners to keep them from hiring Italians who would accept starvation wages and rob them of work. The foreigners were accused of not joining the Unions in order to avoid the $100 annual dues and the high monthly fee. In reality, aside from the stratospheric sum that no one was in the position to pay, the Unions did not accept foreigners who didn't know English, and they could not become American citizens without renouncing their own citizenship, and then only after a residence of at least five years. There was nothing for them to do but take up the same work as before: pick, shovel and wheelbarrow. They settled for the novelty of living in the city, and felt sure things would improve with time.

The Italian district—aside from a large diagonal street, Columbus Avenue, where a green and white skyscraper of six floors with a dome hat, next to Amedeo Giannini's Bank of Italy, and a series of shops, restaurants, cafés, jewelry stores, pretentious pastry shops—was a maze of badly kept and nondescript little streets, with rows of modest homes.

The three friends rented a room in a boarding house run by Caterina, a middle-aged woman who had come to America with her husband and two children years ago from Rovigo. They had built the little house themselves, and their little sons had even carried stone and bricks. She was still paying off the loan. Recently her husband had been killed in a fall from the scaffolding of the same quarry where his adolescent sons were working, and after the accident the widow had made ends meet by running a boarding house for Italian workmen. Out of necessity she knit children's socks in the evening at a dollar a dozen, and mended her renters' clothes. For their meals she raised vegetables in the few square yards of land behind the house, so thickly planted there wasn't an inch of wasted space.

Rather than a room, they had rented a cubbyhole with barely

space for three beds, and one window that looked onto a wall. The nice thing about it was not having strangers around, so after work Gildo could play his accordion in peace as much as he wanted, and that made a big difference.

In the beginning they cautiously explored the unfamiliar city on Sundays. They happened on the business district, but left at once, intimidated by the ten-storey skyscrapers bursting with an overpowering sense of wealth. They hiked up steep little streets that passed over the hills and, breathless, had contemplated from a summit the immense green and foaming ocean; and on the opposite slope they had seen residential quarters stretching along the coast as far as the port and docked ships, and the blue bay curled by the currents and the long shore enclosing it, thick with fog-bleached houses. Myriads of streetlights came on in the evening, and from that height the proud twinkling metropolis seemed to lie tamely at their feet.

Curiosity won out and they took a ride on a cable car, a railway tram painted red and yellow like a toy, which slowly and determinedly climbed up the difficult hills. At the end of the line the driver turned the car around on a revolving platform and went on its way again in the opposite direction: the descent was so vertiginous that the car seemed to be falling straight into the sea, and the boys, hearts in their mouths, held onto the back of the seat ahead of them with both hands.

On Sunday afternoons they wandered around the lively streets bustling with automobiles, tilburies, sulkies and gigs, mingling with the crowds listening to the firemen's band in the bandstand in a shady square. To Gildo that wind and percussion music seemed to possess the dignity of real art: graceful melodies, some of poignant melancholy, sometimes with a happy, strong beat. Anxious to increase his repertoire, and trembling with excitement, he stored marches, polkas, mazurkas, and waltzes in his head to replay on his accordion. He stood for some time reading and rereading the program of the Washington Square Theater, a Russian church some Italians converted into a theater with a thousand seats. *L'Elisir d' amore* was playing. He was dying to buy a ticket, but had to postpone the desire until he could afford to buy a proper suit for the occasion.

One evening, at a second-hand store where a gramophone stood in front of the little shop, he had stopped to listen to Caruso's flute-like voice singing "Una furtiva lacrima." He noticed some musical scores in the window and without giving it a second thought he went in and bought them. Reading music was a superior and complex knowledge that fascinated and frightened him, comparable in difficulty to learning a new language from the indecipherable characters without a guide. But his ambition to become a professional musician drove him to tackle it. He realized that those mysterious black symbols on the five lines — some above and others below — wouldn't mean a thing to him, bereft as the was of the most fundamental knowledge, if he didn't decipher the writing of a piece that he already knew by heart. For many evenings he went over and over the score of *Poet and Peasant* by von Suppé and Strauss' *Blue Danube Waltz*, comparing it note by note with the music in his head. It took much time and persistent concentration to assign the correct meaning and value to each of those signs, to identify those that established the pitch of the sounds, low or high according to their progression from low to high on the lines, the duration of each note as well as the pauses between them; and the secret reasons why some of those little empty or full circles are alone and others are in clusters of two or even three, four, or five, sometimes decorated by one or more commas on the rod; or the meaning of those curved lines that embrace the notes above and below. Still more difficult to penetrate the meaning of certain odd signs — sharps and flats — and when he finally understood that they were semitones that he found with eyes closed on the black keys of the instrument, he let out a whoop of victory. The final riddle had been the symbols at the beginning of the lines, the musical keys that determine the pitch and the tonality of the notes, which he puzzled over for entire evenings. The light dawned when he realized that the accordion spontaneously changed register by moving a lever.

Proud of his singular success, Gildo burst out laughing and began to sing. He had started from zero and had been terribly disadvantaged by not having anyone to teach him the basics. To make some sense of that complicated writing had been very fatiguing mentally, but finally, by faithfully following the written notes, he had managed to play a composition very slowly and with somewhat disappointing results compared to playing it by ear. The melody came out labored, uncertain, faltering. He needed much practice to learn to read the score with the same speed as the words and to translate the notes onto the buttons and keyboard quickly. With time, he told himself, he would be able to do it, and he already felt encouraged by the hard-won progress.

He seemed to have finally landed in the right place to cultivate his passion, and his heart swelled. Work at the quarry was exhausting, but the excitement that possessed him replenished his energy and wiped out his weariness.

In the meantime he continued to play the melodies he already knew, and gradually added the new ones he had heard the firemen's band play. For example, Strauss' *Radetzky March*. Along with the clatter of pans and skillets in the kitchen while preparing supper for the boarders, Caterina would hum the tunes he was playing. At the table she would greet him with a big smile. Music was soothing, she said, it was like a powerful balm that eased the unpleasantries of the day. The renters also enjoyed the music. They urged him to play, requesting favorites, and he didn't wait to be begged. Those musical flurries spread a peaceful happiness, calmed minds, and sweetened the daily trials.

On Sundays Gildo eagerly read the announcements in the local Italian newspaper, as if sticking his nose in the unhappy affairs of his countrymen, giving him an idea of other's difficulties, consoled him a little for his own. Cooks, farmers, miners, nannies, maids offered their services. One looked for an inexpensive house, another wanted to buy a horse or a cow; some were selling dry mushrooms, sardines, olives, salami, ham, olive oil, macaroni and other pastas, another had alfalfa, wheat and corn seeds to sell. There was a notice asking for news about old, absent-minded parents swallowed by the city, another for information about a missing daughter with descriptions of her clothes and physical appearance; another wanted information about a brother not heard from for some time. One man complained about his stolen billfold and pleaded for the documents to be returned at least; a worker was in despair over his stolen bicycle, indispensable for getting to work, and pleaded for someone to come forward with information about it. And at the bottom of the page, a green grocer in their neighborhood was in urgent need of an accordion player for his daughter's wedding, and was willing to pay well provided the musician was good and had a broad repertoire.

In Saint Francis church, still smelling of fresh plaster and varnish, the just-inaugurated organ played the wedding march, which started the ceremony off on a happy note. For the wedding dinner Aniceto, who came to San Francisco ten years ago from Salerno, transformed his fruit and vegetable warehouse into a cheerful hall festooned with colored paper, garlands of evergreen and jasmine, satin ribbons and rosettes, huge flower arrangements, an Italian flag on the wall and a strip of red velvet on the floor. Planks on sawhorses, covered with embroidered white tablecloths, occupied half the room. The other half was left free for dancing and a battalion of chairs against the walls. One hundred people were invited — relatives, witnesses, godparents, neighbors, important customers and good acquaintances, and more than ten noisy children of various ages. The most distinguished and revered guest was

Aniceto's son-in-law's American boss, accompanied by his wife.

After eating at the table with the guests and drinking a couple of glasses of Monticello red wine from Napa Valley that made his ears burn, Gildo left the table and began playing the *Royal March*. Aniceto requested it so he could tactfully explain to the American couple, in his primitive and ungrammatical English, how Italy was not a country of backward shepherds, but a country of ancient traditions, including an honest-to-goodness king, descendent of the very ancient and noble dynasty of Savoy, who go back to the year one thousand. He would have liked to add that he found it very difficult to swallow the Americans' arrogance and presumption when they bragged about their civilization still in its infancy, considering it superior to the thousand-year-old civilization of the European emigrants. But he was a prudent and practical man and kept silent.

It was an intense and solemn moment. The guests jumped to their feet in reverent homage to the distant country. The children were even silenced. Some eyes grew damp, furtively dabbed by handkerchiefs. Enthusiastic applause greeted the conclusion, which was followed by many warm and generous toasts.

At the first chords of the *Merry Widow* waltz, the bride practically ripped off her veil, grabbed her new husband, and in a kind of wild fury amid deafening applause, dragged him off to dance. The dancing went on late into the night. The children danced awkwardly with each other; the older guests, as light as feathers in spite of the weight of their years and aching feet from old calluses, whirled untiringly through the waltzes and mazurkas, staring straight ahead without exchanging a word. With a gallant bow, Aniceto invited the American lady to dance a waltz. She laughed loudly, as though she had never enjoyed herself so much in her life. A couple of girls buzzed coquettishly around Gildo with smiles and compliments, but he blushed up to his eyes and stammered in confusion, intimidated by such casualness and withdrew like a snail in its shell. The young men, already a bit tipsy, after spinning around like tops, had begged for mercy and requested slow dances, tangos, the fox trot and one-step. The men removed their jackets and let their shirttails swing outside their trousers. The girls threw off their too tight new shoes and in bare feet jumped like crazed grasshoppers. They loudly begged him to play the "chicken polka," and the dancers galloped up and down the large room making the room reverberate with their thudding heels. Those nostalgic for old times insisted on a quadrille where the whole family could dance — grandmother, mama, and daughter — a dance with couples facing each other, disorderly and hectic, commands yelled at the top of the voice, bows, about-turn, reverse, faces flushed, hands sweaty, breathing rapid, ties loosened, hair undone and hairpins falling on the floor. Finally, worn-out and gasping for breath, they collapsed on the chairs. Aniceto asked Gildo to play 'O sole mio. The wine had its effect and the off-key chorus sing-along seemed more like a lament for a lost and beloved shore than a song.

It was late when the party broke up. Aniceto, glowing over its extraordinary success, kissed the American lady's hand as he told her and her slightly dazed husband good night. He embraced Gildo with an enthusiasm intensified by the wine, slapped him loudly on the back, and covered him with compliments for his skill and the variety, richness, and beauty of his repertoire. He said he would speak about him to his customers and acquaintances so they might call him for weddings, baptisms, confirmations, first communions, silver anniversaries and patron saints' days, as he furtively thrust a well-folded ten-dollar bill into his hand. Gildo, shy and embarrassed, smiled sweetly and stammered around trying to thank the generous green grocer. On the day of his debut he had earned more than a whole week's pay. It was truly an unforgettable day.

15

Ninetta found work in a bottle factory, and as long as she could she kept her pregnancy hidden in shapeless smocks. By the end of the seventh month it had become so obvious that her boss noticed and fired her on the spot. Full of anger over that injustice, and incapable of remaining idle, she accepted ridiculous pay to scallop buttonholes on already made shirts. And as she threaded a needle, she was thinking that if she bought a Singer sewing machine on time — an American way of paying that didn't exist in Italy — she would be able to make the shirts from start to finish and earn more. Since that crowded house didn't have room for even another pin — much less room for a sewing machine and even less for a baby's cradle — the only solution was to move to a larger place and take in ten boarders to pay the rent and time payment. She tried to persuade her husband who turned a deaf ear: it was only a matter of having debts for the first month, and then the income would cover the expenses.

Giacomo was afraid to bite off more than he could chew and made one excuse after the other for not going into debt: whoever sold on time required a solid guarantee and his modest pay wasn't enough, Americans refused to rent houses to Italians because of their bad reputation, they couldn't be sure of finding the number of renters needed to pay off their debts, without mentioning the risk of taking in the kind that don't pay regularly or even not at all.

The baby was born in that state of uncertainty. Ninetta's water broke while she was scrubbing the floor. The delivery was so quick that she hardly had time to lie down on the cot, and with the help of the landlady, after a few pushes, the newborn came out easily.

She was named Lucia, in honor of her paternal grandmother.

The little one cried all night long, and consequently the angry boarders couldn't get a wink of sleep. The annoying episode was unfortunately repeated the next night, so the landlady told the little family they had to find another place, the men worked all the blessed day and had every right to sleep at night.

They found a dilapidated wooden house at the edge of town that hadn't been lived in for years. Perhaps the owner was confident that he wasn't taking much of a risk. Giacomo repaired and straightened the lopsided roof, adjusted the gutters, patched the caved-in floors and the disconnected fixtures, covered the cracks in the ceilings and walls, replaced the broken window glass, whitewashed the rooms and unplugged the drains. Ninetta, still feeling weak after the delivery, cleaned and polished the dusty rooms, bought beds, mattresses, blankets, a table, a dozen unmatched chairs, pans and cutlery on credit from a junk dealer. She wanted to do things right, to offer clean, proper lodging and decent food to the boarders at a fair price. Poor devils everywhere were forced to live in squalor and filth. Giacomo spread the word around at the cement factory, and ten men moved in.

Ninetta's calculations turned out to be shrewd. Money from the boarders easily paid the house rent. They gradually paid off the junk dealer, and the debt contracted with the valley provost. They sent a little money to her sister who was taking care of Daniele and even put a few dollars aside. The Singer sewing machine was never mentioned. What with the house work, the shopping, meals to cook, and the baby to care for, she didn't have time to breathe. She was worn out by evening, arms throbbing from fatigue, back aching and legs like lead. Because of the overwork she had for some time been without milk.

1914 was a lucky year for Gildo. Although the quarry at Telegraph Hill, scrapped to the bone, had closed, and he, Luigino, and

Giusepì had lost their jobs, the requests for playing at Italian events had multiplied, thanks to Aniceto's enthusiastic recommendation. In addition to weddings, the Italians celebrated engagements, birthdays, baptisms, high school graduations, inaugurations of businesses, visiting relatives. Any occasion was excuse for a party. Groups of fellow Italians would chip in to rent halls for partying and dancing, and cafés to supply the food. They much preferred live music to a gramophone or player piano.

Each time he earned from two to five dollars, and often some guest would slip him a tip. It was enough for his expenses and a little extra to save. More than the money — or at least the same — was the joy he got out of it. He played for himself, not for the others, though they obviously enjoyed it. As soon as his fingers touched the keys, as though enchanted, he went out of himself and migrated elsewhere, in a land all his, where nothing reached him, his mind in symbiotic fusion with the music, his body welded to the instrument as though they were one. Absorbed and oblivious, his face was transfigured, his lost and empty expression almost followed a vision into a place inaccessible to the others, his whole being seemed concentrated and at the same time absent. He was alone during those moments, but his solitude fed a vivid flame that burned and renewed him. Sometimes he improvised. His total mastery of the keyboard inspired him to experiment the endless possible combinations, and melodic inventions flowed with an intuitive naturalness that surprised even him. When he stopped playing he seemed dazed, estranged from the world around him, unsure of his footing.

Most often the festivities took place on Saturdays and Sundays. He didn't feel right not having anything to do for the rest of the week, so he found work at the port unloading merchandise from ships. Luigino and Giusepì moved to Oakland on the other side of the bay to work on a new road. They left Caterina's boarding house and Gildo rented from Rosa Cencini, a middle-aged woman from Tuscany, petulant, greedy, and obsessive, a little room all to himself: a bed, a chair and a wobbly, worm-eaten table, a pitcher and flaking basin for washing. The toilet was on the other side of the house at the end of the stairs. There were no electric lights. An old gas lantern survived and she heated breakfast and cooked something for supper on a spirit stove. The entrance to his room was right on the street, and when, happy and proud of that solitary and independent arrangement, he closed his door and put the key in his pocket, he seemed to finally be master of his own existence and even a little bit master of the world. He had made it, he flattered himself, and maybe someday he would be a soloist in a little orchestra that played in elegant restaurants, or in open-air cafés in nice weather. And so he would earn his living just by playing music, and even the Americans would know and appreciate him. At the end of his day he shut himself up in his little room and played late into the evening, the music flowing into the streets from the open window, putting the neighbors in good spirits.

Because of his natural distrust of people — Luigino called him a cynic, with a laugh — he was happy not to have anyone underfoot he would have to talk to. It was enough for him to meet a couple of friends once in awhile. When he could he crossed the bay in a steamer and met them in an Italian café, Il Vesuvio, facing the sea. They would drink beer and go their ways after strained efforts at conversation. However, the conversations heated up at the end of June when they read in the newspapers that Archduke Franz Ferdinand of Austria and his wife Sophie were killed at Sarajevo. And there was even more to discuss a month later when Austria-Hungary, out of retaliation for that despicable assassination, declared war on Serbia. Russia took their side, Germany aligned itself with Turkey and mobilized against Russia and then against France. Events came to a head, and one after the other and one against the other, as in a relentless chain, all the European states went to war, including Belgium and England. Italy declared itself neutral and kept out of it, while America stood by watching.

All of Europe was in flames; a giant massacre was taking place on the battlefields, but from so far away those events seemed remote and unreal. So while they were butchering each other over there, the three friends congratulated themselves on their good fortune to be sitting here calmly downing a pitcher of beer.

Sometimes it was the two brothers who would cross the bay, say hello to Caterina, and they would all take a walk around the neighborhood. After a policeman had severely scolded Luigino for talking too loudly and gesturing in the street, they began to stay in Gildo's Spartan little room, sit on his bed and talk about the news from the war fronts while quietly munching a sandwich accompanied by a glass of wine.

One evening Luigino suddenly changed the subject, as though propelled by an urgent need he couldn't postpone: blushing to his ears he went boldly into the thorny subject, observing that he was now more than twenty years old and had never been with a woman. What were they waiting for, to become decrepit old men? He had noticed a whorehouse of Italian prostitutes not far from there, with Italian customers, and what was to stop them from going there? It was time to try it. They had saved some money, they worked like slaves—didn't they have the right to some enjoyment?

Gildo turned red at those words. It was such a private subject that he found it embarrassing to talk about even with friends. It was better handled alone. He was continually pulled between two extremes: a tormenting desire that fomented wild fantasies, inevitably frustrated, and the fear of finding himself alone with a female body, as alien and as distant as the moon. He was uncomfortable when he had to talk to a woman he had never seen before, and who knows what one says in such a situation. He was ashamed of his absolute, too-long inexperience and boundless ignorance. He was afraid of being disappointed, of appearing green and unskilled, of arousing ridicule and sarcasm, and of leaving the encounter feeling humiliated rather than satisfied. Torn between opposing feelings, not the least the fear that his two friends might consider him a coward, he didn't know which way to turn and remained in embarrassed silence. Which Luigino broke with a sudden outburst: Go on, live! It seems like we're going to a funeral instead of visiting women! Come on, get moving! And because Gildo was hanging back, he took him by the arm and pushed him out the door.

It had not been a thrilling experience. The woman had taken his hand and led him like a baby to a filthy, disorderly room with an unmade bed and dirty sheets. She had him take off his trousers and underwear and energetically washed his genitals in a basin of dirty water. And since he hesitated with eyes averted, upset by that annoying and brutal effrontery and tempted by the desire to put his clothes back on and leave, she told him to hurry up, she didn't have time to lose, other customers were out there waiting for her. She had taken off her clothes and was stretched out on the bed, legs apart, snorting with impatience, as if she were dealing with a mental deficient. Calling him over she took his hand and put it between her legs. Gildo, paralyzed by her callous ways and disgusted by that obscene display, lost every desire. The woman went to work mechanically to arouse him and in a few minutes the sad business was over.

In a corner of his mind, along with his fears, he had cultivated visions of gentleness, smiles, tenderness, a dash of friendship, and he had imagined an incandescent desire that rose as spontaneously as in his solitary fantasies. What a fool. He had experienced only haste, coarseness, even aversion. Consequently he had been subjected to the old, painful conviction of being incapable of provoking kindness, but to that depressing thought he immediately contrasted his recent successes: Aniceto's lavish praise, the sympathetic audiences, the warm welcome, the flattering comments, and he felt cheered. He mustn't misunderstand or be deceived. That was a business and nothing more, a service for pay in which the less pleasant part certainly fell to the women closed up there inside. Now that he knew what it was about he could reduce it to what it was, a mechanical release that did not include courtesies or sentimental fluttering, and much less conversations which neither wanted. The next time he returned to the brothel, having produced the appropriate protective antibodies, he chose a younger woman, a fledgling like himself, and mastered the encounter with sufficient casualness. She was nineteen years old, from the Marches, named Maria, but at the brothel they had rebaptized her Suzy. At the third meeting she told him about a fellow countryman who, after getting an advance from her poor parents, had convinced them to let her leave with the mirage of honest work as a seamstress. When she arrived in America he took her passport and clapped her in the prison from which it was impossible to escape. That kind of work disgusted her. She was obliged to offer herself to obscene, slobbering old men. Thank goodness every once in awhile a nice, well-mannered man like him would come along. He had sympathized with her and treated her kindly, but the need for love, attention, affectionate consideration that crouched in his veins and sometimes drained them dry, would be found elsewhere. But he didn't know where or how or when.

Around Christmas and New Year's Eve he was invited to play more often than usual and earned more than he had ever imagined. He was happy and proud of himself. Since he was seen in public he took better care of his appearance. He liked to appear clean, well combed, and neat. He shaved carefully on Saturday and Sunday to the last whisker. He bought a new suit, jacket, trousers, and vest, a shirt with starched, detachable collar and cuffs, a matching tie, a pair of shoes and a hat with a narrow brim trimmed with a grosgrain ribbon. He seemed like another person: distinguished, slender, elegant, almost a gentleman. Certain that he wouldn't make a bad impression in the audience at the Washington Square Theater, he bought a ticket for the premiere of the *Barbiere di Siviglia*.

The theater was incredibly full of chattering, restless people: Italians, Irish, Russians, Hungarians, Polish, and even a small handful of Chinese. Gildo sat stiff and eager in his cheap seat almost at the back of the theater. He held his new hat on his knees, watching the heterogeneous, multicolored public chattering animatedly, and could barely contain his impatience for it to begin. For the first time he was going to see a lyric opera, a genre he knew only by word of mouth and from some arias heard on a record. He also allowed himself to buy the libretto for the occasion, and leafed through it to get an idea of the plot. Adelina Patti, Malibran, Enrico Caruso, celebrated singers dead or alive, heroes of a legendary myth from the celestial spheres, descended among the mortals to display their sublime art. However, those who would soon appear in flesh and blood were not well known, but that wasn't important. The event in itself was enough to thrill him, and the novelty to intoxicate him. Chills ran down his spine when, in a dissonant prelude to the harmonies of a magnificent living organism, the instruments in the orchestra pit began tuning up in a jumble of sounds. In the seat in front of him, a bare-shouldered young woman restlessly shook her brown curls, fiddled with an unpretentious necklace, raised an arm to straighten her hair, and with every movement spread an odor of hyacinths in the air. As if his look had pricked the back of her neck she suddenly turned, looked at him for an instant and smiled. Gildo became red as a lobster and quickly averted his eyes.

Suddenly the instruments were silent and the orchestra conductor entered, bowed, and the audience exploded into thunderous applause. Gildo listened rapturously to the fascinating overture: the scintillating arabesques of the strings, the triumphant power of the brass, the thunderous rumble of the drums, the tempestuous crescendo of the finale. When the curtain rose, Count Alma-viva intoned the serenade "Ecco ridente in cielo" under beautiful Rosina's balcony, Figaro sang his cavatina at the top of his lungs "...ah, che bel vivere, che bel piacere, per un barbiere di quali-tà...," the young soprano embroidered sweet notes, trills, warbles, enchanting embellishments in "Una voce poco fa," Don Basilio thundered hints of slander, Don Bartolo declaimed "A un dottor della mia sorte." At the end of each aria the spectators clapped their hands raw. Gildo's eyes grew moist and instead of applause he would have preferred a religious silence.

Between acts people went to the buffet. The young woman passed in front of him and gave him another look and smile. Gildo sank his eyes in the pages of the libretto and remained in his place. But at the end of the opera, when people began to swarm out of the theater he was sorry to have lost sight of her. With long, exul-tant steps, happy as he could ever remember being, he walked home through the silent and deserted streets, whistling the arias. As he unlocked his door he asked himself how did one say "feli-ce" in English? "Eppi," he answered his question and laughed.

Advised by Caterina, Gildo went to a banker from the Veneto, Innocenza Biachin, to whom she had for sometime turned over her savings, and recommended as honest and trustworthy. Bit by bit, he had saved almost one hundred dollars, and planned to buy a new accordion when he had scrapped enough together. Bigio's was becoming steadily more toneless, the bellows were beginning to gap at the joints, and the leather now worn by age was thin in some places and about to break. Recently the body was slightly damaged and he had repaired it as best he could, but it could break at any time, perhaps while he was playing.

One day he happened to pass by a store that sold musical in-struments. In the middle of the window, along with a guitar, man-dolin, violin, flute and trumpet, was a shiny accordion made in

Oregon by an Italian, Francesco Peranzi, as was stamped on the front. It cost an enormous amount, but it was worth it. It had keys of ebony and ivory, bellows of soft leather, a body with floral designs in embossed silver studded with colored stones that looked like emeralds and rubies, and straps of shiny black leather. As soon as he had a moment free he would run to plant himself in front of the object of his desires, brood over it, scrutinize every small detail, anticipate the moment when it would be his, and imagine that an instrument so precious, shiny and neat, would produce heavenly sounds. Beyond the window he sometimes exchanged glances with the owner who was watching him, at first indifferent, then curious, and finally frowning and suspicious. Did he, because of Gildo's patched old clothes, think he was a thief plotting a crime? A thief so reckless as to show his face? As the days went by the shopkeeper seemed reassured, his expression became more relaxed and friendly, and beyond the window he had even motioned a greeting. Until, at the hundredth ecstatic pause of that lanky young man with feverish eyes, he went to the door and invited him to come in. They didn't understand each other very well. Gildo's English was still basic, but his gestures were eloquent. At his request to try the instrument, the man was taken aback. He hesitated, perhaps doubtful about a stranger who didn't seem oozing with money, but softened by the ardent devotion that governed his behavior, he took the accordion out of the window and handed it to him.

From the first chords the sound of the instrument was magnificent, powerful, and as harmonious as a church organ. Gildo played the symphony of the *Barbiere di Siviglia* from start to finish with great enthusiasm. It seemed like a whole orchestra. At first Mr. Clifford listened to him incredulously, and then more and more amazed, realizing he was before real talent—and anyway, it was well known that music ran in Italian veins. When he finished the man nodded energetically, pleased and full of admiration.

With big smiles he applauded vigorously and launched into an animated discourse to congratulate him for his rare gift of absolute pitch, his fine ability to recognize and reproduce a sound with no need for the printed score. He really had a true, authentic musical talent. He had a sure future ahead of him, provided he could study with a good teacher. If Gildo had understood very little of that discourse, Mr. Clifford's passionate manner was enough to communicate his enthusiastic appreciation which filled Gildo with joy. Wildly excited, stumbling over his words, he did his best to explain that he intended to buy the accordion, but he didn't have the money yet; however, he played at different events and in several months he planned to buy it. Mr. Clifford, now won over, offered a discount on the spot, but Gildo sadly shook his head. Even that amount was beyond his reach. At that point it seemed like the deal was dead. Broken hearted, he was ready to leave in defeat, when the man suddenly, as if in a hurry before he changed his mind, enunciating clearly so as to make himself understood, proposed that Gildo give him what he had now and pay the remainder when he got it together. And he added that he would speak about him to some of his friends who owned a popular café that had dancing and he might be able to play there.

Beside himself with joy Gildo left the store and went running and jumping down the street. In a few days he withdrew a large part of his savings from Bianchin, and the precious jewel was in his room filling it with light. He kept the accordion near his bed, and at night its intrusion into his dreams woke him with a jolt. In the dark he touched it, caressed it, feeling the keys and the silver tooling, and when pacified went back to sleep. The lock and chain that had secured the old accordion to a leg of his cot in camp he now fixed to the door handle and to a hinge on the door jam. Now he had two keys in his pocket.

During Carnival he was hired to play at dances. His new accordion with its powerful sound was very much appreciated. He earned a good deal and the dollars added up, but the amount was still far from paying off his debt. He forced himself to be calm, like someone who has a secure future, but from time to time the fear gnawed at him of falling back into the miserable existence he had known, and he didn't dare give up the dirty, hard work at the port, as difficult as it was. There were alarming signs around. For some months the winds of disaster had been blowing in the county. Many jobs had been shut down and the workers let go, while others slowed down and some men worked only three or four days a week. The pinch worried Luigino and Giusepì who for fifteen days had worked off and on, and they had spent one week with arms crossed. The only construction sites that went at a mad pace were those of the lavish Panama-Pacific International Exposition, put up in the cove of Harbor View to celebrate the opening of the canal to take place on August 1914.

For too long he had not been in touch with his family. They didn't even know his address, and the more the months went by the more ashamed he was of his unjustifiable silence. And the more ashamed he felt the more he procrastinated. While he brushed his new suit before going to play at a birthday party, it occurred to him to include in the letter he would send to them a picture of himself in his elegant suit and hat. He was anxious to show his family how he had changed from that ragged fellow he had been when he left.

At the photographer's shop he chose a background with the prospect of a totally imaginary square in San Francisco, a building with shop windows and signs of shops and cafés shaded by awnings next to the Broadway Theater; behind the building, as though the sea were in the distance, sprouted masts of moored sailboats, on the right a two-storey second building topped by a tower. All fake, of course, but he hoped it would give those at home an idea of what a big city was like.

On the other hand, the topless automobile, a model-T Ford, was real, and on the front of the hood "San Francisco-1915" was written in large letters. The photographer had him sit in the driver's seat, one of the four seats of black leather quilted with lozenges. And he told him to hold his hands firmly on the wheel and look straight into the lens, as if he were really in that square and driving his own automobile. He had become a little sullen, staring as though frightened, but his suit was perfect. It gave off bright reflections of good quality material. The jacked collar framed the immaculate shirt and well-knotted tie. The crease of the trousers at his knee was straight and definite as if just ironed.

In May 1915 Italy entered the war against Austria-Hungry. The Italian-language newspapers, in block letters, celebrated the armed intervention, invoked the liberation of the countries oppressed for some time by foreign invaders, exalted the patriotism of those in favor of the conflict and expressed contempt for the lazy, worthless, slackers who opposed it.

In a few days the same newspapers published appeals to the emigrants residing in American to return to Italy and enlist in the army. The war would be short, they guaranteed, the government would pay their trip back and the return ticket to America at the end of the conflict. So there was nothing to worry them about the future. It was only a matter of a slight parenthesis, and every honorable citizen had the duty to respond to his country's call without delay.

Later the tone changed and became stern if not threatening: it warned that those who do not return from overseas to fight would be declared draft dodgers and would be unable to set foot on their native soil until thirty-two years old, not even for a quick visit to their family. If they returned before the time limit they would be arrested and imprisoned. For years.

Gildo was flabbergasted. He hadn't given a thought about returning, especially now that things were going so well and offers to play came from right and left. He lacked ten years from being thirty-two, the years of one's youth, those in which you struggle to reach your goals, because after that it's too late. It was unthinkable to toss it all away to go fight for the country you belonged to, certainly, but one that you felt absent and hostile, because it forced its people to emigrate to keep from dying of hunger. He had earned the very bitter bread of strangers since he was thirteen. What had his country done for him? Nothing. What obligations did he have? None. What would he get in exchange if he went back? Nothing. He felt only bitterness towards those politicians that didn't think twice about sending men to be slaughtered, while they stayed home sitting comfortably in their armchairs. Why had they never lifted a finger to get work for the thousands of desperate men who were hanging on to life by their fingernails? Why couldn't they do more than send them far away to suffer?

He met with Luigino and Giusepì, also alarmed by the news, and they discussed it at length. The two brothers had worked irregularly for two months. They were afraid the work site would close definitely, leaving them unemployed and looking for other hard-to-find work. Unemployment spread among the unqualified workers. The cost of rent, food, clothes had gone sky high, but salaries remained as they were and in some cases reduced because the owners took advantage of those in need. They heard that an employment agency was asking five dollars up front and twenty percent of the first month's pay, and in the end offered work unplugging a sewer, a two-day job.

Luigino raised the subject that a man who fails to report for military service couldn't go back before he was thirty-two, without ending up in prison. But Gildo said he was sure there would be an amnesty: if few or no men went back what would the government do? Would it keep hundreds of thousands of men from stepping foot in their own country? Maybe in the meanwhile the situation would get better and they would find work. They had to get busy asking and looking around. If they needed help he would gladly lend them some of his savings.

They say the war will soon be over, the usually silent Giusepì observed. Ordinarily he was the shadow of his older brother and let him do the talking while he listened reverently. They pay for our trip back, we do what we have to do, and then come back here. Anyway, we could see our family. Papa's gone, I haven't seen mama or my brothers and sisters in years.

His voice broke as if he were on the verge of tears and Luigino nodded. They had already decided, Gildo thought, and he felt awful. If they left he would be all alone.

That evening they went to Caterina's boarding house to hear what the other Italians had to say. They were all at home and a feverish discussion ensued, nourished with an ample supply of wine. No one seemed to be burning with patriotism, and much less by the desire to go fight, except one man from Trentino and two from Gorizia who had had a taste of occupation and couldn't wait until the Krauts were kicked out. They described the Austrians as sauerkraut eaters, fat as pigs, drunk on beer from morning to night, violent and arrogant.

The older men felt safe and handed out opinions and advice. The young men, reluctant to leave, worried about not being able to return home before they were thirty-two years old, that is, almost old. As if he were begging them not to leave him, he endlessly repeated that the shirkers of military service would be given amnesty. They couldn't put thousands of thousands of men in prison for years. The people would rebel. But no one paid attention to him.

Although no one had settled on a date to return, since it didn't depend on them but on the amount of money they could accumulate, they worried about it a great deal. They pretended to be free to go and come whenever they wanted, even if it was only wishful thinking. They were disparagingly called "birds of passage," accused of not putting down roots, of staying in one place just long enough to get a little money together—the amount determining how much feeling they had about America. The few who were convinced that America was now their country and intended to stay there, because their own country had nothing to offer but hunger and misery, boiled with rage and homesickness at the thought that their return was blocked for years under pain of imprisonment.

Supposing, as was said, that the war lasted only a year. A man from Como asked who would make up for the loss of twelve months pay? The ridiculous soldiers' pay? Or the disgusting military rations that still made him want to vomit just thinking about it? And if it lasted longer—two, three, four years? How could you know? Who would provide for their families left without the money they sent? The government? And the families where all the men had emigrated and where there were only old people, women and children—how could they manage? And if they didn't go, the villagers would say they were stinking cowards that didn't give a damn, while those in Italy were forced to sign up with no way to avoid it.

Oh, comrades, in war you go to die, a Tuscan had interjected. After those matter-of-fact words there was a long dismayed silence. Gildo held his breath, but no one replied. Go back? Not go back? The question still hovered in the air when they took leave of each other late at night.

Luigino and Giusepì embarked on a ship at the San Francisco port on July 1915, along with a large group of their fellow countrymen. That there were so many of them surprised Gildo. Only later did he learn that there had been three thousand. Suddenly he felt excluded, as if relegated to a corner. He went with them to the wharf, helping with their baggage and waited there until the ship pulled away. He had been miserable while he waited. Giusepì, all keyed up, kept walking back and forth with his hands in his pockets and his cap pulled down to his eyes. Luigino had kept his arm around Gildo's shoulder all the time, every once in a while looking at him, smiling sadly, and hugging him tighter. Be good, he had whispered, be good, you'll see I'll come back soon. Now his only friend was gone and he didn't know if he would ever see him again. He felt an agonizing desire to hold him close. He could barely hold back his tears, his mouth trembled, his arms hung inertly, his eyes stared into nothingness. Separation was an unbearable pain.

They had never spoken of that horrible evening on the train track, when Luigino had struggled to the last moment to snatch him from death, and he had succeeded. Gildo owed his life to him and felt embarrassed about that moment of weakness. If he hadn't saved him he would never have known the joy that music had given him, but only the brutal exhaustion of the pick and shovel. The two unfortunate brothers, in what for them had been a cruel adventure, had lost their father and kept with pick and shovel work. They were going back home nearly as poor as had they left, and a war was waiting for them over there. He remembered Luigino's convulsive sobs when he hit him on his chest and they lay in the dark on the escarpment. The only person in the world who had ever cried for him. Now he was alone, and gasping like he was drowning. Stock-still on the wharf he waved at the ship that was moving out of the bay thick with fog until it disappeared.

After reaching the Genoa port, as soon as they got off the ship, the two brothers were loaded onto a train, unloaded at a barracks and then sent to the front. They didn't get even a minute at home.

A month later a letter arrived from Carolina: mama and all of them had been very worried about his long silence. They didn't know what to think. Thank goodness the photograph with him driving that magnificent automobile had reassured them about his good health and excellent situation. They were glad about his good fortune and hoped he would send money as soon as possible. Lorenzo had come back from prison March '14, thin and haggard... and as soon as he had put on a little weight he was called back into the army and had just left for the front in the Isonzo valley. It had been almost six years, between military service, war in Libya, and prison, and now he was starting all over. He was truly unfortunate. Early in 1913, Giacomo and Ninetta had gone to America, leaving their baby with relatives. Giacomo was in Concrete, in the state of Washington, working for a cement factory, and his wife Ninetta kept a boarding house for Italian workmen. They had had a little girl, and named her after grandma Lucia. She was pregnant again and would have the baby in six months. She included his brother's address and advised Gildo to write him. They had finally received word from their father in Montana, but he didn't give a return address. Perhaps he had forgotten. He said he worked as a master mason in charge of many workers, but he had sent them such a small amount of money they didn't know how they could manage. Many of the young men of Abbazzia and nearby villages had left for the war. Only old people, women and children were left and people were dying from hunger. On Sundays the priest prays for the safety of the soldiers on the front. However, the sons of Berto della Calchera's widow had come back in a box. She hoped that the war would end soon and the men would return home safe and sound. Giacomo had written that he would not enlist. Had Gildo decided whether to come back or stay there?

16

When he thought back over the last eight months after Luigino and Giusepì left for the war, Gildo seemed to remember that the signs of the financial crisis had been almost imperceptible at first, so that nothing seemed to have really changed. Only with the passing of time had the signs become more obvious, but he had purposely ignored them or underestimated them, as if he wanted to shake off his uneasiness and feel a confidence that sometimes vacillated. He listened gladly to those who said that America was always having highs and lows but they were nothing to worry about. It is a prosperous country, strong, determined, resolute, capable of rising up from the most ruinous slumps in the blink of an eye.

At a certain moment the worsening situation had become so apparent that you'd have to be blind not to see it. Salaries were reduced, much work was suspended definitely and others were off and on, unemployed men loafed around aimlessly in the streets, or crowded the bars and, discouraged about their uselessness and unemployment, drank their last penny and staggered around drunk on the sidewalks. Stores had few customers. Those with some income bought the bare necessities or inferior food at bargain prices. Women often importuned the shopkeepers for scraps, rancid pork rind, moldy cheese crusts, animal organs, leftover fat and bones for broth. Gildo was more careful about how much he spent, also. He noticed that men and women who looked down-and-out walked to work instead of taking a tram, so as to save a few cents.

As a result the number of burglaries had risen in the city. Rumor had it that some of the laid-off workers, not knowing how to make ends meet, stole whatever they could get their hands on and resold it to fences for whatever they could get.

Caterina's boarders who remained after others left for the war asked for a reduction in rent since their salaries had been cut. To make a profit she was forced to take in more boarders and add straw mats even in the kitchen and hallway, making the house so overcrowded it was hard to move.

At first the celebrations went on as before, but the compensation became less generous. Two dollars normally, and sometimes three. Then the events rapidly became fewer and less elaborate, and he had to face facts. Not only was it lack of money that tightened the purse strings, but also expanding bad humor, tension, anxiety that took away all desire for celebrating. People seemed to be shut up inside themselves, fearful and circumspect, as though waiting for the worst. Those who had families in Italy in the war zone or relatives fighting on the front had further reason for a heavy heart.

Between Christmas and New Year's Eve he had been called to play only twice, and at Carnival for one dance only. Two brothers from Abruzzi opened a restaurant in the neighborhood and hired him for its inauguration, but pulled out at the last moment. They had spent more than they had planned to and couldn't afford any more. Those who had thought about celebrating golden or silver wedding anniversaries had to give up the idea. Wedding and engagement parties were postponed or took place quietly. Baptisms and First Communions were downgraded to private ceremonies with a few close friends and relatives.

Before the financial slump got so bad he had left his work at the port. While unloading a cart he had slashed the palm of his right hand on the corner of a steel box. The wound wasn't serious, but it was two weeks before he could play again, and the company didn't pay his salary. Aniceto, the fruit and vegetable salesman had urged him to quit, it was heavy work and dangerous for a musician. There was always the risk of permanently damaging a hand, and then you could kiss your musical career goodbye. They called him to play often enough, didn't they? And he earned enough, didn't he? Why break his back like that for a little bit of money? If Gildo needed more money later he would help him find work.

He bought new sheet music to study. Now he could decipher the notes easily, but he was still slow and hesitant in translating them onto the keys. He had time now to practice and did so meticulously every day. He was determined to learn all he could about music, musicians, singers, composers. In a secondhand shop he found a book in Italian about the life of Gioacchino Rossini and swallowed it in one gulp.

Gildo had not yet been able to put the sum aside that he owed Mr. Clifford, even though he had an engagement as soloist on Tuesdays and Thursdays for four dollars an evening in a café of someone he knew. The Americans did not seem touched by the economic squeeze, and not even by the war in Europe. The place was always full of happy and noisy people who shoveled in the food and drink. Mr. Clifford had been kind and understanding: not only did he never hurry him, but also he had been agreeable to his offer to pay the money a little at a time as he could save it up. Don't worry, he said, he could wait. Gildo went to Bianchin to deposit his savings. He still lacked forty dollars and couldn't wait to pay off his debt and finally breathe freely.

March 1916: he would never forget those early days of spring. It was like being struck by continual, booming rounds of thunder, sinister messages of disaster, because that's when it all started.

A short letter from Carolina announced that Lorenzo had been killed on the front at Isonzo. Gildo had felt a terrible blow to his chest, and before his eyes, instead of his brother's image, appeared that of Luigino on his back with his guts ripped open, his uniform soaked in blood, his face smeared with mud, his dead eyes wide open. Except for a Christmas card he had heard nothing from him, and he often worried about what had happened. But why, he chastised himself, had he thought of Luigino instead of Lorenzo? His brother was practically a stranger; he hadn't seen him in ten years, since he had gone to Switzerland. The distance certainly didn't help them get to know each other. They had become strangers and being of the same blood didn't matter. He could vaguely remember his features, his tall and robust body and a tuft of brown hair following over his forehead. As solitary and silent as he, they had almost never talked when children, so he couldn't blame himself if news of his brother's death had made so little impression, like a distant event taking place in a distant world. When he delved far back in time he felt neither touched nor saddened, almost as if the present difficulties had forced him to bury the past. Carolina's scanty letter mentioned the sorrow of their mother, sick and bent with fatigue. Angry remorse had suddenly overcome him and he took the ten dollars he had hidden in the pillowcase and sent it to them with a letter. The last letter they would receive from him.

A couple of weeks later he ran into Aniceto, followed by one of his sons who trudged behind him out of breath. Aniceto was beside himself as he toured the neighborhood searching for his stolen bicycle. It was practically new and had cost him a fortune. He had furnished it with a basket for his son for making home deliveries to his rich American customers. Each evening he had locked it up inside the warehouse next to his store. That morning he had found the door broken, and along with the bicycle, two cases of oranges, his weighing scales, bunches of oregano and basil were missing—a sure sign that the thieves were fellow countrymen from the south. What would polenta eaters from the north do with those herbs that the southerners use in pizza and tomato sauce? Gildo followed him in his furious search, even though Aniceto thought it unlikely that even the most careless thief would leave stolen goods in plain sight on the street. He knocked on the doors of people he knew and with a voice altered by rage asked for information, but with no result. Even though they knew they wouldn't rat on anyone, as was the custom where they came from. He didn't report it to the police because not only would they not move a finger, but they would laugh their heads off at the immigrants' misfortune. They had no sympathy for them and snickered among themselves as if to say: that's just too bad. Instead of coming here to be a nuisance you should have stayed in your country. They were sure that the Italians stole from each other, and they weren't entirely wrong. Aniceto thought so too. So what if they were poor wretches out of work. What did that have to do with him? For years he had been just as poor and had worked like a slave to be independent, but now people were beginning to feel the business slump and they only wanted overripe apples and leftover vegetables.

In May he went to deposit fifteen dollars with Bianchin. Just another ten and Mr. Clifford would be paid in full. He expected to do it by the end of the month. That debt weighed on him heavily and he couldn't wait to get out from under it.

Bianchin wasn't there. In his place sat a young man with greasy hair and a pretentious mustache. The boss had gone to Sacramento for important business and would be back in a few days. He took deposits, he replied to a man who wanted to withdraw money, but he wasn't authorized to make withdrawals, which Mr. Bianchin would tend to personally. He should be back by the end of the week. The man had grumbled, but then resigned himself and went away.

Gildo deposited his dollars, and as he was leaving he met Caterina with her dirty deposit book in hand, She was coming for the second time to withdraw what she needed. Bianchin would soon be back, she had been told, but now almost a week had gone by and the answer was always the same. She was beginning to feel uneasy: what was the banker doing in Sacramento all that time? She really needed that money. How could he expect people to wait his convenience? And who was that young man no one had ever seen before in the neighborhood?

Gildo turned pale. What was going on? The two of them went back into the office to demand their rights. At Caterina's peremptory questions the young man scratched his nose, and with the greatest calm answered that the boss had unfortunately been delayed longer than expected. It was very important business, it took time to finish, she had to be patient and come back within two, three days at most, and she would find him as always at the disposition of his customers. Exasperated, Caterina told him off, but the guy remained unperturbed, shrugged his shoulders, opened his arms, said he was sorry but there was nothing he could do.

The next day they went back together. Gildo asked for the fifteen dollars he just deposited, as surely he still had it, but the substitute refused. He had to respect the orders he had been given, he babbled. Gildo trembled with rage. It was now clear that something was wrong, but he forced himself to keep his suspicions to himself. A group of people had formed outside who demanded to see Bianchin, each one wanting to withdraw money. Caterina was enraged. She seemed to be suffocating. She held a hand to her throat and excitedly whispered some prayers, which she interrupted to incite the others: Something fishy is going on. I smell a rat. I've never seen anyone disappear like that, taking so long to come back, and leaving someone in his place without authorizing him to pay. It's our hard-earned money, for heaven's sake, not his!

The young man sat tranquilly at the window, scribbling on a sheet of paper, glancing at a newspaper, and from time to time nonchalantly looking at the rebellious crowd, and to anyone who questioned him he serenely responded that they should be patient and return the next day, or better, in two or three days, and the boss would certainly be there as usual.

That night Gildo woke up many times nagged by terrible premonitions. In a cold sweat, his heart pounding wildly, anguish washed over him. He paced the floor until dawn without being able to calm down.

He went back the next day and the next, and as the news spread and hopes dwindled, the waiting group expanded until it became an ever noisier and more agitated crowd. Some swore, others cursed the banker, Caterina cried without restraint, Gildo forced himself to be calm, but he felt he was going crazy. Honest and trusting, he had turned over all his money to that crook who had cleared off. It was the worst thing that could have happened to him.

The young man, left alone to face the furious crowd, decided at a certain point it would be prudent to lock the office, and from there looked through the glass in fright. His fear must have grown because he got up from the table, closed the dusty torn drapes and disappeared from view. Those outside, even more angry, furiously shook the handle, knocked on the glass, shouted insults, threatened bodily harm, threatened to tell the police, waved their fists. Someone made a throat-cutting gesture. They shouted: Bastard, thief, coward, scoundrel, come out if you have the courage!

When it grew dark the substitute didn't turn on the light. He must have been crouching in a corner waiting for them to leave. For a while they waited for him to come out. They were so angry they would have lynched him, but he didn't risk it. Only late at night, when they were worn out from waiting and went home to sleep, did he go look warily up and down the street, and then slip along the wall like a shadow and vanish.

After a sleepless and anxiety-ridden night, Gildo hurried to the place the next morning. He found the door locked and the office deserted and he was devastated. Struck by a pain that cut him in two, he kept a certain distance from the livid crowd of silent, glaring men and weeping women. At one blow he had lost all he had. Now he was left with nothing. Stunned, inert, he contemplated his ruin. Caterina was leaning against the wall, holding her now useless bankbook to her breast and sobbing. What will I do, she moaned, Lord, what will I do. It's the end. I'm finished.

They kept on gathering there for days, as though those tricked out of their life's savings were expecting some kind of a miracle. Gradually the crowd thinned as the victims became sadly resigned to their fate. A group of them went to make a complaint at the police station. The police took down everyone's name and the amount they lost, but that's as far as it went: the dirty business of cheating between cheating Italians. Better to let them work it out.

The news of Bianchin's flight fell like lightning on the community. In a panic people ran en masse to withdraw their savings entrusted to other neighborhood bankers, which were sadly bankrupt in a couple of days.

The night in which he lost the last of his illusions, Gildo hadn't closed his eyes. Lying on his bed prostrated by that misfortune, he accused himself of ingenuousness, gullibility, and even stupidity, for trusting in Bianchin, even though many others had done the same. The bugbear of poverty, so feared and thought buried forever, became frighteningly real. After that blow that had impoverished him he realized how his situation, which had seemed secure, was really fragile and precarious, how exposed to injustice and arbitrary power it was, and how everything that he had won could suddenly be taken from him, including his accordion, whose shape he could see in the darkness by his bed. He was afraid that when Mr. Clifford found out that he couldn't pay what he owed would want it back. He supposed he had the right, since he hadn't kept his word, even if it wasn't his fault. At that thought he shuddered and his hair bristled. It would be lost. He clung to the hope that Mr. Clifford wouldn't take it back considering his talent: perhaps his music, his beloved music, would be saved. But he mustn't forget Mr. Clifford was a businessman, and therefore his interests would override hypothetical impulses of generosity.

Then he scolded himself for not paying his debt all along when had the money; if he had done that he would now have it nearly paid off and he wouldn't have lost everything. At that time he had appreciated the shop owner's faith in him, but in the end he would turn against him. Gildo had spent more than a year saving what he needed, and now he seriously doubted Mr. Clifford would be willing to wait for an undetermined period. How could he blame him?

With his eyes wide open in the dark he had made an accounting of his earnings. After that disaster he was left with the eight dollars a week he earned at the café and what he got for the occasional party. Enough to get by on and some to give the shopkeeper. A tenuous ray of hope was lit in his desperation. However, he couldn't find the courage to go face his reaction, which even in the best of scenarios would not be indulgent: He had to give himself time to digest that shock, resign himself to it, encourage himself to overcome it.

On Tuesday he shaved and combed his hair with special care, put on his new suit and went to play in the café. He played the latest dance tunes and to please the customers, passionate and tireless dancers, he concluded with Offenbach's wild cancan. It was met with loud applause and, in addition to his regular pay, he received larger than usual tips.

With that money he hurried to pay rent for June, and to be at ease he also paid for July. Food was no worry: he would be satisfied with bread and cheese, as in the past, when he worked in the northern construction sites, and it wouldn't kill him. Rosa Cencini, the skinflint landlady, as bullheaded as a tax collector, always came for her money on the evening of the last day of the month: she knocked insistently on the door, almost tore the dollars out of his hand, counted and then recounted them before putting them in her bodice, and never said thank you.

Overcoming his shyness Gildo went to a couple of bars with his accordion to see if they wanted him to play in the evenings. He played them a dance tune, a waltz, and to impress them he finished with a lively Strauss march, but the only result was a curt dismissal. On his way home, feeling downhearted, it occurred to him that if he really hit bottom he could play on street corners of fashionable neighborhoods. He had often run across mediocre players of barrel organs, guitars, mandolins; they would leave their hats upturned on the sidewalk and the passersby would throw in five, ten cents, and sometimes even a quarter. He was a professional, he could play a wide repertory well, and his hat would surely be filled. Like a beggar, he thought, without having the guts for it. But the important thing was that he could do it without hesitation if he had to. Maybe some important person who loved music would notice him, take him off the street and hire him for parties or concerts. He had heard stories like that. Not all was lost, he consoled himself. No one could steal his precious resource, a fact rooted in his head, blood, muscles, ears, hands, and every single finger.

When he felt he had built up enough energy and a dash of daring, he went to Mr. Clifford, resolved to fight his battle. He would tell him about his financial disaster and beg him to give him more time to pay off the debt. Another year, he figured. As he spent most of his time with Italians his English hadn't improved. He forced himself to remember the few words he knew and to assemble them in an appropriate speech. As he walked he became bolder and convinced himself that not only would the shop owner be sympathetic about what had happened, but as a lover and connoisseur of music who admired him, he wouldn't have the heart to refuse him help. He wasn't just any accordion player. He was an expert musician endowed with real talent, which Mr. Clifford had fully appreciated.

When he reached the store his heart began pounding like a drum. In front of the man who stood there waiting, he fell into a state of confusion. His elementary English was terribly mangled, broken, and incomprehensible. So much so that the man told him to calm down and begin again. When he finally understood, he arched his eyebrows, and in his look of annoyance Gildo caught a flash of mistrust, as though he didn't believe him. He hadn't expected this and he couldn't understand it. Why did he doubt him? Why would he want to lie? Disconcerted, gnawed by feverish anxiety, he didn't know what to say.

Mr. Clifford looked away quietly lost in thought. What was he brooding about? Why didn't he say something? He stood stiffly with his arms crossed, and on his stern face Gildo saw a hostility he didn't know how to handle. In the face of that prolonged, devastating silence he had forgotten to beg and plead and just waited in agony for him to speak.

Finally the man pronounced the coldhearted sentence: he had put the greatest faith in him, though he was a perfect stranger and what is more, a foreigner, unfortunately, as he was beginning to realize. But he was a man of good intentions. He had had the goodness to wait more than a year to be paid, and then to find out that he did not intend to keep his part of the bargain. The reason for this was of no concern to him — that was his business. At this point he had to consider his own interests, and Gildo should return the accordion at once, otherwise he would report him for fraud. In the meantime the instrument had been used and he couldn't sell it as new; therefore he would keep down payment to compensate his loss.

Gildo stood rooted to the ground. He hoped he had misunderstood, but Mr. Clifford's glacial expression cancelled out every illusion. Floundering and stumbling over his words, he tried to defend himself: if he returned the accordion he wouldn't be able to earn his living and would be condemned to starvation. And besides music was his passion and reason for living that he could never never never give up.

The stiff-necked Mr. Clifford didn't give an inch. Sorry, he said automatically. Those were the rules for someone who reneged on paying for what he bought. He must bring the accordion back at once or he would get a visit from the police.

For the last time he went to play at the café, intending to tell the owner that he wouldn't be coming any more, without explaining the why and wherefore. But the owner beat him to it and went up to him as soon as he came in the door, curtly informing him he didn't need him any more. Gildo glanced around the room and noticed a group of musicians already sitting on the platform. Did the storekeeper have a hand in it?

Slowly he headed back to the house and collapsed fully dressed on his bed. The next day he didn't leave his room. He picked at a piece of stale bread and some leftover cheese. For the last time he picked up the instrument and performed for himself. As always the music burst from the instrument like a tongue of flame, but it faded away in lacerating sadness. He dedicated himself to shining the silver, and cleaning the black and white keys one by one so there wouldn't be the slightest sign of use. He dusted and rubbed the case and leather strap with care and said goodbye with a long caress. The next morning it would go back to Mr. Clifford.

Toward sunset he went to the port to ask to be rehired, but the foreman told him that there was no need for more men. Later, after the sun had set, he went to Aniceto in search of any work whatever. The fruit and vegetable man was surprised: why in the world did he want to go back to backbreaking work? Now he was a musician, it was his profession, it was how he made his living. Did he want to injure his hands again? He should take care of is hands, because they were so important.

Gildo had trouble getting the words out, but he briefly summarized the latest installment of his misadventures. Aniceto was flabbergasted and angered by Mr. Clifford's ruthlessness, just like everyone here, with a few exceptions. All they thought about was making money. That was all that interested them. He would have been happy to lend him the money to finish paying for the accordion, but unfortunately he didn't have it. He was broke. Business wasn't good. He didn't even have the money to buy a new bicycle. He had to tighten his belt. People weren't buying anything and he didn't know how they lived. They had to eat, didn't they? Some poor devils go around with faces the color of hunger, that yellowish and grayish color of someone who doesn't get enough to eat. Others who couldn't pay their rent have been evicted and sleep on the street. "Omeless," they call them. If they were Americans they would live on some kind of public assistance, but emigrants without money who have lived in America less than five years, risk being sent back to their own country. Luckily the weather was nice, and they could sleep in the open without fear of freezing. But what will those poor devils do in the winter? As far as work goes he concluded, scratching his head, it was a bad time. He didn't know anyone looking for workers, but he would spread the word.

Sometime after nightfall he reached home. He rummaged in his pants' pocket to find the key, found it, and felt blindly in the dark for the chain and lock. But he couldn't feel them. Surprised he groped around the keyhole and under that light pressure the door gave way. At that moment he had a terrible premonition and the blood froze in his veins. He pushed the door open, which squeaked on its hinges as always, and felt his way to the shelf with the small stove, took a match out of the box, and lit a gas light. It lit up the room, but he hesitated before turning. Suddenly he had a sharp pain in his temples, like a knife buried in his flesh. He squeezed his head in his hands, breathed deeply a few times, and slowly turned.

The accordion was not there. Nor his hat, shoes, and new suit that he kept on a coat hanger hung on a nail in the wall. He sat bent over on the bed, his elbows resting on his knees. In this position he remained for some time without moving, staring at the floor. Then he got up and with a candle went to inspect the door. The lock had been forced, the rings that he had screwed to the door-jamb, along with the ripped off chain and lock, were lying on the floor.

17

Ninetta's boarding house now had six men who worked in a brickworks factory, added to the ten cement factory workers. All Italians, crammed into three rooms. The house was chockfull and no one could turn around. She dreamed of having a bedroom to herself to share with Giacomo and another for the children. Instead they all had to sleep together, one at the head and one at the foot of the same little bed. For fear the children might awaken and be startled, she and Giacomo didn't often get intimate, and when it happened they took a thousand precautions, trying not to talk or breathe, and it all took place quickly and in silence. They pined for the passionate hunger that had once possessed them, that reciprocal, wild frenzy for each other's bodies that flamed up, swept them away, made them entirely forget the world, and they felt a great longing for that fever, like a precious thing lost.

The problem was not entirely the children's presence, or the noisy group of men that invaded the house at certain hours, or the exhaustion that made them collapse like dead weights in bed at night, with just a slight caress before falling into deep sleep. The bitter truth was that desire had gone out like a burned candle.

Ninetta fantasized that it would rise again intact and even more passionate if they were left alone and had the time and peace for themselves. While she bustled about she daydreamed that at night, after straightening the kitchen and putting the little ones to sleep, she would sit with Giacomo on the veranda steps to enjoy the cool and quiet of the night animated by the crickets' song, her head resting on his shoulder, whispering something. Wrapped in the smell and warmth of his body, a faded languor would sweep her veins, a burning hand of desire would reach inside her dress, a shiver would run down her back.

Mornings she got up at five o'clock in the dark, and she didn't stop running until midnight, blinded with fatigue. She did everything herself: cooked lunch and supper for twenty people, made the beds, cleaned the rooms, once every two weeks she did an enormous washing. She refused to sew and mend her boarders' clothes. Each man could manage for himself, she only had two hands. She was precise, orderly, demanding, and didn't tolerate dirt. What is more, after the birth of her second daughter, Giuditta, a year ago, she had become terribly sensitive to smells. The reek of dirt and sweat turned her stomach. She expected the men to wash up before supper and appear at the table neat and combed as if every day was Sunday. In the big cellar room she had had a row of sinks installed, each with a piece of soap, and she watched to make sure that from the first to the last, including Giacomo, took off their clothes down to their belt, carefully soaped their face, neck, underarms, head, to remove the filth that encrusted their skin and stuck to their hair. Once a week she demanded they wash their feet. She couldn't stand the disgusting stench that permeated the house.

At first some had rebelled at those extravagant demands. They had never washed so much in their life. All that bother to clean up when they just got dirty again the next day, and everyone knows that too much soap was not good for your skin. What was her problem? She commanded like a general, as though they were a platoon of recruits in a barracks. Eventually they got used to it and even developed a liking to appear at the table fresh and clean.

She forged on with bowed head, somber, hard, brooding over her great disappointment. The land of plenty so raved about had turned out to be a mirage, something that had seemed within reach, but which gradually moved farther away. She hadn't seen a sign of good fortune. Giacomo had the same job and earned barely enough to make ends meet. Thanks to the sixteen boarders she not only paid the rent, but also had paid off the debt to the secondhand man and the priest and had set aside a nest egg for emergencies. She worked like a beast of burden. Some days she just couldn't take anymore and wondered how long she could keep it up before collapsing.

The little girls required constant care. She had to watch Giuditta every moment: adventurous and fearless, staggering around on her little legs she poked her head into every thing, risking serious harm to herself every time. Lucia was jealous of her. When she thought no one was looking she enjoyed pulling Giuditta's hair and ears, pinching her cheeks, pushing her and knocking her down. And she laughed boisterously every time her little sister broke into sobs. Sometimes when they made a commotion or messed up something Ninetta had just put in order, her eyes would grow dark and she would grab them and slap their faces. Afterwards she would be sorry, take them on her knees, console them, and dry their tears. And when they calmed down she would hug them so tightly they would begin to cry again and struggle to get away. From a safe distance they would look at her like she was a witch and for a while wouldn't let her come near. Sometimes while she held them she would burst into tears and the little girls, frightened, would join her in chorus.

One morning while in the backyard hanging up the two weeks of laundry, she fainted from exhaustion. When she came to, she found little Lucia beside her, calling her name and crying, pounding her chest to wake her up.

In July of 1916 she discovered she was pregnant again.

All the anxieties he had ever known came back to attack him like hungry wolves. For days, like a mad man, with an exertion that squeezed his throat and stabbed his throbbing temples, he wandered around from morning to night in search of the stolen accordion. He knocked on neighbors' doors, those whom his music had so cheered, and questioned everyone he met, but everyone just shrugged. No one had seen anything. To hear them tell it on the night of the theft they were shut up in their houses or even asleep, including the landlady who bristled angrily as if the question hid an accusation or suspicion. She ordered him to get the damaged lock repaired and reminded him that she would be there punctually on the last day of the month to get the August rent.

He walked as far as the business center. Many times he had crossed the seemingly endless Market Street and adjacent California and Montgomery Streets, where strolling mandolin, guitar and hand organ musicians played, sometimes accompanied by pale and ragged children who held their hands out to the passersby. When the sound of an accordion would reach him his heart would leap, and short of breath he would run in that direction, inflamed by the mad hope for some miracle, even though he knew he was fooling himself. The sound of his instrument, full, warm, sonorous, was unmistakable even at a distance, and in fact he was always disappointed. It was just any old second-rate instrument, nothing like his dazzling beauty. Determined, inconsolable, with a dazed look, and gripped by unceasing torment, he continued to wander through the streets at random.

Every morning, as soon as the stalls were opened he would search the market around the port where used and stolen goods were sold, and where there were receiver's warehouses crammed to the ceiling, but he never found a trace; nor did he in the places where he had played on some evenings. Sticking his head in just to have a look was enough to be shown the door because of his shabby appearance.

He didn't go to the police. He remembered what Aniceto had said when his bicycle disappeared, about how useless it was to report a theft, considering that the most you would get out of the police would be cynical disinterest if not downright meanness. Nothing but dirty business between foreigners who can sort it out between themselves. He couldn't have stood their rudeness, their mocking little smiles and looks of contempt. Swallowing his rage had made him tense and coiled as a spring, close to exploding at the slightest rudeness or annoyance, often at the wrong moment or the wrong person. He didn't even go to Aniceto. It would be a waste of time to go to someone who had been robbed with no good outcome. And much less would he go to Caterina, as crushed as he by a similar disaster.

Gildo would return at night, destroyed by anguish, feverish. He shut the door as best he could, but the forced lock hung crookedly to the side. Lack of money had kept him from getting it repaired, and for a makeshift sort of protection he propped a chair against the door before going to bed. Anyone could have come in, but he didn't care. He wasn't afraid of losing anything now that there was nothing to steal. He would throw himself on the bed without lighting the lamp and lie there for hours with eyes wide open in the dark, staring at the pale light coming in the window. The blood pounded in his throbbing temples, and frightening visions of abandonment, poverty and hunger swirled in his brain. He would decide to go to Mr. Clifford the next day to tell him what happened, and the next morning he wouldn't have the courage and would postpone it until the following day.

Finally he made up his mind and left for the store. For the entire way he felt like an axe was hanging over his head about to drop. He knew beforehand that the shop owner would doubt his honesty and accuse him of stealing it, and he even imagined the flash of anger that would spring from his eyes and the sharp look of a deeply offended person being told deceitful lies. He felt the apprehension of not being believed when he was telling the pure truth, of not being able to convince him, of suffering a wrong and not knowing how to defend himself.

Then Mr. Clifford had spoken. The theft of the accordion according to him was a clever way to get out of paying for it, a stunt to trick him. He was convinced that he had hidden it waiting for the waters to calm. Gildo replied that if it really was that way, he could have left without coming, it was easy to disappear, to change cities, to lose every trace. Instead he had come.

The shopkeeper had suddenly gone berserk. He gestured, yelled, swore. Gildo didn't grasp the meaning of the words of that virulent outburst, but the infuriated tone and bulging eyes were enough. He threatened to report him to the police, just what he feared the most, he understood perfectly, and he knew very well that the officers would believe the accusations of an American citizen over the excuses of an immigrant, furthermore one who was unable to express himself in proper English. There was no escape. He had never stolen anything in his life, not even a piece of bread when he was hungry in Renton. And although he had suffered two crushing thefts, he was the one who was accused of thievery. An atrocious mockery of fate.

In the face of that burning injustice, he felt a violent burst of rage and thought that he had the right to defend himself in any way he could, even dishonestly, even by disappearing. Who could find him in this enormous America if he left San Francisco? But where would he go? To whom? He thought fleetingly of joining Giacomo in Concrete, but with a surge of pride he immediately rejected that. There was no way he would run to the family that had thrown him out without a second thought. He was too ashamed of being down and out, and preferred that those at home went on believing in his good fortune, as the picture of him at the wheel of the Ford convertible attested. And even if he let himself be tempted by the idea of going to his brother, he had only a little change left, barely enough for food, never mind a train ticket. And work was out of the question. Swarms of unemployed men and women milled around, and the refusals he could imagine would have wounded him further. No one needed him. He was superfluous, useless. He had no future. Everything ahead was darkness.

July was nearly over. He had paid the room rent until the end of the month, but in a few more days he wouldn't have a place to live. He would join the 'omeless in their nightly lairs, and like them would dig in garbage cans for leftover food and in garbage bins at restaurant backdoors. He felt a shiver of horror. He was beaten, finished, defeated. What was left for him to do?

On the evening of July 31 he closed the window and stretched out on his bed. The summer heat was stifling in the room. He was waiting for the police sent by Mr. Clifford to break into the room, arrest him and take him to prison in handcuffs. The chair would fall with a great crash, but it wouldn't wake him up.

He listened to the quiet hiss of the gas, a low whisper like a light sea breeze. The smell of boiled cabbage made him think of his mother who would fry the garden cabbage with onions and a bit of lard because the children hated the smell of boiling cabbage. The knife would strike the cutting board with the steady rhythm of a horse ride. When a child he would whistle a happy little song to that gallop, a meaningless nursery rhyme that the mothers in the valley sang to their children while she bounced them on her knees. He could only remember the beginning: *Flic floc ol terloc d'ol sberloc...* But he could never remember riding on his mother's knees.

A pleasant drowsiness weighed on his eyelids and loosened his contracted muscles. He seemed to be floating in mid air, in a confused half-wakefulness of jumbled thoughts. The noises outside were muffled: the cartwheels rolling in the street, the horses' hooves thudding in the stalls, the children yelling in the alley, a woman's voice calling, a door slamming, a hammer pounding rhythmically on a nail. Everyday life.

Gildo wondered what sorts of noises Luigino heard at the front. Rifle shots, cannon roars, wounded soldiers crying, officers' barking orders, and trumpets blasting. Who knows what war was really like.

Now it was summer there also, and instead of cold trenches they put up with the heat, fought under the burning sun, their uniforms soaked with sweat. Or blood. He had never received a letter from Luigino, only that Christmas card without a return address. A few words: I am fine as I hope you are. Maybe he had forgotten about him. He was easy to forget, as if he were insignificant. He didn't leave deep tracks or strong impressions, with his way of staying at the edge of the scene, reluctant to show himself, to let himself be noticed, like someone would who has a small opinion of himself. From childhood he had dragged a sad anchor behind him. The foreign country had given him a sad, dull, crushing heartache, accompanied by the constant feeling of being out of place, in the wrong, perhaps ill. The painful uneasiness that continually kept him hanging on the edge of despondency had been relieved and then dissolved when he arrived in San Francisco, to resurface from time to time. In the beginning he had been excited by the hustle-bustle of the city, as Luigino and Giusepì were, and at the surprising discovery of a way of living completely different from what they had known. Only when he had begun to play in public did he feel truly peaceful, proud of earning his livelihood in a more congenial way, a right way for him, cut to measure. From that pride had sprung new energy, new optimism, faith in the future, and in certain moments of exaltation he finally felt sure of himself, like someone who had found his place in the world. He felt like he had come out of a dark corner where he had been holed up like a frightened animal, but life had pushed him back into that hole again, and this time forever.

He stared at the square window lit by the pale light of the city. His eyelids grew heavy as lead and everything seemed fuzzy. The usual sounds of the people hurrying along before nightfall came to him stifled, remote, as from an enormous distance. The hiss of gas was almost imperceptible, the odor of cabbage less pungent. His thoughts were foggy, like when one drops unconscious into sleep. A gentle sensation, almost soft, like a smooth, warm hand placed on his face.

He saw the lantern's yellow eye again that cut through the darkness and illuminated the thick forest of fur trees that the train ran through. He heard the clack of locomotive wheels on the track again, the rhythmic puffs of the steam, Luigino's insane screams as he tried to tear him from the tracks: stupid, stupid, stupid, get off from there, what do you think you are doing, goddammit… He had saved his life, but what good had it done except prolong the agony fate had in store for him? There had been one lucky break that didn't last long, as though he didn't deserve it, as though he didn't deserve anything good.

Thoughts of Susy came to mind, or rather thoughts of Maria, the girl from the Marches he met in the brothel that he hadn't gone to since the banker's flight. Her smile and her kind ways, her voice whispering his name and calling him darling (which meant "caro," so she had explained, but that was a word he didn't even know existed). She had a way of addressing him tenderly, with a caress that moved him every time, almost as though expressing affection she wasn't sure where to place. Just like him she had no one, and no one cared for her. He had never known a woman's love, and now there was no more time, but he ached with regret. He hadn't deserved even that.

In the hazy fog the knocking at the door had trouble making its way, a far off knocking, muffled, as though someone were knocking on a door at the end of the street. They were repeated stronger and more impatiently, and he was annoyed to think that by mischance the police had come too soon, before he expected them. He had to hurry. Everything would be over with their eruption: he breathed deeply the gas-saturated air many times, filling his lungs. He felt his mind fading, his thoughts reduced to fragments slid away, his body sank into nothingness, soft, inert, insubstantial. He tried to close his fingers in a fist, but couldn't do it, as if they didn't belong to him anymore.

Rosa Cencini was tired of knocking. An unpleasant odor was coming from the half closed door. She pushed it open and the chair fell to the floor. From the threshold, in the shadows of the room, she saw her renter asleep on the bed. She was amazed the noise hadn't wakened him. He must really sleep soundly, and she wondered how he could breathe in that terrible stink. What was it? Something rotten or rancid, some food gone bad or moldy, the air stale from filth accumulated for how long? Men alone keep house like a barn, she had had occasion to observe.

She looked around, advanced two steps, went up to Gildo and shook him by a shoulder, wanting to tell him that she had come for the August rent, when she realized that there was something odd about that stillness. Suddenly she recognized the smell of gas and heard the hiss. Frightened, she shouted, ran to turn off the gaslight, and threw the window open. Turning again to Gildo she called him and shook him, and since he did not respond but lay there motionless and seemingly unconscious, she took him under his arms, braced herself, grit her teeth, and pulled him out of bed. The mattress slipped to the floor with him and kept his head from hitting the floor. Gasping for breath, she hurried to open the door wide and breathed deeply, swallowing mouthfuls of fresh air. Then she hurried back to him, and taking him by the arms, she dragged him outside with great effort and laid him carefully on the sidewalk. She kneeled down beside him and put her head to his chest to listen for his heart beat. It was irregular and weak, just as his breathing, but there was a light, barely audible movement that seemed to fade from one moment to another. Thank God he wasn't dead, but close to it. In the dark street faintly lit by a distant streetlight, she couldn't see his face, but only the striking pallor. She began to shake him, unbutton the collar of his shirt, slap him, pinch his cheeks, furiously massage his hands and feet. Vigorously moving his arms and legs, she spoke his name, begging him to wake up, it was Rosa, his landlady. In the name of God if he would only open his eyes, say something, she couldn't stand it any longer. What was he thinking of? Or what possessed him? Didn't he know that it was a mortal sin that the Lord didn't forgive? Did he want to go to hell with the devils? There is a cure for everything in this world but death. And she caressed his hair, his cheeks, rubbed his still cold hands. Poor little fellow, she murmured crying and sniffling, poor little fellow, if your mother hears about this.

She allowed him to stay in the room for another two weeks; he could pay for it after he found work. More than that she could not do. After all, she wasn't swimming in gold either. Every once in awhile she came to see him, afraid he might try it again. She brought him a little warm food and begged him so much to eat that a knot in his stomach kept him from swallowing. Couldn't he see how bad he looked? He seemed like a decrepit old man, not a young man of twenty-three. And he should go outside for some fresh air, take a little walk to stretch his legs, it would be good for him and give him an appetite. Outside was the sun and a nice little wind off the sea. And besides he should talk to someone instead of staying quietly on his bed all the time mulling over bad thoughts. At his age he shouldn't waste his life like that. The Lord who sees and provides would help him; he only needed to have faith and pray.

Gildo vomited for days. The intoxication had left him dazed, weak, lifeless, dull. He constantly felt nauseated and dizzy. The stabbing pain in his temples had worsened. It caught him off guard, by surprise, lasting a long time and leaving him exhausted. Melancholy enfolded him like a sticky shroud. He didn't feel grateful to Rosa who had saved him. If she hadn't come everything would now be resolved. Instead he had to start all over. Life was too hard, unjust, cruel, meaningless, a never-ending trick. As soon as you got something someone would snatch it out of your hand. There was no God who saw and provided. You were always alone from the time you were born to the time you died.

When his head had cleared and he was himself once again, he was surprised the police hadn't come and arrested him, and he waited anxiously for knocks on the door. But the police were nowhere to be seen. Could it be that Mr. Clifford hadn't reported him? Out of pity or out of a kind of musical fraternity? Or had he believed him in the end?

At first he had spent hours lying stupefied on his bed staring at the ceiling. Then he had dragged himself here and there aimlessly and listlessly, his eyes as empty as his mind. Losing weight, pale, dirty, unkempt, not shaving for days, he saw no reason for taking care of himself, and alone he didn't know what to do. He had nothing to do but let time pass, a time that was worth nothing. Ashamed to be seen in his bad condition and not wanting to be pitied, he avoided the few people he knew. He was determined not to ask for help. He had almost forgotten about the music he loved so much. He had been so wildly ambitious, so overconfident, to expect to change his own situation, to get away from the daily blind drudgework that was his destiny. Brutal facts had slapped down the foolishness of his aspirations, and as everyone is held to the place he was assigned at birth, life had punished him severely. What he wanted now more than anything else was to sink to the bottom like a wreck, to touch the bottom of solitude, distress, misery, to the point of self-annihilation. His was a bitter, self-destructive vendetta against the whole world that had shot him down and tossed him aside like filthy garbage.

When the two weeks were up, at sunset he gathered his few things in a bundle: a razor, a piece of soap, a box of matches. He took the blanket that belonged to him, left the door ajar and without telling Rosa goodbye went to look for shelter for the night.

Now he too was a "'omless" person, like so many others. In the port area there was a run down, abandoned warehouse where a crowd of homeless slept, wrapped in rags. He spoke to no one and paid no attention to the grumbling of those who didn't appreciate new arrivals or to the disgusting smell of urine. He didn't answer any questions. He chose a dark, out of the way corner, laid old cartons on the floor dirty with trash of every kind. He used his bundle as a pillow, wrapped himself in his blanket, and tried to sleep.

In the morning he gathered his miserable belongings, loaded them on his shoulder and went out in search of something to eat. He felt weak, as after a serious illness that affected his thoughts as well as his body. He wandered around muttering meaningless words, looked around wild-eyed and everything seemed confused and blurry. He staggered on unsteady feet through unknown streets until he entered Chinatown's labyrinth of lanes where he had never been before. An ant hill swarming with hard-working people, pagoda roofs and lanterns, colored houses jammed up next to each other, brightly-colored balconies, glowing signs in indecipherable characters, butcher shops with roast duck hanging from hooks, eating joints, numerous laundries, barber shops, myriads of little restaurants, and over the entire district the aromatic odor of incense.

Hunger gnawed at his guts. He stared greedily at the carts selling cooked food, rice and smoking soup, and the stalls crowded with customers and overflowing with fruit, vegetables, shrimp, live fish. The venders weighed the merchandise and rapidly calculated the price on an abacus. No one paid any attention to him. Slender little men carried baskets on a balancing pole. Yells and conversations criss-crossed in a language of quick high tones. Chicken and suckling pigs walked around freely, white-haired old men played cards or mah-jong.

He roamed around for some time, becoming more tired and

hungry. His stomach was cramping, but he didn't dare go to the garbage bins outside the restaurants. Exhausted by that fruitless wandering, he stopped at the door of a joint where a woman was washing the sidewalk, and when she went back in he got up his courage and began to rummage in a bucket, grabbing a handful of rice with vegetables. Like a stray dog.

After that first time, in which he felt he had reached the depths of abject poverty, he grew used to it and became more daring, but the leftovers that he managed to get his hands on were not enough to satisfy him and he was tormented by hunger day and night. He made two daily incursions to a couple of restaurants in the elegant area behind Columbus Avenue, after lunch and after dinner, just as soon as the waiters had finished clearing the tables and had filled the tubs to the brim. He had a greasy cloth sack for squirreling away pieces of bread, meat, cheese, leftover fruit and sweets to eat in peace in his corner. In the morning he would be wakened from the precarious pallet with a hole in his stomach and would gobble that little bit he had set aside. He moved cautiously, careful not to let himself be surprised by the owners who chased beggars away without pity; but most of all by the police, even more unfriendly. When he saw them coming from a distance, handcuffs swinging from their belts, with the slow steps and wary eyes of someone surveying his legitimate territory, he slipped away in a hurry to hide in his shelter. Like a hunted animal.

18

Autumn was announced by dense skeins of dripping fog that enveloped and obscured the bay from dawn to late afternoon, when the east wind rose, and tempestuous gusts swept the sky clear.

Soon the winter made great strides. For entire days and nights rains fell without let up. From holes in the roof it rained onto the floor, soaked clothes and mats and congealed the dust into slippery mud. Furious quarrels broke out in the evening over the few dry places, disputes that came close to blows at times. At night a piercing wind entered the cracks in the crumbling walls. Gildo put on all the clothes he owned, wrapped himself tightly in his blanket, but still couldn't get warm or fall asleep. In the morning he would get up stiff and bent, bones and muscles aching as though he had been beaten, making it difficult to get moving. Hunger drove him out. He gathered up his things and wandered chilled to the bone for hours in search of food.

He was unrecognizable, aged, bony, his hollowed face a yellowish pallor, his beard unshaved, his clothes filthy and torn, his sleepwalkers gait unsteady and wavering. His headaches gave him no respite; pains pierced his temples and left him dazed. If in that derelict community he seemed the same as the others, in the streets he noticed that the passersby avoided him, and in case they suddenly found themselves facing him, they turned away with looks of disgust, censure, and reproach which hurt. As if he was responsible for his miserable condition. What did they know about him? He was deeply wounded each time by those pitiless faces, those glances that immediately turned away.

The police continued to be a problem to contend with. One of the men in the shelter told him that people like them, without a fixed address, could be imprisoned according to law, or interned in a camp at the edge of town so they wouldn't disturb the decorum and respectability of the citizens. Others disagreed. If they committed no crime — and to be poor was a serious misfortune, but not a crime — the guards had no right to arrest anyone. In the uncertainty, to avoid a danger of unknown consequence, it was good to take to your heels when a uniform appeared.

The two fancy restaurants in the neighborhood of Columbus Avenue where he usually went to find leftovers kept their garbage bins inside to be free of the assault of the hungry beggars who bothered their moneyed customers, making the daily hunt for food even more difficult and frustrating. Toward the end of the morning, when the customers in the open markets thinned out, he would retrieve the discards piled around the stalls: rotten fruit, moldy grapes and oranges, cabbage cores, wilted lettuce, yellowed stalks of fennel and celery, cracked eggs, spoiled sausage and rancid cheese. He also rummaged around in the garbage barrels of stalls at the port where he found rotten fish, leftover vegetables and meat, and in the gigantic pyramids of garbage unloaded every day by carts in a depleted quarry. But the competition there was ruthless. Dozens of tramps foraged there along with a battalion of rats, ravens, and crows.

One morning he ran into three fellow countrymen that he already met in his wanderings. One of the three, a young man his age, as ragged and thin as he, invited him to join them. They were going to a place where they could eat all they wanted, and it was free. His generosity surprised Gildo. The lack of food and the trouble of getting it were such that everyone kept his sources to himself and jealously guarded his survival strategies. The goal was the Chinese cemetery at Colma, on the southern edge of the city, where the yellow faces, according to a custom in their country, placed already cooked food on the graves, convinced that their dead needed to eat even in the other world. Every religion, the young man commented, had its beliefs and traditions: the Christians put flowers and oil lamps on the tombs to honor their dead and provide them company. And they recited requiems and rosaries to insure that the Lord would open the doors of paradise. Unlike the Chinese, we know that when one loses one's life one also loses one's appetite; so all those good things would be wasted if the hungry didn't take advantage of it. With so many tombs there was food for everyone. The rumor had spread among the poor devils who passed it along and in that way they managed to stay alive.

They walked for a while along endless straight streets across unknown neighborhoods, and after skirting San Bruno Mountain, a long green hill, came to the cemetery. Entering the gate, Gildo was surprised to see colored porcelain bowls with chopsticks stuck in rice mixed with meat, fish, and vegetables on every grave. They were not the only beneficiaries of that provident and curious custom. Some other down-in-the heels men furtively circled the graves, grabbed bowls and, using their fingers for a spoon, stuffed it in their mouths so furiously they nearly choked. He too hurled himself ravenously on the fragrant spicy dishes. He ate until his stomach, long unused to being full and satiated, rebelled with sharp spasms and contractions that took time to subside.

After that first rewarding incursion, he made the long walk through the streets every day, and for a couple of weeks was sufficiently fed—pleasantly relaxed and satisfied feeling that made him feel like a new man. He never saw a Chinese in the cemetery. He imagined that they worked hard in their quarter during the day and only found the time to cook and bring the food to their dead in the evening; most of all he was surprised that they allowed that daily looting, unless they really attributed it to their dead that came out of the tombs to empty the bowls.

Very soon he got the answer: with great consternation of the poor fellows who had depended on that resource, one morning they found the entrance barred by two brawny guards armed with clubs standing there to stop access to those not belonging to the community. And so the providential restaurant closed its doors, and the affectionate customers were obliged to return to the daily, difficult rummage in the garbage bins.

One day of battering rain and desperate hunger, during which he had eaten only a wormy apple, Gildo took shelter in the lobby of the train station. A beggar sitting with crossed legs held out his left hand to the hurried and indifferent people coming and going. His right hand was empty and lifeless, resting in full sight on a knee, but a lump in his torn jacket led one to suspect a fake mutilation devised to arouse pity. Occasionally someone would hand him a coin. The man bowed in obsequious and servile gratitude, nearly prostrating himself humbly to the floor. A real professional. Gildo was tempted to imitate him and he put some distance between himself and his rival so as not to interfere with him. He noticed a secondary exit and positioned himself there. People trickled by, and when he saw a well-dressed man approaching in the distance, he gathered all his strength, his forehead pearled with sweat, and forced himself to stretch out his hand. But as soon as the man was no more than two feet away he suddenly lowered his hand, turned and looked at a far point in the lobby as though to appear he was there for an entirely different purpose.

The sequence was repeated with everyone that entered his trajectory: in a resolute manner he would stretch out his hand and at the last moment withdraw it. And while he squirmed and struggled between two opposite impulses, his irritation grew for his own inability to bend to circumstances, for his vain pride, that misdirected self-esteem that was unbending, that withstood everything and that grew stronger in spite of his will and the hunger that gnawed at his guts. Why was he incapable of adapting to bare necessity? What difference was there between picking through garbage and asking passersby for a handout? Why did that seem to be so dishonorable? And if it really was dishonorable, hadn't he chosen to sink into degradation and self-annihilation? Now he was forced to change his mind and to observe that, in spite of his intentions, an obstinate knot of pride and dignity resisted inside him that not even hunger could affect.

As regards his powerlessness to compromise he could be happy only if it led to slow self-destruction. He remembered the time when he thought that at the worst, if he fell into the deepest misery, he could play the accordion in the streets and leave his cap turned up on the sidewalk; but in that case he would have simply offered his music in exchange for compensation, and his dignity, self-esteem would have been left intact.

After that exhausting battle—won or lost?—there was nothing left to do but to continue rummaging through the garbage. He had tried going to the more modest eating joints in lower-class neighborhoods, but he suspected that the leftovers were reused and served to the customers in other ways, in meat balls, for instance, because he could find only pieces of stale bread and fruit cores without pulp. More often he found raw inedible food, yellowed leaves of cauliflower and spinach, half-rotten potatoes, scraps of fat, bone, legs and heads of chicken, which boiled all together would have made a delicious soup. But he had no way to cook them and he left them where he found them. Then the idea came to him that if he could build a fire in the warehouse and get a discarded pot, he could cook the soup and eat it in peace inside, and to that end he collected odd pieces of wood and scattered paper. After a relentless search he retrieved from a pile of abandoned things an old pan with handles and from a pile of rubble two bricks to rest it on. Among the leftovers fished from a bin he found six chicken legs and three heads he cooked over the fire to get rid of the tough skin and leftover feathers, and in spite of the fact that he had no salt and didn't know how to get it, the piping-hot soup was delicious. In the broth he immersed some stale bread, devoutly chewed the legs, stripped the flesh from the heads and sucked them down to the last little neck bone, and after devouring the tasty crest and wattles he smashed the head to extract the brain. His hunger was finally satisfied, as were the others he had invited to the banquet.

The success of Gildo's soup reanimated the poor souls who set about finding wood and chips outside lumber mills, paper, cardboard, fruit crates and anything that could be burned. They collected edibles of all sorts, and every day that warm collective meal restored and reinvigorated them. The crackling fire, besides cooking the daily soup, warmed a part of the warehouse not in use and the numbed men gathered around and rubbed their frozen hands. The smoke easily escaped out the holes in the roof. The walls were smoked and on the floor the cinders had blackened a circle, and a piece of wall became the hearth. In good weather the kitchen was moved outdoors.

That initiative had stimulated the others to make their desolate refuge more comfortable. The first thing they did was to stop urinating in the corners of the warehouse, and the smell gradually evaporated. At an appropriate distance away they dug a rectangular hole, spanned the two banks with a plank to put their feet for their corporal needs and set up some boards around it for privacy. In the accumulated piles of rubbish around the port and in the city's alleys, they salvaged receptacles to keep water for drinking, washing, cooking and for a hasty and occasional laundry, as well as cartons for the damp floor; in a box outside a laundry they found discarded sheets they tore to use as towels, and in a pile of rags they found worn and holey blankets and pieces of wool to soften their pallets. And even a real horsehair mattress, though torn and stained, chosen by lots to avoid envy and argument. They had also found old suits that still had some wear, wool socks with holes and old shoes. One man refitted himself from head to toe. He still didn't appear presentable, but everyone agreed he was transformed, and they nourished ardent expectations for spring that would soon come.

That daily activity, beneficial for survival, had also rescued them from idleness and pernicious apathy. It sprouted seeds of solidarity, if not friendship, and nourished an unusual sense of community among the outcasts; they no longer looked daggers at each other, didn't quarrel over the slightest thing, didn't contend for space. Everyone had his own cozy spot, considered that dilapidated warehouse his home, and was beginning to feel affection for it. With old bricks, metal scraps, rusty tin sheets, and wooden planks they built shelves for the kitchen things, and the food and water receptacles. In their encampment they had added other comforts: fruit crates served as stools, a wobbly piece of furniture and a flaking basin functioned as a toilette, completed by a broken mirror nailed to the wall and by the pieces of cloth hanging to use as towels. A rope was stretched from one wall to another to hang the laundry. Gildo had unearthed some stumps of candles. Evenings during supper they lit a couple and those trembling weak lights reminded them of the tepid stalls back home. The lights of the last steamships cut through the bay. The buzz of motors and siren blasts broke the nocturnal silence. Lazzaro, originally from Udine, patiently doing his best with a file and a sharp rock, had made rudimentary soup plates and spoons from a sheet of metal. Thus they had the consolation of eating the soup as it should be eaten, each one with his own dish. Actually someone did complain that Lazzaro had gone too far. If you weren't careful the sharp edges could cut your mouth and even your fingers.

Like a civil confraternity they reached the point of taking turns keeping their abode neat and clean. They swept the floor and removed the trash, and anyone who dared to hawk and spit or throw refuse on the floor was bitterly reprimanded and made to clean it immediately.

Gildo continued to feel like his soul was frozen, deaf to joy as well as pain, but that collective industriousness had gradually given his spirits a tentative boost. Now they were talking, telling each other the sad stories of lonely and rejected men, each one different from the other and yet so similar.

Filippo, an eighteen year old, had had a job washing dishes in a restaurant. One day his skinflint boss who skimped on the food caught him stuffing his mouth with stewed beans. No sooner than you can say Jack Robinson he was shown the door, and the boss had kept his final week's earnings to pay for the beans. The Americans have an easy dismissal policy. The smallest infraction is grounds for losing a job.

Emilio, a southerner who worked in the vineyards of Napa Valley during the harvest, and harvested orchards in the surrounding area summers, was unemployed in the fall. Not knowing where to go he had decided to find refuge in the city where he thought things would be better. But it didn't work out that way. San Francisco was tough as lava after it has cooled and hardened. In the spring he would go pick artichokes in Santa Cruz County, a hundred kilometers south, but in the meantime he had to get through the winter.

Bartolomeo, a middle aged, sad and taciturn man from the Veneto, after being urged for some time, told of having entrusted his nest egg to a countryman who swore he was about to return to Italy and would turn it over to his family. But actually that so-and-so never left and had kept the money. Someone said they had seen him in San Francisco, so Bartolomeo had come here to hunt him down and get his money back. That was why he left every morning and came back at night. So far he hadn't caught sight of him, but he wasn't discouraged. When he met up with him he would break his neck with his bare hands.

Without even a day's notice, only a note in English on the barred door, Lazzaro lost his job because the factory closed during the dead season not to reopen until spring. And that crook hadn't even given him his final pay.

Fedele, a laborer from the province of Pavia, had a similar story: his factory didn't let them go with words, but in deeds, by reducing the daily work hours. The bosses expected the workers to be there every morning at seven, and kept them with teeth chattering in the cold without anything to do until late afternoon, and then they worked for only two hours, half an hour, or not even a minute. Long enough to drive you crazy. In the evening he would be exhausted without having done a darn thing all day, and had barely put fifty cents or a quarter in his pocket. Sometimes the foremen, with the bosses right behind them, would interrupt their work before an hour was up to rip them off, or demand they hurry and finish before the hour was up, and this way they didn't see a red cent. On their part, in order not to be cheated, they would slow down until it was a full hour. A covert and vicious war was fought between the foremen and workers. The atmosphere was tense and sometimes it lead to fisticuffs. Anyway, it wasn't worth complaining or arguing about. At daybreak a crowd of unemployed men were there waiting to replace them, willing to accept any condition. In the end the factory went bankrupt and closed its doors.

Leonida, a white-haired man with a lined face, listlessly told about having been assumed as foreman for a street construction on the condition that he turn back a third of his salary. Forced by need, he had agreed. Then he found out that the superintendent had blackmailed his subordinate and extorted money from him — a chain of tyranny that involved everyone, from the lowest to the highest in the hierarchy. The boss, under the threat of firing, set one against the other so they would work harder. After two years of that killing rhythm, he couldn't stand it anymore; he was dead tired, worn out, weak. He slowed down; he held back, produced less. And so, when he was distracted for a moment, they used that as an excuse to let him go. It was easy to get rid of old workers, squeezed and used up like he was. There was no end to the supply of strong young men ready to replace them.

Gildo listened but said nothing. He was ashamed of his own misfortunes. It made it worse to have achieved a certain success, to have earned a lot doing something he liked, and then to be rolled to the bottom of an abyss. If he told them he was a musician without being able to prove it he was afraid no one would believe him, and he couldn't bear the surprised or mocking comments of those who could see how far he had fallen.

In March the police came. On a damp, bleak dawn a squad of guards raided the abandoned warehouse while the men were still asleep. The sudden commotion woke them with a start. They sat up frightened and still groggy with sleep. In the dark they could barely make out human shapes moving around, heard irritated male voices shout: out, out, hurry up, hurry up! But they couldn't grasp what was going on. Filippo was the first to recognize the uniforms and he yelled: The police! The police! This was followed by frantic commotion. The terrified men blindly groped for their clothes, leapt about trying to get their trousers on, and ran wildly back and forth like crazed sheep.

The officers seemed to be blinded by rage; barking like angry dogs they deliberately and with great pleasure devoted themselves to a systematic demolition of the encampment, destroying every-thing in a terrible racket. They struck their clubs savagely at any-thing within range. They broke the two large windows, they kicked the stacked wood in every direction, as well as the soup pot, dishes, spoons and the rudimentary kitchen utensils; they scattered the ashes and the remains of the fire, poured the containers of water on them and in that muck threw the rags used as towels, the clothes hanging on nails, and the blankets they ripped off the pal-lets. With two strong blows they smashed to smithereens the piece of mirror attached to the wall and cut the rope with drying laundry, and all fell in the mixture of water and ashes.

Speechless, the men watched the ruin of their refuge, loved and cared for as much as they could; they witnessed the destruction of that semblance of a home that had nevertheless sheltered them, fed and warmed them, and they saw their poor belongings cruelly scattered in gratuitous malice, unjustified, actually perverse. Agostino and Lazzaro, in a flash of rebellion, rushed to save some items of clothing that had escaped the assault, but a wave of clubs sent them back. No one else tried to do anything.

When that insane outburst of brutality was over, the police ordered the men to line up against the wall, but they didn't understand a word. They hesitated uncertainly, looking at each other, until the policeman who seemed to be the head, a sergeant to judge by his status, started yelling and took the nearest man by the arm and shoved him against the wall, making a sign to the others to do likewise. When they were all lined as before a firing squad, speaking each syllable distinctly to make them understand, he formally accused them of illegally occupying private property where they had no right to be. Therefore they must get out of there immediately or else they would be arrested and sent to jail.

While the sergeant was talking, one of the policemen at his side, with a sneer that revealed two gold incisors, exhibited a pair of shinning handcuffs and gave them a jingle. His colleagues broke into laughter, entertained by the fine joke. The sergeant checked their documents, and then his subordinates surrounded the men, pushing and kicking them out of the warehouse. Leonida and Fedele, with gestures, asked permission to pick up the blankets left on the floor. It was still cold and would help at night, but that was not allowed.

Before leaving the building Gildo turned, and out of the corner of his eye saw one of the guards kicking the precious soup pot around like it was a ball. He must have noticed the box where they kept the stale bread to dip in the broth. He picked it up and flung it across the room. Pieces of bread scattered on the muddy floor. Outside it was pouring.

Standing on the sidewalk in the middle of the pedestrian hustle and bustle Gildo looked in the shop windows and the coming and going of customers. A jeweler exhibited rings with diamonds, emeralds, rubies, pearl necklaces and semi-precious stones, pins, pocket watches and wristwatches. Next to him a men's and women's shoe shop displayed models of the latest fashion: laced ankle boots, women's boots with laces, footwear of shiny patent-leather. Just a little beyond, in the open door of a tailor's workshop was a headless manikin dressed in a gray suit still basted with white thread. A man bent over a large table marked the cloth with chalk and began to cut it with a pair of enormous scissors. Next to that was a pastry shop with shelves piled high with cakes and trays of little sweets. People came out with packets tied with brightly colored ribbons. Every time the door opened out came a sweet smell of chocolate, vanilla, candied sugar.

The sun was shining, but Gildo shivered with cold after his long fast. Hunger had tortured him for days: weak and exhausted, his head foggy, rocky from lack of sleep, his legs as pliable as a soft pastry, he was afraid of collapsing on the ground. He fought to keep his eyes open. He would have liked to lie down on the sidewalk, curl up and sleep, but he forced himself to stand up and concentrate on that important thing left for him to do. When he noticed a policeman coming his way he had staggered to an adjacent alley and hid behind a pile of boxes. The moment had not yet come. He must first figure out the best thing to do, chose the right place, and be careful not to make mistakes.

Beside the pastry shop was a dry goods store. At the counter two elegantly-dressed women in hats and coats leaned on their elbows and felt the fabric with the tip of their fingers, discussing it in soft voices. The clerk brought one fabric after the other to the window that overlooked the street, so the customers might see the colors in natural light. The women nodded, sighed hesitantly and looked up at the stacks of fabrics. The clerk climbed up a wooden ladder and came down with a roll in her arms.

He moved a few meters to look in a café with a yellow sign. Two men were sitting at the counter, looking absent minded and dazed staring at the drinks half full of an amber liquid. He was reminded of Filippo: when they had gone their own ways after the police raid, Filippo had told him, disconsolately, since he hated such work with his whole heart, he would try to get hired as a kitchen boy in a café where there were only cups and glasses to wash, because in a restaurant you always kept your hands in soap and grease. Your skin broke and the sores never healed. Gildo wondered if Filippo had found work. He hadn't the energy and determination to look for the impossible job to keep from starving to death. As unpresentable as he was, reduced to exhaustion, weak, worn out, as though bloodless, without even the strength to work, he would just be refused. Now only that single, extreme solution remained.

After they were barred from the warehouse no one knew where to go. They had talked it over for a while. The idea of looking for another abandoned building where they could all be together was rejected by the majority. They would be seen, someone would report them, and sooner or later the police would find them and kick them out once again. Downhearted, they scattered in different directions, each one on his own in search of whatever shelter he could find.

The first night and those following, he slept cramped in an abandoned quarry at Telegraph Hill. It was still bitterly cold and without a blanket he had shivered until dawn. With the sun he went out on the usual itinerary in search for food, but he didn't find much. And on the days following he had also been atrociously hungry. He couldn't stand it any longer and felt exhausted. He yearned for a roof over his head, a real bed where he could rest his aching bones, a pillow to lay his head, a wool blanket for cover, a faucet where water always ran, a piece of soap to wash off the dirt, a bathroom where he could go in peace whenever he wanted. He couldn't remember the last time he washed, and he was sick of his smell. More than all he yearned for piping-hot meals served on plates and eaten with real utensils, he yearned passionately for vegetable soup, plates of stew, steaks, roasted potatoes, cups of hot milk, glasses of wine, crisp bread, slices of fresh cheese. Visions of food stalked him. Nights, with his stomach empty, he would roll around without closing an eye. He dragged himself around the streets in the day gripped by confused hallucinations. He had swallowed his pride and forced himself to beg, but he was awkward, wooden, surly, unable to arouse compassion. And anyway, people were tired of so many beggars and, except for the rare occasion, they turned and walked away. And so the step he was ready to take, though risky, seemed inevitable. The last attempt before giving up and letting himself starve to death.

Next to the bar a bakery spread a wake of oven smells. That bakery could be what he was looking for. The jeweler was not to be considered, in order to avoid any misunderstandings that could cost him dearly; and the same for the pastry shop, the tailor, the dry goods shop or shoe store. Shops so luxurious they didn't offer him the necessary justification.

In the bakery window, bright as a mirror, on the polished wood shelves were baskets of golden brown bread just out of the oven. And dark and compact loaves of rye, round hamburger buns, loaves with brown, slightly burnt crust, bunches of breadsticks in baskets decorated with dry flowers, small cotton bags of wheat flour, barley, corn. That sight before his eyes drove him crazy, filled his mouth with saliva, moved his jaws to chew something that was not there. Inside were women lined up with their shopping bags. A young clerk with a white cap covering her hair smiled as she quickly waited on them without superfluous chatter and nimbly rang up the sale.

He moved to the outer edge of the sidewalk and waited, his right hand in his trousers' pocket. That was the right distance. At the opportune moment he would take another couple of steps back into the street. People hurried along on their business and paid no attention to him. They looked straight ahead, perhaps afraid to see the umpteenth beggar with his hand out.

Gildo desperately hoped no one would come between him and his line of fire. He firmly intended to limit the damage to avoid worse consequences, and above all to make his real motives as evident as possible.

His squinted his inflamed eyes to search the street in both directions as far as he could see, on the lookout for a blue uniform in the distance. But he didn't see him yet. Normally the officers only patrolled back and forth watching people. Now, however, he was a few minutes late. But before long a policeman did appear at the end of the street, walking at a leisurely pace, swinging his club. Gildo's heart began to pound. Now is the time, he thought.

Gildo took a few steps to the middle of the street without taking his eyes off him, judged the distance, made sure no one was passing, took a deep breath, closed his eyes to conquer the dizziness that gripped him, opened them again, staggered slightly, looked the officer in the face now that he was a few feet away, took the rock out of his trousers, raised his arm, took aim and threw it with all his strength at the bakery window. With a sharp, rifle-like explosion the window shattered. Slivers of glass scattered over the bread on the shelves and fell on the sidewalk with a tinkling sound. The clerk in the shop screamed in terror, jumped back, her cap slipping sideways. Mouths open, yelling in fright, the customers quickly grouped against the far wall, and raised their arms to protect their heads. To reassure them Gildo showed his empty hands.

The stone hadn't hit them. Maybe some fragment of the rain of glass had touched them, but thank goodness no one seemed to be hurt.

The policeman leapt at him like a coiled spring. He pushed him hard and his massive weight made Gildo lose his balance. He fell face down on the sidewalk, hitting his nose, forehead, and one cheek, and was bleeding copiously. The officer had a knee on his back, and while crushing him with his weight, he savagely grabbed his hair with one hand and beat his face repeatedly on the pavement, swearing between his teeth: son-of-a-bitch, bastard; fuck you, dago—the rosary of insults that he knew very well. Gildo did not move, flat on the ground, meek and submissive, he didn't offer the slightest resistance. He hadn't expected such brutality. He had imagined the capture differently, bloodless, handcuffs on his wrists and straight to jail, where he could eat and sleep. But it didn't happen that way. His face was dirty and bloody, his mouth covered with dust from the street, his body aching from the hard fall on the sidewalk. When he thought it was all over, the officer landed a blow of the club on the back of his neck that nearly knocked him senseless. He twisted his arms violently behind his back, as if ripping them from his body. He slipped on the handcuffs, and holding him by the nape of his neck, he yanked him up and dragged him away.

The next day, April 6, 1917, the United States entered the war, but Gildo didn't hear about it. President Wilson, after having long cultivated the illusion of a diplomatic solution to the conflict and defending the country's neutrality, was forced to intervene on the side of the Entente because of the repeated attacks by German submarines on American ships: the sinking of the Lusitania with its hundred passengers lost at sea, then the Sussex and others. Congress enacted the Selective Service Act that instituted obligatory military service for American and foreign citizens between the ages of 21 and 31. As soon as the day was fixed in May for the beginning of army registration, a certain number of immigrants who opposed the war, anarchists in particular, fled to Mexico, but the majority of Italians of the required age didn't avoid the draft. The first expedition, hurriedly trained in Texas and elsewhere, left for Europe to disembark in the French port of Brest and from there joined the Aisne-Marna western front near Nancy. Actually that tardy help served most of all to guarantee predominance in a new international order realized at the end of the conflict. Thanks to the war, industry was revived, the economic crisis began to improve and unemployment to diminish.

Even so, industry required fewer non-specialists. To this end Congress, in February of the same year, passed the Immigration Act aimed at reducing the most bothersome and unwelcome immigration, the dagos coming from the southern Mediterranean and the hunkies and bohunks of central Europe, using as an excuse the widespread illiteracy among those populations. From then on when the Italians arrived at the ports, though it wasn't at all necessary for the humble work they were destined to do, they had to take a "literacy test" to demonstrate they knew how to read from thirty to forty words in English or in another language or dialect. Should they fail the test they were sent back to their country.

19

The ardent hope that as soon as he stepped foot in the station the police would offer him food to placate his aching stomach was disappointed. Bewildered and exhausted, sitting on a bench in a cell along with a half dozen handcuffed men arrested that same day, he waited a long time in vain for someone to pay attention to him. Besides the primary reason, to remove his hunger pains, he burned to explain why he broke the bakery window, an act otherwise unjustifiable. But he wasn't asked anything. The irons rubbed on his scraped skin, a painful bump was on his neck where the club had struck him, blood dripped from his cut head, from his forehead and swollen nose, splattering his clothes and encrusting his skin as far down as his belt. He would have liked to wash, but there was no water in the cell.

The prisoners waited calmly and silently, each one enclosed in his own thoughts, faces tense, limbs contracted, a snort, a sigh, a cough from time to time. He hoped they would talk among themselves so he would know if there was an Italian among them, but no one said a word. When their glances met they immediately looked away, almost as though it was a reciprocal intimidation. He asked himself who they were, where they came from, what crime they had committed: they didn't look like calloused criminals, ugly mugs that collected convictions and went in and out of prison like it was home, but just seemed to be poor devils like him who had slipped up occasionally. He didn't dare ask anything: not only because of the certain lack of a common language, but out of fear of breaking that silence in which they seemed to find protection, and of arousing hostile reactions for violating their privacy. Therefore he didn't speak, but contemplated his wrists rubbed raw by the handcuffs.

Through the bars he could see part of the lobby where a sergeant was bellowing in the unceasingly noisy confusion: a man obviously drunk, with his complaining wife who showed the officers the results of the fight: a black eye and a pummeled face; four men arrested for fighting in a bar, still burning with rage, exchanged curses and threats. A fifteen-year-old boy guilty of stealing two apples had been grabbed by the greengrocer, manhandled, and dragged there by an ear. He stroked his bright-red ear and glanced around him with a childishly lost and imploring look. Five scantily dressed prostitutes taken in a brothel raid were waiting for the madam to come and pay the fine. While they waited they winked at the policemen and told them vulgar jokes. When the madam came and put up the money, they left laughing and slammed the door, and for some time a wake of cheap perfume floated in the air.

Somewhat later a harried officer took the prisoners from the cell one by one, along with the drunkard, the fighters, and the boy half-dead from fear, and wrote down the pertinent information of each. Gildo waited to be asked why he had done such a thing, and had his words ready — jobless, I was very mad — to make him somehow understand that he was dying of hunger, but the man took him back to the cell without asking him a thing. Because he had gone without food for days and had been waiting so long, the need to eat something had reached unbearable proportions. It seemed like his body was breaking up into pieces, as though flesh and bone had lost its consistence and cohesion. His vision danced and his head spun. Everything was blurred; sounds were amplified and boomed in his ears. Starvation had altered his perception, affected his awareness and slowed down his reactions, like a mechanism losing its steam before it stopped completely.

It wasn't until evening that they were given a couple of cheese sandwiches and water. Gildo swallowed his down at once with a few big bites, but it didn't help his hunger pangs very much. Short-ly after the lights were turned off they stretched out to sleep on the benches or on the bare floor. In the morning, after a hurried breakfast of sandy-tasting coffee and two pieces of stale bread, again handcuffed, they were taken to the court and enclosed in a cell of provisional detention, next to the courtroom, together with prisoners coming from other police stations. Twenty unkempt, shab-by men were crowded there, half of them foreigners. In the stag-nate air hung the foul odor of unwashed bodies and clothes, in addition to the stench of urine, feces, and disinfectant that rose from the latrine, a hole in the cement in a back corner.

The judge had rushed through the proceedings as quickly as possible. Consulting the prisoner's papers—largely accused of minor offenses—he informed them of their rights to public coun-sel for those unable to pay for a private lawyer, and of the possi-bility of provisional freedom while awaiting trial, released on bail. In other words, those who had money were free to go.

There were no interpreters and the foreigners, including Gil-do, hadn't understood half of what was said. But even if they had understood it wouldn't have made any difference. Not one of those poor unemployed, lost and isolated souls who managed as best they could, knew anyone who could loan them the necessary five hundred dollars. For Gildo it was not a problem: he had acted deliberately to end in jail, the last, extreme expedient to survive, and he intended to stay there.

The drunk with free hands, who must have had a lot of exper-ience, had immediately requested a meeting with his badly treat-ed wife, certain that she would be sorry she had made the com-plaint and would give him the bond money. The apple boy was separated from the adults to be sent to a reformatory for minors. The four brawlers who had made up during the night talked softly to each other, dismayed by their getting in so much trouble because of a stupid fight.

The noontime meal had to be skipped because of a series of mishaps, and Gildo, along with a dozen others, were escorted to prison. They were taken into a large reception room with benches along the walls. Prison guards hung a card on the new arrivals with name, date of entrance, a serial number to be memorized, and had them photographed in profile and facing front. Their names became superfluous, as they were called and identified by that number. Then their fingers were rolled in ink and transferred to paper. When the preliminaries were over, the guards ordered them to strip off their clothes and throw them in a container. The Salvation Army would pick them up to be distributed to the poor.

Since Gildo, humiliated and shamed by that unexpected request, hesitated to undress and took his time, dillydallied and blinked his eyes in confusion. One of the guards lost his temper and let loose a torrent of abuse. Embarrassed, beet-red, not looking at each other, the men naked as the day they were born, sat on the benches waiting to get dressed, covering their genitals with their hands. They were given garb made of rough cloth — without pockets so they couldn't hide anything — cotton socks and cloth-soled slippers without laces. As he was putting them on Gildo, with a sinking heart, realized that those housewife soles, thin, vulnerable, that were no buffer against humidity, rain, rough surfaces, and that muffled the footstep, were a symbol of the enclosed and restricted space where he would have to move from now on. For the first time he had a clear idea of the deprivation of freedom, segregation and anguish that would govern and stifle his days.

In addition to two wool blankets, they were given a canvas bag containing a clean mattress cover, soap for washing and shaving, a safety razor, pencil, some writing paper, envelopes and stamps as well as the prison rules written in English and a form for requesting visitors.

Two officers, one at the head of the line with a great bunch of keys, and one at the end, escorted the prisoners through a labyrinth of corridors, barred from time to time by heavy iron gates, each one bolted with three locks, until they came to a wing of the prison where the detainees were kept while awaiting sentencing — a dimly lit, booming cavern, the cells aligned on the ground floor and perched on the floor above.

His cell door closed and locked three times, Gildo immediately collapsed exhausted on his bed without the strength even to look around his new dwelling. Only later were they handed two aluminum plates with the long awaited meal. Revived a bit, he gulped it down like a ravenous animal, without chewing, without wondering what he was eating, much less guessing what it might be. Only when his stomach was full did he realize that it had been a mixture of rotten smelling chopped meat and vegetables. On the plate of cooked prunes in a swill that pretended to be syrup floated whitish worms. He fished them out one by one and laid them on the edge of the plate. The only utensil, a heavy soup spoon with thick rounded edges made him wonder: was that to keep them from cutting their throat or wrists? Like the house shoes without laces kept them from hanging themselves?

Dead tired, before throwing himself on his bed again, he looked around the cell: two bunk beds were secured to the walls with iron chains, the little table where he had placed his toilet articles was nailed to the floor. Instead of the sink and faucet with running water he had imagined, there was a bucket of water for drinking and washing; instead of a latrine, there was a second bucket with wooden cover. He washed and put the clean cover on his greasy and spotted mattress of lumpy horsehair, the signs of many bodies that had spent months or years there. Half asleep, before he drifted into a deep sleep, he tried to convince himself that the essential thing was to have a roof over his head, a place to sleep, and a place to eat. That was all that was important.

When he woke up he was holding the form for requesting visitors — there was space for ten names — making it glaringly evident that he had no one in the world to come see him, no one who knew where he was, no one who would think to look for him there. He had disappeared from the face of the earth, swallowed by a hostile place about which he knew nothing. He thought of Giacomo and Carolina who might have written him at his old address, and if they had the letters would certainly have been returned. The pencil and paper were nagging him to get in touch with them. But where would he find the courage to explain to his family why he had ended up in prison? How to tell about the misfortune that had dogged him and reduced him to extreme poverty before that? How to overcome the shame of confessing such a failure, and now stained with dishonor. He knew that when he got out of prison he would be marked forever. He had to face the fact that, by avoiding death by starvation, he had sentenced himself to a civil death, whose consequences he had not considered. Growing evermore anxious, he had to believe that he would get out of there quickly, stubbornly repeating that breaking a window wasn't serious enough to require a long sentence. What came after that he didn't care to think about. Not now anyway.

A month went by and nothing had been said about a trial. A public defense lawyer had not been assigned. The days followed monotonous and exasperating in their repetitive regularity, divided between meals in the dining hall, the hour of fresh air in the courtyard in the morning and afternoon, empting the slop bucket and distributing water, cleaning the cells and corridors by the detainees themselves. The three daily roll calls to be counted, the segregation until the next morning after the six o'clock supper, when lights in the cells were off and a faint glimmer came from the slit in the door.

In the evening he couldn't wait to be locked up in his little space. He preferred to be alone, and dreaded the times when he found himself elbow to elbow with the others. The atmosphere was thick with threats and mean looks were thrown like knives. Gestures and words in code he didn't understand; allusions, challenges, mysterious underground business and exchanges. Groups were formed which excluded him, complicities with the guards that showed preference or open hostility of one over the other. He soon learned that no one was trusted. He kept to himself, never asking anyone what crime he had committed, but only what he had been accused him of—unjustly, of course. In short, everyone was innocent and no one admitted he was guilty in order to keep some stool pigeon from ratting on him. Because there were spies ready to tell anything to the prison guards in exchange for privileges kept strictly secret to avoid ferocious vendettas by his companions at the slightest shadow of suspicion. It was enough for someone to start the rumor, whether true or false, that so and so was an informer for him to be in serious danger.

He even felt excluded from a trio of Italians, as if common origin was not enough reason for trust. Impenetrable groups were formed in the dining room, where he had an assigned seat at a table with another six prisoners; in the hours in the courtyard, or in the corridor when the cell doors were left open and the prisoners walked back and forth chatting, or played cards sitting on the pavement, he felt left out and sometimes in danger, even though he didn't know exactly why. An innocuous look seemed sufficient, a casual gesture, a careless word, to arouse anger, hostility, inexplicable animosity, as in every concentrated universe. He was afraid. In there he had no friends or allies. He stayed in the background, moved cautiously, and said little. But his reserved and wary behavior, far from arousing sympathy, earned him bitter distrust.

Some time later, in order to thin out the population when room was needed for new arrivals, he and a group of prisoners were transferred to San Quentin penitentiary, in Marin County, north of San Francisco. In that prison they were mostly criminals, already judged and sentenced to long detentions, perpetrators of serious crimes like theft and armed violence, homicides, rape, arson. The mammoth prison was too costly if not filled to the brim, so in one section were those accused of minor crimes and awaiting trial: thieves, counterfeiters of art, signatures or documents; swindlers, card sharks, receivers of stolen goods, peddlers of counterfeit coins, rowdy drunks, thieves of all sorts, or probation violators.

At the port they were loaded on a special steamer, chained to each other and then locked in a cage. The bay crossing was done in the middle of the night. From the narrow slits at eye level, Gildo watched the lights of San Francisco slowly fade. At a certain point he saw the beacon on the island of Alcatraz pierce the darkness, and he was reminded of Sundays some years ago when he gazed at the military prison from the quarry on Telegraph Hill, disturbed by that gloomy spur of rock rising out of the sea. He hadn't understood the reason for his morbid attraction for the island prison, but now it seemed like a premonition, a dark, obscure warning of the destiny awaiting him. At that time, a time that now seemed remote and unreal, he had had a job and two faithful friends, Luigino and Giusepì, and now he was left with no one and nothing.

It was still night when they disembarked on the peninsula's Point San Quentin wharf, and from there they were taken to the huge penal complex that occupied the other slope of the tongue of land jutting into the sea—a fortified citadel defended by high walls topped by barbed wire and towers for the armed guards. The prison officers took them in and the usual rigmarole began all over again. While Gildo doggedly waited for them to ask him why he broke the window and was ready to reel off the words he had memorized, he was brusquely ordered to take off his clothes and put on the prison uniform. A prison guard advised the new arrivals that every time they were spoken to they were to answer respect-fully: yes sir. Every transgression of the rule would be severely punished.

A chorus of male voices in a discordant mixture of languages rose to greet the new arrivals from the dark cells along the corridor, among which he caught a sarcastic phrase in Italian: "Benvenuti in paradiso!" "Welcome to Paradise!" someone shouted, and the echo of a snicker had reverberated against the walls and ceilings.

In the damp, cold, and dark cells space was limited. About three yards long and not even a yard and a half wide, windowless, the walls and ceilings covered in steel, a rough cement pavement. Two iron bunk beds were fixed to the wall with strong chains, the coarse wooden table nailed to the floor. One chair in a corner and a broom. Here also was a bucket with water for washing, and a second, lidless bucket, for the piss and shit, with a stink to turn your stomach. The straw mattress and pillow were bristling with lumps and spikes, the scratchy sheets were like sand paper, the two blankets dirty, faded, and frayed, stiff enough to stand alone. It was no worse than the shacks he had lived in for years, and fortunately that hole was all his.

While taking possession of the cubbyhole and laying out his few things, the racket from the nearby cells made his skin crawl. A mixture of shouts, raspberries, belches, farts, hysterically mad laughter, coughing fits, monumental hawking and spitting, curses, foul jokes, obscene songs, running water, undefined noises and rustling. The prisoners talked to each other without seeing each other, called each other by name or nickname, made rhythmic taps on the wall that sounded like a secret code. Grim, anxious sounds of segregated lives, forced to manifest themselves in contorted, degraded ways. The guards yelled insults from the hall to impose silence. They threatened punishment, banged on the bars with clubs, made a din loud enough to break the eardrums and stun the brain.

All in response to a declaration of war. It had the beat of a reciprocal, bloody ruthlessness, of a hate without respite, a mortal duel between savage beasts ready to snap at each other's throats. Terrified, he wondered again if his gesture, which had seemed the only solution to hunger and desperation, had been wise, and if he had not got himself into a predicament that would end by crushing him.

Lying in bed in the dark after the six o'clock supper, the idea of having to start all over again in that immense fortress where he knew no one made it difficult to breathe. It was not easy to adapt to living with a crowd of criminals, who he supposed were guilty of crimes much more serious than his. And it was not easy to figure out the rules, habits, pecking order, alliances, complicities, hostilities, dangers, agreements among the prisoners at the slightest involuntary slight or transgression, according to the practices and codes that, as previously, escaped him. Not only that: he had to learn to deal with new guards walking around armed with lead-tipped clubs. He noticed how impatient, irritable, and tyrannical they were in this isolated place where they were obliged to live and where, in different ways, they had to put up with the same kind of confinement. He had to learn to bend to their bad moods, arrogance, cruelty, power, and unabashed inclination for bullying.

The prison guards enjoyed absolute, uncurbed power. They doled out sympathy, dislike, punishment, and retaliation as they pleased; they encouraged under the table trafficking, collusion and complicity among the criminals. By nature he was not at all made for such things and kept aloof from them, but he guessed that his behavior did not earn him indulgence from either the guards or the inmates. They hated anyone who stood out from the majority, interpreting their behavior as refusal to recognize the supremacy of the chiefs of either side. One guard in particular picked on him — a big brute with a jutting jaw they nicknamed Pig, who met him with a sneer, his lip raised over his hyena-like canines, who beat his club on the palm of his hand to intimidate him. Dago, shit, son-of-a-bitch, bastard were the insulting epithets he habitually pinned on him, threatening without reason to lock him inside the famous and feared isolation cell underground, adjacent to death row, and as soon as he got his hands on him, he would stick the club in his ribs or stomach. Gildo could see angry dislike on his swinish face, a sort of disgust, as for a filthy and repugnant being, and he tried in vain to understand its origin. It seemed to have begun when, instead of answering Yes, Sir, as he was supposed to, to a rebuke he hadn't understood, Gildo had just stood there gawking at him, and he, interpreting the silence as an offense to his authority, yelling Go fuck yourself! in his face, had taken him by the collar and shaken him with homicidal fury. He wondered if it was his dreamy and distracted air that irritated him, the slow and uncertain way he moved, that could be interpreted as laziness or provocation. The repeated vexations, the daily oppression and insults, made him continually more insecure, fearful, and awkward; he didn't understand the orders, didn't know how to follow them, stumbled, ran into things, knocked them over.

He couldn't get to sleep. His bed seemed like a burning grill. Hounded by anxiety about the next day and the countless days to come, he listened to the night sounds in the crowded wing: whispers, low voices, and above it all the rasping snore of many sleeping men, a gargling chorus that at times swelled into a roar. In sleep laments slipped out that seemed like cries or calls for help, hoarse groans springing from some nightmares, restless sighs. Nighttime relaxed defenses, relieved tensions, and the prison was revealed for what it was: a concentration of sorrow, unhappiness, and unrelieved, inconsolable solitude.

The bell rang at six. A half hour later armed guards opened the cells and escorted the prisoners into the mess hall for breakfast—

corn syrup, a slice of black bread, an unfathomable mixture called hash, a dark tasteless liquid baptized coffee, sometimes two fried eggs with bacon, two times a week oatmeal with milk. The tables and stools had been fixed to the floor from the time of an unforgettable fight in which a handful of prisoners had cracked several heads with them.

Gildo found himself next to the fellow countryman who had launched the sarcastic welcome at his arrival, a man from Valtellina by the name of Paolino. He told him a man had accused him of stealing his jacket containing his billfold. He hadn't stolen it, but they hadn't believed him. What sense was there in swiping a jacket when it was much easier to take the money out of the billfold? You'd have to be really stupid to do it. He was waiting for trial, but knew that the word of an American was worth more than a hundred Italians.

He didn't ask questions and didn't express opinions; he learned to accept his prison companions' version of their innocence. Paolino told him that every week they were allowed to receive a small sum from relatives to deposit in an account or to spend in the prison commissary where, for a very dear price, cigars, cigarettes, tobacco, canned food, chocolate, candy, drinks and other things were sold. He lowered his voice: a few mean, dishonest prison guards, including the odious Pig, sold the same things under the table, and if they didn't want trouble it was advisable to buy from them.

Those who had family in California managed pretty well: in addition to dollars they received letters and visitors, but that was not his case. He didn't know a soul in America. He also suggested it was not advisable to talk to the black asses; no one liked them, not even the guards of the same color. The Italians were accused of having no dignity, of lowering themselves to mingle with that inferior, dangerous, ignorant and lying race, and no one liked that. And then if you didn't want to surrender in prison, you shouldn't let yourself be intimidated by the guards or prisoners. You had to show you were bold, arrogant, and determined, ready to defend yourself. At San Quentin only contacts with power counted. And if some tough threatened to kill you and scared you shitless, you should never ask the authorities for protection. Otherwise you would be stigmatized by cowardly spies and could pay dearly.

Paolino was amazed that Gildo didn't know that months ago the United States had sent an expeditionary force to fight in Europe. That was all the newspapers had talked about for some time. They said that people in the old continent were spineless namby-pambies incapable of going it alone. So it had been up to the Americans to intervene. He concluded the bulletin of information with a wicked wink: did he know that there was a women's section in the prison? Rumor had it that one of the prison guards had organized encounters with the prisoners at night in a small room and took his cut as procurer. He didn't have a plugged nickel and hadn't tried to do it, but would be glad to.

After breakfast and a wash long hours stretched out until evening which the prisoners didn't know how to fill, except for the few who for good behavior had been assigned work in the kitchen, laundry, storerooms, infirmary, or in shops where they made shoes and work pants, or outside with private road construction. Very desirable jobs because of the weekly pay.

In the mornings the elect got busy — those who not only toed the line and didn't cause trouble, but who conspired secretly with the guards and thereby enjoyed special favors. They got out of unpleasant jobs, gave orders, sometimes resorted to physical force. They were entrusted with managing the section: they assigned cells, distributed jobs, and supervised the food and daily roll calls. For the rebels, the disorderly, the troublemakers, they served as examples to imitate so that they might enjoy the same privileges: actually they were hated as collaborators with the detested authority.

At roll call the prisoners lined up in front of the cells, and after answering to their serial number shouted by the elect and checked by the guards, they were counted in case some wit answered for another who had vanished, as had happened. Once a day, at a different time each day, the cells were thoroughly searched for penknives, knives, forks, and pieces of glass or metal used by the thugs to attack or defend themselves that could be hidden a hundred crafty ways. When the guards' raid was announced, the prohibited objects were tossed through the bars into the hall so it was impossible to know to whom they belonged.

Gildo especially hated the exercise hour in the windy courtyard, mornings and afternoons, when the prisoners, watched over by guards with rifles positioned on a ledge high overhead, congregated in groups of unapproachable alliances. They talked among themselves, walking slowly up and down, while those isolated like him didn't know what to do or how to behave. No one spoke a word to him. He felt an unreasonable hostility, a vague danger. Murderous looks cut through him like knives. There was an emaciated little man almost toothless, maybe a Polack or Lithuanian, who slid against the wall in hesitant little steps, and sometimes, blinking his eyelids over colorless eyes, would sign an imperceptible greeting with his hand.

A skeletal, gangling, wild-eyed young man of unknown provenance always stayed in a corner, immobile, head down, hugging his shoulders as though numb with cold, even though the air was warm and the sun was shining. Perhaps he hugged himself as a substitution for embraces he didn't receive.

A cell neighbor, middle-aged, neat and composed, with the appearance of being well off, eyeglasses on his nose, would bring a book to read. He spoke to no one and would hurry back in as soon as the bell rang to end the exercise hour. He wondered what crime such a distinguished man could have committed to have him end up in prison. These and other solitary souls thought only of completing their sentence and getting out of there. They didn't make friends, didn't participate in the feuds, conspiracies or wheeling and dealing. For that reason they were more likely to be considered spies and risked punishment by the hardened criminals. But the prison guards hated them also, just because they didn't participate in the brutal prison practices.

Gildo felt their eyes on him and was afraid of being attacked, beaten, killed. He would lean against the sunny side of the wall, staring at his feet, fingernails or the ground, or he would walk swiftly without looking anyone in the face. Sometimes he would go up to Paolino, who moved among the crowd with ease, and say a few brief and banal words. The boy had found an older protector, certainly repaid by his youthful grace, as frequently happened, who didn't lose him from sight an instant and who was obsessively jealous.

They could not see the ocean from the courtyard, but could smell it, while on stormy days the powerful sound of the surf reached their ears. To give himself something to do, Gildo was in the habit of taking a piece of bread with him to distribute to the gulls that wheeled low over the courtyard launching shrieks and cries. And together with flocks of pigeons they glided over the concrete to fight over the crumbs. They had become tame and pecked right up to his feet.

Dark and cruel settling of accounts took place in the crowd during the hour outside. Someone would suddenly attack another from the back and try to strangle him or wound him with a piece of filed metal or sharp glass, and while the guards rushed to separate them, striking out right and left and dragging the aggressor away for a private beating, Gildo would freeze in terror, turn his back and get as far away as he could, staring at the wall until the fight was quelled. Witnesses would be interrogated, and to avoid fierce vendettas, it was imperative to keep their mouth shut and swear they had seen nothing. Beatings were frequent. At the slightest sign of insubordination, a wrong word, a show of anger, and they were trounced on: the guards would drag the guilty one to his cell and massacre him with punches and kicks. Then the guards would insist they had been attacked, sure that their deceitful version of the facts would be accepted by their superiors and, out of fear, not contradicted by the other prisoners.

One evening in the racket that broke out in the cells as soon as the lights were out—the prisoners noisy farewell to the day just ended before they sank into harsh nocturnal solitude—someone began to whistle. Gildo sat upright and held his breath to listen. After the first timid, almost muted notes, a clear, pure sound as lovely as a silver flute soared in the air with all the vigor and assurance of a triumphal hymn. Entranced, he recognized the aria "Soave sia il vento" from the opera *Così fan tutte*. The entire wing suddenly grew quiet, the astonished prisoners drew near the bars and listened silently to the melody that from some unknown cell rose up whole and perfect: the whirling sounds spread through the enclosed space, ascended to the balcony and the dark vaults ceiling vaults, pierced armored breasts, loosened knots and snarls, softened resentment and acrimony. Who was the companion whistling in the dark? Even the most hardened men yielded to the magic sound, and the guards fell silent under its spell and didn't dare interrupt the mysterious whistler. In that place of never-ending brutality spread a long suspended interval of peace and sweetness, a serenity close to a miracle. The placated prisoners abandoned themselves to the caress of the song, as clear as fountain water that stretched out, soared, died away, recovered breath, power and vigor, and again fell pianissimo, like a whisper.

Gildo had tears in his eyes and convulsively wrung his hands; he happily breathed in the music that he had missed for such a long time, deeply moved by the precision of the intonation, the interpretive savvy of the executor, the shared musical knowledge of beloved Mozart, and he prayed fervidly that the unknown whistler wouldn't stop. Suddenly it occurred to him that it was the man with the eyeglasses and the aura of wellbeing who was in a cell close to his, the one who buried his face in a book in the courtyard and paid no attention to anyone. For the first time since he had entered that place he felt united with someone and enjoyed a long intense moment of comfort. When the tender melody ended and the last vibrations had hesitated and then vanished in the dark hall, he got up quickly, went to the bars, and began to whistle in turn.

At first, face and ears flaming, heart pounding, he was afraid that emotion would cut his breath short and the whole thing would be a fiasco. But gradually he worked up confidence; his mouth sweetly formed the polished notes that flowed from his memory one after the other with prompt precision. And when he had whistled the last note and the echo was about to fade away in the air, the other one began all over, and he impulsively followed; the amazing duet in the tomb in which the unfortunate men were buried rose like a hymn to the lamented and invoked beauty of life, to the freedom forgotten and long-awaited, to the hopes nourished and disappointed. As though the prisoners were afraid of breaking the spell, an astonished silence greeted the conclusion of the duet. Then an isolated handclap began and right after it a cascade of applause, whistles and enthusiastic cheering that seemed endless. At first the guards were hesitant, then they couldn't restrain themselves and joined the collective frenzy, and like a miracle the entire wing was infected by an unfamiliar joy, a sort of feverish elation. From the darkness came laughter, questions, comments, a confusion of sounds, until the guards took control and demanded silence.

The next day in the courtyard Gildo tried to catch the eye of his companion in sorrow, to attract his attention and talk to him, to let him know in case he didn't realize it, that he was the second performer, and shared the same great passion for music. He also proposed to tell him that he played the accordion, had taught himself, had even begun to study music on his own, but he hadn't made much progress and perhaps the man could help him. But with consternation and surprise, when he got closer to him, the man merely looked at him with a cool nod of his head and turned his back. Didn't he recognize him? Or did he want him to know that it was an episode to put aside and forget? That in prison it was unwise to cultivate friendships for affinities or establish alliances over a common passion, because friendships were built on quite other things? And if it is better to avoid those things, it was still better for each one tend to his own business.

A week later the man was released after serving his time. Passing by his cell with his few belongings, he smiled at Gildo and made a friendly sign, while beginning to whistle "Soave sia il vento." Gildo felt a surge of joy for that sonorous farewell meant for him. So after all the man knew very well who the second whistler was. Now he seemed to understand that that anarchic evening concert that broke every prison rule was the challenge of a man who knew he had nothing to lose or to fear, and the whole thing was a festive paean to freedom restored. And the snub that he had taken as hurtful rejection could have been an act of kindness toward the one who was remaining. It looked as if the man's intention was to prevent a friendship from flowering in the few days remaining to him, so it wouldn't cause pain at separation, an unnecessary pain. He had been wise: and yet while his footsteps grew faint in the hall and the guard nosily unfastened the bolt, Gildo felt a sharp sadness, as for a good glimpsed and immediately lost.

20

Gildo was tried and sentenced to a year in prison, an uncon-scionable length of time considering the trivial crime he had committed. He had recounted his story to a listless public defend-er, a thin, poorly dressed little man with a smattering of Italian. The lawyer hadn't understood much of what he said, except for an occasional word. He had tried to convince the judge that his client was not by nature a vandal or a criminal, but an honest and up-right young man who had not caused trouble to anyone and had earned his living with music. Unfortunately he had been robbed of all his savings and his accordion, indispensable for his work. He had almost died of cold and hunger until he decided to break the bakery window in order to be sent to jail just to stay alive. He should be given mercy and understanding. He wasn't the first man nor would he be the last forced by grim poverty to break the law.

The judge appeared unmoved by that pathetic cock and bull story, and without losing time to hear more, he passed the sen-tence, to which he added restitution to the baker for damages. The lawyer explained to Gildo that the courts were much more severe with foreigners than with natives, and so passed exemplary sen-tences to the immigrants as a means to discourage them from com-mitting crimes. On the other hand it was well known that his Ital-ian compatriots were distinguished by the large number of large and small criminal activities, beginning with the Mafioso Black Hand. And this undeniable reality had not helped him. As far paying the damages, he didn't know what to say except that if he didn't have a cent he should get some paid job at the prison and work it off in time.

Gildo felt lost and as loose-limbed as a puppet. How could he bear up under Pig's relentless persecution without reacting? He was on him more than ever, making fun of him, provoking him, and even taunting him about his harsh sentence. And how could he protect himself from the hostility he inhaled with every breath like a poisonous vapor, from the solitude that exiled him from the world, discarded and forgotten like garbage left to rot? If previously, because of crowding, the promiscuity, the everlasting racket and continual violation of any privacy whatsoever, he couldn't wait to be alone in his cell, now he suffered from the isolation, the lack of friends, of attention, deprived of all affection. A smile once in awhile would have been enough, some encouragement, a kind word. And furthermore, now that he was filling his stomach three times a day, even if the food was disgusting, the awful hunger he remembered having suffered seemed bearable, and he wracked his brain trying to understand why he had dreamed up that wild scheme to solve his problems by going to prison. In his stupidity and gullibility he had thought that that horrible place was a kind of free bed and breakfast, where the only inconvenience was not being able to leave.

When mail was distributed in the morning, the prisoners read their letters in their cells and you couldn't hear a fly buzz. During prescribed days and hours, the guards shouted the serial numbers of those with visitors. Gildo watched them hurrying down the hall, their faces suddenly as radiant as a child with a new present. It was then he tasted the bitter gall of abandonment and fell into a deep depression.

After the final judgment he was assigned to the laundry: he went to the cells with a cart and collected the dirty laundry, and along with other prisoners saw to the washing in tubs underground. It was an unpleasant work, all those filthy, spotted, stinking clothes to handle, but it distracted him from his gloomy thoughts, it filled that lost and wasted time in which his uselessness weighed on him like a rockslide. After a short while that work was inexplicably taken from him, and he wondered if Pig had something to do with it.

In order to earn the money to repay the baker and fill the poisonous idle time that was destroying him, he asked to work outside on street repaving or clearing forest paths in the vicinity, boasting previous experience; or else inside in the shops making furniture, shoes, or work clothes, but he supposed that because of an unfavorable report by Pig to the prison director he was denied that. Work was much in demand, in spite of the ridiculous pay, because every day of activity reduced two days of punishment.

These unjustified refusals inflamed him with a bitter rage that gave him no peace. The final straw had been denial to join the prison choir, something he could not understand. It was a privilege given for good behavior, like access to the library or playing on the baseball team. Didn't he deserve it? Didn't he always manage to maintain a correct attitude, obey orders, respect the rules and the hours? He suspected that officer Pig meant to make him pay for the license he took by whistling the aria with the man who had been discharged, even though he had also enjoyed it.

Everyday the guards unleashed pitiless vendettas against the prisoners who didn't bend to their crooked schemes, or they kept on the sidelines those who could be accused of having an irritating, aristocratic detachment toward the powers that ruled in the prison. A power that was actually only fear. Their arbitrary reports to the director, taken as pure as gold, made the good and bad times and determined the destiny of everyone. They seemed to have a sadistic taste for acting in a way that denied even the smallest amount relief to the lead-gray days, as if the slightest breath of normality must be eliminated. He had borrowed from the library an English-Italian dictionary, to try to decipher the prison regulations: where it was written that the most important aim of imprisonment, besides completing the just sentence for harm to the common good, was the re-education and elevation of the prisoner, so that when released he could take his rightful place in society.

He mulled over the wrongs done him that he couldn't digest, an incessant nagging, like a worm devouring his brain. His physical and mental conditions were declining, he felt completely worn out, and he lost his appetite. At lunch he barely tasted the boiled beef, the liver with onions, or the stew with potatoes; the suppers of burned and unseasoned macaroni or a piece of bread with molasses stayed in his stomach like rocks and kept him awake for hours. When he finally managed to fall asleep nightmares would waken him. He dreamed that someone was following him with an enormous sharp knife and hands grasped his neck, or that his mother fell dead in a ditch, and once his little sister Adele was bleeding from her mouth and sobbing convulsively.

He felt increasingly more confused, less master of himself. He did what was expected as though followed by a pack of angry dogs. He was always looking over his shoulder, waiting to be attached. When Pig came around, sneering, wheeling his club in the air, Gildo felt blind terror. In the courtyard he was assailed more frequently by attacks of panic that left him trembling, weak, and debilitated as though he had a high fever. He developed tics, automatic reflexes, which he hardly realized, such as keeping an eye on the hands and clothes of the prisoners to see if they were hiding a weapon, straining agonizingly at the sound of a slammed door or at the footsteps of approaching guards, counting the gulls and pigeons that pecked at the bread crumbs in the courtyard, or obsessively avoiding the cracks in the hallway bricks, or endlessly murmuring the same word like a magic charm to ward off his annihilation. Sometimes he seemed to lose his reason. He tormented himself with obsessions of persecution, delirious visions of brutalization, devastation, death, terrifying ghosts ready to seize and destroy him, which magnified with time until they wiped out every other thought.

As soon as the prisoners were gathered in the courtyard and the wing was empty, Gildo began to scrub the floor at one end of the hallway while another prisoner worked at the opposite end. It was the second day of his weekly turn to clean the section. He worked backward without looking over his shoulder, moving the bucket every time a part was washed, while he counted the bricks and in spite of himself, obeying a fixation he couldn't control. He was careful not to step on the cracks between them, as if it were a question of life or death. Aware of his own mental breakdown, almost as though crossing a border with no return, he was no longer master of his thoughts or actions, and was afraid of quickly losing all control. He didn't know what to do, how to defend himself, how to repair the harm that time had aggravated. And if he lost all control over his own existence, it was inevitable he would lose all control over himself.

Officer Pig kept watch leaning against the wall chatting with a colleague and from time to time would break into a loud laugh like a dog barking. Preoccupied by the need to do his work well, an anxious need for perfection that lately had been transformed into a mania, he bent over to polish the wet floor that shone in the dim light, searching for the smallest dry segments he had missed where some dirt might be lurking. He scrutinized the bricks one by one, to the farthest wall, and behind him, muffled as though very distant or passing through a thick curtain of fog, he heard sounds coming from the other man, scraping feet, the gurgle of the water when he immerged the rag, the dry slap when it hit the floor, the whack of the brush, the rattle when moving the bucket.

Stepping too far as he took a backward swipe, and determining with a sidelong glance how to miss the cracks, his heel hit and overturned his cohort's full bucket. The foamy blackish water spread over the pavement and quickly reached the shoes of the two guards. The two jumped away with curses, while the other prisoner, flying into a rage, cursed him: stupid cretin, where's your head, you ruined my work and now I have to start all over, why couldn't you look where you put your damn feet, stupid dago? Mortified, and anxious to set things right, while repeating sorry, sorry, he bent over to straighten the empty bucket and wipe up the water from the flooded floor. At that moment Pig and the other guard, after an exchange of looks, strode across the hallway, clubs at the ready. The first whack fell on Gildo's neck and shoulder, the second one, aimed at the back of his knee, made him lose his balance and flung him on the ground. Pig was on him. With one hand he grabbed the nape of his neck and pushed his face in the dirty water. Gildo gasped, mouth open, in the effort to breathe, swallowed water, coughed, struggled. The guard raised his face to allow him to breathe and then slammed it again in the filthy water. The guard kept it up for a while until he felt he had taught him a lesson. Only then did he release him and order him to get up and clean the entire hallway from end to end. The order was reinforced by a kick to his hip.

The two guards stood there looking at him with amusement while he got up, his wet uniform sticking to him and his face dripping with dirty water. Pig winked at the prisoner who had witnessed the scene and had laughed like a madman. With his colleague Pig moved a further away and began chatting as though nothing had happened. Gildo, trembling with rage, boiling with hate, while trying his best to squeeze water from his jacket and pull his dripping trousers from his thighs, plotted bloody revenge against those two disgusting animals. Irrational and useless fantasies, pure and simple wanderings of an unstable mind that had lost sight of reality and would alter it to his disadvantage. He knew very well that someone who dared rebel against a beating could be shut up in solitary confinement for weeks, starved, tortured, and even raped. Just like he knew it would be useless to complain to the prison director about the beatings he had received:

the guards would swear he had attacked them and they had only acted in self-defense. The prisoner who witnessed it, out of fear of retaliation, would testify against him, and the reprisal of the guards would be ferocious. There was no way out. He was helpless in their hands: protected by law and the conspiracy of silence, they could do what they wanted with him and no one would ever ask for an accounting.

In the ensuing days his furor was transformed into despondency. A desolate sense of impotence prostrated him, dragged him into apathetic dejection: the beatings, the humiliation, the insults he was forced to bear had deeply undermined his self-respect. If no one showed him the slightest esteem and consideration, how could he have any for himself? He counted the months and days that were left to serve before he could get out of that hell and go back to living: it wasn't important if he would be hungry again. Anything was better than prison where he was forced to put up with all sorts of injustice.

Bewildered and weakened, he moved slowly, dragging his feet, his legs heavy as boulders. His tormentor did not let him out of his sight. He interpreted Gildo's slow pace as a provoking insult to his authority. He slapped the club on the palm of his hand and shouted hurry up, shit, son-of-a-bitch. Gildo would move faster, but was immediately short of breath; he felt dizzy and slowed down again. For a week Pig had ordered Gildo to empty the slop buckets of all the cells on the ground floor, and his prison mates were delighted to be spared that repulsive job and openly made fun him. A scapegoat was useful to them all. It made them feel special and privileged, and gave them a sense of superiority in the prison hierarchy. Besides, anyone who let the guards shit on them showed they had no balls and it meant they deserved it.

Next the guard assigned him the job of collecting the trash. After everyone swept his own cell and piled the trash next to the door, among the sadistic snickers of the others, he had to pick it up with his bare hands — moldy food, rotten fruit and peels, cigarette butts, filthy paper sticky with spit or nameless body fluids — which he put in a garbage can and took to a receptacle in the cellar.

One afternoon, while he was bending over to pick up the trash, Pig, sneering with pleasure, had jabbed him in the back several times with his lead tipped club. Gildo suddenly stood up, blind with rage, and without considering the consequences of what he was about to do, he turned, and giving the guard a look of hatred, he grabbed hold of his baton and held it in mid air. If another guard had not intervened swiftly to block his arm and twist it behind his back, he would have torn it from Pig's hand and struck him. Pig's face had a look of immense surprise. He never would have suspected such an act of open rebellion from that stupid retarded dago. The line of prisoners hurrying to the courtyard suddenly stopped. An impressive silence fell, and incredulity and surprise could be read on their faces as well. The sheep had finally decided to bite the hand that tormented him. They were very curious to see how this would end and how dearly that fool would pay.

Pig, quickly recovering from surprise, angrily blew his whistle to call his colleagues to give him a hand. And while the other guard held Gildo's arm, Pig gave him a tremendous blow on his head, followed by a knee to his testicles. Gildo fell to the floor curled up, knees bent, hands at his groin, screaming from the pain that shattered him. Four guards came running. They took him under his arms, dragged his dead weight into his cell where they massacred him with their clubs. The prisoners had paused a few minutes to listen to the dull thuds and Gildo's screams before moving on to the courtyard. One man shook his head in compassion. It could be their turn one day.

That hand raised to block the club, reported to the director as a premeditated, unreasonable attack aggression a guard who was doing his daily job honestly, was punished with ten days in solitary confinement.

The guards went out slamming the door with a racket that made the whole wing shudder. The keys turned three times in the lock and everything fell silent. Gildo lay supine on the floor, immobile, with eyes closed, his body swollen and painful from the savage, bone breaking kicks. He breathed slowly and carefully. With every breath a sharp pain struck his chest as though his ribs were cracked. If he tried to move his right arm, ferocious shooting pains ran through his elbow. The blood flowing from his nose ran along his neck. He stayed like that for hours. In the course of the afternoon the silence was broken by the footsteps of the prisoners as they came in noisily from the courtyard, by the noise of the cell doors slamming, reopening for roll call and then closing, by the men going to supper in the dining room, and later by their return, by the last roll call, by the last turns of keys, by the last chatter and shouts of the day.

When the lights went out, they could hear a continual, muted moan like a mournful lullaby that made their skin crawl. Someone shouted: silence! But the lament went on. Gildo still lay on the floor, moving as though rocking himself. The sorrowful singsong came from his throat without his realizing it, an indomitable flow of sadness, of grief for his lost life. As though his heart was broken. He didn't even hear the complaints of the others calling for silence. Immersed in his delirium, he didn't even know where he was.

In the middle of the night he was suddenly overcome by a wild frenzy and began howling like a wounded animal, punching himself in the face, kicking like a crazed horse, heedless of the pain. He ground his teeth, foamed at his mouth. Like a possessed man he rolled on the floor biting his hands, wrists, arms, until he had incised crowns of bloody teeth marks. Floundering in the dark he came to the wall and began banging his head on it—

shocking, dull thuds that echoed through the whole wing. The terrifying howls like a butchered dog woke the prisoners who hung on the bars asking from cell to cell what was happening. Someone, supposing it was Gildo, called him by name. Others stuck a mirror between the bars to see down the dimly lit hallway. This time the guards had gone too far, someone murmured. Who knows what they had done to him to make him scream like that. Maybe he is crazy and is killing himself by breaking his head against the wall. Some of the prisoners started yelling for the guards. Those howls were unbearable; they broke their ears and stunned their brain. Shortly afterwards the guards came running with a great clanging of keys, shouting angrily. They ran the length of the hall to the cell where the noise was coming from; throwing open the door they ran to Gildo who was raving, biting his tongue and lips. He kicked and rolled around like he was possessed.

It seemed like an epileptic fit. Four men picked him up and tossed him on the bed, and while they held his shoulders and legs, Pig, cursing angrily, pulled the sheet out from under him. With expert hands he twisted it into large ropes and tied his ankles to the foot of the bed. The second sheet he passed over his chest and under his arms, tying it to the head of the bed. A colleague helped pull it tight so that he couldn't make the slightest movement. He seemed like a tranquil subject, but was actually dangerous. One guard ran to the infirmary and returned with an attendant armed with a syringe filled with a tranquilizer; which he emptied into his vein, and Gildo fell into deep unconsciousness. After prudently chaining his left ankle and right arm to the bed, they transported him to the infirmary. He slept for two days.

When he emerged from his torpor he realized he was trussed up and he again began to rave, struggle, and howl like an animal being slaughtered, so the nurse gave him a second sedating injection. When the calming effect passed he tried to slip out of the chains to sit up. Luckily he couldn't do it. Otherwise it might have raised all kinds of havoc. He kicked angrily in the air with his free leg, grabbed the iron head of the bed and shook it against the wall, he scratched his face with his fingernails. To make him stop hurting himself, the nurse bound him up like a sausage. Then he began to bite his tongue and lips until they bled; his body suddenly flinched and jerked; his head twitched continuously on the pillow. And again those bone-curdling howls that never seemed to stop. At times he would shout incomprehensible words in Italian, as though calling someone, or he would mutter something softly through thick lips like a prayer. Who knows? Who can understand these foreigners who don't speak English even after they've lived here for years. They offered him water, but he refused. He kept his teeth tightly clenched, and when they forced them open and managed to pour a little water into his mouth he furiously spit it out as though it were poisoned. They asked him if he wanted to pee, and since he gave no sign of having understood, they gave him a bedpan but not a drop came out. According to them he was an intractable mad man, dangerous to himself and others.

They sent for the prison doctor who asked him some questions that he did not answer: what was his name, where did he come from, how he did he feel, did he hurt some place, did he need something, did he want them to notify some relative? To quiet him the doctor spoke gently, but he soon gave up. It was clear that not only did he not understand English, but also that he wasn't listening, as if he were estranged from the world where nothing could reach him. The doctor shook his head and went to consult with the director. In his opinion that young man was insane and should be transferred quickly to an institution where we would get the care he needed — providing he was curable, which he seriously doubted. He was convinced he had harbored his insanity for some time and had exploded in the prison by chance or for some insignificant reason. What he meant was that he would have had the fit in any case: that young man, like so many emigrants coming from Latin countries, more fragile and excitable than northern Europeans, was affected by hereditary defects, which because of the frequency in which they were manifested in the people could be considered constitutional psychopathic personalities. You only had to consult the statistics to realize that in proportion there were many more foreigners in psychiatric hospitals than natives. The most typical form of mental alienation of these immigrants is the delusion of persecution: they feel rejected, marginalized, exploited by the country that welcomed them, a country that offers them not only freedom and democracy, which they are not accustomed to, but infinite opportunities to make their fortune and reach a well being that they couldn't dream of in their own country. To tell the truth, it is useless to try to integrate them into an economically advanced country, coming as they do from a simple, rough, primitive peasant culture, with rigid and antiquated customs and habits. For their own mental health it would be better for them to stay in their own villages.

Affected by a hereditary taint, and therefore inadequate, the director thought as he filled out the form for the judge to request internment of the prisoner in the state psychiatric hospital. He signed it with a flourish, shaking his head and thinking with irritation that one way or another these human rejects end up on public dole and by doing so cost the state, that is, honest tax payers like himself, a lot of money.

21

Giacomo, disconcerted, held in his hands the third letter sent to Gildo in the past year and a half at the San Francisco address and returned like the two preceding ones, marked by a blue stamp: Unknown. What happened to him? Where could he be? It's true that America is big and easily swallows people it doesn't spit back, but why had he never gotten in touch? And yet Carolina had given Gildo his address in Concrete when he went there, just as she had given Gildo's to him. She said the last letter she had received from him was last March, and after that complete silence. That brother had always been a little bit strange, but this was going too far.

It was fall of 1917, and Giacomo and Ninetta had been planning a trip to Italy for quite some time, to bring back their first-born left with her sister. Giacomo couldn't wait to have him there. By now he was big, reasonable, and ready to learn the many things that fathers have to teach their male offspring. In April a third daughter had been born, whom they had named Teresa in honor of her maternal grandmother. That third female was the last straw. Could it be that Ninetta was incapable of giving birth to a beautiful boy? They already had one, that's right, but since he didn't live with them it was as though he had never been born.

Ninetta was insistent; the time had come for them to see their family, now that they finally could afford it. For more than a year the entire debt had been paid off to the priest at Val Seriana, and by saving penny after penny, thanks to the boarders who paid on time, they had put aside enough money for the trip. For one person, naturally, don't even consider it enough for two. She would have liked to see her parents and sister again, to show off her pretty, bright little daughters to them and the village, but after a long debate between reason and desire, she had concluded that it was unthinkable to face the long and tiring trip by ship with two young children, and one of them only a few months old and still nursing. She thought about going with just the smallest and leaving the others with some woman available to take care of them for the two months necessary for the trip there and back and the time spent there. But she hadn't found one. And then, who would take care of the sixteen men boarders in her absence? Who might even find some other arrangement in the meantime? If she couldn't go, it was up to Giacomo. He had talked it over with Terenzio, who warned him that he couldn't guarantee him a job when he returned. He might be forced to replace him with another worker who would be difficult to get rid of. He should think it over.

There was little to think over. The prospect of losing his job scared him. It wouldn't be easy to find another one, and besides they thought well of him there and the pay was fair. When he was leaving Terenzio after their talk, the latter called him back: had he forgotten about the war still raging in Italy? Did he forget that if he returned to his country, since he wasn't yet thirty-two years old, by law he would be sent to prison for not serving in the army? Or in the best of circumstances, considering that the government needed men desperately, they would pardon him and send him straight to the front? Rather than risk jail or his skin, wouldn't it be better to postpone the trip until the fighting was over?

Giacomo was petrified: how could he have forgotten that sword hanging over his head? The third child had saved him from obligatory enlistment in the American contingent, but the blade would fall as soon as he stepped foot in Italy. And so the plan to go get their son went up in smoke, and it took him quite a while to resign himself to that reality.

However, Ninetta was as determined as ever. She wanted her Daniele back at any cost. Why have him if she couldn't enjoy him?

The photograph that her sister Camilla sent showed a beautiful, curly, dark-haired boy, with a serious look and the pouting face of one who isn't at all pleased. It was sad to see a restless, frowning expression on that little one who at that age should be happy and smiling. She was afraid her son was resentful about being left. By now he was big enough to think about things and he certainly must wonder why they didn't want him with them, while his little sisters, born after him, lived with their parents.

What could a boy understand about adult problems, about the difficulties of managing so many things, about the terrible fatigue of beginning a new life in a strange country that took all your time and energy, about the need to take one step at a time? She had no doubt about the affection and care of her sister, who still hadn't had the baby she wanted, but she was afraid that Daniele would become too attached to her and her husband and would forget about his own parents. Deep in her heart, like wormwood, gnawed the doubt that they didn't talk to him enough about them, in a way that he might keep memories of them. Sacrificing sleep she wrote him tender letters and asked Camilla to read them to him over and over, especially just before he went to sleep, and show him the photograph of the whole family she had sent. A nice portrait: she and Giacomo dressed in their best clothes, sitting on two large velvet-backed chairs. On the painted backdrop a shady, blooming garden. Two little girls sat on their father's knees, two little dolls with ribbons in their hair and identical dresses decorated with frills sewn by her own hands for the occasion. She held the last born in her arms, wearing a white baptismal dress, her little round bright eyes wide open from the magnesium flash. All this so their images would be stamped in Daniele's mind and when they finally got together again he would recognize them.

In thinking it over the idea occurred to her that since it was impossible for them to go to Italy, maybe someone could bring him to America. Surely some honest man in the village or surrounding area who had decided to emigrate could be entrusted to bring him.

She wrote at once to Camilla, who replied that the young men were all being called to arms and sent to the front, so no one could emigrate even if he wanted to. She had asked around in the valley villages if someone old enough to avoid the draft had plans to go to America, but she hadn't found anyone. These were troubled times. People preferred to go hungry as long as they could remain in peace where they were, waiting for the end of the war against the Krauts, an end impossible to foretell. And to think that the government had promised that it would last only a few months! Alessandro Azzola, engaged to Rosina dei Seresì who had gone to school to be a teacher, had been killed at the front. A fifth young man from Abbazzia to come back in a wooden box. The whole village was in mourning. Not to mention how dangerous sea travel had become. They talked about passenger ships being sunk by German submarines. There was a woman from Albino who, in spite of everything, had decided to leave with her children to join her husband. But she went to Argentina not knowing how far Argentina was from Concrete. Maybe they knew better, having seen the world. From what the secretary of the Albino commune said, many problems could arise in accompanying a child if you weren't a parent or relative. Too many underage males and females had disappeared, had even been sold by their parents to unscrupulous people who passed them off as their own children and exploited them as manual laborers, beggars, or prostitutes. As a consequence it was a long and costly process to get a passport. The father had to give his consent in writing to the Italian consulate in America and they had to communicate it to both the Italian and American authorities. That took months, they said, maybe as much as a year. And then, providing the person could be found, could they entrust a child to someone they didn't know well? Would that person take good care of him? Wouldn't the boy be afraid? And what if he got sick on the ship? And what if they didn't watch carefully and he fell into the sea? To let him leave in that situation seemed like a really crazy idea to her. The boy was growing nicely, he had started his first year at school, he was already covering entire pages of his notebook with notes and soon he would begin writing with pen and ink. The teacher was very pleased with him. She said he was intelligent, conscientious, and disciplined. Was it good to take him out of school to begin all over in America? Wouldn't he be very confused between Italian and English?

It was clear to Ninetta that her sister was reluctant to be separated from her nephew and she resented it. Camilla could have found someone who was leaving, but she didn't try and instead thought up one excuse after the other because she wanted to keep him. Not that Ninetta didn't realize the difficulties of such a long and complicated trip. To help move things along, she suggested Giacomo take a few days leave to go meet the boy at the port in San Francisco. Her exasperated husband told her those were daydreams. The real job was to get him to the port in the first place. In time she grudgingly became resigned to waiting until the end of the war that, unlike her sister, she thought would happen soon.

In late autumn, Gildo was transferred from the penitentiary to the state psychiatric hospital of Sacramento County. To keep him from having a recurrence and hurting himself during the trip, the doctor filled him with sedatives. In addition, the prison director ordered him to be put in handcuffs and chained to a seat of the van. Drugged, rocking with sleep, Gildo opened his eyes from time to time and through blurry eyes looked at the woods that were losing leaves, the blades of light that poured between the trees, the dry leaves that covered the road. For months the prison walls had blocked the sight of open spaces in the country and now he rediscovered them with dazed surprise. He thought how much he had missed the sight of the night sky; he had burned with the desire to contemplate the moon and the stars and feel the fresh evening breeze on his face. They passed well kept vineyards turning a harsh yellow, herds of grazing cows, large freshly plowed fields with brown clods gleaming in the sun's rays, scattered farm houses on the horizon, plumes of clear smoke rising from the chimneys. Not a living soul in sight.

The psychiatric hospital was deep in the country, a vast edifice surrounded by white walls in the middle of a large area fringed by thick trees and marked by dirt paths. Green benches were placed here and there, and a garden of still-flowering roses enclosed in geometric box bushes was at the main entrance. At the bottom of a gradual decline was a pretty gazebo with a wooden floor. In his state of torpor and prostration, compared to the prison, this seemed a calm, welcoming place swimming in light, and with a flash of irrational hope, he imagined that in the gazebo a band played opera lyrics and waltzes on Sunday. He saw a brown squirrel cross the yard quickly with tail erect. It climbed up a sycamore tree and huddled on a branch to chew something it held in its paws. He heard the distant croak of frogs that suggested the presence of a pond, the trill of blackbirds that swooped down and pecked the thick shinny green grass; the complaining clank of a horse-drawn mower, the rhythmic chop of the hoe of a gardener who broke the clods in the rose garden, the silvery ring of a bell were all sounds that came to him. Domestic, familiar, reassuring sounds.

At that moment a group of hatless men dressed in gray came out of the main entrance, escorted by two caretakers in white jackets and trousers. They marched in twos on the dirt path that crossed the yard and sloped down to the woods, in silence, with a strange mechanical gait like marionettes pulled by strings. One of them gestured strangely, as if shooing away annoying flies, another laughed with open mouth without making a sound, and another covered his ears with his hands. One of them tried to take off his jacket and trousers, stopped at once by the attendant.

The guard and nurse walked him around the building to a back wing, the special section for mentally ill prisoners. Through the massive door in the lobby they went to a dressing room where he was turned over to two attendants; they took off the handcuffs and gave them to the guard. They took off his clothes and photographed him nude, and as he had instinctively covered his genitals with his hand, the two held his arms. After dressing him in the gray uniform of the institution and replacing the handcuffs with a wrist cuffs — a contraption of canvas and leather straps that imprisoned his wrists, with a locked buckle at the end — they shaved his head. He's dangerous to himself and others the guard had warned the attendants before he and the nurse turned on their heels. Not word or sign of goodbye.

Inert, dazed, head heavy with disconnected thoughts, Gildo sat on a bench with his elbows on his knees and his eyes fixed on the wrist cuffs: that instrument of immobilization that reminded him of a dog's leash. From the floor rose whiffs of Lysol-soaked sawdust that a very thin, bald, toothless man was sweeping into a garbage bin. He moved his gaze to the solid bars and metal screens on the windows that allowed little light to come through. The bare walls were blindingly white, the table legs as well as the benches fixed to the floor with sturdy bolts. No different from San Quentin, it seemed to him. The lovely area he had seen outside didn't seem to have anything to do with the special section. He sighed and lowered his head onto his chest.

One of the attendants, after having consulted his papers, asked him some questions to which he did not reply although he understood them: he had nothing to say, he lacked the words, his brain was empty, his tongue swollen, his mouth dry, his face muscles paralyzed by the drugs. Useless questions, always the same, although they knew all about him. The attendant repeated them loudly, as if he were deaf, and since he continued to be silent, the two picked him up under his arms and carried him into the room of the psychiatric assistant on duty, who summarily checked his heart and lungs, lifted his eyelids, palpitated the muscles of his arms. When, waving a tongue depressor, he ordered him to open his mouth, Gildo clamped his teeth shut so the doctor immediately lost his patience and returned him to the attendants.

In the special section there were ten rooms with measures of maximum security for patients considered unpredictable. Their rooms were kept locked, the window equipped with bars and metal screens was too high to be reached, the glass peek hole on the door opened from the outside, the bed and table were fixed to the floor. The two men forced him down on the bed, the leather straps of the wrist cuffs were attached to wide strips of rough canvas on the head of the bed, and they went out locking the door behind them.

Crucified on the lumpy straw mattress all humps and valleys, drowsy and stupefied by the sedatives whose affect was lessening, his condition now changed rapidly into frightening nervous tension: he trembled from head to foot, his arms and legs pricked by myriads of burning needles jumped involuntarily. The impulse to massage them in order to relieve the torment was hindered by his bound hands. There was no heat in the room and his teeth chattered from the late autumn chill that the cotton uniform did little to alleviate. He would have liked to get under the blankets and wrap himself in their warmth. He tried to force the straps, but they were soundly tied to the bed. The inhuman, offensive measure of immobilization, as though he were a ferocious dog to keep on a chain, made him furious. He supposed it was due to the lies about his behavior in prison, written on the chart given to the attendant, while they certainly left out any mention of the terrible way he had been treated. He churned with powerless fury, shook his legs to free them from the prickling sting, wriggled his feet numb with cold. A painful cramp went from his neck down his left arm to his wrist. He shook and twisted his hand as much as the ties would allow, but couldn't get free. He struggled to get into a position that would relieve his back and shoulders.

From the room next door he could hear a monotonous, weak, exhausted lament, as if coming from underground passages. Time stood still. It must have been time to eat supper but he had no appetite. The sedatives had left him with a bitter mouth, an upset stomach, and a knot in his throat. He only wanted to cover himself, be warm, turn on his side and sleep.

After a while, the peek hole opened, a pair of eyes surveyed the room, the key turned in the lock, and one of the attendants entered with a supper tray: two meat balls, overcooked rice, the boiled prunes he was all too familiar with. Maybe he would have swallowed something if the man, a stony-faced youth, had untied him and let him eat by himself. Instead he had loosened the straps just enough to allow him to raise his chest and head, ready to be spoon-fed. As if Gildo's skin was tanned leather, he had unthinkingly placed the boiling hot aluminum plate on his chest, and at his loud protests had removed it with the greatest indifference.

Among the innumerable humiliations so far, being spoon-fed was a first, completely unexpected and unacceptable. He closed his mouth tight, and when the spoon grew near, he turned his head abruptly. The attendant, after many attempts, insults, and curses, went to call a colleague, who with one hand planted firmly on his forehead, grabbed his chin with the other, pressing it down to force his jaws open. Gildo clenched his teeth until it hurt, but he didn't surrender.

Suddenly, the man holding him down gave him a whack on his nose, and on the rebound his head hit the iron head of the bed and a rivulet of blood flowed from his nose. The brutal ceremony was resumed as though nothing had happened, but Gildo was determined and kept his mouth clamped shut with all his strength. They had to understand. He was an adult perfectly capable of feeding himself, and that treatment disgusted him. He was tempted to bite the hand of the attendant that clutched his jaw, or spit in the other man's face but, reasoning clearly, he rejected the idea, certain that the two would massacre him. Perspiring, red in the face, pushed beyond endurance, the attendants let fly a stream of abuse. If he continued that stupid game, he threatened, they would force-feed him with a rubber tube up his nose. A practice that was very painful and unpleasant; think it over, Italian shithead, and out they went.

In the next room a patient that had been moaning for hours was being spoon-fed. They urged him to hurry up, they didn't have time to waste. As soon as he chewed and swallowed he began to moan again in a dreadful way until they filled his mouth once more.

Gildo imagined that the patients in the other rooms were eating. A clatter of pans and flatware, then the attendants' cross grumbling, and when the doors were slammed and the keys turned in the locks the coarse shouts and strange laughter would begin. One strident voice begged the Lord to give him peace and to take him into heaven with him. Another sang at the top of his lungs a song that sounded like a desperate entreaty. One of them chanted and another had the hiccups. The lights went out. A tenuous light came from the high barred windows. Maybe there were stars, or maybe a full moon. Not even there was anyone allowed to see them. Silence fell, interrupted only by heavy breathing and an occasional cough.

All night long Gildo shivered with cold without being able to cover himself. Before daybreak he felt the uncomfortable need to urinate. His full bladder hurt and seemed about to burst. He held it as long as he could before giving up. Although he felt ashamed of wetting his bed like a baby, the warm liquid had been a comfort, but as it turned cold the dampness became unpleasant, as did the pungent smell of urine. He moved the best he could to a dry part, but his clothes and sheets were soaked through. The agonizing night cold chilled him to his bones and kept him from going back to sleep.

When barely dawn the early-rising patients awoke. Sounds coming from the rooms were chaotic, a continuous tumult until breakfast time: shouts, cries, prayers, songs, curses, kicks at the doors, knocks on the walls, feet shuffling, things being moved. The same attendant from the evening before brought his breakfast. Smelling the stink of urine, he had an expected fit over the wet bed. He loosened the straps from the side of the bed, leaving his hands bound, and with a volley of swear words took him to the latrine in the hall, a filthy room without a door. He didn't take his eyes off him for a minute while Gildo bent over and tried to defecate in the hole. His bound wrists made his equilibrium precarious, so that several times he had been about to fall in, and the presence of the attendant didn't help the process, who kept yelling Hurry up! Hurry up! He closed his eyes in order not to see him and to concentrate on the painful function that for the first time in his adult life he was forced to perform in the presence of a stranger. But his body fought back, wouldn't respond, rebelled at the violation of its privacy. The attendant led him back to his cell, removed the wet mattress and made him lie on the bare spring. He left the breakfast on the table and went out slamming the door.

No one came until evening. In addition to feeling cold his back ached from the diamond shapes on the bedspring poking him, and he couldn't turn on his side to find a moment of relief. A cruel torture that had all the earmarks of punishment.

When he returned the attendant seemed disposed to treat him more gently: he began a calm discourse explaining that he had been spoon-fed for a few days until they could be sure he was not violent or dangerous to himself or to others. After that not only would he be untied, but he would be able to eat in the dining room along with the peaceful patients, and like them go outside to stretch his legs and breathe fresh air.

Gildo understood what he was saying. The effects of the drugs had worn off, he was hungry as a wolf, he was dizzy from the long fast, his back hurt from the tormenting springs, so he made a temporary truce and docilely gulped down some semi-liquid slop, along with a strange tasting cup of cold coffee and a piece of stale bread. He was in their hands and it was only reasonable to keep that in mind. The attendant untied the straps and had him stand up. He took off the wrist cuffs and brought him clean sheets for the bed and dry clothes to put on. He put the mattress back in place, and before stretching out on the bed to be tied again, he was allowed to cover himself with a wool blanket. It was miraculous that he met no resistance because it seemed like the rule of that place was to make the patients' days an ordeal

Strangely enough the pain from being immobilized began to ease after the attendant left. The drowsiness that rapidly overtook him, taking away his strength and making him sink him into an indistinct fog, made him suspect that they had put some sedatives in that bad coffee. In a residual flash of consciousness before falling into sleep, he decided to refuse to take it from then on: it was tyrannical, a subtle way to control, abuse, suppress the patients. He wasn't crazy. He was perfectly sound mentally. The problem that broke out at San Quentin was the result of unbearable badgering, not loss of reason. He wanted more than anything to preserve his lucidity and be respected.

When the attendant returned for lunch and then for supper, he was still groggy with drugs and refused to eat. To his surprise the man didn't insist. Because he was unsteady on his feet, the attendant helped him out of bed, took him kindly by the arm, accompanied him to the latrine and kept his distance with his back turned.

The next morning the assistant psychiatrist appeared, the one who had checked him on his arrival, and two attendants he had never seen. He asked him why he refused to eat. He should understand that they would take the wrist cuffs away only when he became cooperative. That incomprehensible defiance went against his own best interests. He did not reply to the questions. Silence was a harmless form of protest that strangely enough made the personnel furious. It cost him a lot and wore him out, but he felt he couldn't do otherwise.

One of the attendants placed the breakfast try on the table, the other, standing beside the bed, held a glass filled with a milky solution. The doctor explained that it was a mixture of hysocyamine and bromide to take on an empty stomach. The latest discovery of medical science, a very efficacious cure for his syndrome, which would restore his health in short order. But only if he ate regularly, because nutrition was extremely important.

He signed for the attendant to bring the glass to his mouth. Gildo was certain it was not a medicinal cure, but one of the usual sedatives that made him as dull and dimwitted as a piece of wood and there was no way he was going to swallow it. Even doctors lied, like everyone else. He wanted desperately to be treated like a healthy, reasonable human being, but unfortunate circumstances had excluded him from a normal existence. He clenched his teeth and twisted his mouth. The other attendant held his head and took hold of his chin to force open his mouth, but couldn't do it. The doctor, livid with rage, gave a signal. One of the two went out and came back with a straitjacket, a jacket made of strong canvas, open in the back, with long sleeves sewn shut at the bottom and equipped with straps. The first man held him firmly down with a knee on his chest, while the second one put his right arm in the sleeve and the other one the left. Crossing them on his chest they turned him on his side and tied them tightly at the back. The assistant psychiatrist, arms crossed, observed the operation impassively. The glass was put to his lips again, and again refused. The doctor said they knew how to make him take the medicine. Had he ever heard of the rubber tube?

He remained tied all day long. After an hour his crossed arms, his joints forced into a contorted position, and his fingers numb at the end of the closed sleeves began to ache. Cramps and spasms like knives in his flesh went from his hands to his neck, from his nape to his back, and as the hours passed they became unbearable torture. From time to time one of the attendants would appear, ask him if he had changed his mind, he would not answer, and the man would go away slamming the door.

They didn't bring lunch and he wouldn't have eaten it. In the early afternoon the pain became so acute that he began to moan. The tight straitjacket squeezed his lungs and he felt like he had stilettos sticking in his chest. In spite of the moans no one came. Before supper three attendants came without the doctor, with a rubber tube and a strange wedge of pointed wood. One man held his head the other forced open his teeth and inserted the triangle into this mouth to hold it open, while the third, after pushing the rubber tube down his throat, began to pour the liquid.

The operation was terribly agonizing and traumatic: he felt he was suffocating, he gasped and writhed to get air. His nervousness increased the salivation, flooding his throat, hampering his breathing and setting off a furious fit of coughing. His neck muscles contracted in paroxysms of retching to expel the rigid tube obstructing his esophagus. The constricting straitjacket greatly increased the cruel treatment he was powerless to oppose.

The sedative ran to his stomach, but the operation was not over. As long as they were there, like force-feeding a goose, they poured a semi-liquid pap of milk and cream of wheat into the tube. When suddenly they ripped the tube from his throat he yelped in pain. The sweetish taste of blood and mucus stayed in his mouth for a long time, as well as the ache in his bruised pharynx and esophagus.

It had been a terrible lesson and he had learned it. From that day on he ate regularly, swallowed the daily dose of sedative, but still remained silent. After a week of good conduct his straitjacket was removed, replaced with wrist cuffs, which in turn were removed in time. He had missed the Thanksgiving Day feast: roast turkey with chestnut stuffing, garnished with cranberry sauce, sweet potatoes, and applesauce, just like he had eaten the first time in Renton, at the protestant church dinner. But he didn't miss the Christmas dinner, after he was permitted to eat in the dining room with forty patients transferred from prisons to the hospital for the mentally unbalanced. And he was allowed to go out into the courtyard to stretch his legs and breath the healthy, sparkling air of the winter countryside.

22

The director of the psychiatric hospital, Doctor Bolton, shared the widespread opinion among cultured and illuminated people that the contemplation of nature's beauties played a redemptive role with criminals, and was therapeutic for patients with mental disorders. Convinced that this commonplace constituted a scientific vision of the question, he arranged for the most peaceful patients to go out two times a day to walk on the paths of the vast park, with the aim of enjoying the lovely woods, meadows, streams and low hills on the hospital grounds. Not only that, but he was also convinced that motion for its own sake, enlivened by simple and efficacious exercise, had a salutary affect on their bodies debilitated by sickness.

In the case of intractable, and in his opinion, irrecoverable illness, naturally the question never even came up: they always wandered around in their obscure, ungovernable deliriums, or broke into senseless violent fits that put the safety of others, and often their own, in danger. Therefore, considering that there was no way they could enjoy it, the sight of nature would have little benefit. In fact, they lived apart and were strictly monitored in a special isolated section where he rarely stepped foot and from which they never left.

He was very sorry, on the other hand, for the mentally ill delinquents in the special section, who combined in a happy way (if you can call it that) both characteristics, the criminal and the psychological disorder. They had to live under the iron rules of the prisons they came from. As they were managed by sedatives and by the unfortunately necessary "persuasive interventions," as he liked to define them, they were allowed hours outside in the courtyard, but not walks in the open with the beneficial effect of contemplating nature. Naturally the hours in the open air were not under armed guards, as they were in prison, but protected by a wall that cut off the view of the surrounding countryside, and watched over with firmness, and at the same time discretion, by trained personnel.

Even religious assistance was offered, essential for elevating the poor disturbed minds to thoughts of faith: every afternoon in the chapel the peaceful patients sang reassuring hymns of glory to the Lord, and Sunday mornings the pastor gave them an uplifting sermon.

The doctor had also thought of the relief that music brings to the melancholy, the depressed, the hallucinating schizophrenics in whose minds chaos reigns, and had provided for it: on Sundays before lunch, when the weather was nice, they gathered at the bandstand at the bottom of the yard to listen to the band from the neighboring town. Then the musicians paraded around the building so that all the patients, even the agitated, could fully enjoy the calming effect in which he firmly believed.

That this mass of forlorn, and for the most part, sick men with terrible histories didn't care a fig about dawns and sunsets, woods, streams and hills was something that had never occurred to him. They cared even less in the middle of winter when on the bare, gloomy landscape, sometimes covered with snow, there was thick fog or rain or freezing cold, and the patients preferred to stay in where it was warm instead of scrambling outside to shiver in the cold. He thought it prudent and healthy to have them march in twos muffled up to their eyes in good and bad weather. The director did not understand why they were so unwilling to go out, and some decidedly recalcitrant, to then run back breathlessly, anxious to squat by the stove in the common room. Access to their rooms was forbidden during the day. They were much easier to control when all together, and anyway, the rooms were not heated.

However, whether peaceful or agitated, they were wild about the music, particularly the martial tunes that generally seemed to reinvigorate them and make them happy. But sometimes those worse off, depressed and introverted, would break into hysterical shrieks and stop their ears with their hands, as if the sound of the instruments was too painful to bear.

On sunny Sundays, Gildo would look out of the common room window that overlooked the garden and watch the village band arrive. He watched the noisy group of authorized patients going down to the bandstand that was out of sight. The first boom of the bass drum and the explosion of brass always gave him a start of pleasure, but as the tunes went on one after the other he would feel a sad sense of exclusion, along with the bitterness of defeat. If things had turned out differently, he might have been part of a group of energetic men like those, and with the same enthusiasm, the same transport and passion, to give life to exhilarating and festive music. Instead he was behind bars asking himself if he would ever get out of there, who and when would some day liberate him, and if he would ever be allowed to finger the keys of an instrument. The music carried him back to the past and the dark shadowy future loomed ahead. The irruption of life into that place of segregation, instead of comforting him, showed him the extent of the separation and contrast between the world of the healthy and that of the insane. Those good and solid citizens on the outside didn't want to be disturbed by the mentally deranged. They put them behind solid walls to vegetate and mold and forgot about them. The band did a good service on sunny Sundays, but they kept a fair distance from the patients, who on those occasions were watched more closely than usual, especially those in the security section. Visits from relatives were very rare: who wanted anything to do with someone who had added to the indelible shame of prison that still more scandalous shame of the mental hospital?

The band, after finishing the concert—marches, polkas, waltzes, mazurkas, one-step, breakdown—walked the perimeter of the hospital playing, and concluded with the sentimental *Home Sweet Home*. From the window Gildo observed the gaily-colored procession—sky blue uniforms with red strips down the sides of the trousers, silver frogs and decorations, bright red caps—led by a drum major who waved his polished golden baton in the air to mark the rhythm. The brass and tympanis flashed in the sunlight, the lustrous brown wood of the drums shone like chestnut shells, the cheeks of the wind musicians were swollen with air, red as ripe tomatoes. The band marched quickly toward houses with tables set for Sunday dinner, the music fading in the distance and silence returning. The festivity was over.

From the same window every day Gildo observed the human wrecks of the "normal" section he could see walking outside two by two. It seemed like a sorry group of chained convicts, and he was almost happy he wasn't allowed to go out to undergo the same humiliation. Winter was raging. Often a low cloud mass as black as pitch covered the sky, and a furious wind shook the trees. The patients slogged on head down, hugging their flapping coats. The squalls tangled their scarves and ripped them from their necks, like the wool caps that rolled on the ground, chased after with wild cries and disjointed, extravagant gestures. The attendants, like guardians of undisciplined sheep, shouted hoarsely and ran to herd them back in line. One patient would dig in his heels and refuse to move, another one would get lost, and another would suddenly sit on the frozen grass crying like a lost child and refuse to get up. They picked him up bodily and obliged him to continue walking. Little opaque breaths of vapor issued from their mouths. Noses, ears, cheeks went the gamut from bright red to a grayish pallor.

The group stopped in a level area for exercise. The attendants worked to line them up in semblance of order. They were told to raise their arms above their heads and to spread them like wings, to bend their knees, to raise and lower their right and then left leg. Some stood stock still as though deaf, others lost their balance and fell to the ground, and some wandered off and had to be brought back.

Gildo watched the sad spectacle of that unfortunate bunch treated like imbeciles, in which he could recognize his same situation: stripped of all will and desire, cut off from every possibility for making decisions and caring for themselves, their dignity demeaned, as suffering ill adults, they were reduced to powerless phantoms, each one with his heinous story. If he had had the permission, he would have wandered alone as he pleased through the park, sat on a bench, leaned against a tree or even climbed a tree, ran as fast as he could, lay on his back in the grass. After a downpour, a rainbow astride the hills, seen from the same window, seemed like a miracle to him.

The fresh air hour in the courtyard was identical to that in the prison, a few steps in one direction, a few steps in the other, a senseless back and forth, always with the wall in front of you. In the common room there was nothing to do all day long. You died from boredom and the stink of sweat and urine; some, prostrated by sedatives and reduced to catatonic states, sat drooling in silence on benches attached to the walls. One man was curled up in a corner in a fetal position, an agitated man walked back and forth chanting disconnected phrases, or alternatively singing at the top of his lungs. Others angrily tore off their clothes. One masturbates. The epileptics wore rubber helmets. Many, without shoe laces or belts for fear they might hang themselves, held up their trousers with their hands, which fell to their ankles when they forgot; they then had to take little baby steps, dragging their pants on the floor. Some, afflicted with tics or ritualistic fixations, continually brought their hand to their forehead or ear, licked a finger, worried their hair, kept looking behind them in case someone was about to jump on them, talked to damp spots on the wall where they saw some phantoms. Others counted their steps in one direction, turned abruptly, and counted them in another direction. And some sat on the floor hugging their knees, hiding their faces, or lay moaning for hours. One patient took off his shoes, urinated, and put them back on. Gildo was afraid of being infected by those signal manifestations of loss of reason. The only way he knew how to protect his residual sanity was by passive resistance: he said nothing and retreated to a corner, closed his eyes and sometimes slept.

The personnel had strict orders never to turn their backs on a patient. Once a completely calm patient jumped on the back of an attendant and sank his teeth in his neck. More often someone in an excess of impotent rage would suddenly sock his neighbor, or fly into a rage and throw himself against a wall in the attempt to smash his head. An attendant would promptly jump on his back and squeeze an iron arm around his throat until he nearly strangled, to be dragged to a padded isolation cell and put in a straitjacket if he didn't calm down.

Most of them waited for lunch passive and afraid, and ran to the dining room when the bell rang. They fell on the food grunting and whimpering like animals and in a minute had devoured the mixture of bread, soup, and chopped meat, one arm around their dish to protect the treasure, their ration of bread gripped in one hand. The most agile stole food from the others and savage fights broke out that were settled by the rough interventions of the personnel. One poor soul took a handful of pap from his dish and rubbed it in his hair. Knives and forks were not allowed, spoons and glasses were counted and taken away before the patients left the room, and immediately afterwards bodies were searched to make sure they had hidden no objects such as nails, pieces of glass, string, even pencils and pens, suitable for harming themselves or others. One time a patient picked up a piece of broken glass from the dining room floor. He kept it in his mouth for days and one night he used it to cut his wrists. He was found half dead just in time and saved. Another man blinded himself with a pencil stub. Searching was a delicate operation, considered offensive and mortifying, so that they often rebelled. Gildo underwent the scorching insult of rummaging hands, but he did not rebel: the straitjacket was a good deal worse.

He ate slowly, reluctantly, uncomfortable in the squalor of that abyss where he had fallen, drugged and exhausted by the pharmaceuticals that killed his appetite. An attendant urged him to hurry up, threatening to take away his plate. Not because he had anything against him, but he was impatient to get them back to the recreation room where it was easier to keep an eye on them. But most of all, he was anxious to turn them over to colleagues at the eagerly awaited end of shift, because even the attendants suffered from the prolonged contact with the mentally ill. They finally became infected and manifested disorders, fixations, prosecution complexes and cruel attitudes, which should have earned them their turn in the hospital: nothing changes one more drastically than being authorized to use violence. The rare attendant who showed kindness toward his patients was ridiculed by his colleagues, accused of being weak and cowardly, and forced to toe the line. To be legitimized to dominate the defenseless leads to the perverse sentiment of omnipotence and the ill are seen as worthless, drifting wrecks without the slightest connection to the human race.

The obligatory bath came around once a week, supervised by the personnel. Gildo held back and tried to pass it up: because of the scarcity of hot water the patients all used the same bathwater, an unhygienic practice that repelled him. He would have preferred washing in the sink piecemeal rather than immerse himself in that liquid with little floating islands of the dirt of others. But in the end he had to give in and be covered with a sticky, oily, disgusting patina.

One Sunday morning he tried to hum a tune along with the band, but a sound wouldn't come out and it scared him. He hadn't spoken in a long time; maybe his vocal chords had atrophied. Afraid of losing the ability to talk, he began to say phrases aloud in the common room.

To his great surprise a pale, gray little man answered, who up to then had always kept quiet and alone in a corner. His name was Eliseo, an immigrant like Gildo, and a few days later he told his story. Seven years ago he had left his hometown in the province of Sondrio after lightning had burned his house down, along with the small amount of money he had hidden under a brick. His older son had died in the fire. In California he had worked in a leather factory, saved all he could and deposited it with a banker who had suddenly closed his office and disappeared. A few months later he saw him in the street and followed him. He found out where he lived and it had been easy to ambush him and beat the living daylights out of him. He didn't think to cover his face, and so that bastard had recognized him and hadn't hesitated to denounce him. He was a sly fellow and had been careful to destroy all the papers regarding deposits and withdrawals, so there was no proof of his business. The receipts of deposits Eliseo had saved were considered worthless, with made up letterheads and illegible scribbles for a signature. He couldn't find any witness to testify in his favor; the other poor hoodwinked souls like him had scattered who knows where and were untraceable. That cheat's slick lawyer managed to demonstrate that he had made up the story out of whole cloth, and the court convicted him of forgery and armed assault. He was sentenced to a year and a half of imprisonment for the thrashing.

In prison he found himself wrestling with an American boss who lorded it over everyone and persecuted him, tormented him, hit him, extorted the little money he had left, and threatened to cut his throat with a jackknife he kept hidden in a sock. He had lived in continual terror until, to save himself, he decided to pretend to be crazy. He shouted and raved for days, beat his head against the wall, tried to hang himself with his sheet. They had believed him and sent him to the mental hospital. He didn't have the slightest idea when he would get out either. He would wake up suddenly at night with anxiety attacks or from certain recurrent nightmares in which the American boss was chasing him with a knife. He ran but his legs wouldn't move, as if he had heavy iron balls on his ankles. Just when he was about to be overtaken he would wake up terrified, bathed in sweat, his heart pounding. Years ago he had had a heart attack. Those nightmares could cause another one that certainly would kill him. Gildo comforted him as best he could, and Eliseo seemed somewhat reassured.

The conversation and quiet fellowship with a fellow Italian as unfortunate as he was a help that accompanied him through spring and summer until fall. One year of detention had passed, but the doctors didn't tell him anything. He felt he was cured. He was reasonable and tranquil. The dose of sedatives had been reduced. So one day he went to the psychiatrist who was handling his case and asked him how long he would have to stay in the hospital. His hands were tied: it wasn't up to them to decide, but the court judge and they hadn't received any instructions concerning him.

That blow knocked him senseless for days. They had buried him in a ditched, marked it with a stone, and forgot about him. Vanished from the face of the earth, as if he had never existed. After days and nights of burning anxiety without knowing what to do, he was overcome by a fit of rage. He tore his clothes, rolled on the ground howling like an animal and bit his hands until they bled. He beat his fists and head against the wall, refused to eat or drink until they once again put him in a straitjacket and took him to a padded cell, and fed him with a rubber tube filled with drugs. Instead of getting well the patient had suddenly regressed into a state of acute self-destructive frenzy that required appropriate cures and continual surveillance.

On November 1918, Austria, crushed by the Italian army in the battle of Vittorio Veneto, signed an armistice. The army that had descended the valleys with proud certainty now, suddenly humiliated and defeated, went back up disorganized and without hope. The horrible massacre was over. The dead on both sides numbered in the millions.

Over the year the exodus of emigrants from the United States to their countries of origin had already begun, and after the conflict ended it suddenly skyrocketed In a few months one million three hundred thousand men of various nationalities had left, among them one hundred thousand Italians, each one of which it was calculated had carried away with him amounts from two to fifteen thousand dollars, saved penny by penny over years or decades of work. An enormous, unexpected drain of around four billion dollars that shook the foundations of the government, equal to four-fifths of the American gold reserve before the war. Politicians and newspapers raged against the ingrates who left with their pockets full of money earned in the country that had so generously opened their doors and offered them grand opportunities, only to have them leave and spend it in their own country.

They were leaving because life in America had become too expensive, because years before the dollar that was exchanged for five lire was now exchanged for twenty. So their modest accumulation allowed them to buy land and build a house in their hometown, where they could still live with little. They left also because many states had imposed restrictions on foreign workers. But most of all because, once the war was over, a wave of hostile feeling rose up against the immigrants. First in line were Slavs, Greeks, Hungarians, Italians — weak races, physically and mentally inferior, rough and uncultured, who threatened to reduce Americans to a minority. They endangered the superior civilization, lowered the level and the tone of daily life, polluted the national culture. With deplorable, shameful frequency, they broke laws, soiled their hands with crimes, crowded the federal prisons, elevated abnormally the number of suicides and the mentally ill. All phenomena that constituted enormous bother and prohibitive costs for the community.

Although many had left the country, the honest American citizen's great bugbear remained the invasion of hordes of Balkans and southern Europeans impoverished by the war. Not only poor, but violent people full of ill will, Reds infected by the subversive ideas of the Bolshevik revolution, anarchists, radicals and dissidents of every kind, determined to overturn the social order of an orderly, civil democratic nation. The press ignited delirious crusades of hate against these miserable dregs and launched catastrophic predictions about the horrors of the communist wave that was ready to pour over the coasts.

Immigrants had always taken work from the natives, but never so much as now, when the veterans were returning home, and the country had to show its gratitude by offering them worthy occupations. American citizens still couldn't understand why so many brave boys had been sent to suffer and die in those distant, unknown places that weren't important to anyone. What did Europe have to do with them? Old, spineless Europe was capable only of starting wars and then of whining and begging American help because it couldn't go it alone.

America for Americans! Foreigners go home! they shouted in the streets, raising placards and banners. The Unions stirred up the fire by asking their organizations to raise the membership fee to discourage undesirables from joining. Protestant ministers, in their austere churches, delivered inflammatory sermons: Lord, why must we receive in our cities the refuse of other nations? Aren't you powerful enough to civilize them in their own countries? Politicians proposed drastic remedies to counteract the invasions: drown them all, beat them, toss them all in prison.

There were also some—but only a few to be honest—who pointed out how those millions of foreign workers had taken on the lowest, dirtiest, hardest, and most dangerous jobs that Americans refused to do, and furthermore they accepted slave-like conditions and poor wages that the natives would not tolerate. Therefore, where was the threat to the local laborer? Have we forgotten how many immigrants have died building bridges, subways, railroads, roads, tunnels, sewage systems, and aqueducts? Have we forgotten the maimed that were forced to go home because they were unable to work, going back poorer than when they left? Like wounded animals that drag themselves to their den to die? And all this for a dollar and a half a day, less than what coloreds are paid now? When newspapers proudly declaimed the glory of the one hundred twelve thousand trains passing in one year alone through the tunnels of New York, ninety-nine per cent of them on schedule and without the slightest problem, they forgot that that this huge operation, like so many others, cost the lives of innumerable foreigners. Meat for slaughter is what they were. The immigration laws had already blown away the "chaff," rejecting those with sickness, physical defects, mental disturbances, or who upon arrival possessed less than twenty-five dollars. And the Literacy Act of the preceding year prevented those who didn't know how to read and write from disembarking. Wasn't that enough? What more did they want?

And the treatment of white women? The thousands of young women attracted by the mirage of an honest job and who ended up on the sidewalks or brothels? Every year in Chicago alone three thousand young immigrants were trapped into prostitution, deprived of passports, blackmailed, beaten, raped, threatened with death. Who were the customers who encouraged that shameful business, who used them and abused them, if not honorable, upright American citizens?

Blaming the immigrants, especially the Italians, of starting criminal organizations did not take into account how the mafia could seem like a social promotion for those who felt rejected, disparaged and scorned by the white Anglo-Saxon and Protestant society that considered them filthy beggars, though they slaved away day and night, overwhelmed by difficulties and fatigue.

But the few voices went unheard.

It seemed right. Ninetta was satisfied and full of hope, the war was over, the dangers of a sea voyage during war had been swept away, and now they could begin talking about little Daniele again. The exchange of letters with her sister was resumed, but certain difficulties seemed insurmountable. Camilla informed them that if Giacomo came to Italy to get him he would no longer be imprisoned as a shirker, but he would be obliged to do three months of military service, if he wasn't thirty-two years old, which she thought he wasn't. The country's punishment of its immigrant sons who had not answered the call infuriated Giacomo. Forget about donating three months to the government, losing work and money, with nothing to show for it. For some time at the Portland Cement Company he had gone from unloading clay and limestone to the cleaner and less fatiguing work with the revolving ovens where material was cooked to obtain clinker. His daily wage of one dollar and a half was raised to two dollars, a very respectable salary for those times. Not to be thrown away for something you had no idea how might turn out. Certainly, he wanted this son he hardly knew back with him, but he had to face reality.

The news that Camilla had not mentioned in order not to alarm them, saying instead that the epidemic had not crossed the ocean, was that the Spanish flue had broken out over Europe even before the war ended: the illness that began like an ordinary case of flu, with high fever and cough, quickly grew worse. The lungs filled with a bloody fluid, making the infected person struggle for breath and soon die a horrible death from suffocation. Tens of millions of human lives were cut short, more than had fallen in four years of war, and there had been dozens of deaths in Abbazzia. Camilla trembled with fear that the boy might get sick and die, and as protection had isolated him during the time when it had been most virulent. Unaware that it had spread in America also, she was convinced that news of it had not reached her sister in the lost corner of the world where she lived. Actually she was right. Only later did Ninetta learn of the mortal epidemic when a few cases turned up in Concrete, at the same time it was fading in Europe.

As she was ignorant of the sword that hung over her son's head, she urged Camilla to find some villager immigrating to America to accompany him: now that the veterans were coming back from the front to find themselves without work and penniless, surely many would emigrate. And those who had returned to Italy at the outbreak of war, what prospects did they have except to go back to America with the government-paid ticket? Wasn't there someone in the village?

Camilla said she had not found any villager ready to leave. Ninetta begged her husband to ask Terenzio to find a job at the cement factory for one of his brothers—Mario, Egidio, or Attilio—now grown and big. Or even all three, so the uncles could accompany their nephew and her worries would be over. Giacomo did as he was asked, but Terenzio's answer was that if he would just look around he would see there wasn't room for one more worker, and Giacomo was lucky they hadn't fired him. He should be careful: if he left to pick up his kid he would lose his job. In this way they had gone full circle and the boy stayed where he was, much to Camilla's great joy.

Who didn't know, or perhaps she knew and kept quiet about it, that Luigino and Giusepì, veterans of the war, trusting in the promise of the free trip, planned to return to America. Luigino had written Gildo at his old address to inform him of his eventual arrival, but had received no reply, and the letter hadn't even been returned. He wasn't particularly concerned. Once he reached his destination he would go see Caterina who would know where to find him. Or he would visit Aniceto, or look for Gildo at one of the places where he played or at the celebrations of their fellow Italians. Everyone knew everyone in the Italian quarters; there was no danger that they would lose all trace of anyone.

Involved with the long and complicated procedure for the new passport now obligatory for the ex-patriot, getting the documents from the recruiting office attesting to his and his brother's participation in the war, and all the exasperating bureaucratic red tape to get the free trip (the states' coffers had been emptied by the enormous military expenditures), Luigino promised himself every day to go ask for information about Gildo from his family, and every day he had to put it off. Only on the eve of his departure did he find the time to scramble up to the bird catching house only to learn that they hadn't received even a line from him in three years. He promised the poor mother who had barely enough to stay alive that he would look for him and persuade him, or rather make him get in touch with her. In the meantime, just in case, he took Giacomo's address in Concrete.

The two brothers weren't able to leave before October 1919. Luckily the Spanish flu had spared the whole family, but because of the epidemic medical checks at the Genoa port were very strict and even more so at the port in New York. The Americans were afraid that the European immigrants might revive it again. The first unpleasant surprise had been the increase in the cost of embarking. The ship went straight to San Francisco across the Panama Canal for a short distance so narrow it made you want to reach out to touch the shores on either side. Their second unpleasant surprise came when they faced the exasperating arrival procedures: ten dollars to fork over for entrance fee. And the third, the introduction of the Literacy test.

Giusepì was first, and when the interpreter asked if he knew how to read and write, he had been scared to death and hesitated to answer: he could barely read, and much less write. He could hardly hold a pen in his hand and make a few chicken scratches that even he had difficulty reading. His teacher had told him that anyone who couldn't read his own writing was a dunce.

He sought his brother's eyes for help in the long line behind him, but in the confusion was unable to see him. Increasingly more anxious and upset, while the impatient interpreter repeated the question, waving a sheet of paper under his nose, he called Luigino loudly, but in that uproar he couldn't have heard. At the third request, this time in decidedly irritated tones, terrified of being subjected to a difficult test he couldn't pass, he said no, he didn't know how to read and write. The interpreter made a sign to a functionary and ordered him to join a group of men standing aside. Upset and terrified of some unknown impending disaster, he broke into a cold sweat, shifted nervously from one foot to the other, and bit his lip. When it was Luigino's turn, the interpreter asked the same question, and without hesitation he answered yes. He was handed a paper and ordered to read. He read, quick and sure, and was passed.

He joined Giusepì, surprised that he was standing there instead of going on, and when he muttered rapidly what had happened, Luigino grew dark and returned to the interpreter, asking for an explanation. According to the Immigration Act of 1817, it had been established that anyone would be rejected who could not read and write. Amazed and infuriated, he went back to his brother, took him by the arm and dragged him back, demanding to see the sheet of paper. He almost snatched it from the interpreter's hand, stuck it in his brother's hand, yelling: Read, read, for God's sake, or you'll get sent back home!

Staring and contorted with fear, he turned it over. Luigino turned it back to the right side, and tense as a slingshot, waited with this heart in his throat for him to read the thirty words that would open the doors of that shitty country to his brother. But Giusepì couldn't do it: he trembled from head to foot, his sight was clouded, he saw mixed and unfocused signs dance on the white paper. His heart was bursting in his chest and blood roared in his ears. He stared at Luigino with the lost look of a drowning man, who with a push on his ribs urged him to begin. His face sweating and flushed, he opened his mouth, closed it, swallowed, opened it again, but only an indistinct stammer came out. The interpreter took the paper from his hands.

Rejected. Foaming with rage, Luigino thought that it had all been useless to fight for his country in the muddy trenches, to be witness to the bloody massacre of so many fellow soldiers, to risk his skin and die of fright every minute for four long endless years. It wasn't necessary to know how to read and write to be killed like animals at the slaughterhouse, just like it wasn't necessary for the humble, backbreaking work that America deigned to offer them. The truth was that America no longer had need of them.

> We have dug your millions of ditches
> We have built your infinite roads
> We have carried your wood and water
> And we have bowed under your loads
> We have done the humble work
> Despised by your race
> And now you don't want to admit us
> Because we don't know how to read.

23

In the final year of the war alcoholism had grown to such an alarming degree that it was on the point of becoming a serious social problem. Women's associations, Methodist ministers, fundamentalist puritans in excited ferment urged the government to take drastic steps to eradicate this serious problem that was tragically destroying entire families. Women and children were the first to suffer, victims of the domestic hell of fathers and husbands brutalized by alcohol that, by squandering their pay check in the bars, left them hungry and without resources, and dumped on them the bestial effects of lack of moderation. Countless were the mistreated, beaten, violated women, children covered with bruises and terrorized by their fathers' violence, houses turned upside down by wild men in prey of the fumes of alcohol. It wouldn't help to close the local bars early, as many suggested, because they would only get drunk faster.

More and more often the police were forced to intervene and pick drunks off the dirty street or settle furious fights in bars or sidewalks: nights spent in the clink and stratospheric fines for disturbing the peace weren't enough to curb the drinking. And it didn't bring anyone to his senses to lose his job, and those who ran up bar debts and got the bum's rush simply changed locales. The only solution was to ban alcohol from the country entirely.

The phenomenon did not pertain so much the Mediterranean immigrants who were content to sip a glass of red wine with lunch and dinner, but the American workers who instead gulped down like water high-grade alcohol drinks—local malt whisky, scotch from Scotland, gin, brandy, rum, or a dozen pints of beer. So the Italians were very surprised, and then very resentful when Congress in 1919 approved the 18th Amendment of the Constitution and they discovered that even that harmless glass that restored them after grueling work and lifted their spirits in rare get-togethers was strictly forbidden.

Ninetta's sixteen boarders also stoutly rebelled. They counted on that benevolent daily drink as much as the pasta or polenta. And while she, who was abstemious, shrugged her shoulders indifferently, Giacomo, who counted on it as much as they, was at once intent on finding a way around that hair-brained resolution. My God, a drop of wine was one thing, a whole bottle of Kentucky bourbon the Americans downed every evening was another.

Certain of being in the right they had lengthy discussions about how to get around the law, even knowing that to break it would cost dearly—high fines and years in jail. They plotted in the dark like conspirators after solemnly promising to keep their mouths shut. Not even a whisper must get out. Lucia, the older girl, in spite of her angry objections, was sent to bed immediately after supper along with her sisters so she wouldn't listen to the grown-ups talking; they spoke in English as well as Italian and were afraid she might tell someone about their plans.

One wit who didn't know what he was saying had suggested pressing grapes and letting the most ferment in the basement. The house was isolated, and except for the black bears that wandered around at night looking for food, there were no neighbors to stick their noses in their business and report them.

And where would they get the grapes? Another one sneered. They didn't have vineyards in Washington state, and not only because of the inclement weather, rainy and humid, but also because of the dense, heavy soil good for fir and alder trees. Grapes needed light, rocky soil. The red wine they had been drinking came from California vineyards, which, according to the law, would soon be eradicated. Selling grapes was also prohibited: and even if they found them somewhere they would arrive in such bad condition they would be ready for the garbage bin. So, transporting them was not economical and too risky. Not an option.

A man from Bergamo had an idea that seemed reasonable: from now on vineyards were illegal, so they had better not even think about making wine. And even if some dimwits continued to cultivate them they couldn't hide what they were doing: grapes were good for just one thing. Something difficult to keep secret. On the other hand, you could still plant grains like wheat, barley, and rye that the Americans ferment to make whisky. So why not learn how to make it? This plan aroused a lot of enthusiasm that was soon deflated. It was a complicated process that none of them knew. They wouldn't know where to start.

However, a boarder from Friuli presented a more convincing argument. Washington State might not have vineyards, but it had wonderful plums, like they had in Italy, where the temperature was almost as cold. For centuries peasants in Friuli distilled a wonderful aquavit from that fruit, and if you drink it down in one gulp you can't breathe for an hour. He had watched his old relatives make it and it wasn't difficult. You just needed a metal boiler, wood for bringing the compote to a boil, some tubing, an alembic with a coil of pure tin in which the passing steam condenses until the distillate comes out the beak. A contraption easy enough for them to put together.

At that point Giacomo remembered that his grandfather distilled a kind of liqueur from strawberry grapes, the only kind that grew and ripened in the Val Seriana, and he made a sort of strange grappa from it that everyone was happy to drink. Strawberry grapes didn't exist here, but there were plenty of plums.

So it was that without being aware of the momentous turning point, the loss of their innocent glass of wine, Ninetta's boarders, to her great displeasure, got in the habit of drinking in one sitting entire bottles of the aquavit they distilled in the basement. The devastating effects were not slow in making themselves felt: they went to bed drunk, got up in the morning staggering with sleep and in a bad mood, gulped down a cup of coffee with grappa and argued over nothing. They dragged themselves to work already exhausted, with stomachs churning, and Terenzio railed against those slobs who ruined their life with their own hands.

Ninetta argued with her husband every day. She reprehended him, blaming him for wasting money on the shameful vice of drinking, just like his father who had lost everything because of it. He should remember his responsibilities to his children. What would happen to them if he ended up in jail? He defended himself calmly, accused her of making too much out of it. He only drank a little drop in the evening. What was wrong with that? Had she ever seen him drunk?

She grew more anxious, afraid the business in the basement would be discovered, and every time a stranger came to the house she grew pale with terror. All you had to do was sniff the air and you would know what was going on. She threatened to smash the alembic with a hammer or pour the aquavit in the toilet. When one of them got high she became furious and refused to serve his supper. But a lot of good that did.

One day, out of fatigue, anxiety, and anguish, she fell senseless to the kitchen floor. When the boarders came home for lunch they found her. The little girls were beside her crying, picking at her dress, pulling her nose and calling their mother who they believed was dead. The older girl, her arm around her little sisters, was crying the loudest.

After Ninetta's nervous breakdown that made them feel like heartless worms without a conscience, they quit distilling grappa for a week. Then they started up at night, taking turns, on the sly, careful not to make any noise that would wake her. But the pungent odor rose up the stairs, impregnated the whole house, went out the windows, and could not be hidden. They drank it furtively, feeling like thieves, unable to give up that burst of euphoria that inflamed the brain.

Elsewhere, most Italians weren't able to produce their own aquavit, but they bought it under the counter from illegal dealers. And if they didn't find it they bought the strong local drink. The impact of strong drink on people used to drinking only wine was disastrous. Aside from the hyperbolic amount it cost them, they could not handle it; it caused bad hangovers, nausea, vomiting, blinding headaches.

Prohibition did very little toward stemming the use and abuse of alcohol. Convoys of foreign ships unloaded at night in the ports where the coastguard, softened up by generous bribes, closed both eyes. Bootleggers prospered. Wagons disguised with innocuous signs, the merchandise hidden under innocent products, delivered the booze to every corner of the country. Smuggling flourished and bloody fights broke out between gangs for the monopoly of the black market. Distilleries were run by organized criminals that made a killing selling the alcohol at double the past prices. Many bars obliged to serve orangeade, lemonade, Coca Cola, Pepsi Cola, transformed themselves into speakeasies, illegal dives where whisky or gin was served in coffee cups to fool the police who made surprise raids, but who were also often corruptible.

Congress was divided between the Drys, supporters of prohibition, and the Wets, in favor of going back to selling alcohol, and the two groups battled long and hard. In a few months the wine producers of Sonoma and Napa Valley, compelled to dig up their vineyards, went bankrupt and fired hundreds of workers who wandered around in search of other work they didn't find.

Early in July Giacomo received a letter from Carolina: she wrote that their mother wouldn't rest until she heard news of Gildo. She was worn out, wasting away, and convinced he had died or been killed in that country. He had to do all he could to find him.

Do what? he asked himself in bewilderment. Who could he turn to? How should he go about it? He talked to Terenzio who couldn't tell him how to begin, and suggested he speak to the American owner of the factory, Mr. Ross, who certainly knew more than they did.

They met with him together. He listened kindly, thought about it, and decided that the only thing to do was to write a letter to the central police station of San Francisco where, at the request of relatives, they looked for disappearing persons. It wouldn't be done quickly, he warned; the central station would have to consult with the various police stations around the city and maybe even in outlying areas. It would take time to get a response. He dictated a letter to his secretary and the wait began.

The reply arrived in two months. It seems that a man with that first and last name, originally from the province of Bergamo, forty-two years old, arriving three years ago from Austria where he had formerly emigrated, after several months in San Francisco had transferred farther north, to a farm in Sonoma country, in Alexander Valley, near Healdsburg where he worked in orchards.

Gildo was half the age of his namesake and had never been to Austria. That was obviously not information about him. Mr. Ross sent another letter to the central police station to inform them of the error, and the wait began all over again

It was the end of November 1919 when the information arrived, and Giacomo was upset. He wrote at once to his mother that Gildo had been located near Sacramento, but he carefully avoided telling her that he was a patient in a mental hospital. He asked Mr. Ross for a few days' leave to go get him and bring him home. Given the seriousness of the case permission was granted.

The encounter in the parlor with the brother he hadn't seen in ten years was a terrible shock. He wouldn't have recognized him except for his mild blue eyes, now red-rimmed and inflamed. He seemed a wreck, his body a skeleton, his back bent and tight, his bones sticking out of the gray gown that floated around him. His too-long sleeves nearly covered his blue and boney hands, his trousers danced around his scrawny legs. He was struck above all by his puffy, pale, and flaccid face of an old man with strange scabs here and there, his chapped, cracked lips, the ooze at the corners of his mouth, the deep shadows around his eyes, his shaved head. He remembered how before they left home he himself had cut his hair close to the scalp. He remembered the slap he gave Gildo's baldhead as a salute, and his burning envy because his brother was going to America and he wasn't. He had been terribly wrong to envy him.

That bare head with nose and ears protruding more than usual gave him the forlorn aspect of a plucked chicken. He had staggered in on the arm of a white-gowned attendant and seemed to have a hard time standing. Trembling from head to foot he leaned against the wall exhausted. Giacomo stared at him in astonishment. What had happened to him? How did he end up in there? What did he do? What had reduced him to such misery?

He wasn't sure Gildo recognized him because he said nothing. He looked around nervously without resting his eyes on anything in particular. From time to time he threw a rapid glance his way and then looked down at his feet. Giacomo took a step toward him, raised and arm to put on his shoulder, but his brother drew back as though afraid of being touched. Then, speaking clearly some words in dialect, he told him who he was. A flash of comprehension seemed to light his eyes, but he didn't move. He had come to get him, Giacomo said, to take him to Concrete where he lived with his family. He would have come earlier but no one knew where he was. It had taken months to find him. He was happy to have finally succeeded. He felt like he was talking to a mentally deficient child. Giacomo told him to be calm, they were leaving on a train. They had just enough time to sign the release papers and get to the train station. At the first store they saw he would buy him some new clothes. Waiting at home were his wife Ninetta and his three daughters, Lucia, Giuditta, and Teresa, very curious to meet their uncle. He didn't need to worry about a thing, he had thought of everything. Gildo would be able to rest at their house, get back in shape and put on a little weight, and then they would decide what he should do.

Gildo listened with eyes lowered. He heaved a big sigh, moved a hand in a vague gesture, but didn't reply. Giacomo felt a deep compassion for that poor tortured human being that seemed to have lost his tongue and perhaps his mind. Suddenly he went to him, opened his arms, and hugged him to his chest. He noticed Gildo's eyes were damp. He didn't return the hug but stood inert, his arms dangling, his face tired, his expression lost. Who knows how long it will take for him to return to his normal self, Giacomo thought. If ever.

For the whole long trip Gildo didn't say a word. However, he had enjoyed a hot dog and the cheese sandwiches and apples that Giacomo bought. From the window he observed the landscape rushing by and with one hand sheltered his eyes from the bothersome sun as though he had lived in the dark for a long time. At times he would sleep curled up in the corner, with his hands crossed tightly across his chest as though protection from some feared attack. From time to time he would jump, murmur, moan in his sleep.

Newly outfitted from head to foot — dark jacket and trousers, a shirt of shiny starched cotton, a pair of shoes with laces, and on his head a felt cap with a grosgrain ribbon to cover his shaved head — he looked almost normal, if it hadn't been for his total muteness and cautious, feverish look.

Giacomo filled the uncomfortable silence with a volley of words about Concrete, about the broken-down wood house he had restored and transformed into a decent home, and which he repainted twice a year because the wind and rain ruined the paint and humidity penetrated the walls, about the sixteen Italian workers that his wife kept as boarders, about his clever girls, intelligent and a little mischievous, about the firstborn Daniele, unfortunately left in Abbazzia with his sister-in-law because it had been impossible to bring him with them, about the cement factory and the big dust cloud that enveloped the town, about Terenzio and the American boss, about the snow that buried them in the winter and the sun that was rare even in the summer, the sky in those parts usually gray as a smoked skillet.

Gildo remained quiet and listened. Giacomo asked him if he was hungry, and then if he liked the hot dog and sandwiches, if he was tired, if he was thirsty or hot or even cold, even though it was August, but he answered only in monosyllables. Giacomo was relieved when his brother closed his eyes and slept; he could give his dry, aching mouth and throat a rest from talking. Later he ventured a few careful questions: where had he been before the hospital, what did he do, if he liked San Francisco, if he had met any fellow Italians, not daring to ask him how he ended up in a mental hospital. But Gildo ignored them. He turned his face to the window and stared at the landscape. At a certain point he seemed about to break his silence. He cleared his throat, coughed, took a breath, but then gave up. Curling up in the corner again he closed his eyes like shutting the door and closing the blinds. In time, Giacomo told himself. But the time never came. Gildo never spoke of his past, as though speaking about it would cost him terrible suffering and shame.

At home Ninetta made room for her brother-in-law by clearing a small storeroom with a little window. There she put a cot, a chair, a little table, and some hangers on a nail for his few clothes. She found him fragile, sad, glum, wrapped in impenetrable solitude, and had immediately understood he could not bear up under the company of the noisy boarders either at the table or in the dormitory. And in fact, as soon as he heard the men's voices coming down the lane he hid in his little room, closed the door and left it only after they had gone. Evenings the boarders would linger around the table with the ever-present bottle of grappa, and he would disappear. So for the first few days she served his lunch and dinner before they arrived; while he chewed slowly and thoughtfully, she spoke to him about this and that in a low voice, and when she met his lost look she smiled like an affectionate sister. So as not to make him feel a burden she was careful not to complain about how expensive life was, and what work it was to keep the house going. She cooked the traditional dishes of their town and that food seemed to give him some consolation. It was certainly good for him, because day after day he gained weight, his hair began to grow out, and he no longer had that haggard, pinched look that had so disturbed her on his arrival.

The girls spied on him, keeping their distance, curious but intimidated by that taciturn uncle who paid no attention to them. Then little Teresa was the first to conquer her fear and she began prowling around him as though exploring, looking him up and down, and exhibiting her little smiling, prattling, coaxing ways that had no affect at all. As soon as he finished eating he got up and closed himself in his little hole in the wall and she was left pouting.

However, Teresa was not one to give up easily: one day she plucked up her courage, went up to him, and with a plump little hand tugged on his trousers. For the first time Ninetta saw him smile, a smile so surprising, so endearing that it brought tears to her eyes. Gildo took the little girl on his knees and fed her some polenta with butter and sage left on his plate. The little one twittered with delight, raised her little round face to him, opening wide her big shining green eyes. Her laughter made charming little dimples in her cheeks. From that day she followed him around the house and outside like a duck follows its mother. She mangled his name, and asked to be picked up. He would put her on his shoulders while she wrapped her plump little arms around his head. Ninetta, busy with her housework, listened to Teresa chirping like a little chick and her uncle's croaky muttering and wondered when there would finally be an opening in his airtight armor. She watched him from the window as he washed his underwear and sheets in the tub outside and hung them on the line to dry: a private laundering she didn't interfere with, even though the result left a lot to be desired.

Suddenly one morning he began to talk: hesitantly, awkwardly, as though walking on burning coals. He offered to help her: he knew how to sweep and clean the floor, make beds, cook, wash dishes, fix something broken, even how to sew and mend. Considering his still precarious condition, Ninetta was about to refuse, but she stopped herself in time: maybe that was the way to get him out of his inertia, to feel useful and begin to breathe again. So, early in the morning, as soon as the boarders and Giacomo left the house, he hoed the garden, pulled up weeds, split wood for the fire and carried it into the house, made beds, washed floors, cleaned and cut vegetables for the soup, peeled and boiled potatoes, stirred the polenta in the cast iron pot. He did everything to perfection, with care and attention. The little girls stayed with him and asked to help. He doled out jobs and they did it, garrulous as larks.

One day, from the next room, while Gildo was working in the kitchen, Ninetta heard him telling them stories about prairies, horses, Indians, buffaloes, bears, wolves, and even chickens, and they listened enthralled. And then he broke out in a big guffaw at something Giuditta said. Still laughing, the girls followed him around with their silvery voices shouting: Uncle Gildo, Uncle Gildo, tell us again about the chickens! He started over from the beginning, two, three, four times, with the patience of a saint, and the girl's shrill laughter fanned fresh air throughout the house.

He still didn't talk to Giacomo, as if he were afraid to, so he asked Ninetta, even though it wasn't good weather, if he could paint the house. The paint was peeling and the wood was rotting in places. She asked her husband, who bought some buckets of white paint and cleaned the old brushes, and Gildo began repairing the damaged parts, and sandpapering all the boards and window frames as far as he could reach. Then he set up makeshift scaffolding to reach the upper storey. When the surface was perfectly smooth, he painted the entire edifice with great brush strokes up to the gutters. In certain crucial places he had to paint a second and even a third coat. He worked sure and fast, with accuracy and skill, as though he had always done this kind of work. When occasionally Ninetta caught herself watching him, she would wonder about the mystery of those long years behind her brother-in-law and if they would ever know.

The girls spent hours with their nose in the air, convinced that his head touched the clouds up there on the scaffolding. They asked what he saw up there. Could he see the bears that came from the woods to steal flour from the sacks? And deer? And when would he be finished? How much longer would it take? Why couldn't they come up? And why couldn't he tell the story about the chickens from up there? He came down with his clothes splotched with white paint and a painted mustache, and they cavorted around him like happy does.

In a few days he had finished a careful and exact job that Ninetta complimented: never had the house been so spanking clean as though brand new. Gildo grew red as a beet, smiled with embarrassment, and seemed a little proud of that just recognition of work well done. Giacomo also appreciated the speed and thoroughness with which his brother had repainted the house, and when he told him so he was taken aback when Gildo looked down and slipped away. As if he didn't believe him. He had no faith in himself Ninetta murmured, shaking her head. Who knows what had happened to him.

The winter cold had arrived; the days grew shorter, the whipping wind raised litter and whirlwinds of dust. Every morning after breakfast Gildo bundled up the girls and they all went for long walks. They loved to hold their uncle's hand, but they were three, and he had only two hands, as he had explained without convincing them. To avoid the arguments that broke out each time, he tied a rope around his waist for them to hang on to. He was their horse, he declared, and he pulled them along behind, their explosions of laughter growing fainter as they went down the country paths. They returned flushed and happy, their red cheeks like ripe apples. They wouldn't let go of the rope and followed their uncle all over the house. It was he who fixed supper and put it on the table, took them to bed, tucked them in. Ninette would come to give them a good night kiss, but expected that the last one would be their uncle's.

One day while in the kitchen she heard a melodious, flute-like whistle. She tip-toed to the door and peeked in: the little girls, curled up on the floor, were listening to their uncle open-mouthed, their little faces full of wonder. He whistled the waltz *Rose del sud*, and still whistling, he invited them to dance one after the other. Bending his tall figure over their short stature, he held them by the waist and whirled them around until they collapsed on the floor giggling wildly.

It seemed to Ninetta that Gildo's mood changed at that moment: when he was alone or with the little girls, she would hear him whistling while he split wood, straightened up the rooms, or shoveled the snow from the path to the street, and that music relaxed her. He would stop whenever she appeared, as though the presence of an adult disturbed him.

For Christmas, closed in his little room, he made three rag dolls from some old material. He filled them with sawdust, embroidered eyes, nose, and mouth. A lock of yellow straw served as hair. Then he made a little dress of different material for every doll, and on Christmas Eve, as a gift from Santa Claus, he put them at the foot of their beds. In the morning when they woke up they hugged them shouting with joy and never let them go. Lucia retired the doll the boarders had given her for her birthday to a corner of her bedroom, and wanted nothing more to do with it. Ninetta had furtively glanced at her brother-in-law: he looked radiant, as though he had received a wonderful present.

From the time the oldest, Lucia, started first grade, Gildo had helped her with her homework and in this way repeated the few words of English he knew: dog, cat, red, sun. They sat at the kitchen table. Giuditta, peeking at the letters that her sister wrote in her notebook, copied them herself; Teresa scribbled on a piece of paper gripping the pencil in her cramped little fingers. Ninetta casually watched the quartet as she worked and thought how having her brother-in-law there was a real blessing. His gentleness, his sweetness with the girls, his inventiveness, the growing affection that tied them to him, and all the heavy work he had taken on had eased that awful daily feeling that she could never get all her work done, which up to now had overburdened and crushed her. She often wondered how in the world he had ended up in a mental hospital, since he appeared to be perfectly sound mentally. And if at first she had been a little worried that he had a secret illness that could explode at any moment, now she thought she had been foolish and began to think that this merciless country, in some unknown way, was the true culprit.

The illness struck her at the beginning of March. She woke up with nausea and an irksome low fever that went up during the day. That evening she had sharp pains in her stomach and the fever grew higher. Her forehead burned and rivulets of perspiration flowed over her body. She thought it was indigestion, something bad she had eaten, though she couldn't remember what, or the flu;

perhaps without realizing it she had caught cold. She had been careful not to bother her husband who worked ten hours a day and needed his rest. She had turned in bed without closing her eyes. With enormous effort she got up at six as usual and, aching and exhausted, dragged herself into the kitchen to make breakfast for the boarders. When they had all gone and she was washing the cups and saucers before waking Lucia for school, she felt a tremendous stabbing pain in the right side of her groin that bent her double. With a moan she slumped to the floor. She rolled around groaning from the spasms that followed one another closely with growing ferocity, as though a knife were piercing her guts.

Gildo ran to pick her up and carry her to bed. White as a sheet, burning with fever, she writhed with the unceasing sharp pains. Her cries had awakened the girls who called to her from their bedroom. In a weak voice she asked her brother-in-law to run to town to get the doctor. Maybe it was colic, who knows; she thought she might be dying she felt so bad.

Without putting on a coat he ran out of the house to town. He had never been there and didn't know where the doctor lived, but had it in mind to ask the first person he met. A woman out to do her shopping gave him instructions. Catching the doctor as he was about to leave, he led him back to the house. Ninetta's stomach was hard as a rock and she yelled the moment the doctor touched it. There was no doubt. It was acute appendicitis and she needed to get to the hospital as quickly as possible. Gildo ran to the cement factory to find Giacomo who, along with Terenzio, frantically tried to figure out a way to get her there. When Mr. Ross heard what they were looking for he ordered a van to be put to their disposal.

Ninetta was operated on immediately at the Sedro Woolley Hospital, and saved by a hair, as the doctor said when she awoke from the anesthesia. The danger in cases like these is the onset of peritonitis from the perforated appendix, he explained, usually fatal. She was fortunate, he said with a smile, neglecting to inform her he had taken advantage of the operation to tie her tubes, without asking her permission or that of her husband. It was in her interest, he was convinced, to free her from future problems, considering that at her young age she already had four children, as he had seen on her chart.

She was put in a room with two beds where another patient lay quietly with eyes closed. The ether had left her head foggy, her stomach in revolt, extremely tired and yearning to sleep. But the doctor seemed to want to talk, and pointblank had asked if her four children were in good health. That question came from far away and it took a lot of concentration for her to understand it. What a strange question she thought with surprise. What did her children have to do with her operation? She concentrated on the doctor's face: perhaps she hadn't understood him. In spite of all good intentions, her English was halting. The doctor continued to talk, but she felt the real purpose of his words was hidden. Four children, at her age, were a lot, and not everyone could manage. For example, the majority of American women, even though their husbands earned better salaries than immigrants, had fewer children. Yes, the immigrants, particularly the Latinos, seemed overly optimistic in this regard, or imprudent, if not downright reckless. She was young, and could turn one out a year for the next twelve, fourteen years, or even more. He doubted she wanted that, or even her husband, who apparently was a common laborer working in a cement factory in Concrete. Children are expensive, he sighed, if you want them to grow up healthy, strong, and educated, and it's best to keep that in mind. And then you have to consider the mother's health: as is well known, too many children too close together, and the drain on her body from nursing them, harms a woman's health who quickly finds herself exhausted to the point of not being able to raise the children as they should. In short, by having so many children everyone loses, the wives, the husbands, and the children.

Ninetta listened with all the attention the effects of the anesthesia would allow, and asked herself where that argument was headed as she watched the doctor walk back and forth, gesturing. This meant, he continued, that for all the years to come until distant menopause, young women must be careful to avoid unwanted pregnancies, and sometimes even precautions weren't enough, as she had surely learned. Unless such a hazard was taken care of, he concluded strangely before leaving. At the door he turned, waved his index finger, and smiled encouragingly. Now she must be quiet and rest.

Ninetta wracked her brain over the doctor's enigmatic monolog for some time, but she couldn't make sense of it. He had talked to Giacomo also, who had been just as surprised and bewildered. As the doctor had prepared for the surgery, he had expressed some passing reflections concerning the excessive number of children born to foreigners. Giacomo had been annoyed by the doctor's interference in business that did not concern him, but in the heat of the moment he didn't dare argue. It really didn't seem the time to annoy someone who was about to cut into your wife's belly.

Only after she returned home was the obscure meaning of those words suddenly clear. She had a hard time believing it. Offended, indignant, infuriated, she felt resentful for days: she had no intention of having more children, but that injustice scalded her. How could pompous Americans act like they were masters of the world and make decisions about something so private and delicate without even consulting the person concerned? Were they afraid they would have to take care of their children with public assistance? She had never asked for a nickel, she had worked like a beast of burden and along with her husband had earned what they needed for the girls and for Daniele her sister was raising. Why did they stick their noses in their business? What were they afraid of? That the foreigners' plentiful offspring would make them a minority? Or were they afraid of a future prevalence of Catholics over Protestants? Had they ever dared tie the tubes of an American woman without her consent? America was a country where freedom was shouted from the rooftops, which was violated all the time where immigrants were concerned.

Giacomo was as furious as she and went babbling on about that son she had never been able to give him, and that now would never arrive. In time he calmed down, relieved not to have to "be careful." Ninetta thought of her womb, infertile forever, and asked herself, if after that mutilation, she was still a woman. And if not, what was she?

24

When Luigino reached San Francisco he immediately started job hunting. For some unknown reason he had it in his head that things had improved and he would be hired as a mason, but he was rejected because he did not belong to a Union. He would have to be content with a job as common laborer.

He still felt bitter about that unfair law that kept his brother out because he couldn't read or write. What good would that be if from morning to night you did nothing but load, push, dump carts of cement, lime, bricks? He found a construction job on the south end of the city, on the opposite side of town from the Italian quarter, and he lived in the construction yard, in a jerrybuilt shack along with forty Greek, Slovenia, and Italian workers. They told him about prohibition and explained that there were illegal dives and pubs where they could drink as before, but they cost more. That was of no interest to Luigino who didn't want to waste a penny.

The work schedule was ten hours a day. On Sundays he collapsed exhausted on his bed and slept until mid-afternoon. And so for months Luigino hadn't found the time or the energy to cross the city and ask Caterina, Aniceto, or Rosa Cencini where Gildo was. He was miserable because he hadn't found anything better than that horrible and poorly paid job, and because his brother had been sent back to Italy. He had gone to the port with him, trying in vain to console him: depressed, disheartened, he whimpered like a lost child, so Luigino teased him a little: Damn! When are you finally going to decide to grow up? Giusepì made an effort to control himself and promised that he would work everyday at home to learn to read and write, and when he was ready he would come back. Luigino spared him the well-founded doubt that the Italian government would be inclined to pay for a second voyage with the way the wind was blowing. Because this much was certain—if the government didn't give it to them they would never have it.

While he went awkwardly up the gangplank, numb and bent as a tired old man, Giusepì had turned to look at him and had smiled. In spite of that forced smile Luigino stubbornly insisted on believing that he had cheered up, or was at least resigned. But later as the ship moved slowly away from the dock and his brother leaned over the rail his face had looked pale, distorted, disfigured by anguish, and a weak wave of his hand seemed more like a desperate call for help than a salute. Luigino had walked away with pain in his heart for that little brother so fragile, so needy; and what if he made the same desperate gesture as their father in the course of the crossing and jumped into the sea?

They had agreed that he would write two lines just to say he had arrived—could he do that much? If not, he could always ask the priest for help. Send it special delivery until he had an address. It took those two lines two months to arrive—those same chicken scratches—two months of pain, torment, and anxiety.

Early one Sunday morning in December Luigino set off for the Italian quarter in search of Gildo, on foot, to save money. The streets he wandered were disorienting. So much had changed during the years he had been away. New buildings, new shops, new streets and squares he had never seen. The house where Caterina had lived was gone. In its place was a brand new five-story building. He went around a long time asking for information but no one had heard of her. Finally he ran into an Italian. After that terrible disaster that had wiped them out, Caterina could no longer pay the interest on the loan for her house, so the bank confiscated it and then demolished it to construct that building. What disaster? The banker running off with the clients' savings, hadn't he heard? Everyone who had trusted that rascal had been left without a pot to piss in and many were forced to leave. A real tragedy. Caterina had moved, but he didn't know where.

However, he found Aniceto: aged, haggard, grayed, but as exuberant and cordial as ever. He had welcomed Luigino with slaps on the back and crushing bear hugs, eager to know how people in Italy were getting along after that shitty war, and if it was really worthwhile to leave America to go fight in their country, risk their skin, and as recompense for all that sacrifice, be forced to emigrate again.

Business was so-so. He managed to make a living selling fruit and vegetables. Some times he had been on the verge of giving it all up and going back to Salerna. But in the end he stayed. Once he went back, he was sure, he would regret what he had left in America, just as now he missed his village on the hill with a view of the sea. Whoever left his country for a foreign land was always divided, half here and half there. So he might as well stay.

Before Luigino could ask about Gildo, Aniceto asked him, and was amazed he didn't know anything. All Aniceto knew was that he disappeared in August 1916, after losing all his savings deposited with that scoundrel Bianchin. Rosa Cencini had told him about his accordion being stolen; he didn't see him before he disappeared. Two blows like that, one after the other, must have been more than he could take, poor guy. A good man, a little too quiet, but with real musical talent. Rosa was the last to see him, but he had seemed all right. He was gone, but he didn't know where. Luigino had the sneaking feeling that Aniceto felt a little guilty about Gildo, and perhaps it was better not to probe.

Why not have lunch with them? There was spaghetti with tomato sauce and an eggplant dish. Luigino, eager to talk to Rosa to find out what had happened, regretfully declined the invitation.

Two Italians now occupied the little room where Gildo had stayed. The landlady had gone to mass, but would be back soon. Luigino saw her coming down the street and ran to meet her. When she recognized him she grimaced as if she was not at all happy to see him. When he asked about Gildo, she warily invited him in where they could speak freely.

And so Luigino learned of the suicide attempt that the woman had told Aniceto to keep quiet about, and he turned white: that idiot had tried it again! She had gone to his room by chance, had knocked on his door but with no response. She opened the door, or rather broke it, had smelled a great stench of gas, entered and found that poor soul on the bed, more dead than alive. She was so frightened she nearly fainted, but she got up her courage, and as heavy as he was, she dragged him out of bed and into the street to breathe the fresh air and was saved. Just in time. If she had waited fifteen minutes he would have been gone. They had taken all he owned, the accordion, suit, hat, shoes. Out of pity she let him stay without paying—and here it became murky, as though she had something to hide or blame herself for. One day she found the room empty. He had gone without saying goodbye and she hadn't seen him again.

Luigino went away oppressed by many gloomy thoughts. If his friend had tried to kill himself again, it meant he had touched bottom. He thought about that evening after the foreman's beating when he had lain on the tracks waiting for a train to run over him, and about his stubborn resistance to being dragged away. What guarantee was there that he hadn't tried it again later after Rosa's intervention? Knowing him as he did there was a good chance of it. Now he blamed himself for abandoning his friend—dearer than a brother to him—to get involved with that filthy, senseless war that gave him nothing but suffering, terror, misery. If he hadn't volunteered he could have stayed here with him and things would have been different. And on top of that, he had never written from the front, and Gildo must have thought he had forgotten him. Alone like a dog in that selfish, unjust, merciless country with no one to help him, after those terrible blows that would have floored anyone, he hadn't seen a way out and had put an end to it.

How could he find the courage to tell his family what he knew? Write his brother in Concrete? He tortured himself, put it off, made up his mind, and then thought better of it. Only in March did he decide to write a cautious, reticent letter, in which he avoided revealing his fears about his friend's terrible end, which as time went by he felt more sure of. He said only that he wasn't to be found in San Francisco and asked Giacomo to tell his family in Italy.

Luigino's letter arrived in Concrete at the time Ninetta was in the hospital and Giacomo could think of nothing else. Gildo was happy to hear of his friend's safe return from the long conflict, but was up to his neck with things to do and put off answering it until he had a moment's peace.

Because during Ninetta's absence, and through her convalescence, the whole house had fallen on Gildo's back, a gigantic landslide that he had confronted with determination he didn't know he had. That hammer blow had worked like an alarm clock, a kindly shake that forced him to face days packed with numerous urgent tasks. It was a mystery to him how his sister-in-law could have handled everything by herself before he came.

At first the most frustrating thing had been dealing with the boarders who he had previously avoided: noisy, disorderly, slovenly. Deafened by their noisy babble, disturbed by their vulgar jokes, by their salacious exchanges, by their strings of curses, he regretted being exiled from his little room because of the circumstances. Then he got used to it. He closed his ears and kept busy. After supper he set the table for breakfast, mixed the bread, covered it with a dishcloth and let it rise all night on the warmth of the stove. He had hidden the sacks of wheat and corn flour under his bed after a bear broke down the basement door, tore into the sacks, and scattered on the pavement what he didn't eat.

While the boarders were eating breakfast, he fixed each a sack of sandwiches to take to work—a change accepted owing to Ninetta being in the hospital, but firmly continued by her later. He sent Lucia to school alone. It was a short, safe walk and she was very proud of that independence. He almost never heard a peep out of Giuditta, who kept busy playing in a corner, and if he asked her, she helped him straighten up and clean the house. From the time her mother left home Teresa dirtied her pants. He didn't scold her, but washed her bottom under the cold-water tap. He rubbed her with a stiff brush, and first she cried because of the cold and then laughed because it tickled. She kept asking when her mother was coming back, and he would say "tomorrow," caress her little face, and she would calm down.

Gildo was touched by the blind faith with which his little nieces turned over their little bodies to the care of his big inexpert and awkward hands. He was moved by their little faces held up to be washed, the little cries when soap got in their eyes, the patience with which, without a complaint, they bore up under the morning ceremony of combing the knots out of their hair, the sighs suppressed when the little dresses pulled over their heads covered their faces and their arms flailed in search of the sleeves. And then the abandon, the familiarity with which they snuggled up to him, perched on his knees, or rested in his arms like chicks with a mother hen. Teresa, when she was curled up against his chest with her knees touching his chin, would put her thumb in her mouth and suck away.

He experienced an unusual sense of paternal responsibility and protection, softened by good-humored indulgence and by his desire to play; and the eager devotion of the little girls comforted and reassured him. Consequently he concluded he was worth something, he was useful for something. Someone needed him.

As soon as everyone left the house he took over as master of his domain and went briskly to work. He lit the oven to bake bread, emptied chamber pots, put clothes to soak in soda before washing them, made beds, swept floors and scrapped spills off the floor-boards, wiped down cobwebs, filled the wood box, chased rats away from the woodpile and out of the basement, took the two little ones to town with him to shop for groceries, and washed, rinsed, and hung up the clothes after his return. For lunch, to make it simple, they ate sandwiches too. In the afternoon he mended shirts and socks, sewed on buttons, ironed, split wood, lit the stove and prepared supper with a zeal for food well made and attractively served. After years of disgusting food in the construction yards, prison, mental hospital, he felt extremely happy while chopping, mixing, seasoning, browning, tasting the dishes, smelling the delightful odors that rose from the pans, intoxicating him: vegetable soup with pork fat, polenta with sauce and sausages, boiled beef or liver, tripe, fried onions, potatoes cooked in the embers, soup of lentils or chick peas, beans with chopped onions. He missed red wine, unfortunately banned by law, which besides flavoring the beans, would be good in beaten eggs and sugar for the girls' breakfast. His mother had always maintained that a drop of red wine worked better than a tonic for children.

The girl's weekly bath, which wasso essential to Ninetta, was a time of great fun for them: he warmed the water on the stove, heated the towels on the back of a chair pulled up to the stove, put the three of them in the steaming tub, narrow as an egg shell, soaped them up and energetically scrubbed them while they laughed. They pinched and teased each other as they chattered and splashed.

Gildo whistled while he cooked, washed, cleaned, sewed. After supper he cleared the table, washed the plates, put the girls to bed, but before going to sleep they asked for the story of the chickens. The evening drinking had miraculously subsided. He suspected that Giacomo had discouraged the boarders from distilling grappa. He had heard him explaining his wife's operation as heaven's punishment for the drinking vice. Some had resented it and protested, but he had stood firm. You can't fool around with God's chastisements.

Before Ninetta came home he made a xylophone in his spare time to teach Lucia and Giuditta to play: two boards supported thin strips of wood of different sounds according to the musical scale and two little hammers for percussion. He was convinced that if someone had done something for him like that when he was a child his life would have been entirely different. That musical toy entranced the girls. Teresa hit the keys like someone possessed, producing a strident noise. The others tried it but were soon bored: not everyone is born with a bent for music, as is well known. And so he played that homemade instrument whenever he could: with those light, limpid, silvery trills, so different from the powerful timber of the accordion, he reproduced old time tunes. Hammering on the keys he found the energy and passion that he was afraid he had lost forever, along with the desire to forget all the bad things he had experienced to start all over.

As soon as Ninetta was reestablished and he had a little more time to himself he wrote Luigino—without imagining those lines would lift him from a nightmare, and that he would begin to dance and shout as though he had lost his mind—however, without mentioning all his misadventures. Modesty and shame as well as his fear of others' judgment, including his friend's, inhibited his speaking of that inexorable disgrace that accompanies one who has set foot in a prison and mental hospital. Perhaps he would feel only like telling Luigino about his second attempt to end it all, given that he had saved him from the first.

For some time Gildo had thought of going to Sedro Woolley to have a photograph made to send to his mother. He wanted to reassure his family so that they would not ask too many questions about his past. Now he looked decent, he had a full head of hair and his face was filled out. He felt reinvigorated, energetic, and held himself back with difficulty from venturing out of his shell.

After his long segregation he was gnawed by the curiosity to see how much the world had changed. He didn't have a cent, and although he tried to repay them with his daily work, he was well a-ware he was living off his brother, who certainly wasn't swimming in dollar bills. Sometimes he scolded himself for those immoder-ate desires, as if he had no right to them. He was living in a limbo that couldn't last forever. He had to find a solution, though he didn't know what that might be.

Taking his courage in hand, he spoke to Giacomo about it, who had already been giving it some thought. While waiting for a labor-er's job to come open, as Terenzio had vaguely promised, he was willing to make him a loan that he could pay back when he started earning some money of his own.

So on a bright morning of May he took a train to Sedro Woolly. Under his jacket he had a typical western shirt of colored checks, a button-down collar, a gaudy flowered tie, both to show his family the American taste, and to camouflage himself in the crowd in town that recognized immigrants on sight. Ninetta, without her hus-band's knowledge, gave him some money to buy a gramophone and a few Enrico Caruso records. It had been a longtime desire and she thought she deserved it for all those years of killing work. Deep down she yearned for it as a just payment for all that she had put up with.

On the outskirts of town the train passed by endless lumber stacks, tree trunks and pyramids of scrap and sawdust, and the squeal of saws accompanied him to the station. At the La Roche pho-tography studio he refused the proposed picturesque backgrounds, remembering the foolish portrait from San Francisco in the driv-er's seat of the Ford Model T, whose falsity, on thinking it over, seemed to be the beginning of his adversities. It was as though he had bragged ahead of time of his success hanging from a thread that was soon broken. A simple portrait would be enough.

Among the whirl of busy people and honking automobiles—

Packard, Hudson, Overland, Ford, Chalmers-Detroit—he wandered around the streets looking for a shop where he could buy a gramophone. Along the way he was attracted by a group of people intent upon reading a newspaper hanging by clothespins outside a shop. As he drew near in curiosity a scowling man in the group uttered to his neighbor: Dammed Dagos. I hope they hang them.

Under the big headlines on the front page a long article told of the arrest of two Italian anarchist immigrants, Nicola Sacco and Bartolomeo Vanzetti, suspected of a serious act of violence on April 15: Frederick Parmenter, cashier of Slater & Morrill Shoe Company, and Alexander Berardelli, private guard at South Braintree, Massachusetts, were brutally murdered and robbed of $15,000, the payroll for employees of the shoe company.

The article raged against the Italian wops, reds, anarchists, radicals, delinquents, agitators, who should all be eradicated without exception. They hadn't heard anything about that crime in concrete. No one in the house bought newspapers, and Italian newspapers were not available. The others might as well be in Arabic for those who didn't know English. Struck by the seriousness of what happened and by the violence of the words, Gildo looked around, fearful of being singled out as Italian, but no one was paying any attention. All eyes were glued to the newspaper. Conquering his fear and calling himself a coward, he entered the shop and bought copy and, to avoid being betrayed by his accent, he pointed to it.

He sat on a bench to laboriously spell out the article. The meaning of many of the words was beyond him, but he managed to understand the general idea. The thought that those two might be innocent wasn't even suggested, as if they had already been condemned, though the trial had just begun. It seemed to him nothing had changed in the Americans' attitude toward Italians. They were the first to be suspected and accused of a crime, even when there wasn't a scrap of proof.

Two photographs appeared side by side: Vanzetti had a long flowing mustache that almost entirely covered his mouth, a receding hairline and premature baldness that sculpted his hard, sharp features as though carved in wood. His look was direct and proud. Under his jacket you could see a white shirt with high collar and a well-knotted tie. Sacco had a clean-shaven face and sunken cheeks, sad dark eyes, a thin mouth, eyebrows thick and straight as though drawn in charcoal. He wore a bow tie that seemed out of place below his austere face. Their appearance was civil, neat, dignified, as if they were dressed for a special occasion.

When they were arrested they each were carrying a pistol, and Sacco also had a flyer announcing a demonstration in protest for the death of an anarchist typographer, Andrea Salsedo. His crushed body had been found on the pavement below windows of the Court of Law of New York where, on the fourteenth floor, along with a friend he had been interrogated for eight weeks. That is to say, beaten and tortured, Gildo deduced with a shiver. They knew nothing of this in concrete, either. The article said that on May 1917 they had fled to Mexico to avoid the draft: two big cowards, like other foreigners who were opposed to the war.

Vanzetti lived in Plymouth and sold fish from a cart on the street. The other ran a sharpening machine in a shoe factory. They both began working at thirteen, exactly like him. And they didn't have a bit of money saved, like him. He wondered if they were in jail because they didn't have a penny for bail. How they lived in there and how they were treated, above all if Italian, everyone knew, but he forced himself not to remember so the fury wouldn't rise in his head and poison his thoughts, and misery wouldn't start devouring his soul again. He knew his balance was fragile and the risk of falling into the well again terrified him.

Only some years later, when it was effectively over and newspapers around the world wrote about it, would it be known that Vanzetti, shut up in the Charlestown prison in a wearying teeter-totter of hope and desperation over his fate that consumed his nervous system, had exploded and was sent to a state mental institution. Just think of it, exactly like him. Certainly, Vanzetti was waiting to be sentenced to death, but wasn't it that constant terror of ending up dead some other way that had made him go crazy at San Quentin?

The thought of the two fellow-Italians suspected of double homicide—one would have been enough to end up in the electric chair—stayed with him like a painful obsession in his search for a gramophone, that now seemed hopeless. He had wanted so much to stick his nose in the world, and look what he found.

He was distracted by the window of a shop where, like Mr. Clifford's in San Francisco, a very fine accordion was displayed, and for awhile he lovingly contemplated the details of the instrument: the bellows of fine leather, the small, shining mother-of-pearl decorations, the inlays of semi-precious stones, the silver tooling. A masterwork. He would have given anything to be able to play a piece, even the march from *Radetzky* or the waltz from the *Merry Widow*. Who knows if his unpracticed hands would respond as they should.

The clerk, to convince him of the good quality of the machine, put on the record player the aria *Mattinata* by Leoncavallo: "Metti anche tu la veste bianca e schiudi l'uscio al tuo splendooor," sang the unknown tenor at the top of his lungs. "Ove non sei, la luce manca, ove tu sei nasce l'amooor..." He left the store with a heavy, large package and a second one with records of Caruso wrapped in many sheets of newspaper to keep them from breaking, a sheaf of music that he wanted to study, the libretti of the *Barbiere di Siviglia* and *La Traviata*, and lives of Verdi, Puccini, and Donizetti.

At home it was the end of the world. Giacomo was furious with his wife for that crackpot expenditure. They didn't have money to throw out the window. At her age and with four children she should have other things on her mind than those stupid operas and dumb popular songs. Ninetta defended herself like a tiger. That money she earned by working like a mule from morning to night she could spend like she wanted.

As soon as her husband went to work and the house was empty, she would dash to the new machine, crank the handle, carefully lower the arm on the record, and while she worked she listened in rapture to the melodic voice of Caruso singing *O sole mio*, *Santa Lucia*, "La donna è mobile," "Una furtiva lacrima," "Celeste Aida," "E lucean le stelle." The addio to his mother from *Cavalleria rusticana* was the last piece: "Mamma, quel vino è generoso, troppi bicchier ne ho tracannato, vado fuori all'aperto..." and Ninetta shivered with emotion. When he reached the high notes that took her breath away and pierced her ears and the ceiling, her mouth would fall open as if they came from her throat. She would raise her eyes to heaven melodramatically and rest her right hand on her heart.

After supper the boarders listened to the records of the celebrated singer, proud of the fame he had earned in America, which redeemed the good name of Italy, so maligned in other ways. The story of Sacco and Vanzetti struck them like a slap in the face. They fell on the newspaper Gildo bought in Sedro Woolley, snatching it from each other without understanding a thing, and for long moments they contemplated the photographs of the two anarchists in glum silence. One of the boarders commented: Either an immigrant toes the line, bends his back and closes his mouth, or else anything can happen to him.

The two had not yet been formally incriminated. The investigation was underway, but everyone knew the death penalty could be expected for homicides. They discussed it for hours after the girls went to bed. The death penalty had been abolished in Italy for thirty years, aside from the military, one informed man declared. In the group were those who were happy about it as a civilized move, and others who were sorry because it was only right that a murderer should die. Otherwise where would we end up? And if in spite of the deterrent of the death penalty many crimes were committed anyway, what would happen if it were abolished? However, everyone was horrified at the thought of the electric chair. A firing squad or hanging would be much better. You died instantly and painlessly. On the other hand with that terrifying shock it took a while to die. The whole body shook violently like an epileptic fit. The heart broke open like a pomegranate and the brain burned to cinders like it was paper. After that macabre discussion a nice bottle of grappa was needed to lift their spirits, commented the sad and sleepy boarders, dragging themselves to bed.

Gildo bought a newspaper from time to time. He apprehensively deciphered headlines dripping with hate for the immigrants. For months those suspected of being communist had been expelled. The "Red scare" spread to the point that people were arrested and mistreated for distributing the Declaration of Independence on the street. Sacco and Vanzetti were still in prison, one at Dedham, the other at Charlestown. The investigations continued. Dozens of eye-witnesses of the South Braintree homicides were interrogated—housewives of the Plymouth Italian community that on the morning of April 15 had bought fish from Vanzetti, or an employee of the Italian consulate in Boston where on that same day Sacco went to renew his passport to return to Italy, along with his wife and son. His mother was dead and his old father being alone worried him. What an awful joke America was playing on him.

A job at the cement factory was not yet in sight. Terenzio was prevaricating. So Gildo went to apply at a house construction site in another part of Concrete, and to his great surprise he was taken on as a mason. They must have had a shortage of skilled workers. In a few days he learned how to put up a wall. He handled the trowel to spread and tamp down a layer of mortar between the bricks, he used the plumb line, the square, the plumb rule, the level, and a hammer to break the bricks into regular rectangles with the greatest precision.

He worked ten hours a day. When returned home he gave himself a quick rinse and helped Ninetta fix supper. The girls danced around him. They couldn't get used to Uncle Gildo leaving in the morning and coming back in the evening and not having time to be with them.

When Gildo's letter reached Luigino he was ecstatic with joy that Gildo was alive and kicking while he had only expected to cry at his grave. In his excitement he wrote right back. What was he doing there in that frozen, moldy, god-forsaken place? Didn't he have enough of forests and meadows in the state of Washington where they had worked so hard and suffered together? Why didn't he come back to San Francisco? Didn't he think about buying another accordion and play again? Aniceto was waiting for him with open arms and was already looking for places where they needed an experienced musician. The city was full of music, day and night, right and left, orchestras and soloists, and surely there was a place for him. He should come back before October 12, when the Italian community celebrated Columbus Day with great pomp and flags flying. Music, dances, marches, parades, just what would be good for him. Even if some Italians said that it would have been much better if Cristoforo Colombo hadn't discovered America. What was he waiting for?

He would wait until the house was finished, and while he tossed trowels of mortar and leveled it until the plaster was smooth as silk, he thought about his future and wondered why he didn't pay attention to Luigino and his vocation that certainly was not to plaster the walls of Concrete. If he didn't listen to his friend and the insistent voice that urged him to abandon mortar and trowel for the profession more congenial to him he would be sorry all his life he hadn't found the courage to start over, and that would affect his life forever. With his earnings as mason he paid back Giacomo and put aside a little money. Would he agree to making him another loan to buy the accordion? He had to try, telling him about the success and his earnings, unfortunately interrupted by the banker's flight and the final theft. Not a word about all the rest. Not for anything in the world would he speak about it to a living soul.

Word got around among the Italians in Concrete about the gramophone. And often after supper someone would come to ask to listen to that famous Caruso, the man who sang for sixteen years at the Metropolitan in New York, and in 1915 had dedicated a concert to the three hundred thousand fellow Italians who went back home to fight. They said it was wonderful, and even that once one of his high notes had splintered a crystal chandelier. And besides he was the son of poor people, going hungry as a child. He began to sing in the church choir, then as a soloist, and tenaciously, one step after another, he rose to great heights and sang in the most famous theaters of the world. Caruso was a national flag to wave under the nose of those presumptuous Americans—just like Rodolfo Valentino, an actor the whole world admired.

Gildo stood aside, ready to crank the handle. He said nothing and listened to the tenor's velvet voice and the lively chatter of the others between pauses. Since Ninetta had taken command of the house he felt superfluous. After work he did as he pleased. Evenings he took refuge in his little room, studied the sheet music, read the lives of the musicians, played the xylophone. But he wasn't content. He hesitated to make a decision that would change his life drastically, but he felt he was wasting his time. Luigino was right. He should pay attention to him, pack up his few things and return to San Francisco.

One evening two self-confident young Italian women knocked at the door. They worked in the bottle factory where Ninetta had worked years before. They had heard about the gramophone and the records of the famous tenor and were excited. At first Ninetta had scowled, then she relaxed, invited them to sit down, and for the hundredth time they listened to the prodigious voice in reverent silence.

One of the women, Giuseppina, dark eyes shining and black hair pulled back, slipped her arm under that of the other, Annetta, brown-hair with lively blue eyes and a dazzling smile who waved her hand in rhythm to the melody. The men couldn't take their eyes off the two young women. In Concrete there were few unmarried women, never mind the American women who avoided them like poison. When the men met one of them on the street and respectfully saluted her she would turn away to make it clear she wanted nothing to do with dagos.

Gildo, stock-still, eyes downcast beside the gramophone, listened carefully, ready to turn the handle at the first sign it was about to run down. At a certain point he raised his eyes and encountered Annetta's smiling and inviting look and blushed.

The women returned, never tired of listening to the same passionate arias and songs. One evening they brought a record of Neapolitan songs and a dance record. They all embarked on a discordant chorus saturated with nostalgia for their distant country, offending Gildo's sensitive ears. Then another disk was put on the turntable. A polka's wild rhythm enflamed the boisterous assembly. The large table was moved against a wall and the men furiously competed for the only three women of the company. The others paired off, and joking and making funny faces, they danced wildly around the room.

At the next piece, a waltz, Annette crossed the room resolutely, and going up to Gildo in his corner, invited him to dance. Red as a beet and deeply embarrassed, he shilly-shallied, but the young woman would not be deterred. She gently took his hand and guided it to her waist, and when his arm was solidly anchored to her back, with a leap she dragged him into the whirlwind. Instead of resenting it every time he stepped on her foot, Annetta laughed loudly. The dance was both a delight and a torment: disturbed by her closeness, by the perfume in her hair, befuddled by the contact with her flexible waist, her elastic and compact torso, by her hand on his shoulder, he didn't follow the rhythm, stumbled over his own feet, perspired, bumped into the other dancers. But she didn't seem to care. She had literally requisitioned him and expected to dance only with him, until the others, resentful, had protested: there were only three women and one was all for that clumsy dolt? They pulled her from his arms while she struggled and protested. Gildo took a deep breath: he felt awkward, clumsy in his movements, scrutinized by smiling eyes, and the interest that the young woman showed him, if flattering, was also frightening. He had had no experience with women. He had kept his distance all his life, too timid and shy to know what to say and do. He preferred dancing with the little girls, and in fact he danced with them one after the other with mutual satisfaction.

Besides the evening visits, Annetta began coming during the day. She showed up Sunday afternoons with a friend. From outside she shouted for Gildo, in his room or sometimes gone for long solitary walks in the country. He pulled himself unwillingly from his tangled meditations: he wouldn't have minded talking with Annetta if she didn't numb him with frivolous and weird talk and assault him with dumb questions. He hated his own taciturn, misanthropic nature, convinced that fortune smiled on the brazen, arrogant, enterprising, loquacious. But he was what he was, he had to realize that and learn to live with it.

Early in September Gildo read that Nicola Sacco and Bartolomeo Vanzetti had been formally charged for the South Braintree crime. He felt numb. He had followed the case with growing concern for the two unknown Italians, sadly identifying with them, and had the idea they were innocent. More than mistaken, the judges seemed to be following a preconceived notion, as if pursuing a real persecution. The two were perfect targets: Italians, anarchists, Reds. Perhaps in the course of the trial the truth would come out.

Two weeks later he received another letter from Luigino urging him to drag himself away from that little town and go back to the big city. The house under construction was almost finished, and with an enormous effort that had cost him nights of worry, he spoke to Giacomo about his plan to leave for San Francisco to begin playing again to earn a living. He needed a loan to buy the accordion. The money he had put aside was only enough for the trip and to live for a while.

Giacomo had expected his brother to spontaneously confide the events that had led to the mental hospital, but it didn't happen. The question was on the tip of his tongue, but it stayed there. He gave him the loan willingly, counting on getting it back as soon as he was settled.

Ninetta and Giacomo were very unhappy to see him leave. The little girls were brokenhearted and gave their uncle pleading looks. He was sorry to leave them. Uncle Gildo, Teresa stammered, twisting a strand of hair, Uncle Gildo, when are you coming back to dance the waltz with us?

25

The Guerrini brothers, makers of accordions in San Francisco, knew how to treat good customers who came with cash in hand. Therefore, they didn't hesitate to lend Gildo a used accordion until his was ready.

Luigino met his train and couldn't stop hugging him and patting him with the overpowering impulse one has for someone come back alive. With tears and trembling mouths they stammered half-sentences as if after the long separation they didn't know where to begin.

Aniceto expected them for supper, impatient to talk to him about the plans cooking in his head. He still blamed himself for not looking for him with the necessary persistence when he suddenly disappeared. Where had he gone? What had happened to him? He grilled Luigino who assured him he knew just as little, and like him doubted that Gildo, so closed and secret, would ever let a single word escape his lips. No matter what, he was determined to help him all he could. Unfortunately Gildo had arrived too late for the big Columbus Day celebration, the toasts, music, parades, the waving of American and Italian flags, but there would be other occasions.

According to Aniceto's business experience it was indispensable to present oneself as a serious professional, as was the custom in America, a strict and pragmatic country where amateurs didn't get much sympathy. To this end he had elegant calling cards printed with Gildo's name, the profession of "musician" emphasized in bold letters, the drawing of an accordion and small, graceful musical notes flying like little angels to heaven. Besides giving them to fellow Italians who he counted on to convince party-givers to hire Gildo, he had gone to many pubs, cafes, saloons, restaurants and hotels where they had music in evenings, or mornings in the hall for an appetizer, or afternoons in tea rooms, insisting in their auditioning the famous talented Italian when he came back to the city. At the moment Gildo was busy with a concert tour in the northern states. A few lies were necessary to convince people, weren't they?

For now, if he wanted to, he could live in his house until he could pay for a room; they could set up a place to sleep somewhere. Domenica, his wife, smiled and filled his plate with pork rinds and pieces of cheese dipped in corn flour, and immediately afterward came pasta with meat sauce. Gildo, confused and at a loss from such an affectionate and caring welcome, chewed and blushed.

The house was empty during the day. Aniceto went to the wholesale market at dawn with his two sons to buy fruit and vegetables. One of his boys went around the neighborhood with a newly acquired bicycle after the theft the year before, receiving orders and delivering groceries. The other loaded the merchandise on a cart and sold it in the street, yelling at the top of his lungs like they did in the country. His father presided over the shop. Left alone with Domenica who was busy stirring at the kitchen stove, Gildo played for hours on the accordion the Guerrini brothers lent him. After the initial stiffness, his fingers got looser and softer and flew quickly over the keys.

Gildo earned his first eight dollars at the engagement party of the oldest son of a barber from Salerno who had his shop on Stockton Street. Then an elderly Sicilian couple celebrated their golden anniversary with a flock of children, grandchildren, great-grandchildren and close and distant relatives. And he played at the baptism of the firstborn of a young couple where Aniceto was godfather. Aniceto himself arranged an evening dance in the warehouse used once for the marriage of his daughter, inviting his best customers so they would spread the word about the extraordinary artist. Advertisement is the soul of business, he exclaimed. A reception was held in the ballroom of Miramare Hotel for the opening of a branch of the Banco di Napoli. A group of workers from the north organized a benefit ball to help a companion wounded in an accident and no longer able to work. A Neapolitan colony staged a lottery to give the statue of San Gennaro a sumptuous dress embroidered with gold sequins.

The brand new accordion was ready just before the Christmas festivities, a precious jewel in silver of superb craftsmanship, the initials of his first and last name in embossed letters: the instrument let loose flashes of fire at the slightest movement and sounds of a magnificent velvety timber, warm, sunny vibrations, passionate and melting tones as though having an entire orchestra in his hands. Aniceto's family, Luigino and a little group from the neighborhood, gathered around the marvel with awe and touched the floral decorations and inlays of mother-of-pearl, the ebony keys those of immaculate ivory with their fingertips. They sniffed the pungent odor of the soft leather of the bellows, and captivated they whispered their undying admiration. Some had requested their favorite song, and Gildo had complied. He played with his heart in his throat. Domenica, to make the event memorable, fried cazuncielli, the traditional pastry eaten at Christmastime in Salerno; she was very disappointed at not finding even on the black market the sweet liquor and anice to perfume them as they should be.

Aniceto seemed like a man possessed and furiously continued his publicity bombardment: between Christmas, New Year's Eve and Epiphany Gildo played every evening, and during Carnival time there had been a whirl of masked balls. It was hard for Gildo to believe what was happening, he seemed to be living an enchanted life, and he wondered if he weren't due for an abrupt awakening. Dumbly he counted his money, felt it, and for a long time contemplated the packet of dollars earned that he had hurriedly sent to Giacomo, keeping out what he needed to buy a suit and vest, shoes, hat, and some shirts. In order to command respect and consideration, Aniceto had advised, one had to dress like a gentleman.

Although he hated being a bother and didn't feel comfortable, obligated to talk when he would have preferred to keep quiet, Gildo had delayed renting a room untl he had paid his brother most of what he owed him. Along with Domenica's insistence that he stay with them—it didn't make sense to waste money on rent—he also had the nightmare that in a room of his own his accordion might be stolen again, while she could keep watch since she almost never stuck her nose out the door.

To introduce the celebrated musician who had finally arrived in town and to get an audition, Aniceto took Gildo to some places where he left calling cards. Mr. Lucchetti, owner of an elegant restaurant on Davis Street that offered "French and Italian dinners" and organized banquets for weddings, clubs, societies, was very sorry he couldn't hire him because the little orchestra already had an accordionist and he certainly couldn't dismiss him. Other places, to Aniceto's great annoyance, appeared rather cold, not at all interested in engaging an accordion virtuoso, even if exceptional. The green grocer couldn't understand. He asked himself over and over if it was a matter of distrusting Italians, appreciated and in demand when it was a matter of humble work or small businesses, but scornful when they offered themselves for art or higher professions. They preferred to keep those for themselves. Until the American owner of a bar on Columbus Avenue explained to him that the fashion had changed. Now the music, ragtime and blues, black bands from the south, were very popular. All these musicians, after Storyville in New Orleans closed, had moved in mass to the big northern cities in search of work. He had hired a black dance orchestra: piano, saxophone, clarinet, trombone, banjo, string bass and drum. There was no place for an accordion. They played pieces from Afro-American folklore or elaborated on European music, marches, quadrilles and the whole works, but in a syncopated, wild rhythm that got feet tapping, so much that people went crazy and danced until dawn.

Blacks? Aniceto asked himself dumbfounded. What music could the blacks have invented that replaced Italian or Viennese or French song and dance tunes known over the whole world? Those poor devils exploited to the core, the worst paid in all America? Was it possible that people had suddenly forgotten the tunes that they had always sung and whistled, to prefer the music of savage ignoramuses? The world really seemed topsy-turvy.

He didn't stop approaching other locales, certain that he would find someone a little behind the times. But that didn't happen. The calling cards were handed back smugly: no, they didn't need an accordion player. He even went to Signor Ghirardelli's chocolate factory, to propose that Gildo play while the workers worked, but he had laughed at that absurd idea, and Aniceto laughed with him. He stubbornly searched the whole Italian quarter inch by inch to find work for weddings, engagements, baptisms, birthdays, spaghetti, sausage, polenta, olive oil, festivals, for fairs and second-hand stores. An accordion, he declared to the disinterested, drew more people than the cries of a thousand barkers.

Gildo wanted to hear for himself that surprising new black music, so one Saturday evening he and Luigino went to the White Horse Dance Club. Sitting at a little table with two big glasses of Coca-Cola and a slice of lemon, they had listened in amazement to the breathtaking rhythms, the trumpet and drum explosions of a band of wild blacks. In their opinion it was hellish music, a cacophony of ripping, unpleasant, strident sounds, completely different from the melodies they were accustomed to. The people, however, went into ecstasy. The women rose on their feet, jumped up on chairs, and clapped their hands raw. The men howled and whistled through their fingers like rooting for a baseball game. They left in a daze. To tell the truth Gildo liked a couple of those pieces, such as *Memphis Blues*, and especially *Crazy Blues*. He was amazed by how much the American taste had changed in a few years and he couldn't understand how it happened. He tried to reproduce on his accordion the wild rhythms he had heard: not to imitate a genre that didn't belong to him, but to test himself and his instrument. No, it was the wrong instrument. As much as he tried he couldn't bring out anything like the furious trumpet solo or the booming assaults of the drum.

Sometime later Aniceto had triumphantly announced that he got him a gig at the Sunrise Hotel where he furnished the groceries, whose owner had not been corrupted by the new musical trend. He had to play in the hall three times a week on alternate days, two hours in the morning and two hours in the afternoon. It didn't pay much, but he should accept.

In a corner of the atrium furnished with divans and armchairs, the floor covered with second-rate Persian carpets, opposite the reception desk where the uniformed clerk met the customers was a wooden platform and chair. Next to that, in round copper pots was a forest of green palms; at the end of the room, against a wall of mirrors, was the counter of the bar. Great confusion reigned in the hall. A continual buzz of voices, people coming and going through the revolving glass door, porters pushing squeaking, heavily loaded luggage carts, the jingle of room keys or ice in glasses, doors opening, doors closing with a bang, the agonizing groan of the elevator going up and down. When he began to play the people crowding the hall continued to chatter, laugh, sip drinks, and walk around with the greatest indifference. No one was listening, as if they were deaf, and much less did they clap at the end of a piece. When he started up again the desk clerk motioned to lower the volume, as if he was annoyed or couldn't understand what the customers were saying.

Gildo was mortified. With good weather, the evening dances were moved outside, in courtyards, squares, even on bocce grounds ruined by the women's high heels. He was asked to play at a banquet in honor of a member of the Mutual Aid Society of Italians from Campano, distinguished by his generous and untiring dedication; then a convivial supper, at two-fifty a person, by a group of Italians who wanted to celebrate the twentieth trip from Naples to San Francisco of Salvatore Santoro, captain of the ocean-going ship San Giovanni.

On Labor Day, the first of May, he played without pay, naturally, and the people danced until late at night. Aniceto's Italian friends organized a jaunt to Sausalito, beyond the strait of the Golden Gate bridge: fifty people, including the children, embarked on a boat with provisions of bread, sausage, salami, cheese, tomatoes and cans of beverages. Gildo played during the crossing, then on the picnic grounds facing the sea, where the children went wild and the adults took off their shoes and danced barefoot on the grass until exhausted. Another picnic took place in the Golden Gate bridge park, near the children's playground. While the children assaulted the slide and the cardboard horses; the older folks, sitting with legs crossed on the silk rug of mown grass, sang nostalgic and passionate songs after lunch, to Gildo's accompaniment.

After a euphoric summer, thanks to Aniceto, Gildo noticed that the requests of co-nationals were growing more infrequent, while those of the local dance locales had stopped completely. He began to doubt that music could ever be his only job. The dollars earned had been almost enough to pay off his debt to Giacomo, and so he had rented a room for a modest amount. The fear that his accordion might be stolen resurfaced, which kept him in a state of tension, a near-paranoiac obsession. Luigino laughed, gently teasing him. Gildo forgave him because he didn't know what had happened. He tried to convince himself that having his first and last name incised on the instrument would make it easy to identify and difficult to sell to the fence.

As an exchange of favors, in his free time Gildo gave a hand to Aniceto in the heavy work that age and chronic bronchitis prevented him from doing. He kept the shop and warehouse in order, unloaded the merchandize bought at the wholesale market, stacked up the cases of pears, apples, oranges, moved and put on display sacks of potatoes and dry beans, put to soak the chick peas for Fridays, inspected the fruit and vegetables and threw away what was withered, rotten, worm-eaten or yellowed—discards like he got out of the garbage in his hungry days. He pulled up the lettuce clumps and cleaned them with a jet of the pump, swept the floor, washed it and scattered sawdust over it, shelled beans and fresh peas for the customers who did not have time to spare. Aniceto maintained that well-off people paid no attention to the price and were willing to buy clean vegetables and polished fruit. He scraped the damp spots off the walls and ceiling of the shop and warehouse and then whitewashed them, replaced the broken or stained bricks on the floor and polished the wooden counter.

While going around town he carefully avoided places that reminded him of the darkest moments of his past. For fear of being asked embarrassing questions, he had not gone to see Rosa Cencini, for whom he had come to feel gratitude for saving him as the time grew more remote. And he had cautiously given Mr. Clifford's music storewide berth.

Sunday afternoons he met Luigino. Sometimes they crossed the north part of town and went as far as Lincoln Park, on the promontory jutting in the sea that faced the strait of Golden Gate bridge. They sat on the grass in the shade of acacia, cypress, and eucalyptus trees and, lost in thought, they contemplated the movement of the white veils of the pleasure boats, the foaming wake of the large ships entering the canal, the people walking back and forth, the breathless children running after them. They looked toward the barren, rocky hills of Marin County. Beyond the ragged coast faded by the fog and deep cove of Richardson Bay, hidden by the Tiburon peninsula opposite Angel Island, rose San Quentin prison. As soon as he saw the gloomy shape of the fortress, twisting his stomach like an iron fist, he resolutely put it out of his mind and watched the purple tongues that the setting sun laid on the calm sea. Would he ever find the courage to tell anyone what he had experienced behind those walls? Or in the mental hospital? He lost himself in imagining a compassionate, serious woman's face that looked at him while he quietly told his story. He seemed to feel the warm light touch of her hand resting on his, and he squeezed it. A woman who like him passionately loved music, and would listen to him play for hours, enchanted. He sighed, putting aside the feverish fantasy. He glanced at Luigino sitting beside him and rejected the temptation to tell him: Luigino's bewilderment, doubt, disapproval would be more than he could take.

As usual they didn't talk much. It was enough to have company. Each kept his melancholy meditations to himself. Luigino frowningly scrutinized his hands, wrists, arms white with lime, the cement dust penetrating the folds, a thick network of whitish wrinkles that wouldn't go away in spite of all the washing and scrubbing. Discouraged, he told himself that all his life he had done nothing but handle a cart, mortar and bricks. Horrible work that barely kept him alive.

The letter Giusepì had written by himself to show how much he had learned made Luigino laugh hard again. Among other colossal blunders, he wrote, the Italian government had refused to give him money for a second trip. Could he send it? Was it possible that Giusepì had forgotten how bad things were here? Perhaps the distance had rekindled the American dream of a thousand promises, which only showed its cruel face up close.

For his part Gildo was thinking over the progressive, inexorable shattering of his illusions: he had invested every hope in affirming his own particular talent with which he could have lived with dignity, and had gradually discovered it was all nonsense.

He had never taken a real step forward. Only his backward fellow countrymen appreciated him, those who tried hard to become integrated and remained entangled in the nostalgia that wrapped their distant country in a pink cloud. The world had changed, progressed, transformed, but they didn't realize it. They clung to memories, regrets, habits, traditions and there was no way to make them give them up. Just like him. It was an ugly business to belong neither to the world you left nor to the world you found.

At the end of May 1921, when the Dedham court in the state of Massachusetts began the trial of Sacco and Vanzetti, Gildo followed the news in the *Voce del popolo* with a kind of morbid curiosity and underlying anguish, as if the judge's accusing finger was pointed at him. In their defense, the newspaper maintained the innocence of the two accused, challenging point by point the accusations and the hasty testimony of those who had seen the crime at South Braintree and the flight of the murderers in the touring Buick. It seemed to him that the two anarchists had been condemned from the beginning, even if a number of witnesses, largely Italian, had furnished solid alibis vindicating them. Testifying were the friends in Boston that Nicola Sacco had eaten lunch with on April 15 at the Boni restaurant on North Square; a journalist that a little later had met him at the Giordano cafe, where he was also seen by the head of a bank's foreign office; the director of the conservative Italian newspaper *La Notizia* who knew him and had also noticed him sitting at the table in the restaurant. To these was also added the grocer who Nicola Sacco had paid for past purchases on that day, and the clerk at the consulate when he went to renew his passport. All Italians. None of which were believed. The court was convinced that they lied out of that famous *omertà* that united the wops. Also not taken into consideration was the testimony of two Americans above suspicion and disinterested, a builder who on the day of the crime had met Sacco on the train for Boston and a publicity agent who was sitting at the same table at the Boni.

It was the same story for Bartolomeo Vanzetti. At Plymouth on that infamous April 15 he had bought fish from a wholesale merchant and had sold it to his usual customers, one man and a dozen women, all Italians. Then he had bought a piece of fabric from a haberdasher in a market, a certain Rosen, and he chatted with Melvin Corl, a fisherman who was painting his boat on the beach, both Americans. Neither man had been believed. On the contrary, the numerous witnesses present at the scene of the crime had sworn under oath that they recognized one or the other accused: Vanzetti's mustache or Sacco's dark coloring, and even their impeccable pronunciation, while it was obvious they spoke English with difficulty. They were contradicted many times, and yet everything they said was taken as gospel truth.

Gripped by that disturbing affair, Gildo followed it anxiously. On the first page of the newspaper was a photograph of the two accused men being led to court handcuffed together. Vanzetti with a Sicilian checked woolen cap, Sacco with a black felt hat. Those handcuffs made him relive the awful humiliation of his time in prison. He felt the bite of the iron teeth on his wrists and the roughness of the shapeless jacket on his skin. Pig's revolting sneer reappeared, the bare walls of the cell, the courtyard for the hour of fresh air, the pale and emaciated faces of the prisoners. The anguish came flooding back. The two accused men also showed signs of the year spent in jail—pale faces, dark circles around their eyes.

It seemed obvious to Gildo that, like the majority of Americans filled with hate and disregard for Italians, Judge Thayer and the jurors shared the same racial prejudices and, backed by conservative politicians, were coldly determined to send those two to the electric chair. A true conspiracy. That trial was necessary as an example and to serve as a warning to the Reds, anarchists, rabble-rousers, the political hard liners who stank up the serene, civilized American society.

The trial ended in July. Sacco and Vanzetti were condemned to death. The newspaper maintained that the whole debate had been widely diffused in the international press. The entire world was aware of the monstrous injustice inflicted by the democratic American nation to two innocent, honest and helpless proletariat, guilty only of professing ideas too upsetting for the susceptible ears of the rich and powerful. Their fight was for bread for every mouth and a bed for every head, as Vanzetti said at the trial. America, the newspaper wrote, was an unfair, violent, arrogant and presumptuous nation, and in spite of that pretended to present itself as a model of liberty, equity and justice for all the people of the planet. In his solitude Gildo had nourished, along with dull resentment, the ideas he shared with the two condemned men against the exploitation, oppression, marginalization of poor people, and now with amazement discovered how widespread it was, a view shared and upheld by many.

A defense committee was formed to collect money in the United States and abroad for a retrial. Money came from every part of the world and from the most remote villages — modest sums, a few dollars that people of little means dug out of their pockets to help those two escape death. The best lawyers in America cost an enormous amount. For some time a well-known lawyer from Boston, William Thompson, had had the civil courage to take that unpopular cause, drawing the ire of the powerful and the disapproval of a large part of his fellow Americans. Well, there was hope, Gildo told himself, trembling with indignation. He made a note of the committee's address in Boston and sent a ten-dollar money order.

From the first request for a retrial — there would be seven, all denied — protests began in many American cities. It was so obvious that they were accommodating political ends that had nothing to do with the guilt of the accused that intellectuals in every part of the world spoke up and signed spirited appeals against that infamous conviction. Some of the finest Americans were also mobilized, along with thousands of Italian immigrants of many generations, to show their solidarity with the two persecuted men.

At North Beach, stirred up by the upcoming demonstration, Gildo had played the *Internazionale*, the hymn of workers the world over, in front of Aniceto's store where a little crowd gathered to sing at the top of their lungs. The greengrocer stood on cases of fruit and had declaimed: let everyone understand. The lives of two innocent Italians were on line, one from Cuneo in Piedmont and one from Foggia in Puglia. Italians of the north and south must unite against that abominable sentence, a dishonor for the American nation. The impressive demonstration — unauthorized — went down the wide downtown streets waving signs and banners: SACCI & VANZETTI ARE INNOCENT MEN — THEY SHALL NOT BE MURDERED!; WE WANT JUSTICE FOR SACCO & VANZETTI; NICK AND BART FREE!; DEFEND, VINDICATE, LIBERATE SACCO & VANZETTI; GHASTLY MISCARRIAGE OF JUSTICE!; ASSASSINI!; CONSPIRACY AGAINST SACCO & VANZETTI!; WE WANT THE TRUTH!; VOGLIAMO GIUSTIZIA PER SACCO & VANZETTI!; NICK & BART NON DEVONO MORIRE!; SACCO & VANZETTI ARE NOT GUILTY.

Gildo, Luigino, Aniceto, his wife, and sons walked with the crowd, eyes shining and knots in their throat. Many people were crying and sniffling, their serious, sad faces showing signs of hardship and struggle, merging with the ruddy, well-fed natives. That procession, it seemed to Gildo, was like a gravestone falling with a great crash on the American dream, on the land of milk and honey, too difficult to seize for anyone who bore the stigma of hunger and poverty on his body and mind. Vanzetti had tried hard to make a living with his fish cart, Sacco managed a little better as a technician: neither one, as poor as they were, was happy to think only of himself, but fought for even the most humble to have his part. For that they were punished.

Some sang the *Internazionale*, and from time to time a demonstrator would call out Nick and Bart! and an ovation would reply: free them! It sounded like a demanding, vibrant, angry request. All those people thirsted for justice and were there to get it. Many looked out their window, waving and shouting greetings. One voice from above shouted: "Salsedo!" and from the street responded an explosion of voices as powerful as a cannon shot.

Suddenly, from a side street mounted police came galloping into the crowd and scattered the procession. Many who had been swept into the crowd fled in terror. The police grabbed signs and banners from the demonstrators' hands, threw them on the ground to be trampled by the horses' hoofs. They waved bully clubs and randomly struck tremendous blows on the heads and shoulders of those they reached. Some fell to the ground trampled by the crowd and got up bleeding. Many of them running for shelter ended up in the arms of policemen on foot crouched in doorways and on side streets, and were soundly beaten. Others were dragged bodily to the patrol wagons waiting nearby and taken to police stations. The terrible thunder of hoofs on the stone pavement muffled the moans and pleas of the bruised and wounded, and the cries for help of those lost in the commotion.

In that bedlam Gildo and his friends found temporary shelter in a store that had promptly lowered the shutters. But as soon as the police left in pursuit of the groups in flight, they went back in the street, picked up signs and banners off the ground and continued marching. As a challenge they sang at the top of their lungs, red in the face, eyes sparkling with anger, pride, indignation.

At sunset they returned to Aniceto's house, exhausted. They sat around the kitchen table and Domenica served them bread and salami. Bitter bread, Luigino grumbled between one mouthful and another. Damn, this American bread is bitter!

In May 1922, out of the blue, a letter arrived from Giacomo:

their father had returned to Italy and had written to say that the government had decided to assign the uncultivated land of the Agro Romano, near the capital, to the ex-combatants of the Libyan war and the world war. Therefore, poor Lorenzo, who died at the front, and he, Giacomo, who fought overseas, had the right. For the moment the Opera Nazionale Combattenti offered them very reasonable annual rent, with provisions to buy as soon as the necessary decree was issued. There was also an old farmhouse where the family could live in the meantime. When sold the land would be divided in equal parts between the seven males, father included—the sisters were excluded as women did not go to war—and everyone could build his own house. As a veteran he was principle assignee, father had written, therefore he urged him to return and convince Gildo to do likewise.

Giacomo wondered where his brothers in Italy would find the money to buy the land eventually. As far as he knew they earned low wages and didn't have a lira saved. And he had serious reservations whether his father had acquired the habit of saving during the years he spent in Montana. He had to decide what to do in a hurry: he certainly was not living lavishly in concrete, but he couldn't complain, even if Ninetta was fed up with working so hard. It is always hard to make a decision to change. To leave the known for the unknown is frightening, especially when you are no longer twenty years old and have a family to support. The girls were doing well. Giuditta was not in school and Teresa often asked why Gildo hadn't come back. On the one hand, it would be an opportunity to reunite the family and change jobs; on the other hand, he was afraid of the risk of falling into poverty, and he didn't know what to do. He asked Gildo what he thought about it. Did he have any money saved? What did he intend to do?

What did he intend to do? His brother's letter had forced him into a strenuous hand-to-hand battle with himself to try to untangle the tumultuous snarl of contradictory thoughts. To go, to stay: he made detailed lists of reasons pro and con each appeared to him well founded and indisputable, only to begin again to evaluate and weigh each one by one, a seesaw that tossed him up and down without mercy and left him tired and confused. What did he want? That dilemma imprisoned his thoughts and robbed his sleep. As soon as he thought he had it resolved, the opposite arguments that he thought he had settled and buried, rose from the ashes and shouted to be heard.

First of all, military service: at twenty-nine it was still obligatory as soon as he put foot in Italy, and he supposed it would last the required three years. And then what would he do? For three long years, at a mature age, he would be shut away who knows where, in a position of subordination, inertia, solitude and dejection, and wouldn't earn a plugged nickel. Wouldn't it be better to wait until he had turned the critical thirty years old, when he would definitely be safe?

The legend of the easy fortune that anyone in a short time and with the minimum effort could accumulate on the American continent was stamped in block letters in the minds of those who remained: therefore to repatriate spontaneously, with his modest savings, was equal to an admission of failure that many would surely criticize. Instead, the paternal command, coming with the offer of land, was an easy alibi and a valid justification.

However, the idea of returning to his family after so many years of being alone frightened him: the hostility that his father had shown him from the time he was a child, his selfishness, his authoritarian ways as an arrogant patriarch, the tyranny he exercised over his mother and his siblings aroused loathing and resentment, and when he thought of their usual daily future his whole being revolted. To a certain degree the prospect of sharing the same house with brothers he hadn't seen in twelve years also disturbed him. Perfect strangers, now adults, whose names and faces he could barely remember. Would they get along? Would they respect him? He knew well that in case they didn't his submissive nature would swallow it in silence. Wasn't it wiser to dodge the risk and stay? His real family, for whom he felt affection, trust and gratitude, if not the confidence of which he was incapable, was there, in San Francisco: Aniceto, Domenica, their children and Luigino. An affectionate, open, industrious family, always ready to help.

On the other hand, the idea of living again with Giacomo, Ninetta, and the girls made him happy. He was grateful to Giacomo for getting him out of the mental hospital and lending him money to buy the accordion, and not least, for that land in Italy on which the whole family, he included, could benefit without any merit of his own. He was grateful to Ninetta for taking him in and treating him like a brother, grateful to the girls who, loving him in that tender way, had saved him from getting lost in an abyss.

That the events might decide for him was a great relief, and the offer of an advantage thanks to a right earned by others, without struggling and working to earn it himself, seemed to him like an award for the many obligations, fatigue and pain. Suddenly, through no fault of his own, he had been tossed out of the house almost as a child, forced into exile, slammed to the other part of the world by fate, and left there to manage the best he could: now they were calling him back, welcoming him, giving him back his place again, and the wound never healed began to ache. It was not a present, because he would have to pay for his part of the land, but a turning point, an opportunity for change, even though he was not able to evaluate its significance. So why not leave?

The uncertainty of the future awaiting him in Italy tormented him. What work could he do? How would he support himself? He certainly wouldn't be able to make a living from his music: here the nostalgia for their country, loneliness, isolation, the common language and customs pushed the immigrants to look for frequent occasions to be together, where familiar music was the essential ingredient, the glue cementing them. But who would ask him to play in an unpopulated area like the Roman countryside? Or populated with poor people who had no money to waste or even any reason for celebrating?

Not that he had reached his expected goals in San Francisco. He got by with the gradually more rare Italian festivities, always the same and by now boring. He scraped out a living, but he didn't get ahead, as if the main road was blocked. In the past few months he had continued to play unwillingly in the noisy hotel hall. Saturday evenings he had found an engagement with the Il Vesuvio cafe in Oakland and returned on the last night boat. He observed sadly that he would always be an amateur. Good, yes, but not a real concert performer. To become one he would have had to go to a good music school, study seriously, pass the exams, understand those in written and spoken English, get a diploma, join the musicians union, pay the unlikely sum of $500 a year, make his way without help and introductions in a clique that defended itself tooth and nail. He was too old and too alone for all that. There was no hope for someone like him. He would be left on the sidelines stuck in the lowest category, because of his background and language. He would grow old playing the same pieces his compatriots liked; or perhaps not even that as new generations would forget them and eventually, ashamed of them, they would repudiate them in order to become fully integrated in the country where they now belonged. That was the aspiration of those who decided to stay: to become true Americans, to lose every connotation that made them different. Certainly, he could have changed his repertoire, keep up-to-date, add new songs as they appeared, insist on opera arias that would never grow old. Could he do it? In Italy he would find his language again, his customs, his roots and he could move at his ease. But what work was waiting for him? What he had always done, manual labor, a mason at the most? Then wasn't it better to stay?

26

He returned at sunset. The children kept their eyes on the road fidgeting with impatience. As soon as they spied him at the curve they ran shouting joyously. Hanging onto the saddle, laughing and eager, they let themselves be pulled along. He would lean the bicycle with the bag of tools tied to the crossbar against the corner of the house, smiling awkwardly at the children that jumped around him like crickets. His mild blue eyes, illuminated by warm affection and restraint, he ruffled their hair and patted them on the cheek. He took his mason's cap wrapped in two pages of the *Messaggero*, stiff and creaking from dry mortar and encrusted cement, and hung it on a branch of the plum tree. His little girl crouched to take the clothes pins that kept the hem of his trousers tight. Then she jumped to grab the hat. He took it and put it on her head. It seemed like a childish game to him, but she loved to breathe in the sharp odor of lime and sweat of her beloved father that soaked the newspaper. The large hat spilled over her eyes and blinded her. His little boy rang the bicycle bell, caressed the leather seat shiny from use and the black crossbar. With a measured glance he saw it was still too high for his stature; he gave the pedal a kick and watched it turn.

He took off his shirt and undershirt, went to the pump, bent over, and water poured over him. He soaped up his chest, neck, face, hair, arms, armpits. He rinsed in a tempest of splashing and reached out blindly in search of a towel. He left his work boots at the entryway so as not to dirty the floor. His children followed him into the house one after the other. From the kitchen mama saluted him with an imperceptible bow without saying anything. He responded with a sort of scraping cough. He blinked and his expression was hesitant, insecure, as if he expected a slap for some unknown reason.

He looked around in the bedroom while putting on clean clothes and hanging the dirty ones on a clothes stand. Parading like chicks behind the mother hen, they followed him to the big room, where every evening he took the shiny accordion out of the case, slipped it on, adjusted the leather belts on his shoulders, opened the slightly yellowing leather bellows, and energetically pressed out vigorous chords from the keys and buttons.

That is the most intense and fascinating time of their day. When he begins to play, their papa's face changes: he frowns, arches his eyebrows, squeezes his lips to a slit, opens his wide eyes on a void as though he were no longer with them and didn't even see them. A somber blush lights his cheeks and ears. His temples pulse as though they might burst. Sometimes to the little girl curled up on a chair to watch him furtively, his shining eyes seem as though about to spill tears. What is he thinking about? Instead of cheering him up the music seems to make him unhappy. Disturbed, distressed, she feels deep sadness for him. But how can that be? Surely she is wrong. Papas are big, strong, solid, tough, and they never cry.

He plays with a passion that carries him into a dimension where nothing and no one can reach him. His gestures are solemn, proud, sometimes violent, but he seems to play only for himself, as if it is entirely unimportant for anyone listen.

He plays for a few minutes when mama calls them: time for them to set the table, clean the plastic tablecloth, get out the plates, cutlery and glasses, cut the bread, fill the water bottle, get the wine in the cellar. Captivated by that musical flood that plunges them in a sort of religious contemplation, they do not obey at once, so that she has to come to the door angrily for her high and imperious voice to reach papa's absent ears. He starts, looks around lost as though returning from a distance and doesn't know where he is or what is going on. He becomes aware of her and his fingers fall from the keys as though dead.

That music always gives me a headache. It's so annoying. All a foolish waste of time. Then she suddenly turns to the two children and orders: Hurry up, move, what are you waiting for? Set the table. Do I always have to tell you twice?

THE END

Acknowledgments

Italian emigration in the United States and elsewhere, from the end of the nineteenth century, to the early decades of the last century, to World War II, has attracted the interest of many scholars who have analyzed it in every aspect. I am grateful to numerous writers for their meticulous and erudite work, which has allowed me to merge an actual personal story with the general picture of a dramatic phenomenon that for nearly a hundred years drastically changed the lives of suffering millions.

My heartfelt gratitude goes to those who in various ways have helped me: my brother Guido, for his skill in the construction of streets, tunnels, and railroads in the past and present; Anna Milano Appel, Italian-American translator, for combing through the Ellis Island archives; Frances Lansing, American artist transplanted in Italy for years, for having taken time from her work to reconstruct the daily life in prisons and mental institutions of her country in the period of interest; Isa and Amedeo Marvelli who, besides furnishing me with detailed atlases of Washington, Oregon, and California, dug up basic information for me on Internet; Albert Schiavi, for lending me indispensable books; Ferdinando Fasce, for information concerning the United States intervention in World War I; Chiara Brauer, musicologist, for the learned excursions into the process of learning music; Roberta Alunni for her diligent research on any subject; Louisa Antonucci for the skillful digital restoration of the cover photo; Maria Grazia Ferrario for her meticulous and accurate finalizing.

VIA Folios

A refereed book series dedicated to Italian Studies and the culture of Italian Americans in North America and other areas of the Italian diaspora.

PINO APRILE
Terroni
Vol. 72, History, $20.00

EMANUELE DI PASQUALE
Harvest
Vol. 71, Poetry, $10.00

ROBERT ZWEIG
Return to Naples
Vol. 70, Memoir, $16.00

LETIZIA AIROS & OTTORINO CAPPELLI, EDS.
Guido
Vol. 69, Essays, $12.00

FRED GARDAPHÉ
Moustache Pete Is Dead
Vol. 67, Oral Literature, $12.00

PAOLO RUFFILLI
Dark Room • Camera oscura
Vol. 66, Poetry, $11.00

HELEN BAROLINI
Crossing the Alps
Vol. 65, Novel, $15.00

COSMO FERRARO, ED.D.
Profiles of Italian Americans
Vol. 64, Essay, $16.00

GIL FAGIANI
Chianti in Connecticut
Vol. 63, Poetry, $10.00

PIERO BASSETTI
Italic Lessons: An On-going Dialog
Vol. 62, Essay, $10.00

GRACE CAVALIERI & SABINE PESCARELLI, EDS.
The Poet's Cookbook
Vol. 61, Poetry & Recipes, $12.00

EMANUEL DI PASQUALE
Siciliana
Vol. 60, Poetry, $8.00

NATALIA COSTA-ZALESSOW, ED.
**Francesca Turini Bufalini:
Autobiographical Poems**
Vol. 59, Poetry, $20.00

RICHARD VETERE
Baroque
Vol. 58, Fiction, $18.00

LEWIS TURCO
La Famiglia/The Family
Vol. 57, Memior, $15.00

NICK JAMES MILETI
The Unscrupulous
Vol. 56, Art Criticism, $20.00

PIERO BASSETTI
Italici
Vol. 55, Essay, $8.00

GIOSE RIMANELLI
The Three-Legged One
Vol. 54, Fiction, $15.00

CHARLES KLOPP
Bele Antiche Stòrie
Vol. 53, Criticism, $25.00

JOSEPH RICAPITO
Second Wave
Vol. 52, Poetry, $12.00

GARY MORMINO
Italians in Florida
Vol. 51, History, $15.00

GIANFRANCO ANGELUCCI
Federico F.
Vol. 50, Fiction, $16.00

ANTHONY VALERIO
The Little Sailor
Vol. 49, Memoir, $9.00

ROSS TALARICO
The Reptilian Interludes
Vol. 48, Poetry, $15.00

RACHEL GUIDO DEVRIES
Teeny Tiny Tino
Vol. 47, Children's Lit., $6.00

EMANUEL DI PASQUALE
Writing Anew
Vol. 46, Poetry, $15.00

Published by BORDIGHERA, INC., an independently owned not-for-profit scholarly organization that has no legal affiliation to the University of Central Florida or the John D. Calandra Italian American Institute, Queens College, City University of New York.

MARIA FAMÀ
Looking for Cover
Vol. 45, Poetry, $15.00 / CD, $6.00

ANTHONY VALERIO
Tony Cade Bambara's One Sicilian
Night
Vol. 44, Memoir, $10.00

EMANUEL CARNEVALI
DENNIS BARONE, ED. & AFTERWORD
Furnished Rooms
Vol. 43, Poetry, $14.00

BRENT ADKINS, ET.AL
Shifting Borders
Vol. 42, Cultural Criticism, $18.00

GEORGE GUIDA
Low Italian
Vol. 41, Poetry, $11.00

GARDAPHÉ, GIORDANO, AND TAMBURRI
Introducing Italian Americana:
Generalities on Literature and Film
Vol. 40, Criticism $10.00

DANIELA GIOSEFFI
Blood Autumn/Autunno di sangue
Vol. 39, Poetry, $15.00/$25.00

FRED MISURELLA
Lies to Live by
Vol. 38, Stories, $15.00

STEVEN BELLUSCIO
Constructing a Bibliography
Vol. 37, Italian Americana, $15.00

ANTHONY JULIAN TAMBURRI, ED.
Italian Cultural Studies 2002
Vol. 36, Essays, $18.00

BEA TUSIANI
con amore
Vol. 35, Memoir, $19.00

FLAVIA BRIZIO-SKOV, ED.
Reconstructing Societies in the
Aftermath of War
Vol. 34, History/Cultural Studies,
$30.00

ANTHONY JULIAN TAMBURRI et al
Italian Cultural Studies 2001
Vol. 33, Essays, $18.00

ELIZABETH GIOVANNAMESSINA, ED.
In Our Own Voices
Vol. 32, Ital. Amer. Studies, $25.00

STANISLAO G. PUGLIESE
Desperate Inscriptions
Vol. 31, History, $12.00

HOSTERT & TAMBURRI, EDS.
Screening Ethnicity
Vol. 30, Ital. Amer. Culture, $25.00

G. PARATI & B. LAWTON, EDS.
Italian Cultural Studies
Vol. 29, Essays, $18.00

HELEN BAROLINI
More Italian Hours & Other Stories
Vol. 28, Fiction, $16.00

FRANCO NASI, ed.
Intorno alla Via Emilia
Vol. 27, Culture, $16.00

ARTHUR L. CLEMENTS
The Book of Madness and Love
Vol. 26, Poetry, $10.00

JOHN CASEY, ET AL.
Imagining Humanity
Vol. 25, Interdisciplinary Studies,
$18.00

ROBERT LIMA
Sardinia • Sardegna
Vol. 24, Poetry, $10.00

DANIELA GIOSEFFI
Going On
Vol. 23, Poetry, $10.00

ROSS TALARICO
The Journey Home
Vol. 22, Poetry, $12.00

EMANUEL DI PASQUALE
The Silver Lake Love Poems
Vol. 21, Poetry, $7.00

JOSEPH TUSIANI
Ethnicity
Vol. 20, Selected Poetry, $12.00

JENNIFER LAGIER
Second Class Citizen
Vol. 19, Poetry, $8.00

FELIX STEFANILE
The Country of Absence
Vol. 18, Poetry, $9.00

PHILIP CANNISTRARO
Blackshirts
Vol. 17, History, $12.00

LUIGI RUSTICHELLI, ED.
Seminario sul racconto
Vol. 16, Narrativa, $10.00

LEWIS TURCO
Shaking the Family Tree
Vol. 15, Poetry, $9.00

LUIGI RUSTICHELLI, ED.
Seminario sulla drammaturgia
Vol. 14, Theater/Essays, $10.00

FRED L. GARDAPHÈ
Moustache Pete is Dead!
Vol. 13, Oral literature, $10.00

JONE GAILLARD CORSI
Il libretto d'autore, 1860–1930
Vol. 12, Criticism, $17.00

HELEN BAROLINI
Chiaroscuro: Essays of Identity
Vol. 11, Essays, $15.00

T. PICARAZZI & W. FEINSTEIN, EDS.
An African Harlequin in Milan
Vol. 10, Theater/Essays, $15.00

JOSEPH RICAPITO
Florentine Streets and Other Poems
Vol. 9, Poetry, $9.00

FRED MISURELLA
Short Time
Vol. 8, Novella, $7.00

NED CONDINI
Quartettsatz
Vol. 7, Poetry, $7.00

A. J. TAMBURRI, ED. & M. J. BONA, INTROD.
*Fuori: Essays by Italian/American
Lesbians and Gays*
Vol. 6, Essays, $10.00

ANTONIO GRAMSCI
P. VERDICCHIO, TRANS. & INTROD.
The Southern Question
Vol. 5, Social Criticism, $5.00

DANIELA GIOSEFFI
Word Wounds and Water Flowers
Vol. 4, Poetry, $8.00

WILEY FEINSTEIN
*Humility's Deceit: Calvino Reading
Ariosto Reading Calvino*
Vol. 3, Criticism, $10.00

PAOLO A. GIORDANO, ED.
*Joseph Tusiani:
Poet, Translator, Humanist*
Vol. 2, Criticism, $25.00

ROBERT VISCUSI
*Oration Upon the Most Recent Death
of Christopher Columbus*
Vol. 1, Poetry, $3.00

www.ingramcontent.com/pod-product-compliance
Lightning Source LLC
Chambersburg PA
CBHW071343020726
47502CB00001B/226

* 9 7 8 1 5 9 9 5 4 0 3 2 0 *